THE USBORNE YOUNG
STARS
& PLANETS

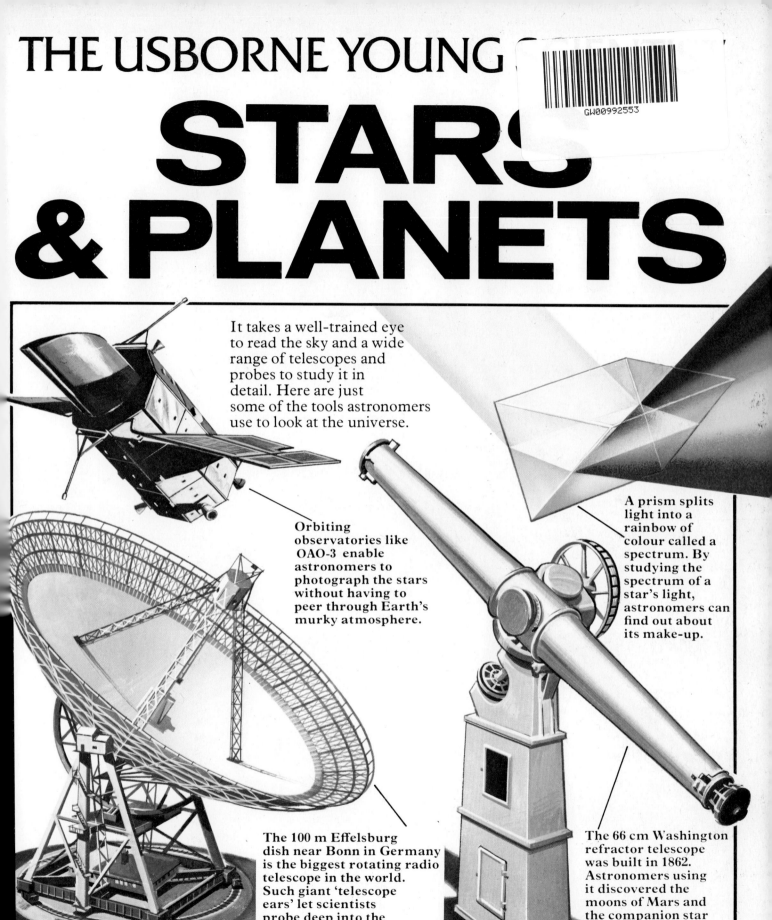

It takes a well-trained eye to read the sky and a wide range of telescopes and probes to study it in detail. Here are just some of the tools astronomers use to look at the universe.

Orbiting observatories like OAO-3 enable astronomers to photograph the stars without having to peer through Earth's murky atmosphere.

A prism splits light into a rainbow of colour called a spectrum. By studying the spectrum of a star's light, astronomers can find out about its make-up.

The 100 m Effelsburg dish near Bonn in Germany is the biggest rotating radio telescope in the world. Such giant 'telescope ears' let scientists probe deep into the universe.

The 66 cm Washington refractor telescope was built in 1862. Astronomers using it discovered the moons of Mars and the companion star of Sirius.

Credits

Written by
Christopher Maynard
Revised text by
Christopher Cooper
Art and editorial direction
David Jefferis
Design assistant
Iain Ashman
Revised edition designed by
John Barker

Scientific advisers
Adrian Berry, FRAS
Kenneth Gatland, FRAS, FBIS
Nigel Henbest, MSc, FRAS
Illustrated by
Michael Roffe, Malcolm English
and John Hutchinson
Copyright © 1991, 1977 Usborne
Publishing Ltd.

The name Usborne and the
device are Trade Marks of
Usborne Publishing Ltd.

Acknowledgements
We wish to thank the following
individuals and organizations for
their assistance and for making
available material in their
collections.
Space Frontiers Ltd.
National Aeronautics and Space
Administration (NASA)
British Interplanetary Society
Royal Astronomical Society

First published in 1977 by
Usborne Publishing Ltd.
Usborne House,
83-85 Saffron Hill,
London EC1N 8RT, England.

Revised edition published 1991
Printed in Italy

On the cover: Voyager space
probe passing Saturn and its
largest moon Titan, whose
surface is hidden by an orange
haze.

The experiments

Here is a checklist of the equipment you will need for
the experiments and things to do included in this book.

WARNING:

Never look at
the Sun directly, either
with your eyes or through
binoculars or telescopes.
If you want to observe
the Sun, use the safe
Sun-scope shown
on pp. 10–11.

General equipment

Scissors
Sticky tape
Ruler
Chair
Binoculars
Felt pen and pencil
If you can afford it, buy a tripod
to mount your binoculars on. Your
arms will not ache, and the view
will be much steadier.

Special experiments

Looking at the sky (p.6):
Deckchair
This book
Torch or bicycle lamp
Thermos flask
Notebook
Warm clothing

Phases of the Moon (p.8):
Grapefruit
Golfball
Torch

Sun-scope (p.10):
Two sheets of white card
Binoculars

Meteorite craters (p.18):
Plain white flour
Shallow tray
Spoon

Sky-Spy (p.26):
Large sheet of tracing paper
A world atlas
A sheet of white card

Weights and measures

All the weights and measures used in this book are Metric.
This list gives some equivalents in Imperial measures.

mm = millimetre
(1 inch = 25.4 mm)

cm = centimetre
(1 inch = 2.54 cm)

m = metre
(1 yard = 0.91 m)

km = kilometre
(1 mile = 1.6 km)

kph = kilometres per hour
(1,000 mph = 1,609 kph)

kps = kilometres per second

kg = kilogram
(1 pound = 0.45 kg)

1 tonne = 1,000 kg
(1 ton = 1.02 tonnes)

°C = degrees Centigrade
(Water freezes at 0°C and boils
at 100°C.)

Speed of light = 300,000 kps
Light year = 9,460,000 million km

Contents

About this book

Stars and Planets is a beginner's guide to the universe we live in. Its clear text and detailed pictures take the reader on a journey through the familiar sights of the night sky and on to the frontiers of the unknown.

Stars and Planets explains how scientists think the universe began and how Earth, a speck in space, fits into the cosmic picture. Readers will visit the still smouldering crater of a giant meteor strike, see the planets of the solar system, and be shown how matter and energy are sucked into black holes.

It also contains safe and simple experiments that can be done at home with ordinary household equipment. They range from simple illustrations of scientific principles to projects like building a sun-projector.

The universe of stars

Earth and Moon

▲ Here is the Earth and its satellite the Moon. The Earth has a diameter of 12,756 km while the Moon is barely one-quarter as large. The average distance between the two is 384,000 km. Yet this is next to nothing. Even the nearest planets are tens of millions of kilometres away.

The Solar System

▲ The Earth, under the red arrow, is just one member of the solar system. Here, within a space of 11,800 million km, are the Sun, 9 planets, over 60 moons and thousands of asteroids and comets. Beyond is a void of some 40 million million km until the closest star, Alpha Centauri, is reached.

The universe is unimaginably huge. Our planet, Earth, is merely a tiny pinpoint in space. As a planet, it is rather small and unimportant. Next to any one of the millions upon millions of stars in the universe, Earth is barely noticeable at all.

In the bubbles above, the red arrows show the location of Earth. Each bubble shows a bigger portion of the universe, the last taking you to the outer limits of known space.

Astronomers know that the universe is expanding. How and why this is happening are still very much unanswered questions.

In the beginning . . .

▲ The origin of the universe has always been a puzzle. Astronomers now favour the 'Big Bang' theory. They think that the universe began about 18,000 million years ago with a colossal explosion.

▼ At the moment of the Bang, all the material in the universe was packed together in an incredibly hot, dense mass. The explosion ripped it apart.

The Milky Way

▲ The solar system (arrowed) is a minor member of the Milky Way galaxy, a spiral cloud made up of about 100,000 million stars. Distances in deep space are vast so they are measured in light years. One light year is the distance light travels in a year, 9·46 million million km.

Galaxies like grains of sand

▲ The Milky Way is some 100,000 light years across. Yet it is just one of many thousands of millions of galaxies, scattered as far as telescopes can see. They have been spotted up to 15,000 million light years away. Yet the actual size of the universe is somewhat larger than this.

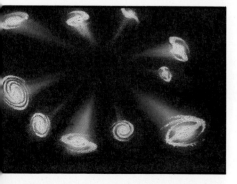

▲ Out of this material the galaxies, stars and planets were formed. But the force of the Bang persists. The universe is still expanding and galaxies everywhere are whizzing apart.

The expanding universe

In 1842, the Austrian scientist Christian Doppler showed why the sound of approaching and receding objects was different.

Movement causes the sound waves in front of a moving object to be compressed. The ones behind are spaced out.

The Doppler effect also holds true for light. Light waves from a receding star are spaced out, making the light take on a reddish colour. This light change is called the red shift — all the distant galaxies have a red shift, proof that the universe is expanding.

▲ Hear the Doppler effect in action! Look up at a jet plane and note how the sound changes from a high whine to a low roar as it goes overhead. This is the 'sound' version of the red shift.

5

Looking at the sky

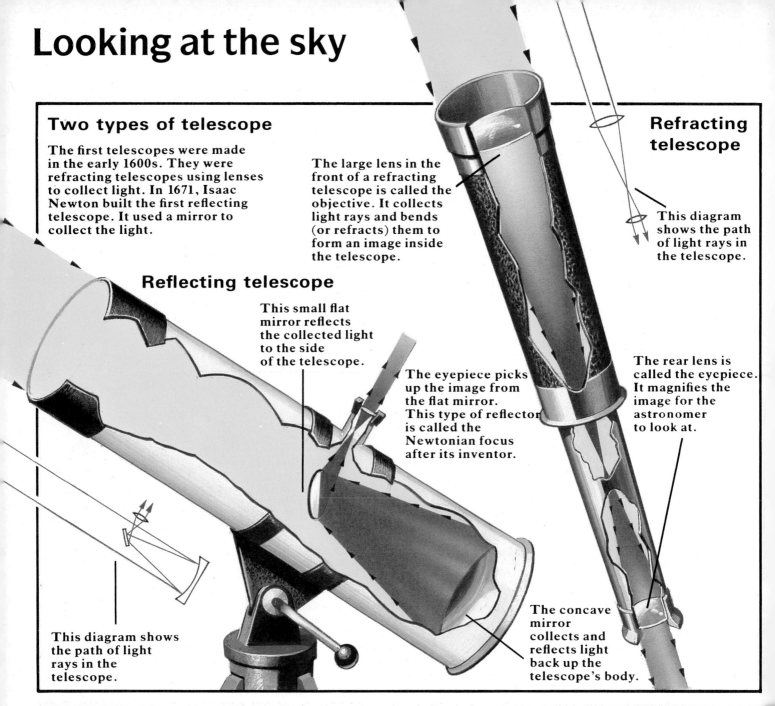

Two types of telescope

The first telescopes were made in the early 1600s. They were refracting telescopes using lenses to collect light. In 1671, Isaac Newton built the first reflecting telescope. It used a mirror to collect the light.

The large lens in the front of a refracting telescope is called the objective. It collects light rays and bends (or refracts) them to form an image inside the telescope.

Refracting telescope

This diagram shows the path of light rays in the telescope.

Reflecting telescope

This small flat mirror reflects the collected light to the side of the telescope.

The eyepiece picks up the image from the flat mirror. This type of reflector is called the Newtonian focus after its inventor.

The rear lens is called the eyepiece. It magnifies the image for the astronomer to look at.

This diagram shows the path of light rays in the telescope.

The concave mirror collects and reflects light back up the telescope's body.

All you need to look at the sky

Amateur astronomers can have as much fun as the professionals. You need an atlas of the stars and a pair of binoculars. Even your naked eyes will do: with them you can see as many as 3,000 stars on a clear night.

From a comfortable spot outdoors you can chart and log the stars and planets. With luck, you might spot a meteor.

Many comets, such as Alcock in 1959 and Ikeya-Seki in 1965, have been first spotted by amateurs searching with binoculars.

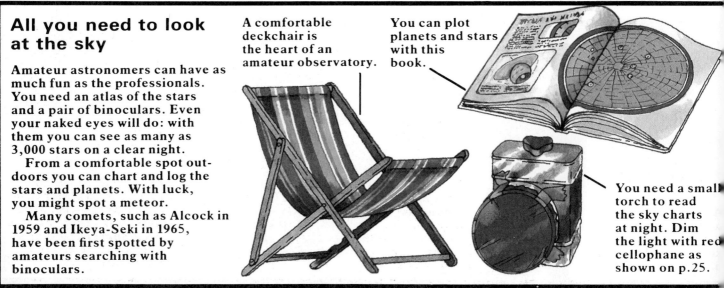

A comfortable deckchair is the heart of an amateur observatory.

You can plot planets and stars with this book.

You need a small torch to read the sky charts at night. Dim the light with red cellophane as shown on p.25.

Ever since Galileo turned his telescope to the sky in 1609, astronomers have been improving the instruments with which they study the stars.

Nowadays, most large telescopes are really 'super-cameras' as film is much more sensitive to dim light than the human eye. Special devices help boost the faintest starlight to a clear strong image.

Stars not only give off visible light, but also emit radio and other waves that are invisible to the human eye. Special methods are used for "photographing" them.

▲ The largest optical telescope today is the 6 m reflector at Mount Semirodniki in the Soviet Union. It can gather starlight 10,000 million times fainter than the brightest star in the sky. It could detect a candle 25,000 km away.

Invisible astronomy

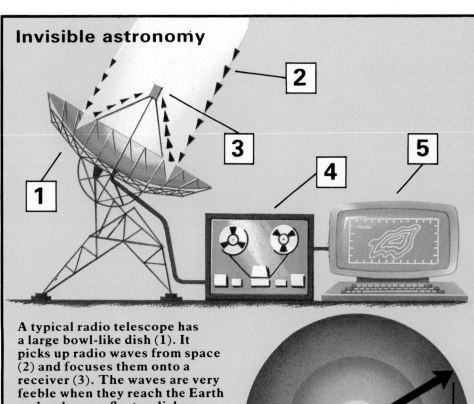

A typical radio telescope has a large bowl-like dish (1). It picks up radio waves from space (2) and focuses them onto a receiver (3). The waves are very feeble when they reach the Earth and so large reflector dishes are needed to collect a recognisable signal. The radio signals are recorded on magnetic tape (4) and later fed into a computer, which turns them into a graph or a picture (5).

▶ Radio telescopes increase the range to which astronomers can probe into space. The picture on the right shows the limits of the naked eye and of optical and radio telescopes.

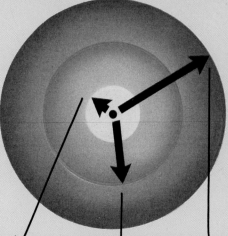

Limits of naked eye   Limits of optical telescopes   Limits of radio telescopes

A thermos flask with something hot to drink will keep away the night-time chill.

Use a notepad and pencil to make notes and sketches during your skywatching.

Wear lots of clothes. A pair of old gloves with the fingertips cut off will let you write as well as keep your hands warm.

A good pair of 7 × 50 binoculars is better than a cheap telescope. With these, you should be able to see some of Jupiter's moons and details of lunar craters.

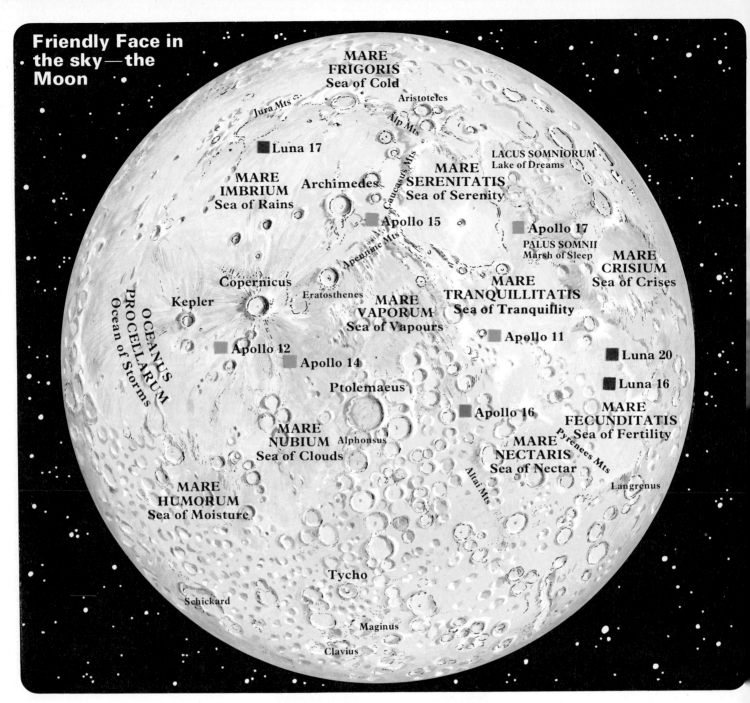

Friendly Face in the sky—the Moon

MARE FRIGORIS
Sea of Cold

Jura Mts

Aristoteles

Alp Mts

Luna 17

Caucasus Mts

MARE SERENITATIS
Sea of Serenity

LACUS SOMNIORUM
Lake of Dreams

MARE IMBRIUM
Sea of Rains

Archimedes

Apollo 15

Apollo 17

PALUS SOMNII
Marsh of Sleep

MARE CRISIUM
Sea of Crises

Apennine Mts

Copernicus

Eratosthenes

MARE VAPORUM
Sea of Vapours

MARE TRANQUILLITATIS
Sea of Tranquillity

OCEANUS PROCELLARUM
Ocean of Storms

Kepler

Apollo 11

Apollo 12

Luna 20

Apollo 14

Luna 16

Ptolemaeus

Apollo 16

MARE FECUNDITATIS
Sea of Fertility

MARE NUBIUM
Sea of Clouds

Alphonsus

MARE NECTARIS
Sea of Nectar

Pyrenees Mts

Altai Mts

Langrenus

MARE HUMORUM
Sea of Moisture

Tycho

Schickard

Maginus

Clavius

Phases of the Moon

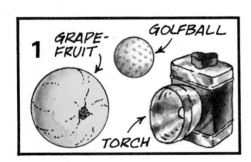

1
GRAPE-FRUIT
GOLFBALL
TORCH

2
GOLFBALL
(MOON)
GRAPEFRUIT
(EARTH)

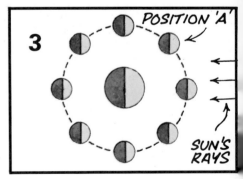

3
POSITION 'A'
SUN'S RAYS

▲ The Moon only shines with reflected sunlight. As it moves around the Earth, we see different parts of its sunny side. For this experiment, you need a torch and two balls— try a golfball and grapefruit.

▲ Balance the torch on a table, or fix it firmly to the back of a chair as shown above. Put the 'Earth' grapefruit and the 'Moon' golfball on the table. Make sure the 'Sun' torch is shining on them both.

▲ Starting from position A shown above, move the Moon around the Earth in a circular orbital path. As the Moon goes around, you will see that the view from Earth goes from shadow to sunlight and then back to shadow again.

Earth's nearest neighbour

The Moon is our closest companion in space and the only one ever to have been visited by Man. Although it is roughly a quarter the size of Earth, the Moon is far less massive. It would take 81 Moons to make up the same weight as Earth.

Gravity on the Moon is quite feeble—only 1/6th as great as on Earth. It is far too weak to hold an atmosphere. As a result, the Moon is a bleak and arid world where temperatures soar to 100 C by day and plunge to a freezing −150°C at night. The Moon's surface is a monotonous expanse of rock and dust.

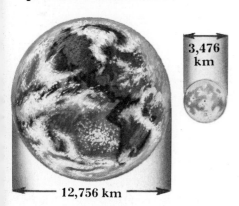

3,476 km

12,756 km

▲ To get an idea of the distance between the Earth and the Moon, trace off the two scale globes shown above onto a sheet of card. Cut out the two circles and knot a piece of string 1.25 m long between them to see the scale distance.

The side we never see

Although the Moon spins on its axis, it always keeps the same face to Earth. It takes the Moon as long to rotate once (27.3 days) as it does to circle the Earth. As the direction of rotation and spin are the same, we never see the other side.

Astronomers had the first glimpse of the far side of the Moon in 1959 when the Russian spacecraft Luna 3 passed behind it and took photographs.

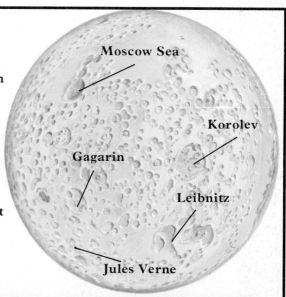

Moscow Sea

Korolev

Gagarin

Leibnitz

Jules Verne

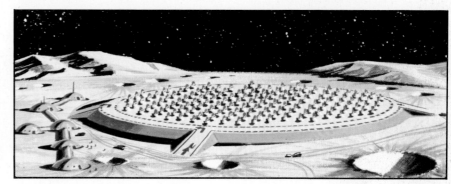

▲ The far side of the Moon is a perfect site for an observatory. Here, optical telescopes would not have to cope with a murky atmosphere. Radio telescopes would use the Moon as a rocky shield 3,500 km thick to protect themselves from the interfering radio waves from Earth. One idea, shown above, is for a vast 'Cyclops-eye' radio telescope to probe into the depths of space.

4

HOW THE MOON LOOKS AT POSITION 'A'

▲ Put the Moon back at position A again, and peer over the top of the grapefruit Earth. If you have got the angle of the light from the torch right, you should see that the lit portion of the golf-ball Moon looks like a crescent.

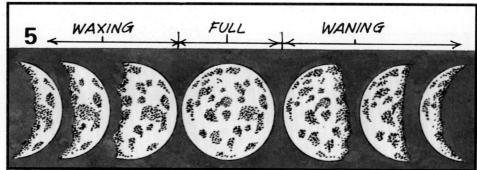

5 WAXING   FULL   WANING

▲ Here are the phases of the Moon as they are seen from Earth. Every 29½ days, the Moon completes a full cycle. It goes through three stages. A waxing Moon is one that is getting larger and brighter. A full Moon is a shining disc in the sky. A waning Moon is getting smaller. When the near side of the Moon is completely in shadow, it is called a new Moon. A crescent Moon in the waxing phase is in the same place as position A in your small-scale experiment model.

9

The nearest star

The Sun is just an ordinary star. The only reason it looks like a huge burning ball in the sky is that it is millions of times closer to Earth than any other star.

The Sun is the source of all life on Earth. The nuclear reactions in its core provide a steady stream of life-giving light and heat. The Earth receives barely 1/2000 millionth of the total radiation of the Sun. Yet this is enough to warm the planet and provide all the energy for plant and animal life.

Though the Sun uses up four million tonnes of fuel every second, it has enough to burn for a good 6,000 million years yet.

At times, long looping streams of gas called prominences arch up from the Sun. They climb into space at speeds up to 600 kps. Small short-lived prominences are called spicules.

Size of Earth to scale

Dark patches on the Sun's surface are sunspots. They are 1000-2000°C cooler than the surface and so shine less brightly. Sunspots usually appear in pairs. They develop in a few hours and may last for many months.

The surface of the Sun is in continuous upheaval. Swirling gas eruptions called flares often occur with sunspot formations. They release bursts of intense radiation causing magnetic storms that disrupt radio communication on Earth.

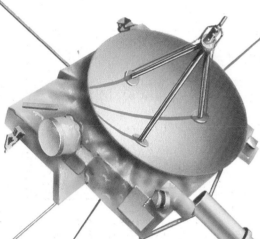

▲ The Ulysses spacecraft was launched in 1990 to study the Sun from a new angle. It was due to pass Jupiter 16 months later, so that the giant planet's gravity would swing the probe over the Sun's poles.

DANGER – DO NOT LOOK AT THE SUN

Never, ever, look at the Sun through binoculars, telescopes, or even just with your eyes. The strong light can easily blind you. Even smoked glass and sun filters should never be used as they do not block out all the dangerous rays.

Make a safe Sunscope

1 7x50 BINOCULARS

▲ It is very dangerous to look at the Sun. Filters exist that screen out harmful rays, but it is easier and cheaper to make this sunscope. You need a pair of binoculars — 7 × 50 are ideal — and two sheets of stiff white card.

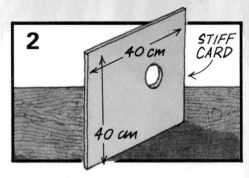

2 40 cm STIFF CARD 40 cm

▲ You need a square of card about 40cm × 40cm. Cut a hole in it as shown above, just big enough to fit one of the binocular lenses. The other lens will not be used in the Sunscope, so you only need the one hole.

Temperatures at the core of the Sun rise to an incredible 15 million°C.

The outer part of the Sun is a 'convection' zone, in which heat is carried outward by hot gases that rise, cool and fall again.

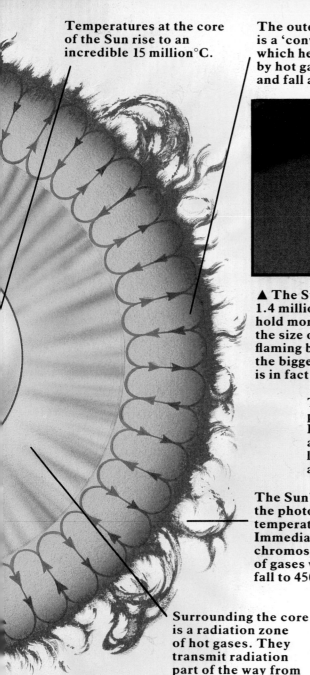

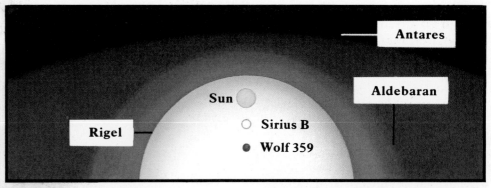

Antares

Aldebaran

Sun

Sirius B

Rigel

Wolf 359

▲ The Sun has a diameter of about 1.4 million km. Its interior could hold more than a million planets the size of Earth. Although this flaming ball of gases looks like the biggest thing in the sky, it is in fact merely a medium-sized yellow star orbiting far out in one of the spiral arms of an average sized galaxy. The picture above shows the Sun compared with some of its stellar neighbours. As you can see, it is a very ordinary star indeed.

The corona is the outer part of the Sun's atmosphere. It can best be seen during a total eclipse when it looks like a glowing halo around the Sun.

The Sun's surface is called the photosphere. Here, the temperature is about 6000°C. Immediately above it is the chromosphere, a thin layer of gases where temperatures fall to 4500°C.

Surrounding the core is a radiation zone of hot gases. They transmit radiation part of the way from the core to the surface.

▲ This picture shows a total eclipse of the Sun. From time to time the Moon passes in front of it and exactly covers the Sun's disc. This is the only time the shining halo of the corona can be seen without special equipment.

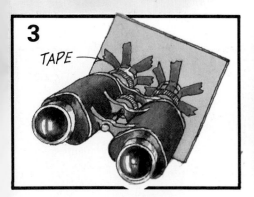

3

TAPE

▲ Lay the card on a table and balance the binoculars on it, making sure that one lens fits over the hole you have cut. Carefully tape the binoculars into place. They must be firm so do not skimp on the tape!

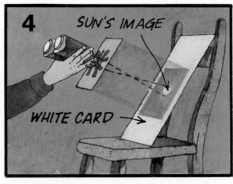

4

SUN'S IMAGE

WHITE CARD

▲ For a screen you need a large sheet of white card. Prop it against a chair at right-angles to the Sun in the sky. Focus the binoculars on infinity and hold them in front of the card. The Sun should appear on it.

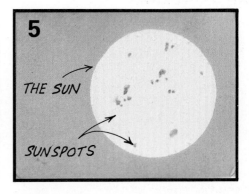

5

THE SUN

SUNSPOTS

▲ This is the sort of image you should get quite easily. Move the binoculars backwards and forwards until the image is sharp. With luck, you will see some tiny black specks on the Sun — they are sunspots.

TAKE CARE – if you adjust the Sun's image to make a pinpoint, you may burn the card.

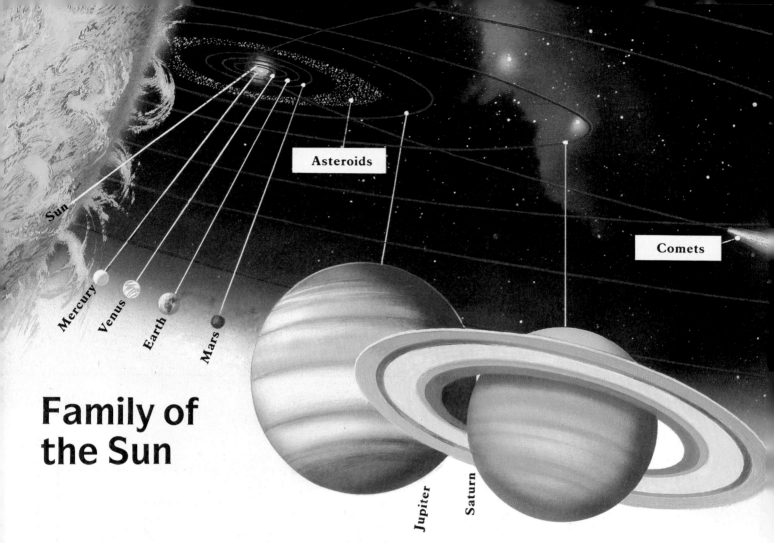

Sun

Asteroids

Comets

Mercury

Venus

Earth

Mars

Jupiter

Saturn

Family of the Sun

The solar system consists of the entire family of planets, moons, asteroids, comets, meteors and swirling dust and gases that circles the Sun. The Sun itself is more than 750 times as massive as the rest of the system combined. Its enormous pull of gravity locks everything within a range of over 6,000 million kilometres into orbit around it.

After the Sun, the most important members of the solar system are the nine planets. The chart below shows you some of the more important facts about each one. Planets' 'days' and 'years' vary because they spin at different speeds and move along in their orbits at varying rates. Pluto, for instance, rotates every 153 hours compared with Earth's rotation time of 23 hours 56 minutes, so Pluto's day is more than six times longer than Earth's.

Facts and figures

Name of planet	Diameter in km	Average distance from Sun in million km	Number of known moons	Time taken to go around the Sun (year)	Time taken to turn on its axis (day)	Speed in orbit around the Sun in kps
Mercury	4,878	57.9	—	88 days	59 days	47.9
Venus	12,100	108	—	224.7 days	243 days	35
Earth	12,756	149.6	1	365.3 days	23 hours 56 mins	29.8
Mars	6,790	227.9	2	687 days	24 hours 37.5 mins	24.1
Jupiter	142,800	778	16	11.9 years	9 hours 50.5 mins	13.1
Saturn	120,000	1,427	19	29.5 years	10 hours 14 mins	9.6
Uranus	52,400	2,870	15	84 years	15 hours 14 mins	6.8
Neptune	50,450	4,497	8	164.8 years	16 hours 3 mins	5.4
Pluto	2,300	5,900	1	248.6 years	6 days 9 hours	4.7

Uranus

Neptune

Pluto

Plotting the planets

The Planets swing around the Sun in regular orbits. From Earth, they seem to move across a narrow belt of sky. This is because the planets circle the Sun in a roughly flat plane, rather like the bands between tracks on an LP record. The only exception is frozen Pluto, the outermost planet which has an angled orbital path.

The planets move through twelve star constellations called the signs of the Zodiac. Once you have spotted the constellations, any extra 'star' will be a planet. The chart below shows where you can see the four brightest planets during the next few years.

Key to the planetary symbols shown below

♀ Venus   ♃ Jupiter

♂ Mars   ♄ Saturn

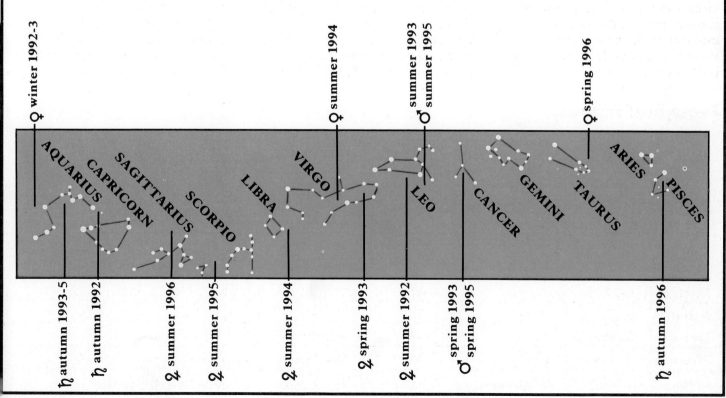

The inner planets

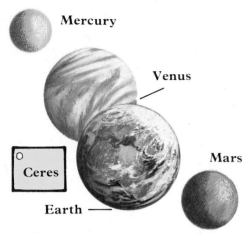

Mercury

Venus

Ceres

Mars

Earth

The four inner planets are the midgets of the solar system. The diagram above shows them all to the same scale, together with Ceres, the biggest asteroid. All are quite dense and, apart from Earth, have barren, rocky surfaces. The features of Earth are softened by the great oceans that cover 71% of its surface.

Only the thinnest of atmospheres exist on Mercury and Mars. As a result there is a great difference between day and night-time temperatures. On Mercury the change can be as high as 400°C. Earth and Venus, however, have shielding atmospheres. Their temperatures are fairly constant. On Earth at the equator, this is about 15°C while most of Venus roasts at nearly 500°C — hot enough to melt lead!

▲ Tiny Mercury is the nearest planet to the Sun which, looming some three times as big as it does on Earth, sears the landscape to a baking 400°C.
In 1974, Mariner 10 passed the planet and snapped the first detailed pictures. They showed a dry rocky surface that was scarred with craters. Instruments on board showed Mercury to have a dense iron-rich core much like that of Earth's.

▲ Venus, the morning and evening 'star', ought to be Earth's sister planet. Its size is almost identical, yet it is a hell-world shrouded by clouds of sulphuric acid and smothered by an atmosphere of carbon dioxide.

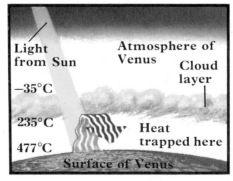

Light from Sun

Atmosphere of Venus

Cloud layer

−35°C

235°C

477°C

Heat trapped here

Surface of Venus

▲ The clouds that blanket Venus trap sunlight like a greenhouse. Light passes through the clouds and heats the surface. The ground radiates infra-red heat waves that are trapped by the atmosphere making temperatures soar.

▲ From nearby space, Earth shines like a blue-white beacon in the sky. Even from the Moon, the brown outlines of the continents, the deep blue of the oceans and the white swirls of the clouds can be clearly seen.

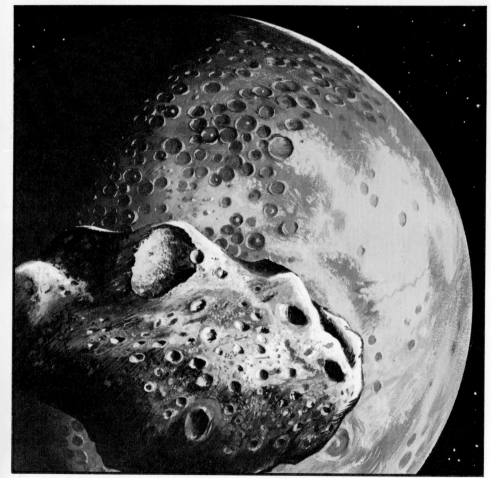

▲ In 1976 two space probes, Vikings 1 and 2, soft-landed on Mars and sent back the first surface pictures. The view above was taken by Viking 2. The horizon is about 3 km away. The fine drifting sand is the result of storms that can rage across Mars.

Lost Planet ?

Orbiting in the 550 million km gap between Mars and Jupiter are tens of thousands of small rocky objects called asteroids. Ceres, the biggest, is only 1025 km across—most are only house or boulder-sized. Astronomers think that the asteroids are the building blocks of a planet which never formed.

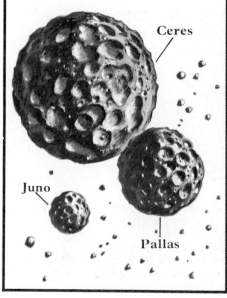

Ceres

Juno

Pallas

▲ This picture shows the largest moon of Mars, Phobos, as it might appear from the viewport of a visiting spacecraft as it approaches the red planet. To give you an idea of the moon's size, the crater in the middle is 6 km across. Phobos orbits 6000 km above Mars, circling it three times every Martian day. The other moon of Mars, Deimos, is even smaller than Phobos. It must appear as little more than a bright moving star from the surface.

The outer planets

Beyond the Asteroid Belt are the outer giants—Jupiter, Saturn, Uranus and Neptune—vast balls of gas circling in the solar system's outer reaches. Beyond them all lies tiny frozen Pluto.

The diagram below compares Earth and the outer planets shown to the same scale.

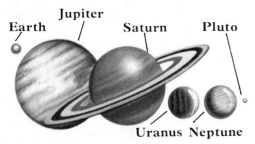

Earth Jupiter Saturn Pluto

Uranus Neptune

▲ Jupiter is the Goliath of the solar system, having a volume 1,312 times that of Earth. It does not have a solid surface. Jupiter's upper layers are a sea of gases that become a denser liquid and finally a solid near the core. In the visible cloud layers, temperatures average —140°C.

The oddest feature is the Great Red Spot (shown on the right in the picture above), first seen in 1666. Astronomers think it may be a long-lasting storm raging in the planet's atmosphere.

Pioneer 10 (shown above) photographed Jupiter in 1973; in 1979 Voyagers 1 and 2 returned more detailed pictures. They discovered a faint ring around Jupiter, two new moons, and seven active volcanoes on one of the larger moons, Io.

▼ Saturn orbits 1,427 million km from the Sun. It is a gas giant like Jupiter, but its amazing rings are what make it really interesting. From Earth, the rings look different from year to year as the planet moves around its orbit. The pictures below show how our view changes.

The rings are barely a kilometre thick, and are not solid. They are made up of countless small pieces

▲ Uranus is an icy world 2,870 million km from the Sun. Latest studies show that in addition to its 15 known moons (two of which are passing in front of it in the picture above), it has 11 narrow rings, much darker than Saturn's.

▲ Neptune is the last of the giant planets. It is similar to Uranus but slightly smaller. Its two largest moons are named Triton and Nereid. Its cloud layers have been calculated to be at a constant and chilly −220°C.

of rock and ice. In 1980, Voyager 1 discovered that the rings are divided into hundreds of separate "ringlets". The two outermost ringlets are twisted around each other like strands in a rope.

Saturn has at least 19 moons, most of them made of ice and cratered by comet impacts. One has a crater a quarter its own size, and another has been smashed into by two smaller moons which now share the same orbit. The largest moon, Titan, has a thick atmosphere of nitrogen, and orange clouds which completely hide its surface. Titan's surface temperature must be about −180°C, and astronomers think it may be covered by oceans of liquid methane (the substance we find as natural gas on Earth).

Arrows show position of Pluto

▲ Pluto was not discovered until 1930. Photographs taken on different nights were compared, and one of the "stars"—Pluto—was found to move. Pluto has a moon, Charon, discovered in 1978, which is half Pluto's size.

Meteors and comets

Along with the planets and moons, a great deal of space debris circles the Sun. Most of it is too tiny and distant to be seen from Earth, but at times some of these objects become spectacularly visible.

The smallest are the meteoroids which range from tiny specks to boulder size. They can be seen only when they hurtle into the atmosphere as streaks of light called shooting stars.

Comets are solitary wanderers. A long shining tail announces their arrival whenever they drift in from space and near the Sun.

▲ The picture above shows a meteor as it streaks into the Earth's atmosphere at a speed up to 70 kps. Friction with the air vaporizes most meteors before they get anywhere near the Earth's surface.

▶ Giant meteorites hitting the Earth are very rare, although thousands of tiny meteors burn up in the atmosphere every day. This picture shows what the scene might be like a short time after a huge meteorite hit. Scientists in helicopters hover over and in the newly gouged crater. Luckily, it is in a deserted area.

Meteorite craters

Astronomers call meteors different names according to where they are. A chunk of rock or stone in space is a meteoroid. The same chunk is called a meteor as it falls through the atmosphere. If it actually hits the Earth (or any planet or satellite such as the Moon), it is called a meteorite.

Meteorites can either land in one piece or explode violently. In 1947, a thousand tonnes of fragments from an exploding meteorite rained down on Siberia, digging impact craters that were up to 30 m wide.

▲ It is easy to make your own meteorite crater with this simple experiment. The surface of your model planet is a bed of flour. Cover the bottom of a shallow tray with a layer of fine plain flour about 2 cm thick.

▲ Smooth off the flour with the edge of a ruler. It is important to have a smooth even surface for the experiment to be a success. Place the tray on the floor. Now cover the floor with newspaper for the next step.

Comets—dirty snowballs in space

Comets appear from the depths of space as glowing balls, sometimes with million km tails. A comet's nucleus is a ball of solid particles and frozen ices enveloped by a coma of evaporating gases. A nucleus a few km wide may have a coma of 80,000 km. The Sun's heat and radiation boils away the gas particles from the coma and spreads them back to form a long filmy tail stretching into space.

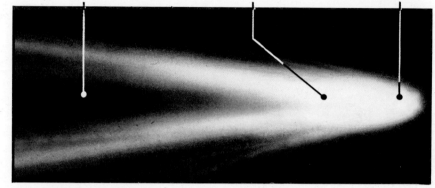

Tail made of gases and dust   Gaseous coma   Nucleus made of rocks and ice

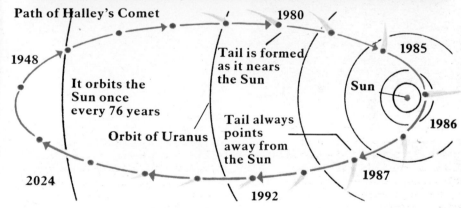

Path of Halley's Comet
1948
It orbits the Sun once every 76 years
Orbit of Uranus
1980
Tail is formed as it nears the Sun
Tail always points away from the Sun
2024
1992
1987
1986
1985
Sun

3 ABOUT 2 m   MAKE SURE YOU CLEAN THE FLOOR!

▲ Climb up on a chair so you are standing directly above the tray. Take a small spoonful of flour, hold it about 2 m above the floor and let the flour drop. Repeat the experiment a few times from different heights.

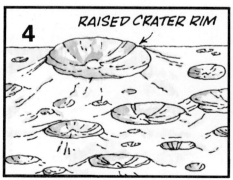

4 RAISED CRATER RIM

▲ The flour ploughs into the tray just like a meteorite hitting the Earth or Moon. You will see that all the mini-craters that are formed in your tray have the same sort of raised lip and sloping sides as real craters.

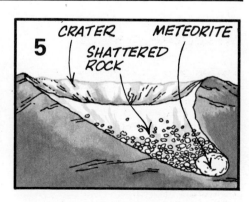

5 CRATER   METEORITE   SHATTERED ROCK

▲ The most famous meteorite crater on Earth was formed 24,000 years ago in the Arizona desert. An iron-nickel meteorite some 80 m wide, blasted into the Earth. It gouged a hole that was 1,265 m wide and 175 m deep.

Star-spotting in the northern sky

There are about 3,000 stars in the night sky that can be seen by the naked eye. Not all are visible at once as only a small part of the heavens can be seen from any single place on Earth.

Only the brightest stars are shown in the map here and on pages 24-25. They are most easily recognised as parts of star groupings called constellations. Most of these were made up by ancient peoples, who imagined pictures of animals and people in the stars. The Plough, part of the constellation of Ursa Major, is easy to spot in the northern sky.

▲ You need the Sky-Spy shown on pp.26–27 if you want to use the sky charts properly. Simply line up the time on the Sky-Spy with the date on the chart. The view inside the oval is what you will be able to see on that night in the sky.

▶ Here are the main constellations of the northern sky. The big numbers on this map link with the pictures on the next two pages.

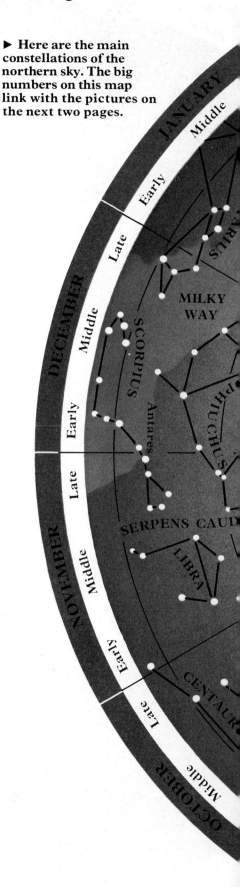

Mapping the heavens

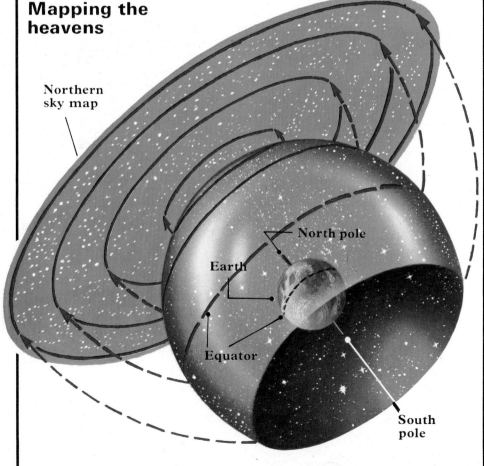

Stars look as though they have been painted on a dark dome. It used to be thought that the stars lay in fixed positions on the inside surface of a hollow globe—the celestial sphere—with the Earth sitting at its centre. The star maps in this book are made by 'folding back' the view seen from Earth to make a flat circle. So, although there is no real celestial sphere, the idea can still be used to make accurate maps of the sky.

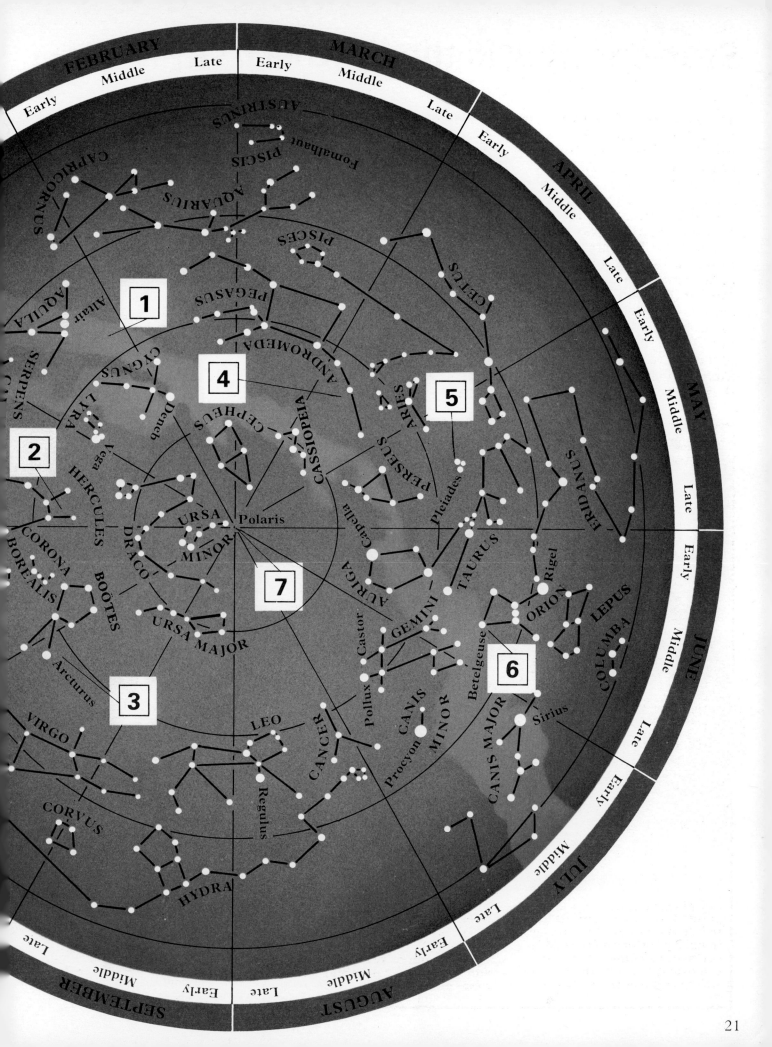

Wonders of the northern sky

Not only stars and planets can be seen in the night sky, but also dark nebulae, star clusters, galaxies and shining clouds of heated gas. Many of these sights are too faint to be spotted unaided. They are only visible with powerful telescopes.

Each object in the sky is ranked according to its brightness, which is indicated by a number called its magnitude. Curiously, bright objects are given low numbers; Venus for example is −4.4. Dim objects have high numbers. The faintest object you can see unaided is around magnitude +6.

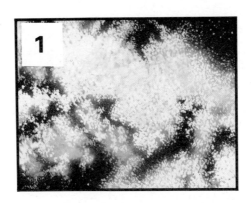

▲ Our own galaxy, the Milky Way, looks like a dim trail of light stretching across the sky. Pictures like the one above show it to be made up of millions of stars so thickly sprinkled that they look like clouds.

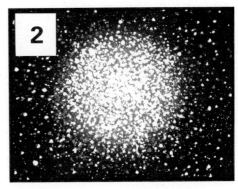

▲ The fuzzy patch in Hercules called M13 is a tight globular star cluster. Here, hundreds of thousands of old dim yellow stars are crowded together. They are packed less than half a light year apart.

▲ The Pleiades are a compact group of stars in the constellation Taurus. They are **about 400 light years away.** The Pleiades are also known as the 'Seven Sisters' since most people can only see seven stars here. However, on a clear night and with very good eyesight, others come into view. Only the sharpest eyes can make out more than fifteen, yet in actual fact there are nearly 400. North American Indians used the Pleiades as a way of testing the keenness of a warrior's eyesight.

The blue-white stars in the Pleiades are 'young'—just a few tens of millions of years old. The Sun is 5,000 million years old in contrast.

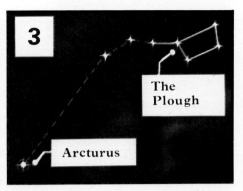

▲ With the Plough as a guide, draw an imaginary line along the curve of its handle. If you continue the line in the same path, it will cross Arcturus, the fourth brightest star to be seen in the skies.

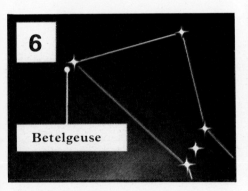

▲ The constellation Orion can be seen in both northern and southern skies. The picture above shows you how to find Betelgeuse at its top left-hand corner. Betelgeuse is a red-giant star 600 times larger than the Sun.

▲ This picture shows the most distant object that can be seen with the naked eye — the Andromeda galaxy. It looks like a faint smudge. The astronomer Edwin Hubble first tried to measure its distance in 1923. It is now known to be two million light years away. Its shape is very like that of our own Milky Way galaxy, complete with spiral arms. The Andromeda Galaxy is almost twice as large as the Milky Way, and it contains three times as many stars.

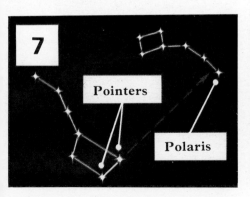

▲ The seven brightest stars of the constellation Ursa Major are called the Plough. A line between the two end stars, the Pointers, runs straight to Polaris when extended upwards. Face Polaris and you always face north.

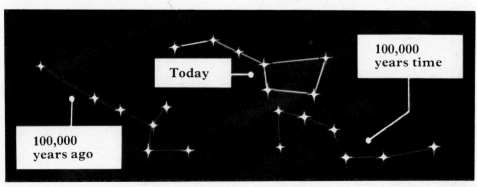

▲ Stars seem to be fixed in the sky. Yet with enough time, movements do become apparent. 100,000 years ago, the stars of the Plough were an unrecognizable jumble. Today, their familiar form is easy to see. In another 100,000 years, the shape will be transformed yet again.

Although stars move at high speeds, they are so far away that any motion is impossible to make out, except with high precision instruments.

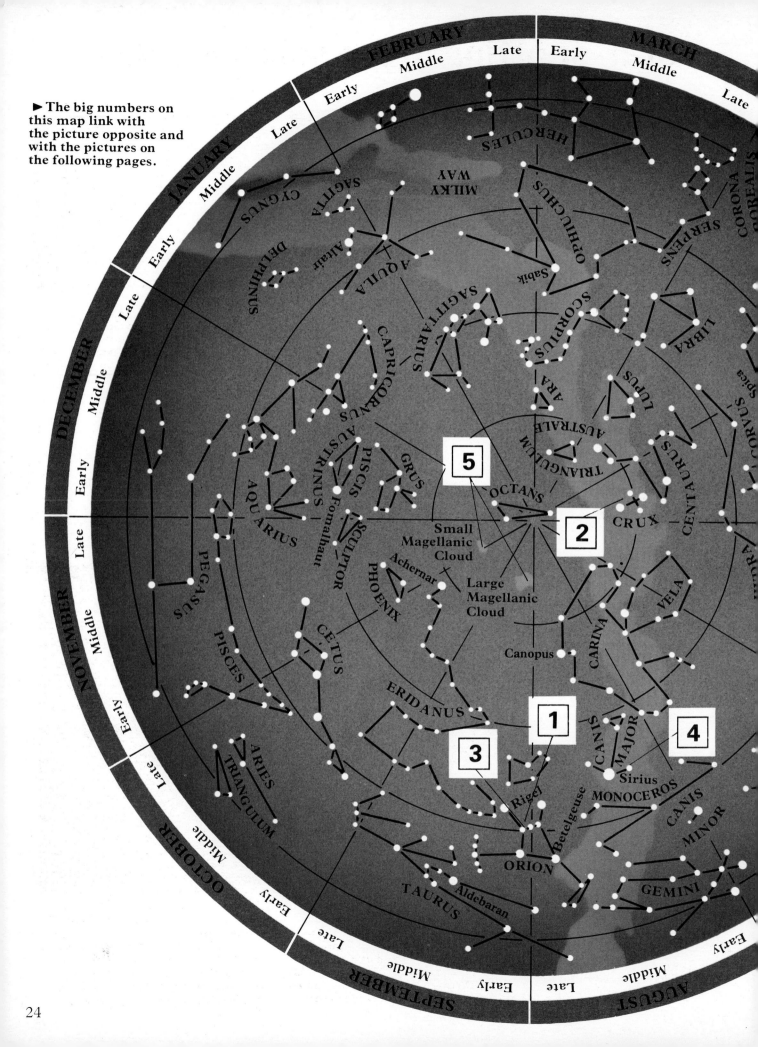

▶ The big numbers on this map link with the picture opposite and with the pictures on the following pages.

FEBRUARY
MARCH
JANUARY
DECEMBER
NOVEMBER
OCTOBER
SEPTEMBER
AUGUST

Early
Middle
Late

HERCULES
MILKY WAY
CYGNUS
SAGITTA
DELPHINUS
Altair
AQUILA
SAGITTARIUS
OPHIUCHUS
Sabik
SCORPIUS
SERPENS
CORONA BOREALIS
LIBRA
Spica
CORVUS
CAPRICORNUS
ARA
LUPUS
TRIANGULUM AUSTRALE
CENTAURUS
HYDRA
PISCIS AUSTRINUS
GRUS
Fomalhaut
SCULPTOR

[5]
OCTANS
[2]
CRUX
AQUARIUS
Small Magellanic Cloud
VELA
PHOENIX
Achernar
Large Magellanic Cloud
CARINA
PEGASUS
Canopus
CETUS
ERIDANUS
[1]
CANIS MAJOR
[4]
PISCES
[3]
Sirius
MONOCEROS
CANIS MINOR
ARIES
TRIANGULUM
Rigel
Betelgeuse
ORION
GEMINI
TAURUS
Aldebaran

24

Star-spotting in the southern sky

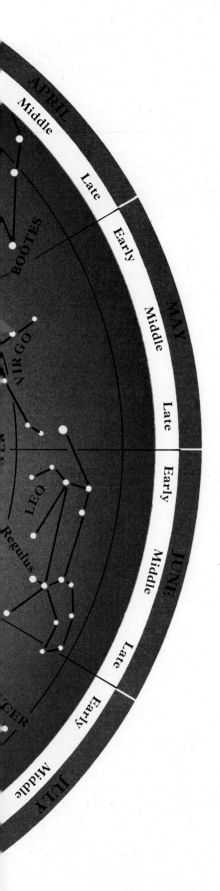

The stars shown on this map can be seen from all the inhabited regions of the southern hemisphere. The stars around the outer edges belong to the northern sky, but at the right times of year they can be seen low on the horizon.

The Greek alphabet is used to name stars. In each constellation one star — usually the brightest — is called Alpha (the first letter), the next Beta (the second letter) and so on. Then comes a slightly altered form of the constellation name. Thus Alpha Centauri is the brightest star in Centaurus.

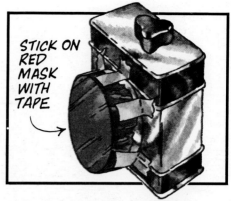

STICK ON RED MASK WITH TAPE

▲ You will need a nightlight to read with whenever you take your sky map outside to go star spotting. So that the glare does not spoil your night vision, take along a torch masked with red cellophane.

Wonders of the southern sky

Because the southern sky was neglected for so long, a number of surprises awaited astronomers when they directed their attentions here. In the constellation Centaurus they found our closest stellar neighbour. Proxima Centauri is a small dim red star just 4.2 light years away. Here in the south are also the nearest galaxies, called the Magellanic Clouds after their discoverer, Ferdinand Magellan.

1

▲ Hanging near the three stars forming the 'belt' of Orion is one of the most magnificent sights in the sky. To the naked eye, the Great Nebula is a faint fuzzy patch. Seen through a telescope, as shown in the picture above, it leaps into view as a vast and colourful cloud of gas 16 light years across.

The young hot stars embedded in the cloud radiate 8 times as brightly as the Sun. They make the billowing clouds of surrounding gas heat up and shine as well.

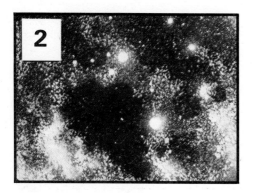

▲ The Southern Cross, shown in close-up above, is a tiny constellation, the smallest in the sky. Two of its member stars point toward the south, just as two of The Plough's stars point north toward Polaris.

▲ Dark nebulae are clouds of cold dust and gases. They can only be seen when they blot out part of a lighter background of stars. The Horsehead Nebula in Orion, shown above, stands out in silhouette against the bright stars behind.

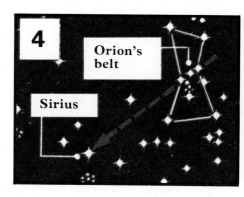

Orion's belt

Sirius

▲ Sirius is the brightest star in the southern night sky. It is also known as the Dog Star because it lies in the constellation Canis Major, the Great Dog. The picture above shows you how to find Sirius using Orion's Belt as a guide.

Plans for your sky-spy

This simple gadget will show you which stars can be seen from your home at any particular time of the year.

Get a large sheet of tracing paper and lay it over this page. Trace off the solid black lines from the yellow half-plan on the right. Now mark on the time arrows from midnight to 6 am.

Flip the tracing paper over. Trace out the other half of the plan. Mark on the evening time arrows from midnight to 6 pm. Also trace on the star where the vertical and horizontal lines cross.

Slide the star on your tracing paper along the degrees of latitude scale until it rests on your own latitude. You can find the latitude of your home in an atlas.

Here are some examples:

Copenhagen	56 North
London	52 North
Munich	48 North
Rome	42 North
Rio de Janeiro	23 South
Sydney	34 South

Now trace out the dotted oval of the horizon line. As you can see, the oval moves north or south depending on where you live.

Transfer your finished tracing onto a sheet of stiff card cut out to the same shape. Lastly, cut out the oval centre. Your Sky-Spy is now complete.

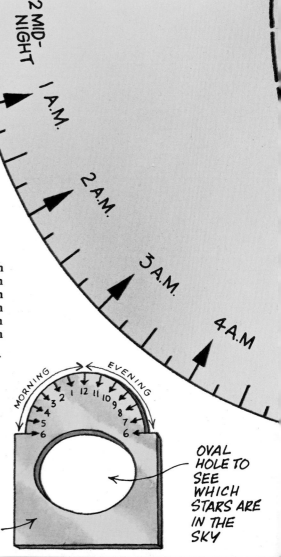

12 MID-NIGHT
1 A.M.
2 A.M.
3 A.M.
4 A.M

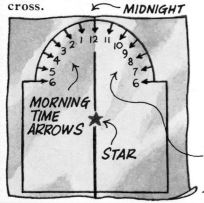

MIDNIGHT

MORNING TIME ARROWS

STAR

EVENING TIME ARROWS

TRACING PAPER

MORNING   EVENING

FINISHED SKY-SPY ON CARD

OVAL HOLE TO SEE WHICH STARS ARE IN THE SKY

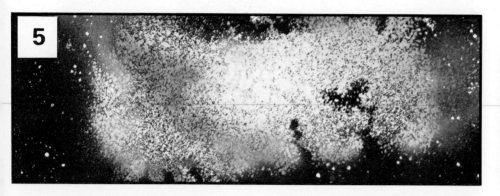

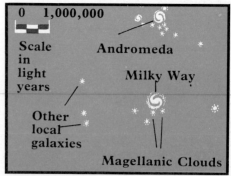

▲ The Magellanic Clouds were first noted in 1521. They are visible only in the southern sky. The Large Cloud, also known by its scientific name Nubecula Major, is shown in the picture above. It is 170,000 light years away from the Milky Way making it the nearest galaxy to us, almost a satellite in fact. It is 23,000 light years across. Unlike spiral and disc-shaped galaxies, the clouds have no particular shape or form. They are classed as irregular galaxies.

▲ The Magellanic Clouds and 30 other galaxies belong to the Local Group. This cluster of galaxies (of which the Milky Way is a member) lies within a 5 million light year diameter sphere. Other clusters can contain up to 2,500 galaxies.

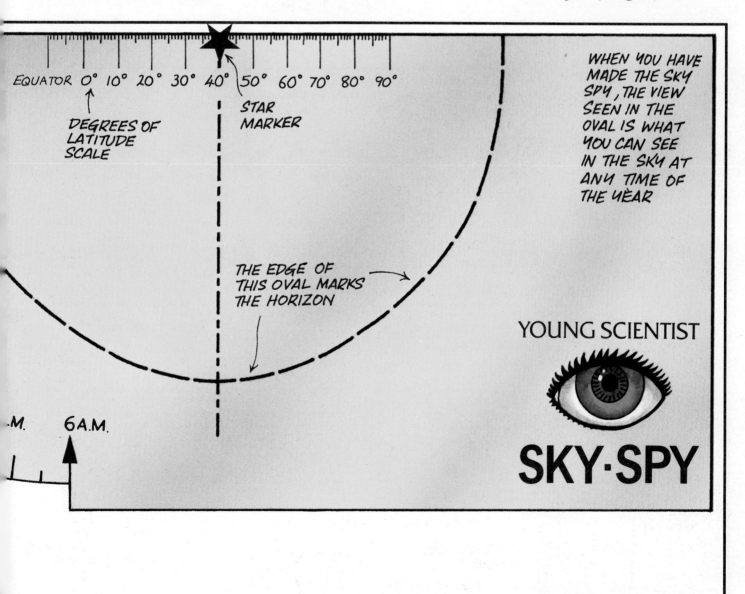

Equator 0° 10° 20° 30° 40° 50° 60° 70° 80° 90°

DEGREES OF LATITUDE SCALE

STAR MARKER

THE EDGE OF THIS OVAL MARKS THE HORIZON

WHEN YOU HAVE MADE THE SKY SPY, THE VIEW SEEN IN THE OVAL IS WHAT YOU CAN SEE IN THE SKY AT ANY TIME OF THE YEAR

.M. 6A.M.

YOUNG SCIENTIST

SKY·SPY

Other things to see

Meteors

At regular times of the year, swarms of meteors cross the Earth's orbit. A heavy meteor shower looks like lots of streaks of light coming from a point in the sky — the radiant.

Name of shower	Where to look	When to look
Aquarids	SW of Pegasus	May 4-6
Geminids	Castor in Gemini	December 11-14
Leonids	Leo	November 16-18
Lyrids	Between Hercules and Vega	April 20-22
Orionids	Between Orion and Gemini	October 18-22
Perseids	Perseus	August 10-14
Quadran-tids	Between Boötes and Draco	January 2-4
Taurids	Between Taurus and Perseus	November 5-9

Man-made satellites

Some of the most successful satellites have been orbiting astronomical observatories, such as COBE (Cosmic Background Explorer), shown here. It was launched to study microwave radiation, left over from the Big Bang, that fills the universe. Other satellites observe infra-red, ultra-violet and X-rays from space, which cannot penetrate Earth's atmosphere. Other types of satellite 'look' at the Earth – to observe the weather, locate resources, relay TV and phone messages, or spy on armed forces.

Comets

Comets travel in long swooping orbits that may take them far into the outer reaches of the solar system. It can be hundreds, even thousands of years before they return.

ENCKE'S: Appears at a regular interval of 3.3 years. This small comet swings as far as Jupiter before turning back to the Sun. Visible only with a telescope.

HALLEY'S: Shown above, this comet returns every 76 years. It last appeared in 1986, when five space probes flew by it to make observations.

HUMASON 1961E: Discovered in 1961, this large comet has a long flat orbit that takes thousands of years to complete. It is next expected in the year 4860.

IKEYA-SEKI: Discovered in 1965 by two amateur astronomers, this bright comet could be seen even in daytime.

Eclipses

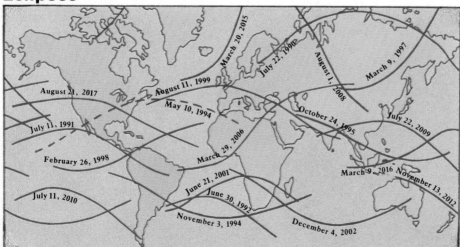

Solar eclipses occur when the Moon passes between the Earth and the Sun, and the Moon's shadow races across the Earth at speeds up to 3,500 kph. On each of the 'paths of totality' shown here, the eclipse is total — the main disc of the Sun is completely blocked out. On each side of the path a partial eclipse can be seen, in which the Moon only partly covers the Sun. The dotted line marks the path of an annular eclipse, in which the Moon is at its farthest from the Earth and the rim of the Sun appears around the Moon's edge.

Strange frontiers

Recently discovered objects in space are stranger than any astronomer had predicted. Scientists know that gravity is the weakest force in the universe, yet they were astonished to find that it can sometimes make matter and energy apparently vanish.

A place where this occurs is called a black hole. In this region, the forces of gravity are so intense that anything which comes near is sucked inside. Even light rays cannot escape its clutches, so a black hole is completely invisible!

Birth of a black hole

Black holes are the result of a process called gravitational collapse. The atoms of a star are squeezed closer and closer to each other so that the star gets ever more dense — a little like the difference between say, balsa wood and lead. One way in which this could happen is when a giant star, shown on the right, explodes violently.

1

The outer layers of the star are flung off into space. If there is enough material left in the core, it collapses inward to form a small super-dense globe called a neutron star. A single matchbox of it would weigh 10,000 million tonnes. A neutron star sends out beams of radiation that swing round like lighthouse beams as the star spins.

2

Some neutron stars shrink still further to become black holes. A black hole is an odd object — incredibly small, yet enormously dense. The picture below shows how a black hole bends the fabric of space, creating a sort of 'plug-hole' effect. Anything falling inside it is likely, as far as astronomers can tell, to be completely crushed or sucked right out of our universe.

3

A world the size of a pea!

If the Earth were crushed as much as the matter inside a black hole, it would fit inside a sphere the size of a pea. From where you read these words, the force of the black hole's gravity would pull you to pieces and swallow you into the page.

Sky firsts

Hundreds of notable landmarks lie scattered through the history of astronomy. Below are just a very few.

140 AD
Ptolemy of Alexandria wrote the Almagest, recording all the astronomical knowledge of the ancient world. He also produced the most accurate star catalogue of his time.

1054 AD
Chinese astronomers recorded a supernova explosion in Taurus. The Crab Nebula is the remnant of this event.

1543
Copernicus laid the groundwork of modern astronomy by showing that the Earth and all the planets revolved around the Sun.

Isaac Newton's reflecting telescope

1608
The Dutchman, Hans Lippershey, used the magnifying power of glass lenses to build the first telescope. The following year, Galileo used his own telescope to observe sunspots, the moons of Jupiter and the stars of the Milky Way.

1671
The first telescopes were crude refractors. In 1671, Newton invented the reflecting telescope. Though only 16 cm long, it was as powerful as a 200 cm refractor.

1937
Grote Reber built the first true radio telescope. He set up a 9 m reflecting dish in his garden to study the radio noises that came from the sky.

1960
Radio astronomers discover quasars (quasi-stellar radio sources). These puzzling objects lie at tremendous distances from us—as much as 15,000 million light years away. They are a fraction the size of galaxies yet hundreds of times brighter.

1967
Unexpected signals from space were discovered by astronomers at Cambridge, England. These unknown pulses turned out to be coming from rapidly spinning neutron stars. They were called pulsars. One has been found in the middle of the Crab Nebula, right at the heart of the supernova explosion of 1054.

1987
In a small nearby galaxy, the Large Magellanic Cloud, a blue supergiant star blew up. This supernova, as an exploding star is called, was 160,000 light years away, and was the nearest to the Earth since the telescope was invented.

1990
The Hubble Space Telescope, with a 2.4-m mirror, was launched into orbit. There were errors in manufacture that would take years to correct, but then it will search for other solar systems and help to measure the size of the universe.

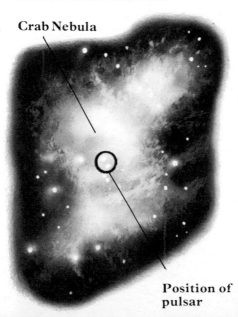

Crab Nebula

Position of pulsar

Sky facts

People have been studying the sky for centuries, yet it never ceases to yield new secrets.

In the last 40 years, radio astronomy has opened up a new side of the universe. Astronomers no longer study only visible light. They can now explore nearly the whole spectrum of radiation. Their findings are proving to be more spectacular than anyone could have imagined.

Here is a list of the ten brightest stars you can see in the sky.

Name	Constellation
Sirius	Canis Major
Canopus	Carina
Alpha Centauri	Centaurus
Arcturus	Boötes
Vega	Lyra
Capella	Auriga
Rigel	Orion
Procyon	Canis Minor
Achernar	Eridanus
Beta Centauri	Centaurus

Although the face of Venus is hidden by an unbroken layer of cloud, the surface is not so dark as was expected. The USSR landed Venus 9 and 10 successfully in 1975. The probes sent back pictures that show the surface to be no gloomier than an overcast day time scene on Earth. Venusian clouds proved to be more like a haze than a blanket.

Quasars are the most energetic objects in the sky, radiating the energy of 100,000 million Suns from compact regions not much bigger than our own solar system. They are explosions at the centres of giant galaxies, probably occurring in a ring of hot gases circling a very heavy black hole. They are also the most distant objects yet discovered, some lying about 15,000 million light years away.

The Sun shivers, but not with cold. Astronomers have recently detected wobbling movements that make the Sun larger or smaller by up to 10 km. At present, astronomers have no idea what causes them.

Pluto is really a double planet—its moon Charon is almost half as large as Pluto itself. Its strange orbit brings the Pluto-Charon double planet closer to the Sun than Neptune between 1979 and 1999. Pluto itself is the smallest planet in the solar system. It is only three-quarters the size of Mercury and is probably made of solid frozen methane (natural gas).

Astronomers estimate that there could be up to 10 million black holes in the Milky Way galaxy.

Time-exposure photograph of a man-made satellite passing overhead. If you see one, it will look like a bright moving star.

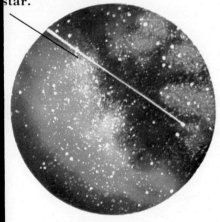

Massive galaxies can act as giant lenses, distorting quasars lying beyond them and even making them look double. The matter we can see in the universe is probably only about 10 percent of what is really present. The 'dark' matter may consist of faint dwarf stars, intergalactic gas, or subatomic particles filling space. Dust clouds that are probably a solar system in the making have been observed around several stars, such as Beta Pictoris.

Sky words

This glossary includes words that are not fully explained elsewhere in the book.

The spectrum

Radio waves · Infrared waves · Visible light · Ultraviolet rays · X-rays · Gamma rays

Astronomical unit (AU)
The average distance from the Sun to the Earth (150 million km) is an astronomical unit. It is a shorthand way of measuring distances within the solar system.

Big bang
Theory which holds that the entire universe began as a vast 'super-atom' of matter and energy that exploded, (the Bang), and sent all the galaxies hurtling through space.

Binary
Two stars in the same sun-system revolving around each other. Three, four and even more stars can link together like this.

Constellation
Group of stars seeming to make a shape or pattern in the sky.

Cosmic rays
Ultra high speed atomic particles that come shooting to Earth from outer space and from the Sun.

Galaxy
Stars are not randomly sprinkled throughout the universe. They are grouped in great clouds or galaxies. Each one contains thousands of millions of stars.

Gravity
The force of attraction that exists between one heavenly body and another. The more massive an object, the greater its gravity.

Light year
The distance light travels in a year (9,460,000 million km).

Magnitude
The brightness of a star or other object shining in space.

Orbit
The path of one body as it moves around another one in space. The pull of gravity keeps objects in orbit.

Radiation
Electromagnetic energy, whose full range comprises the spectrum described below.

Red shift
When the light of a star shifts to the red end of the spectrum, the star is receding from us. This is an example of the Doppler Effect.

Satellite
Smaller objects which revolve around a larger one and are held by its gravity are called satellites. The Moon is a satellite of Earth.

Spectrum
Visible light is one kind of radiation. Radio waves, infrared, ultraviolet and X-rays are other kinds. The entire range of radiation is called the spectrum. Visible light takes up a very small slot somewhere in the middle.

Solar wind
Clouds of atomic particles streaming away from the Sun at high speed.

Index

Going further

Organizations

BAYS
(British Association Youth Section)
Fortress House
23 Savile Row
London, W.1

British Astronomical Association
Burlington House
Piccadilly
London, W.1

Junior Astronomical Society
35 Fairway
Keyworth, Nottingham

Books to read

Spotter's Guide to the Night Sky
by Nigel Henbest
Usborne, 1985

Illustrated Dictionary of Astronomy
and Astronautics
Longman, 1987

The Greenwich Guide to the Planets
Stuart Malin
George Philip, 1987

The Sky at Night
by Patrick Moore
Harrap, 1989

The Monthly Sky Guide
by Ian Ridpath and Will Tirion
Cambridge University Press, 1990

The Skywatcher's Handbook
edited by Colin Ronan
Corgi, 1985

The Greenwich Guide to Stargazing
Carole Stott
George Philip, 1987

THE USBORNE YOUNG SCIENTIST
SPACEFLIGHT

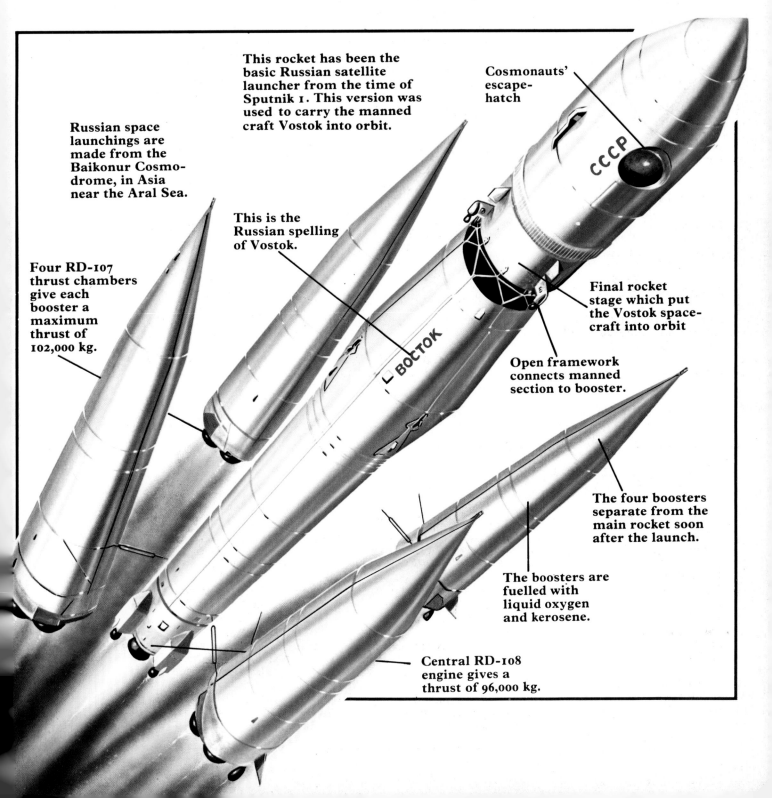

This rocket has been the basic Russian satellite launcher from the time of Sputnik I. This version was used to carry the manned craft Vostok into orbit.

Cosmonauts' escape-hatch

Russian space launchings are made from the Baikonur Cosmodrome, in Asia near the Aral Sea.

This is the Russian spelling of Vostok.

Four RD-107 thrust chambers give each booster a maximum thrust of 102,000 kg.

Final rocket stage which put the Vostok space-craft into orbit

Open framework connects manned section to booster.

The four boosters separate from the main rocket soon after the launch.

The boosters are fuelled with liquid oxygen and kerosene.

Central RD-108 engine gives a thrust of 96,000 kg.

BOCTOK

CCCP

Credits

Written by
Kenneth Gatland
Revised text by
Christopher Cooper
Art and editorial direction
David Jefferis
Revised edition designed by
Paul Greenleaf
Text editor
Tony Allan
Educational adviser
Frank Blackwell
Scientific adviser
Ian Ridpath
Illustrators
Sydney Cornford, Gordon Davies,
Malcolm English, Brian Lewis,
Chris Lyon, John Marshall,
Michael Roffe, David Slinn,
Craig Warwick

Acknowledgements
We wish to thank the following
organizations for their assistance
and for making available materials
in their collections.
British Aircraft Corporation
British Interplanetary Society
European Space Agency
Genesis Space Photo Library
Grumman Aerospace Corporation
Hawker Siddeley Dynamics
Martin-Marietta Aerospace
Messerschmitt-Bölkow-Blohm
National Aeronautics and Space
Administration
Rockwell International

On the cover: a Space Shuttle
takes off riding on the back
of a huge liquid-fuel tank.
On this page: Pioneer 10 flew by
Jupiter, biggest of the Sun's
planets, in 1973.

The experiments

Here is a checklist of the equipment you will need for the
experiments and things to do included in this book.

General equipment

Notebook and pencil
Rule or tape-measure
Sticky tape
Glue
Scissors
Watch
Rubber bands
Paper-clips, used matchsticks
Sheet of thin cardboard

Special experiments

Action and reaction (p.4):
Sausage-shaped balloons
Thin wire (fuse-wire is ideal)
Nylon fishing-line or thread

Air expansion (p.6):
Some small balloons
Narrow-necked glass bottle
Bucket and cloth

Satellite orbits (p.11):
Ballpoint pen case
Plasticine
Fishing-line or thread

Heat insulation (p.13):
Polystyrene ceiling tile
Two ice cubes

Space Shuttle glider (p.18):
**Balsawood, craft knife and
balsa cement OR stiff paper,
scissors and tape**

Mars Roving Vehicle (p.24):
**Two plastic bottles (washing-
up liquid bottles are ideal)**
Polystyrene foam
Stiff wire
Ballpoint pen case
Four necklace-beads

Rotating space station (p.26):
Three plastic bottles
Thick wire
Glass or plastic necklace-beads
Two small balsawood blocks
54 cm length of cardboard
Model astronaut

Weights and measures

All the weights and measures used in this book are metric.
This list gives some equivalents in imperial measures.

cm = centimetres
(1 inch = 2.54 cm)

m = metres
(1 yard = 0.91 m)

km = kilometres
(1 mile = 1.6 km)

kph = kilometres per hour
(1,000 mph = 1,609 kph)

sq. km = square kilometres
(1 square mile = 2.59 sq. km)

kg = kilograms
(1 stone = 6.35 kg)

A tonne is 1,000 kg
(1 ton = 1.02 tonnes)

kg/sq. cm = kilograms per
square centimetre
(1 pound per square inch =
0.07 kg/sq. cm)

1 litre is 1.76 pints
°C = degrees Centigrade

Contents

About this book

Spaceflight is about the exploration of mankind's new frontier. In simple language and with more than a hundred full-colour illustrations, it tells the story of the Space Age from the V-2 rocket to the present day and beyond.

It explains how rockets work and why satellites stay in orbit. You will find out about the dangers of travelling through space and what astronauts can do to overcome them. There are detailed descriptions of America's re-usable Space Shuttle, and how an industrial base may look when men finally settle on the Moon.

Spaceflight also includes lots of projects and things to do. There are safe and easy experiments involving such principles as heat insulation and the expansion and contraction of air; you will also learn how to make working models of a revolving space station and a Mars Roving Vehicle.

The rocket engine

No-one knows who invented the rocket. Perhaps the Chinese have the best claim. They are said to have shot 'fire arrows' at invading Mongols in AD 1232 at the Battle of K'ai-Fung-Fu.

For the next five centuries, rockets were used chiefly as fireworks but sometimes also as weapons.

An Englishman called William Congreve made improved solid-fuel rockets around 1800, but the big step did not come until the start of the 20th century when the Russian Konstantin Tsiolkovsky suggested the use of liquid propellants.

▲ **Dr. Robert H. Goddard (1882-1945) did extensive research with solid and liquid fuels. In 1920 he proposed sending a rocket loaded with flash powder to the Moon, and observing the flash through a telescope when it hit the Moon.**

▲ **It was Goddard who launched the world's first liquid-propellant rocket, in March 1926. Fuelled with liquid oxygen and gasoline, it was in the air for just 2½ seconds, covering a distance of 56 m at an average speed of 103 kph.**

Action, reaction and rocket racers

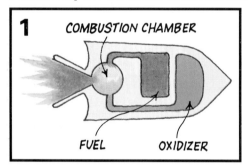

1 COMBUSTION CHAMBER
FUEL   OXIDIZER

▲ A liquid fuel rocket has fuel and an oxidizer, which are fed to the combustion chamber by gas pressure or, more often, by pumps. They ignite there. The oxidizer is needed to provide oxygen, without which nothing can burn.

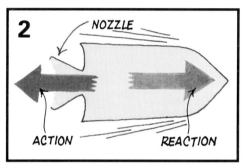

2 NOZZLE
ACTION   REACTION

▲ The burning liquids produce a powerful exhaust, which expands backwards through a nozzle. The action of the exhaust causes a reaction of equal pressure pushing in the opposite direction that drives the rocket forward.

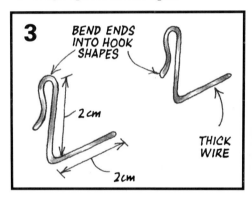

3 BEND ENDS INTO HOOK SHAPES
2 cm
2 cm
THICK WIRE

▲ This experiment is a quick and simple way of demonstrating the principle of action and reaction. You will need a few sausage-shaped balloons, some thin wire, and a length of nylon fishing-line or thread. Bend the wire as shown.

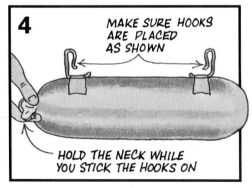

4 MAKE SURE HOOKS ARE PLACED AS SHOWN
HOLD THE NECK WHILE YOU STICK THE HOOKS ON

▲ Blow up a balloon and seal the end with tape. Fix the two hooks carefully to it, making sure they are in a straight line with one another and with the balloon. Ease the tape off the neck and let the air out slowly.

5 TAPE
TAUT NYLON FISHING LINE

▲ Attach one end of the fishing-line firmly to a wall or door. Stretch the line across the room, and tie or tape the other end to a chair-back or wall fitting. The line should be taut and should slope downwards a little.

6

▲ Blow up the balloon again. Hold the neck firmly. Hook the balloon over the line, then let go and watch it speed forward. With several lines and a packet of balloons, you can have rocket-races with your friends.

Europe's unmanned rocket launcher— the Ariane 4

Ariane 4 is a three-stage launch rocket, which when fully fuelled and carrying its payload weighs over 415 tonnes and stands about 60 m tall. It is built by the member countries of the European Space Agency (ESA), listed below.

Ariane 4 can place satellites weighing 4 tonnes or more into 24-hour orbit, 35,880 km above the equator.

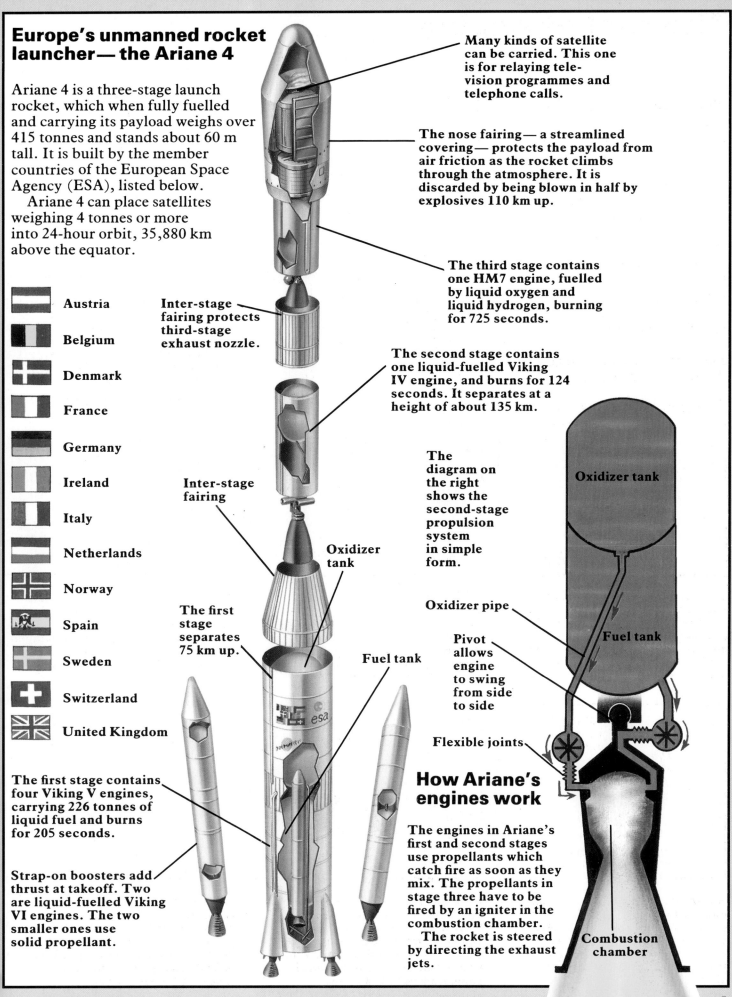

Austria

Belgium

Denmark

France

Germany

Ireland

Italy

Netherlands

Norway

Spain

Sweden

Switzerland

United Kingdom

Many kinds of satellite can be carried. This one is for relaying tele-vision programmes and telephone calls.

The nose fairing— a streamlined covering— protects the payload from air friction as the rocket climbs through the atmosphere. It is discarded by being blown in half by explosives 110 km up.

The third stage contains one HM7 engine, fuelled by liquid oxygen and liquid hydrogen, burning for 725 seconds.

Inter-stage fairing protects third-stage exhaust nozzle.

The second stage contains one liquid-fuelled Viking IV engine, and burns for 124 seconds. It separates at a height of about 135 km.

The diagram on the right shows the second-stage propulsion system in simple form.

Inter-stage fairing

Oxidizer tank

Oxidizer tank

Oxidizer pipe

Fuel tank

Pivot allows engine to swing from side to side

Flexible joints

The first stage separates 75 km up.

Fuel tank

The first stage contains four Viking V engines, carrying 226 tonnes of liquid fuel and burns for 205 seconds.

Strap-on boosters add thrust at takeoff. Two are liquid-fuelled Viking VI engines. The two smaller ones use solid propellant.

How Ariane's engines work

The engines in Ariane's first and second stages use propellants which catch fire as soon as they mix. The propellants in stage three have to be fired by an igniter in the combustion chamber.

The rocket is steered by directing the exhaust jets.

Combustion chamber

5

Ball of life

Planet earth, our island home in space, takes 365¼ days to travel around the Sun, and rotates once every 23 hours 56 minutes. These are our years and days. Oceans cover seven-tenths of its surface, and its poles are always covered by ice.

The air we breathe is mainly nitrogen (78%) and oxygen (21%). It is warmed by the Sun during the day and cools off at night. Temperature alterations cause movements of air, as the experiments below show. The constant interchange of air between sea and land is the main cause of changes in the weather.

◄ Nine planets revolve around our Sun, the closest being Mercury and the farthest Pluto. Earth is the only one with an atmosphere that can support human life. Water, vital to us, would either boil or freeze on the other planets.

Pluto

Neptune

Uranus

Saturn

Jupiter

Mars

Earth

Venus

Mercury

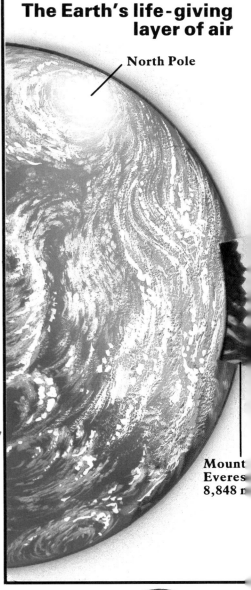

The Earth's life-giving layer of air

North Pole

Mount Everes 8,848 n

---

1 Expanding and contracting air

The Earth's layer of air is thin. Just 10 km from the surface there is already too little of it for men to survive. Manned spaceflight is only possible because man has learned how to take air into space with him.

Our air is a mixture of gases, and like all gases it expands when heated and contracts when cooled.

Movements of air in the atmosphere create our weather. Nowadays satellites are used to keep watch on this (see p.16).

STRETCH SMALL BALLOON OVER NECK

COLD BOTTLE

▲ This experiment with a bottle and a balloon shows how air expands when heated. Cool the bottle by running cold water over it, then stretch the balloon tightly over its neck. It will dangle loosely, empty of air.

HOT WATER

▲ Now fill a sink or bucket with hot water, and stand the bottle in it. As the air in the bottle heats up, it will expand upward into the balloon, blowing it up. Take the bottle out of the bucket, and the balloon will slowly go limp again.

6

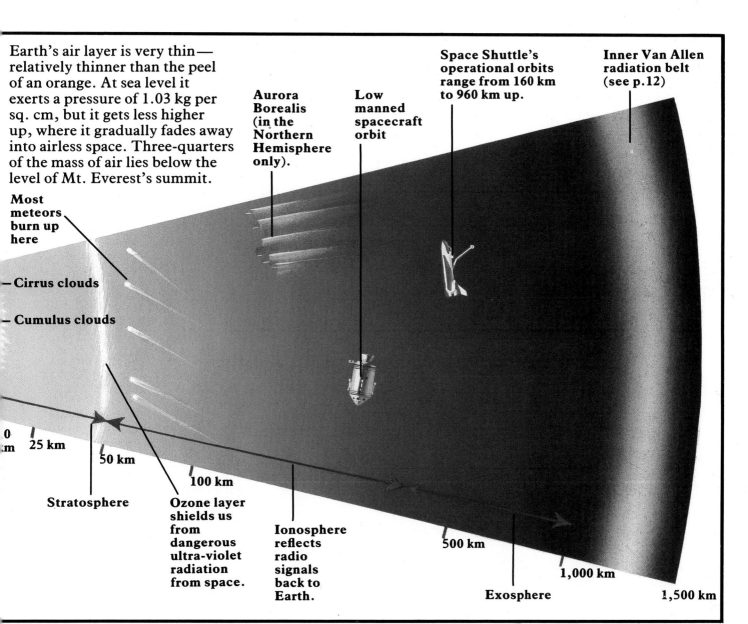

Earth's air layer is very thin—relatively thinner than the peel of an orange. At sea level it exerts a pressure of 1.03 kg per sq. cm, but it gets less higher up, where it gradually fades away into airless space. Three-quarters of the mass of air lies below the level of Mt. Everest's summit.

Aurora Borealis (in the Northern Hemisphere only).

Low manned spacecraft orbit

Space Shuttle's operational orbits range from 160 km to 960 km up.

Inner Van Allen radiation belt (see p.12)

Most meteors burn up here

— **Cirrus clouds**

— **Cumulus clouds**

0 km

25 km

50 km

100 km

500 km

1,000 km

1,500 km

Stratosphere

Ozone layer shields us from dangerous ultra-violet radiation from space.

Ionosphere reflects radio signals back to Earth.

Exosphere

4

HOT WATER

FILL TO OVER-FLOWING

▲ You can reverse the experiment by first pouring hot (**NOT** boiling) water into the bottle. Leave it to stand for a minute while the air inside warms up, then empty it. Stretch the balloon by blowing it up a couple of times.

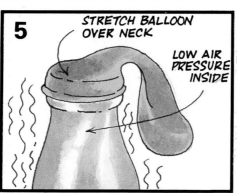

5

STRETCH BALLOON OVER NECK

LOW AIR PRESSURE INSIDE

▲ Fasten the balloon over the bottle's neck. As the hot air in the bottle cools down, it will contract, causing low pressure inside the bottle. There is now higher pressure outside the bottle than inside.

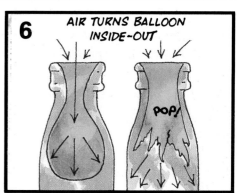

6

AIR TURNS BALLOON INSIDE-OUT

POP!

▲ The higher pressure outside pushes the balloon down into the bottle. In a pressurized spacecraft the higher pressure *inside* presses out against the craft's sides towards space. So it needs a strong hull to keep the pressure in.

Dawn of the Space Age

The big advances that made space travel possible were made in Germany in the 1930s and '40s. After experimenting with liquid-fuel rockets with the Society for Space Travel in the late 1920s, a young enthusiast called Wernher von Braun took his ideas to the Army.

Within a few years, improved rockets were being fired in secret from Griefswalder Oie, an island off Germany's Baltic coast (see map below). This then led to the creation of the big rocket research station at Peenemünde, where the V-2 weapon was developed.

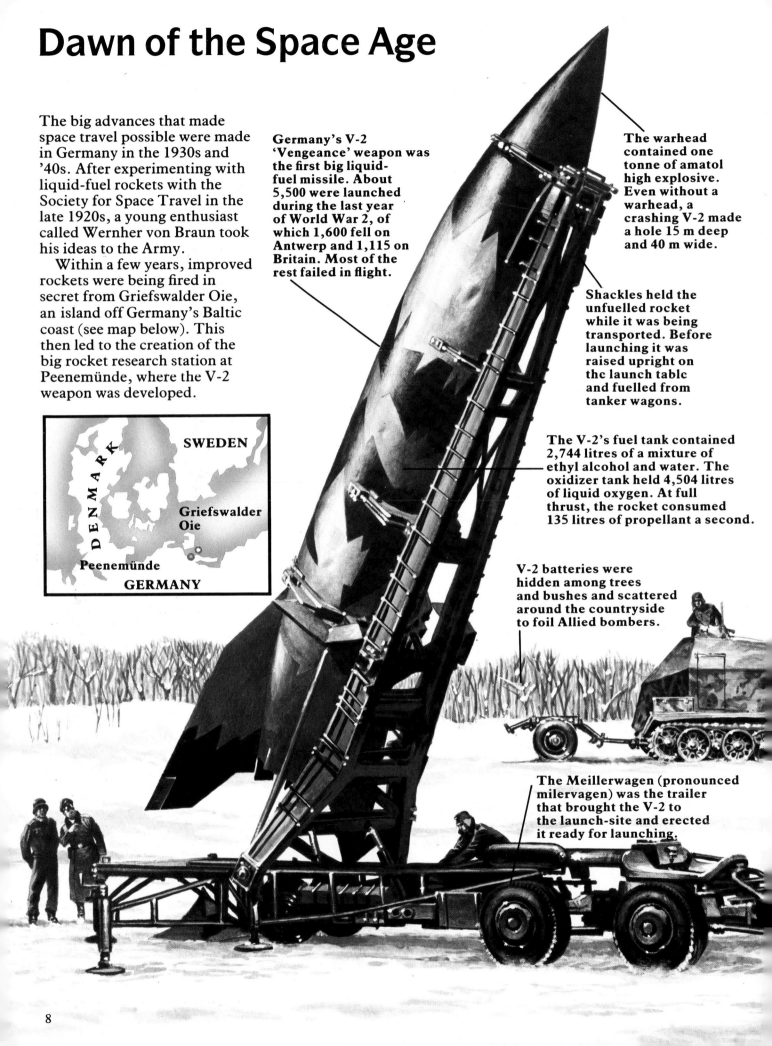

Germany's V-2 'Vengeance' weapon was the first big liquid-fuel missile. About 5,500 were launched during the last year of World War 2, of which 1,600 fell on Antwerp and 1,115 on Britain. Most of the rest failed in flight.

The warhead contained one tonne of amatol high explosive. Even without a warhead, a crashing V-2 made a hole 15 m deep and 40 m wide.

Shackles held the unfuelled rocket while it was being transported. Before launching it was raised upright on the launch table and fuelled from tanker wagons.

The V-2's fuel tank contained 2,744 litres of a mixture of ethyl alcohol and water. The oxidizer tank held 4,504 litres of liquid oxygen. At full thrust, the rocket consumed 135 litres of propellant a second.

V-2 batteries were hidden among trees and bushes and scattered around the countryside to foil Allied bombers.

The Meillerwagen (pronounced milervagen) was the trailer that brought the V-2 to the launch-site and erected it ready for launching.

SWEDEN

DENMARK

Griefswalder Oie

Peenemünde

GERMANY

▲ A Russian schoolteacher called Konstantin Tsiolkovsky worked out that rockets would travel in airless space. Although he never fired a rocket, he drew up designs in 1903 for a spaceship powered by liquid oxygen and liquid hydrogen.

▲ Wernher von Braun went to the USA after World War 2. There he led the team that launched America's first successful artificial satellite, Explorer I. He also developed the Saturn rockets that took astronauts to the Moon.

▲ A big step was taken as early as 1949, when a small WAC-Corporal rocket was launched from the nose of a V-2 high above White Sands Proving Ground, New Mexico. It reached a record height of 393 km and a speed of 8,286 kph.

A London-bound V-2 blasts off. About 500 of the missiles fell on the city.

The V-2's launching was controlled by the missile site commander from this armoured vehicle.

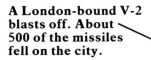

Launch table for V-2

▲ Sergei Korolev was a pioneer of Russian rocketry in the 1930s. He later developed the rockets which put Sputnik I and Yuri Gagarin, the world's first spaceman, into orbit.

▲ Russian scientists rocketed dogs into space in the 1950s to find out more about space travel. Laika, shown in the picture above, was sent into orbit in 1957.

Tow truck for Meillerwagen

A V-2 with wings

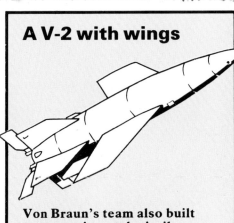

Von Braun's team also built two experimental missiles called A4bs, designed to glide for up to 750 km. The A4b was shelved in 1944, to make way for the V-2.

Into orbit

On October 4, 1957, Russia shook the world by launching the first artificial satellite, Sputnik 1.

American scientists had already made plans to launch their own satellite during the International Geophysical Year (1957-58). But their first attempt failed when the US Navy's Vanguard rocket toppled over on the launch-pad and burst into flames.

Von Braun's Army team was called in. Its four stage Juno 1 rocket put Explorer 1 into orbit on February 1, 1958. The 'space race' had begun.

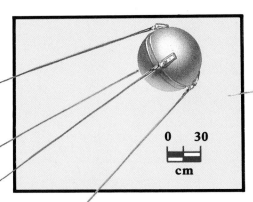

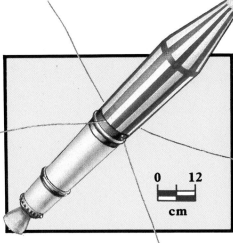

▲ Sputnik 1, a sphere 58 cm in diameter, weighed 83.6 kg — the weight of a large man. It was little more than an orbiting radio transmitter, with long 'whip' aerials. It circled the Earth for 92 days, then burned up.

▲ The instruments supplied by Dr. James Van Allen of Iowa University for Explorer 1 included a geiger counter which led to the discovery of the Earth's radiation belts (see p. 12). The satellite stayed in orbit for 12 years.

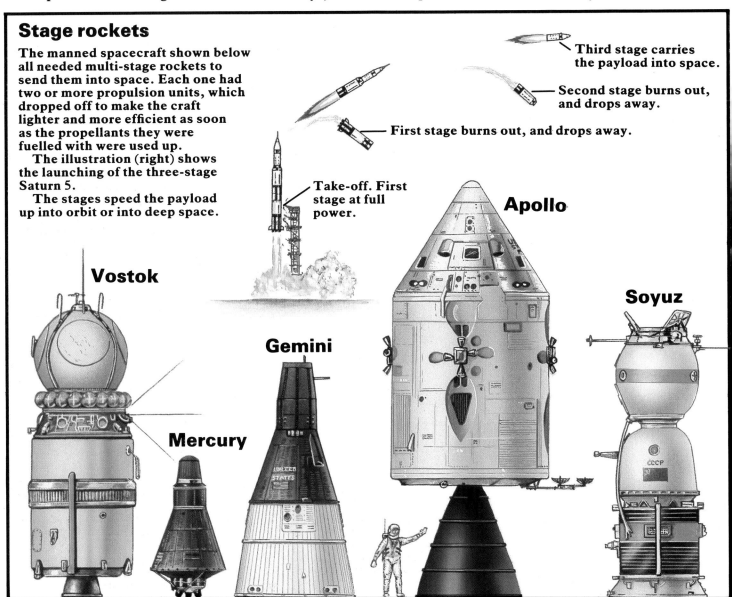

Stage rockets

The manned spacecraft shown below all needed multi-stage rockets to send them into space. Each one had two or more propulsion units, which dropped off to make the craft lighter and more efficient as soon as the propellants they were fuelled with were used up.

The illustration (right) shows the launching of the three-stage Saturn 5.

The stages speed the payload up into orbit or into deep space.

Third stage carries the payload into space.

Second stage burns out, and drops away.

First stage burns out, and drops away.

Take-off. First stage at full power.

Vostok

Mercury

Gemini

Apollo

Soyuz

▲ To understand how a satellite goes into orbit, imagine a gun firing shells from the peak of a high mountain. While a shell travels away from the gun, gravity constantly pulls it down, and it finally hits the ground.

▲ Suppose the gun is powerful enough to fire a shell halfway around the world. Gravity still acts on the shell, stopping it from flying off into space. It follows a curved path until it hits the Earth's surface.

▲ To go into orbit, the shell would have to travel very fast indeed— at about 29,000 kph if it were 100 km up. Gravity would still try to pull it down. But at that speed the outward pull of centrifugal force balances gravity exactly.

Centrifugal force

A satellite in orbit is exactly balanced between two forces pulling in opposite directions. One is the Earth's gravity, which pulls it downwards. The other, which pulls it outwards towards deep space, is called centrifugal force. The size of this depends on the speed at which the satellite is moving.

Because the forces are equally balanced, a change in either one will swing the satellite out of orbit—unless the other force changes too.

The pull of gravity is stronger the closer the satellite is to the Earth. This means that satellites near the Earth have to orbit faster than those farther out for their centrifugal force to balance the stronger pull of gravity.

Satellite speeds

Distance from Earth (in km)	Orbital speed (in kph)
160	27,950
800	26,650
16,000	15,050
35,880	11,070

(At this distance and speed, a satellite seems to stand still over a fixed point on Earth. It is called synchronous orbit.)

382,000	3,620

(This is the Moon's orbit.)

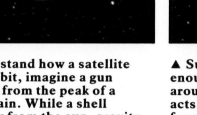

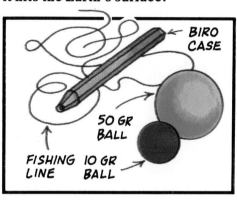

▲ You can make a model satellite with some plasticine, a ballpoint pen case, some fishing-line or thread, and two paper-clips. Split the plasticine into two lumps, one five times heavier than the other.

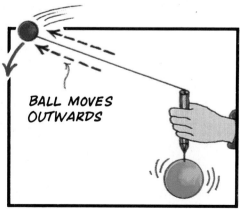

▲ The small ball will swing out, pulling the big ball up. The outward pull of the small ball is its centrifugal force. For a satellite, this must exactly balance gravity if it is to stay in orbit.

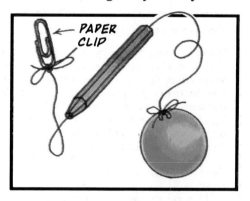

▲ Thread the line through the pen case. Tie paper-clips to each end, and push one clip into each ball of plasticine. Holding the pen case upright with the small ball on top, swing the case fast in a circle.

▲ Hold the case steady. As the small ball slows down, its centrifugal force lessens and it moves back towards the case–like a satellite slowed by atmospheric friction spiralling out of orbit.

Dangers of space

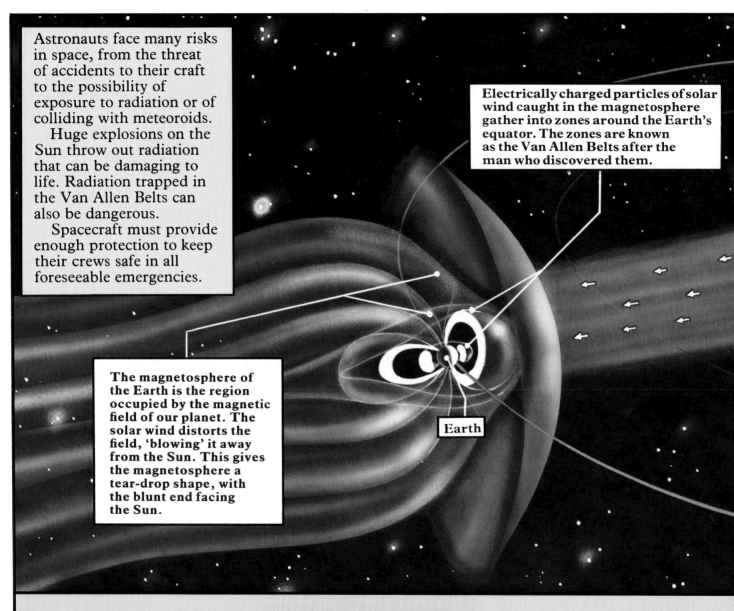

Astronauts face many risks in space, from the threat of accidents to their craft to the possibility of exposure to radiation or of colliding with meteoroids.

Huge explosions on the Sun throw out radiation that can be damaging to life. Radiation trapped in the Van Allen Belts can also be dangerous.

Spacecraft must provide enough protection to keep their crews safe in all foreseeable emergencies.

Electrically charged particles of solar wind caught in the magnetosphere gather into zones around the Earth's equator. The zones are known as the Van Allen Belts after the man who discovered them.

The magnetosphere of the Earth is the region occupied by the magnetic field of our planet. The solar wind distorts the field, 'blowing' it away from the Sun. This gives the magnetosphere a tear-drop shape, with the blunt end facing the Sun.

Earth

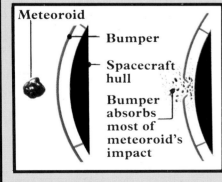

Meteoroid
Bumper
Spacecraft hull
Bumper absorbs most of meteoroid's impact

▲Spacecraft can be protected from meteoroids by a double skin or meteoroid bumper. When a particle strikes the ship, the outer shield takes the force of the blow.

Sunshade

▲Meteoroid shields also give protection against the Sun's heat. Skylab's astronauts had to put up a sunshade to keep the craft cool after its shield was torn off during the launch.

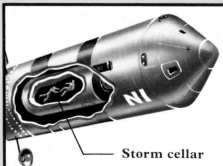

Storm cellar

▲Astronauts on long voyages could avoid dangerous radiation when solar flares erupt by getting into a 'storm cellar'. Inside they would be protected by radiation-proof walls.

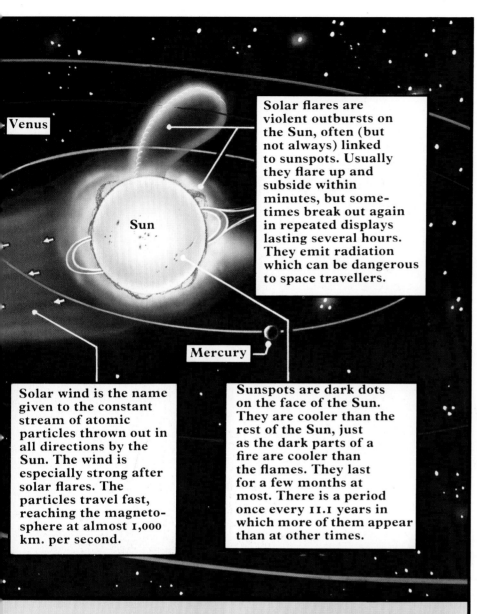

Venus

Sun

Mercury

Solar flares are violent outbursts on the Sun, often (but not always) linked to sunspots. Usually they flare up and subside within minutes, but some-times break out again in repeated displays lasting several hours. They emit radiation which can be dangerous to space travellers.

Solar wind is the name given to the constant stream of atomic particles thrown out in all directions by the Sun. The wind is especially strong after solar flares. The particles travel fast, reaching the magneto-sphere at almost 1,000 km. per second.

Sunspots are dark dots on the face of the Sun. They are cooler than the rest of the Sun, just as the dark parts of a fire are cooler than the flames. They last for a few months at most. There is a period once every 11.1 years in which more of them appear than at other times.

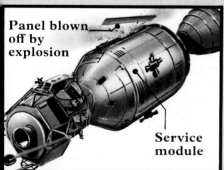

Panel blown off by explosion

Service module

▲An explosion partly crippled Apollo 13 when it was 330,000 km. from Earth. Mission control worked out a return path and sent instructions by radio. The astronauts got back safely.

▲Spacecraft unprotected from air friction would burn up as they re-entered the Earth's atmosphere at speeds of up to 40,000 k.p.h. Thick heatshields are needed to prevent this.

Keeping cool in space

SHADOW TEMPERATURE - 160°C.

TEMPERATURE IN THE SUN 83°C.

▲It is lethally hot in space in the glare of the Sun's rays, and unbearably cold in the shadows. To prevent astronauts from freezing or burning, spacecraft must be protected by insulating materials. Polystyrene is one that is used.

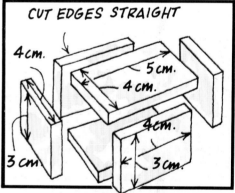

CUT EDGES STRAIGHT

4cm.

5cm.

4cm.

4cm.

3cm.

3cm.

▲Test polystyrene for yourself like this. Make a box as shown above from a ceiling-tile (you can buy these at do-it-yourself shops). Glue the base and sides together with polystyrene cement. You will also need two ice-cubes.

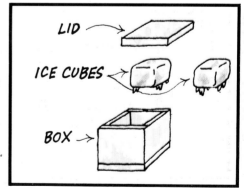

LID

ICE CUBES

BOX

▲ Put one cube in the box and put the lid on. Leave the other in the open. Now wait for them to melt. You will find that the insulated cube will melt much more slowly, as it is shielded by the polystyrene.

What astronauts wear

A human being cannot step out of a spacecraft without the protection of a spacesuit. It wraps the astronaut in its own protective atmosphere, providing oxygen to breathe and keeping the body under pressure. Without this the astronaut would die.

The Apollo moonsuit (right) held oxygen in a backpack that kept the suit's pressure at 0.27 kg/sq.cm. Though it looked cumbersome, the suit was flexible enough for the wearer to walk, jump and bend. Beneath it, the astronaut wore a cooling garment in which water circulated in plastic tubes.

▲Wiley Post, who in 1933 became the first man to fly solo around the world, was also a pioneer of pressure-suit development. His experience helped his sponsors, Lockheed Aircraft, to develop an experimental pressure-cabin plane.

▲The first moonsuit was designed in 1948 by Harry Ross of the British Interplanetary Society. It had a backpack oxygen supply, flexible joints and thick-soled boots. A silvered cape was draped behind it for temperature control.

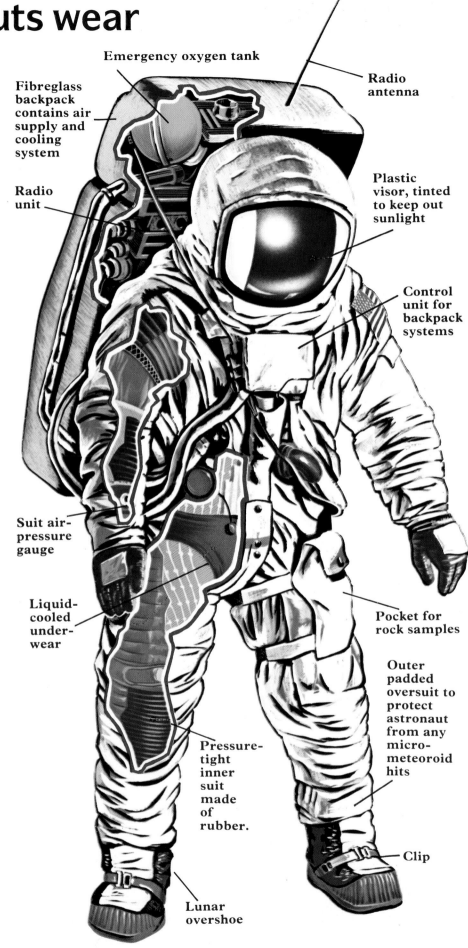

Emergency oxygen tank

Radio antenna

Fibreglass backpack contains air supply and cooling system

Radio unit

Plastic visor, tinted to keep out sunlight

Control unit for backpack systems

Suit air-pressure gauge

Liquid-cooled under-wear

Pocket for rock samples

Outer padded oversuit to protect astronaut from any micro-meteoroid hits

Pressure-tight inner suit made of rubber.

Clip

Lunar overshoe

First flights

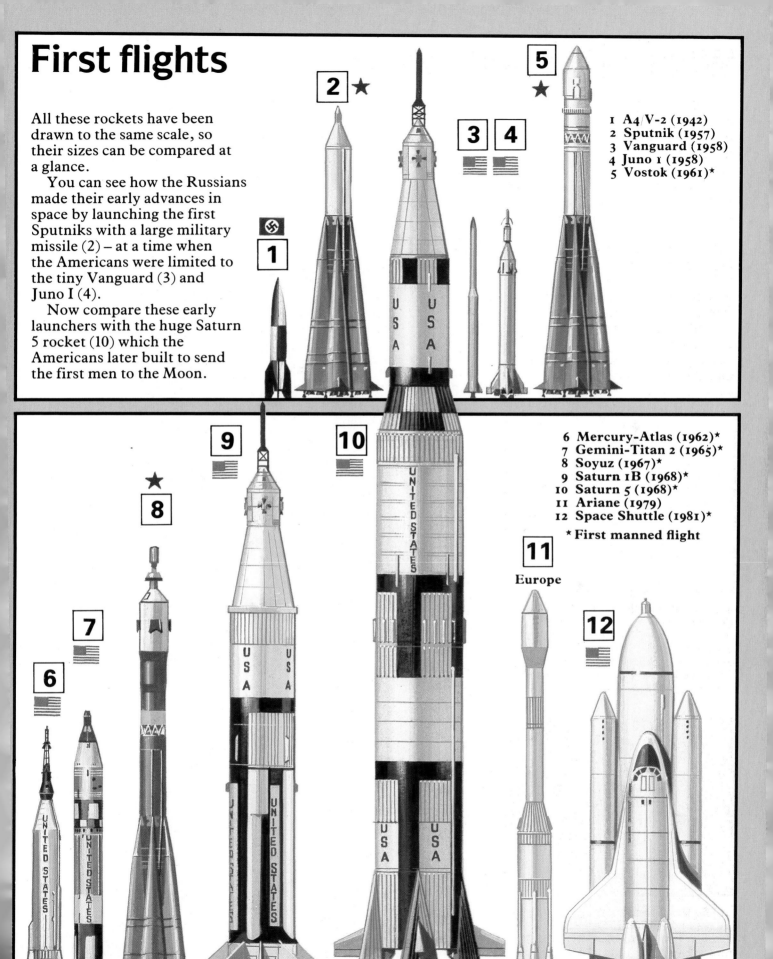

All these rockets have been drawn to the same scale, so their sizes can be compared at a glance.

You can see how the Russians made their early advances in space by launching the first Sputniks with a large military missile (2) – at a time when the Americans were limited to the tiny Vanguard (3) and Juno I (4).

Now compare these early launchers with the huge Saturn 5 rocket (10) which the Americans later built to send the first men to the Moon.

1   A4/V-2 (1942)
2   Sputnik (1957)
3   Vanguard (1958)
4   Juno I (1958)
5   Vostok (1961)★

6   Mercury-Atlas (1962)★
7   Gemini-Titan 2 (1965)★
8   Soyuz (1967)★
9   Saturn 1B (1968)★
10   Saturn 5 (1968)★
11   Ariane (1979)
12   Space Shuttle (1981)★

★ First manned flight

Europe

Servants in the sky

Every day artificial satellites are helping to improve life on Earth. They help us to keep watch on weather changes and storms, or to locate deposits of minerals, oil and natural gas. They observe military build-ups and check that arms agreements are kept.

Others form a global web of communications. They carry millions of international telephone calls every year, and relay television programmes and computer data around the world.

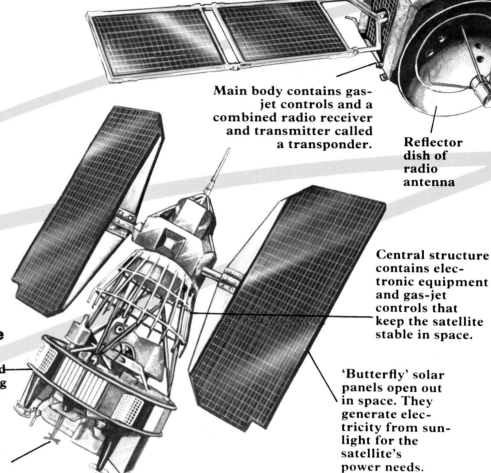

2 MAROTS

Maritime Orbital Test Satellite

Main body contains gas-jet controls and a combined radio receiver and transmitter called a transponder.

Reflector dish of radio antenna

Central structure contains electronic equipment and gas-jet controls that keep the satellite stable in space.

'Butterfly' solar panels open out in space. They generate electricity from sunlight for the satellite's power needs.

1 LANDSAT

Earth resources satellite

Sensory ring holds cameras and other instruments for collecting data about the Earth's surface.

Landsat's systems can map more than 161 million sq. km. a week.

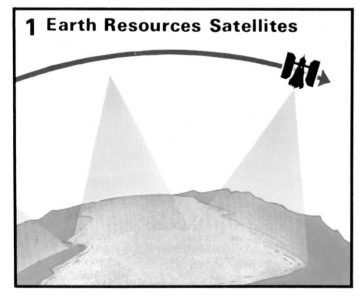

1 Earth Resources Satellites

▲ Besides locating natural resources, these satellites keep track of pollution and give warning of drought, floods and forest fires. Photographs they take have many uses—for instance, they can show whether food crops are diseased or healthy. Blighted crops show up blue-black, healthy crops pink or red.

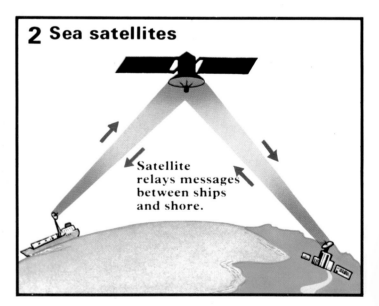

2 Sea satellites

Satellite relays messages between ships and shore.

▲ Satellites keep most large ships, and many small ones, in touch with the shore at all times, and relay distress calls instantly. Special navigational satellites serve as 'radio stars' that allow ships to navigate accurately in all weathers, and help to control the movement of jet aircraft on long-distance flights.

16

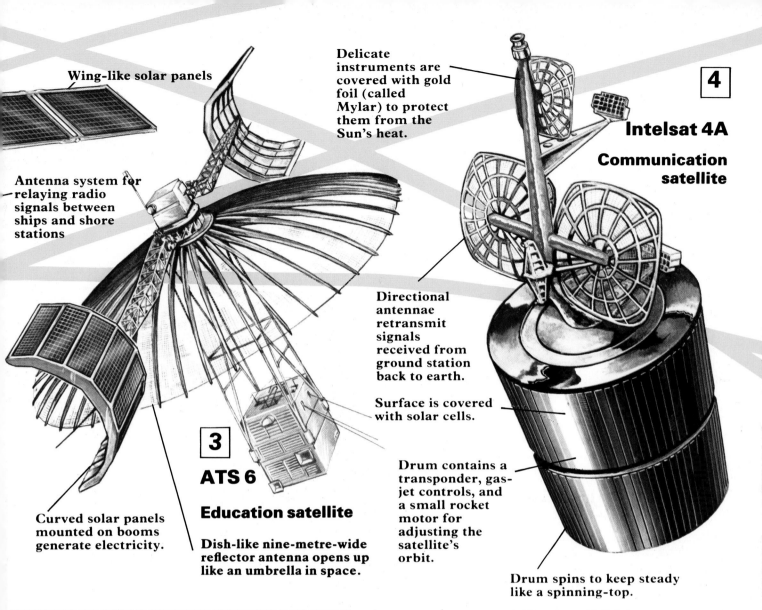

Wing-like solar panels

Antenna system for relaying radio signals between ships and shore stations

Delicate instruments are covered with gold foil (called Mylar) to protect them from the Sun's heat.

4

Intelsat 4A

Communication satellite

Directional antennae retransmit signals received from ground station back to earth.

Surface is covered with solar cells.

Curved solar panels mounted on booms generate electricity.

3

ATS 6

Education satellite

Dish-like nine-metre-wide reflector antenna opens up like an umbrella in space.

Drum contains a transponder, gas-jet controls, and a small rocket motor for adjusting the satellite's orbit.

Drum spins to keep steady like a spinning-top.

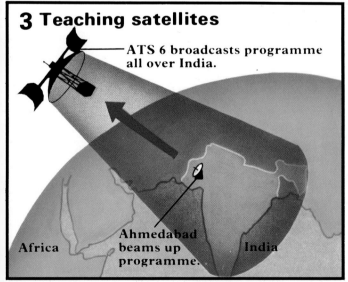

3 Teaching satellites

ATS 6 broadcasts programme all over India.

Ahmedabad beams up programme.

Africa

India

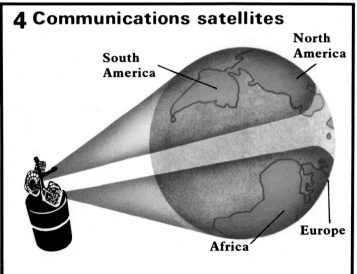

4 Communications satellites

North America

South America

Europe

Africa

▲ Satellites can be used to educate people in out-of-the-way places.
 A powerful satellite stationed 35,880 km above East Africa has been used to broadcast educational programmes beamed up from a transmitter in Ahmedabad to 5,000 towns and villages in India. Each of them has its own dish aerial and TV set.

▲ Dish aerials on houses point at satellites 35,880 km high, which keep pace with the Earth's rotation and seem from the ground to stand still in the sky. The satellites relay TV and radio programmes around the world. Telephone calls are also relayed by satellites in the same orbit.

The Space Shuttle 1: how it works

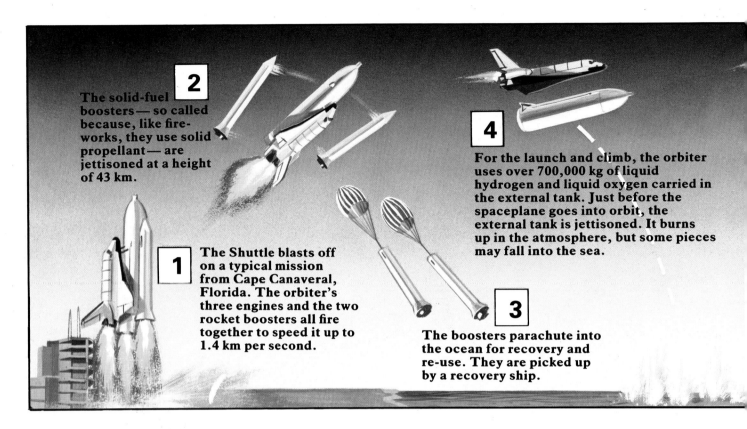

2 The solid-fuel boosters — so called because, like fireworks, they use solid propellant — are jettisoned at a height of 43 km.

1 The Shuttle blasts off on a typical mission from Cape Canaveral, Florida. The orbiter's three engines and the two rocket boosters all fire together to speed it up to 1.4 km per second.

4 For the launch and climb, the orbiter uses over 700,000 kg of liquid hydrogen and liquid oxygen carried in the external tank. Just before the spaceplane goes into orbit, the external tank is jettisoned. It burns up in the atmosphere, but some pieces may fall into the sea.

3 The boosters parachute into the ocean for recovery and re-use. They are picked up by a recovery ship.

The Space Shuttle is designed to cut the cost of space travel by making it more like normal aircraft flight. Unlike earlier launch rockets which fell to destruction, the major parts of the Shuttle — the orbiter, or spaceplane, and rocket boosters — can be recovered and re-used.

The crew consists of a pilot and co-pilot, and one or more mission specialists. When it carries the four-person European Spacelab (see p. 20), the orbiter becomes a miniature space station.

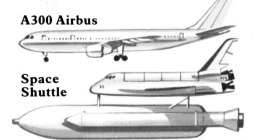

A300 Airbus

Space Shuttle

From the nose of the external tank to the tip of the orbiter's tail, the Shuttle is roughly the same length as an A300 jetliner.

1 Build your own Space Shuttle glider

▲ This model is a 1:200 scale replica of the Shuttle spaceplane. Trace it from the plan on p.19. You can make it from stiff paper, using adhesive tape to stick the parts together, or from balsa wood, using balsa cement.

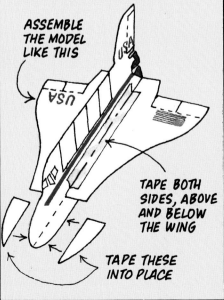

ASSEMBLE THE MODEL LIKE THIS

TAPE BOTH SIDES, ABOVE AND BELOW THE WING

TAPE THESE INTO PLACE

2

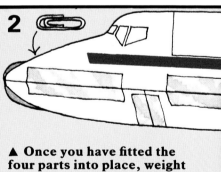

▲ Once you have fitted the four parts into place, weight the model with two or three paper-clips. Slide them onto the nose just over the wings.

3

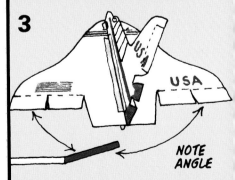

NOTE ANGLE

▲ Now test the model. First make sure that the fuselage and wings are at right angles to one another. Tip the outer elevons to the angle shown above.

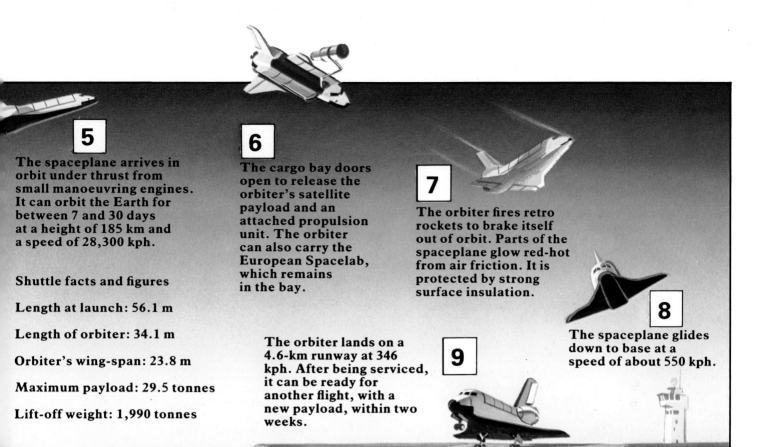

5
The spaceplane arrives in orbit under thrust from small manoeuvring engines. It can orbit the Earth for between 7 and 30 days at a height of 185 km and a speed of 28,300 kph.

Shuttle facts and figures

Length at launch: 56.1 m

Length of orbiter: 34.1 m

Orbiter's wing-span: 23.8 m

Maximum payload: 29.5 tonnes

Lift-off weight: 1,990 tonnes

6
The cargo bay doors open to release the orbiter's satellite payload and an attached propulsion unit. The orbiter can also carry the European Spacelab, which remains in the bay.

7
The orbiter fires retro rockets to brake itself out of orbit. Parts of the spaceplane glow red-hot from air friction. It is protected by strong surface insulation.

8
The spaceplane glides down to base at a speed of about 550 kph.

9
The orbiter lands on a 4.6-km runway at 346 kph. After being serviced, it can be ready for another flight, with a new payload, within two weeks.

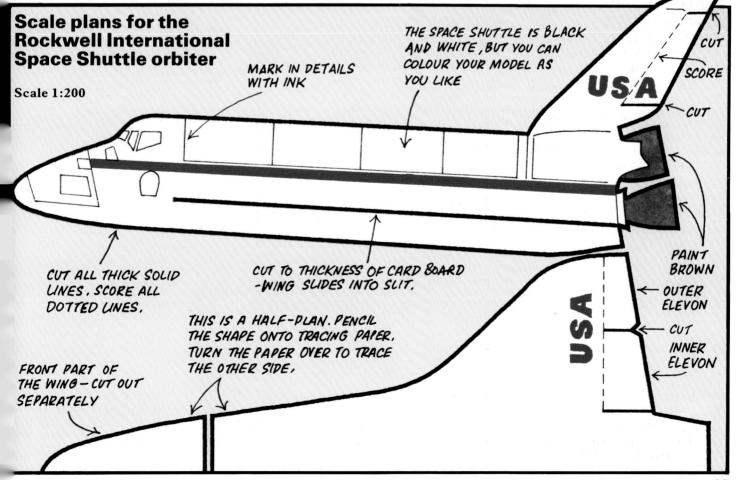

Scale plans for the Rockwell International Space Shuttle orbiter

Scale 1:200

MARK IN DETAILS WITH INK

THE SPACE SHUTTLE IS BLACK AND WHITE, BUT YOU CAN COLOUR YOUR MODEL AS YOU LIKE

USA

CUT

SCORE

CUT

PAINT BROWN

OUTER ELEVON

CUT

INNER ELEVON

USA

CUT TO THICKNESS OF CARD BOARD -WING SLIDES INTO SLIT.

CUT ALL THICK SOLID LINES. SCORE ALL DOTTED LINES.

THIS IS A HALF-PLAN. PENCIL THE SHAPE ONTO TRACING PAPER. TURN THE PAPER OVER TO TRACE THE OTHER SIDE.

FRONT PART OF THE WING — CUT OUT SEPARATELY

The Space Shuttle 2: workhorse in orbit

The Space Shuttle has many commercial, scientific and military uses. It can deliver, service and retrieve satellites of all kinds, and can handle several different jobs on a single mission.

Though most payloads are unmanned, the Shuttle cargo bay is big enough to carry a manned laboratory, the European Spacelab. Scientists of many countries will be able to go into orbit in Spacelab. Unlike earlier space stations that were abandoned in orbit, Spacelab will return to Earth after each mission.

The Shuttle will also play a key role in the construction of the permanent Freedom space station.

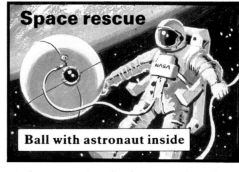

Space rescue

Ball with astronaut inside

▲ Astronauts who have to abandon a crippled orbiter could be carried to safety in NASA's 85-cm 'Personal Rescue Enclosure'.

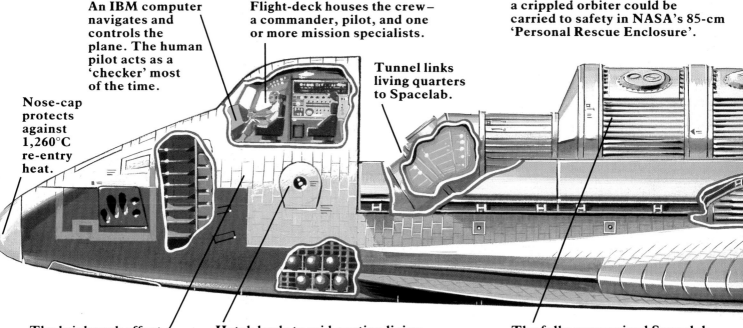

An IBM computer navigates and controls the plane. The human pilot acts as a 'checker' most of the time.

Flight-deck houses the crew – a commander, pilot, and one or more mission specialists.

Tunnel links living quarters to Spacelab.

Nose-cap protects against 1,260°C re-entry heat.

The brickwork effect is caused by heat insulation tiles fixed to the outside of the orbiter.

Hatch leads to mid-section living quarters and to flight-deck. The mid-section has four sleep bays (the crew take turns to sleep), toilet and washing spaces, and galleys with food and water.

The fully-pressurized Spacelab is 4.17 m in diameter — big enough for four people to work in shirt-sleeve comfort. It allows scientists to work under weightless conditions in orbit.

▲ Space crew normally stay securely tied to their craft during EVA (extra-vehicular activity). Shuttle astronaut Bruce McCandless made the first untethered 'spacewalk' in 1984, using an MMU (manned manoeuvring unit), or 'flying armchair'.

▲ Two of the Shuttle crews' tasks are the repair and retrieval of satellites. Here the craft has rendezvoused with a communications satellite, which two astronauts are inspecting. One is tethered to the Shuttle's long robot arm.

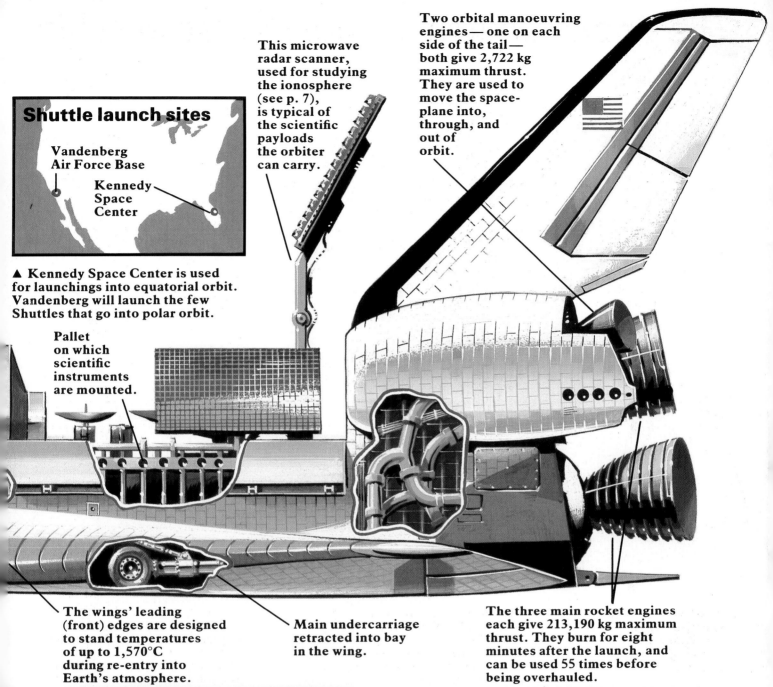

This microwave radar scanner, used for studying the ionosphere (see p. 7), is typical of the scientific payloads the orbiter can carry.

Two orbital manoeuvring engines—one on each side of the tail—both give 2,722 kg maximum thrust. They are used to move the space-plane into, through, and out of orbit.

Shuttle launch sites

Vandenberg Air Force Base

Kennedy Space Center

▲ Kennedy Space Center is used for launchings into equatorial orbit. Vandenberg will launch the few Shuttles that go into polar orbit.

Pallet on which scientific instruments are mounted.

The wings' leading (front) edges are designed to stand temperatures of up to 1,570°C during re-entry into Earth's atmosphere.

Main undercarriage retracted into bay in the wing.

The three main rocket engines each give 213,190 kg maximum thrust. They burn for eight minutes after the launch, and can be used 55 times before being overhauled.

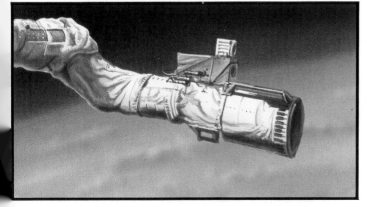

▲ The Shuttle's robot arm has three sections, with a 15-m reach overall. It can position an entire cargo of over 29 tonnes to within 5 cm. The arm can be controlled by a computer, by a human operator, or by the two working together.

▲ At takeoff the three main engines on the Shuttle orbiter and the two solid-fuel boosters fire together, giving over 3,000 tonnes of thrust. The boosters burn out after two minutes, while the main engines continue for a further six minutes.

Into the depths of space

Spacemen may not go beyond the Moon this century, but robot craft are increasing our knowledge of other planets by leaps and bounds. Not only are they cheaper to build than manned ships, they can also be abandoned if they break down.

We can fly to the Moon in three days, but reaching the planets is much more difficult. Interplanetary spacecraft must swing round the Sun. They can only be launched when the planets themselves are in the right positions in their orbits. Journeys of this sort last for months or even years.

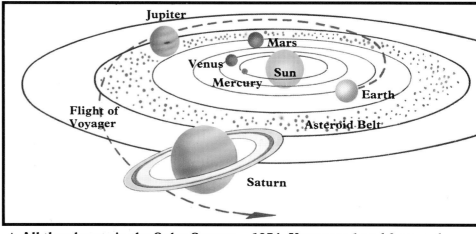

▲ All the planets in the Solar System except Pluto have been visited by space probes. America's Mariner 2 was the first craft to fly past Venus, in 1962. Mariner 9 looked at Mars from orbit, and Mariner 10 passed Mercury on its way from Venus in 1974. Voyagers 1 and 2 passed Jupiter in 1979 before flying on to Saturn, and Voyager 2 later encountered Uranus and Neptune. Both Voyagers have left the Solar System, like Pioneers 10 and 11 before them.

▲ Space-probe photographs of Mercury show a Moon-like world of craters, mountains and valleys. The planet has a diameter of 4,878 km and spins very slowly. It is baking hot by day, and freezing cold at night.

▲ Before Russia's Venera 9 and 10 swung into orbit around Venus in 1975, they sent landing capsules through its thick carbon dioxide atmosphere. Each one sent a panoramic picture by television to Earth. The first showed sharp-edged rocks, the second (above) a view showing rocks that looked like huge pancakes. The surface temperature was far above the melting point of lead, and the atmospheric pressure 90 to 100 times that of Earth.

▲ Saturn and its rings were photographed by the Voyagers. From Earth the rings look like broad bands, but from close up they are seen to consist of thousands of narrow rings. These are swarms of ice-covered rocks orbiting the planet.

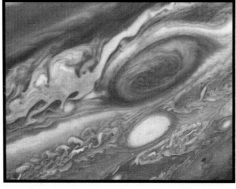

▲ When Voyager spacecraft flew past Jupiter, they obtained breathtaking views of the giant planet's cloud systems. They photographed the Great Red Spot, a storm larger than the Earth that has been observed by astronomers since the 17th century.

▲ A Voyager craft saw an active volcano on the horizon of Io, the innermost of Jupiter's four major satellites. Jupiter's powerful gravity stretches and squeezes the tiny world, heating it and causing the volcanic activity.

Missions to Mars

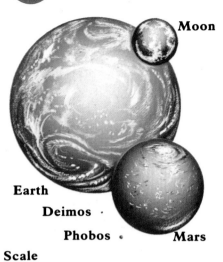

Earth

Moon

Deimos ·

Phobos ·   Mars

Scale

0   6,400   12,800 km

◀ The diagram (left) shows the Earth and Moon to scale with Mars and its two tiny moons, Phobos and Deimos. The cameras of Mariner and Viking space probes have revealed mountains, canyons, and features looking like dried-up river beds.

▲Olympus Mons (above), an ancient volcano 24 km high, is the highest known peak in the Solar System. Two Viking robot craft landed in 1976, analysed the soil and observed the weather. They failed to find signs of life.

The Galileo Mission to Jupiter

The craft first curves in towards the Sun to pass near Venus, where the planet's gravity boosts its speed. Later Galileo passes the Earth again and is speeded up still more. It will reach Jupiter in the mid-1990s after a six-year flight. Five months before arrival, it will launch a probe that will enter Jupiter's atmosphere. This may survive for an hour before being crushed by the pressure.

Meanwhile, the main craft will tour Jupiter's satellites, including the red world Io (below).

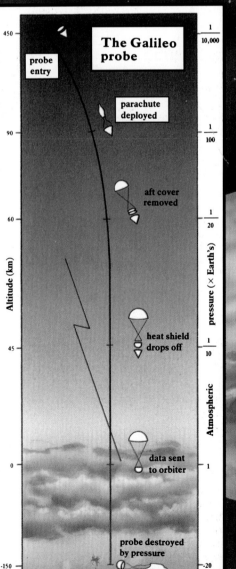

The Galileo probe

probe entry

parachute deployed

aft cover removed

heat shield drops off

data sent to orbiter

probe destroyed by pressure

Altitude (km)

pressure (× Earth's)

Atmospheric

23

Driving on another world

When astronauts eventually land on Mars, they will want to explore farther afield than they can go on foot. They will need transport for the search for minerals and for ice or permafrost, which could be a source of water and oxygen.

The future Mars Roving Vehicle may well look like the one shown here, which is a development of the Moon Rovers already used successfully for lunar exploration. It is equipped with a pressurized cabin and a laboratory, and is electrically powered by rechargeable storage batteries.

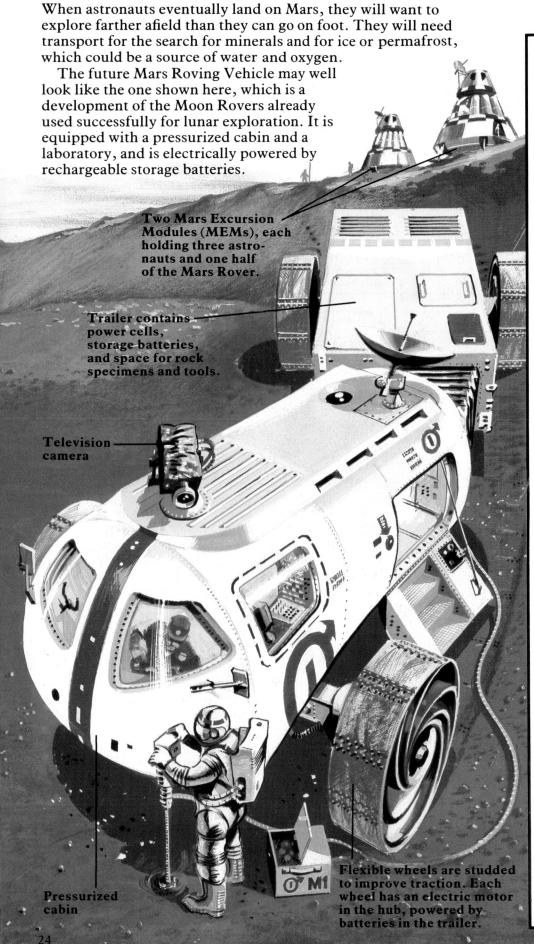

Two Mars Excursion Modules (MEMs), each holding three astronauts and one half of the Mars Rover.

Trailer contains power cells, storage batteries, and space for rock specimens and tools.

Television camera

Pressurized cabin

Flexible wheels are studded to improve traction. Each wheel has an electric motor in the hub, powered by batteries in the trailer.

1 Build a Mars Roving Vehicle

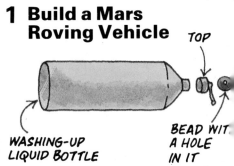

TOP

WASHING-UP LIQUID BOTTLE

BEAD WITH A HOLE IN IT

▲ You will need two plastic bottles, some cardboard, a little polystyrene foam, a matchstick, a rubber band, some thick wire, an empty ballpoint pen case, and four beads with holes through them.

5

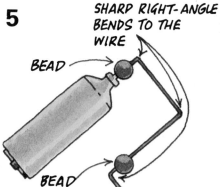

SHARP RIGHT-ANGLE BENDS TO THE WIRE

BEAD

BEAD

▲ Holding the band taut, pass the bottle-top and then a bead along the wire. Fit the top back on the neck. Bend the wire to the shape shown above, and fit a second bead onto its trailing end.

9 Testing trials

FOAM STRIPS

▲ Lift the body off again, and wind up the driving-wheel wire about 50 times. Replace the body, then test your MRV. If it skids, you can glue two foam strips around the drivng-wheel.

2

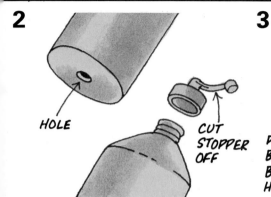

HOLE

CUT STOPPER OFF

▲ Make a hole in the exact centre of the bottom of one bottle. Ease off the bottle-top. If there is a stopper, cut it off. Select a rubber band that is about two-thirds as long as the bottle.

3

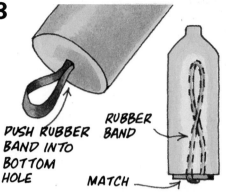

PUSH RUBBER BAND INTO BOTTOM HOLE

RUBBER BAND

MATCH

▲ Use the matchstick to push the rubber band through the hole. Once it is nearly all inside the bottle, loop its end around the matchstick. Tape the matchstick to the bottom of the bottle.

4

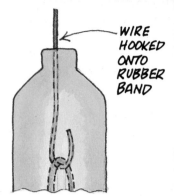

WIRE HOOKED ONTO RUBBER BAND

▲ With a pair of pliers, cut a piece of wire about one-and-a-half times the length of the bottle, and bend one end of it into a hook. Pass the hook through the bottle's neck and catch the band's loose end.

6 Making the body

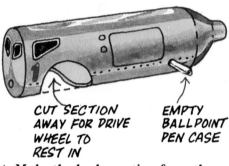

CUT SECTION AWAY FOR DRIVE WHEEL TO REST IN

EMPTY BALLPOINT PEN CASE

▲ Make the body section from the other plastic bottle by cutting a circular section into which the first bottle can fit (see above). Cut holes for rear axle, and slide ballpoint pen case through them.

7 Rear wheels

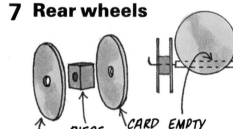

WIRE

CARD DISC

PIECE OF POLYSTYRENE FOAM

CARD DISC

EMPTY BALL-POINT PEN CASE

▲ Make each wheel by glueing two cardboard discs cut to the same size around a small square of poly-styrene foam. Pierce centre holes. Attach to the body with wire through the pen case, as shown.

8 The finished MRV

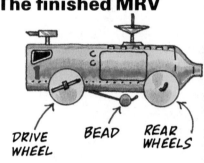

DRIVE WHEEL

BEAD

REAR WHEELS

▲ Fit the driving-wheel into the body, with the trailing bead midway between the two sets of wheels. Decorate the top of the MRV with a model TV camera and radio aerial cut out of cardboard.

10   Obstacle course for MRVs

GIANT CARD DISCS SLIPPED OVER WHEELS

OLD SHIRT

FLOOR TILES

SAND

CARPET

▲ You will find that different ground surfaces will affect the performance of your MRV. The wide driving-wheel works well on smooth floors, for instance, but not on carpets. Test it over an obstacle course like the one shown above.

One way of making it go better over rough surfaces is to put giant cardboard discs over all the wheels. Cut a hole of the same width as the bottle in the centre of two of the discs. Then slide them over the driving-wheel, one on each side of the body. Pierce a small hole in the centre of the other two, then attach them to the rear axle wire with pliers.

Space stations

Factories in space sound like science fiction. But already new alloys and near-perfect crystals, which can only be made in zero gravity, have been manufactured in space.

This early 21st century space station revolves to produce artificial gravity in the living quarters. In the control hub, which does not revolve, people are weightless.

The United States has designed a permanent space station, to be built from modules carried by Shuttles.

The station revolves 3.5 times a minute to simulate Earth gravity.

Space Shuttle orbiter carries supplies to the station from the Earth.

Lift between floors

Crew of 50 walk on vertical 'walls' held fast by centrifugal force.

Make your own rotating space station

1

LEAVE POWER WIRE BENT OVER

TAPE BALANCE FINS TO SIDE

The space station works in the same way as the Mars Rover see (p. 24). You can re-use its driving-wheel if you want. Tape cardboard fins to the base to make the station stand securely.

2

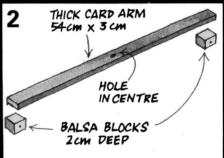

THICK CARD ARM 54cm x 3 cm

HOLE IN CENTRE

BALSA BLOCKS 2cm DEEP

Cut an arm out of thick cardboard to the size shown. Punch a hole in its exact centre. Glue two balsa blocks, as shown, to the two ends. Make a small hole through the centre of each block.

3

TAPE WIRE FIRMLY

Unbend the power wire, and poke it through the hole in the centre of the arm. Bend it down and tape it firmly to the arm. Wind the arm up a few turns to test that it rotates freely.

7

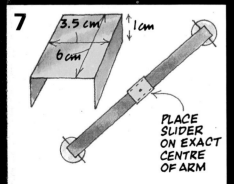

3.5 cm   1cm
6 cm

PLACE SLIDER ON EXACT CENTRE OF ARM

Cut a slider out of postcard to the dimensions shown. Bend the edges over. Wind the arm up, and put the slider on its exact centre. Let the arm spin. The slider will stay in place.

8

CENTRIFUGAL FORCE

Try it again with the slider a little-off centre. As the arm speeds up, it will move away from the centre hole. This outward momentum is called centrifugal force.

9

MODEL ASTRONAUT

Wind the arm up again. This time put a plastic model astronaut in one tub, balancing the other tub with plasticine. Let the arm speed up gently, as in frame 6.

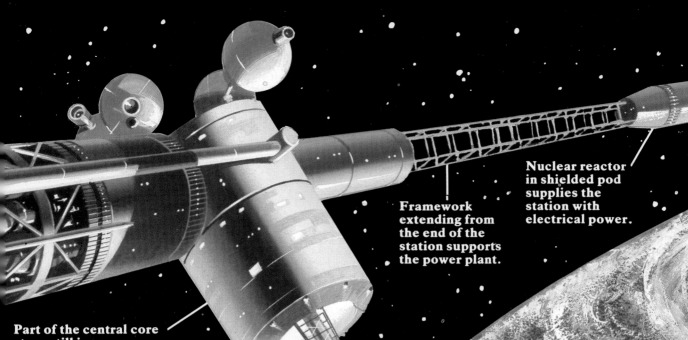

Nuclear reactor in shielded pod supplies the station with electrical power.

Framework extending from the end of the station supports the power plant.

Part of the central core stays still in space, so that visiting spacecraft can dock easily and safely. Zero-gravity workshops are in this part of the station.

Docking arm

4

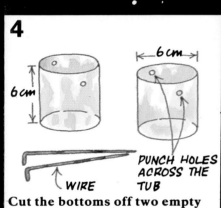

6 cm

6 cm

PUNCH HOLES ACROSS THE TUB

WIRE

Cut the bottoms off two empty plastic bottles – transparent ones if possible. Punch two small holes in them, as shown. Cut two lengths of wire, about 1½ times the width of the tubs.

5

PUSH WIRE THROUGH HOLES

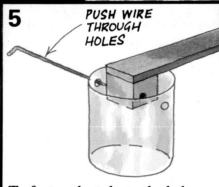

To fasten the tubs to the balsa blocks, thread the wires through the holes as shown. Then twist the ends over the rims of the tubs. Check that the tubs can swing freely.

6

WIND UP ABOUT 50 TURNS

HOLD FIRMLY TO TABLE

Testing time! Wind the arm up, then press a finger over its centre to serve as a brake. Keeping a firm hold on the base, ease your finger off. The arm should gain speed gently.

10

ASTRONAUT SHOULD STAY STANDING

As the arm turns faster, the tub will swivel outwards. Yet because of centrifugal force the astronaut will remain on his feet – like those in the space station shown above.

11

WATER

You can do the same trick with almost anything. Try it with water. Fill the two tubs about half full. Make sure there are no leaks. Take care that the arm speeds up at a steady rate.

12

WATER IN TUB

ASTRONAUT IN TUB

If space stations do not rotate, there is no force to hold things down. They float weightlessly. But in one that rotates, astronauts can even have baths!

27

Moonbase

When astronauts return to the Moon, it will be to set up a colony. A possible site at which to search for minerals would be near the Leibnitz Mountains (see map below).

Scientists and moonminers will live and work inside pressurized shelters. There will be solar furnaces for smelting lunar ore, and solar cell 'farms' will be used to make electricity from sunlight.

This is how Man's space frontier might look in your lifetime. After the moonbase, the next step will be the planets, and perhaps the stars.

Apollo landing sites

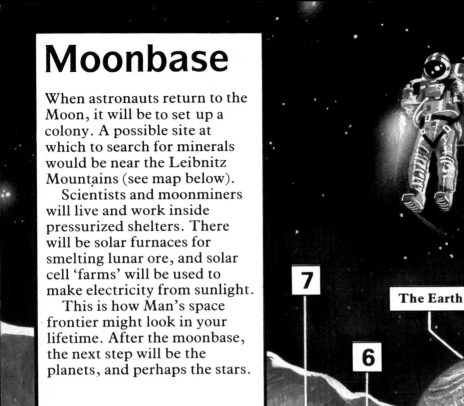

15 17

12 14 11

16

Site of base

▲ Twelve men have walked on the Moon—two each on Apollo missions 11, 12 and 14-17 (number 13 failed). The last manned mission was in December 1972. No more are planned.

Astronaut using rocket backpack for quick journeys in low gravity-one-sixth of Earth's

7

6

The Earth

Departing cargo pods bound for Earth orbit

5

Hydroponics dome. Fresh vegetables grow here, using special liquid in place of soil.

TV camera

8

Container loaded with lunar minerals

9

10

Fabric-covered wire wheels

What's what in the moonbase

1 Moondome living quarters, offices and administration centre. Domes are mostly buried underground to protect them from heat and meteoroids.

2 Radio and radar antennae.

3 Command communications centre maintains contact with Earth and supply craft. There is a three-second delay in talking to Earth because of the distances involved.

4 Lunar module shuttles between the moonbase and orbiting supply ships.

5 Solar-cell 'farm'. Panels swivel to follow the Sun.

6 Refinery used to obtain useful materials (oxygen,

calcium, aluminium etc.) from moonrocks.

7 Hillside drilling leads to mining area.

8 Overhead cable conveyor carries ore from the mines to storage area.

9 Astronaut-geologists take core-samples in a survey of fresh lunar terrain.

10 Moon Rover mobile laboratory.

11 Traffic lights give warning of spacecraft approaching to land or taking off.

12 Electromagnetic catapult launches lunar materials in computer-controlled modules towards a space factory in Earth orbit. Take-off speed is more than 2,400 m a second.

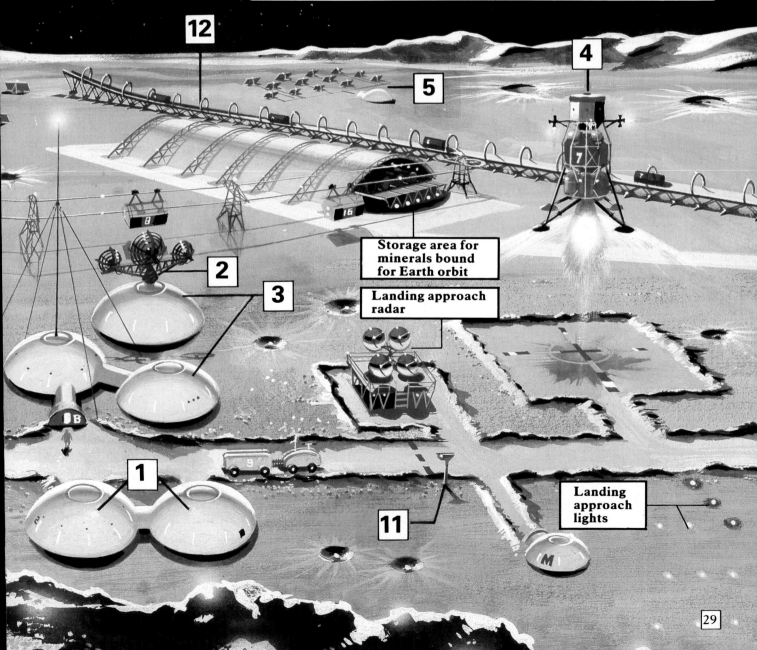

The Sun

Storage area for minerals bound for Earth orbit

Landing approach radar

Landing approach lights

Star Wars

The opening battle of a future war might be fought in space. Here ICBMs (intercontinental ballistic missiles) carrying nuclear warheads (1) are intercepted by satellites, anti-missile missiles (2) and other space weapons.

As a wave of ICBMs is launched, their rocket exhausts are detected by orbiting early-warning satellites (3), which relay the information to ground control (4) via communication satellites (5). Defenders have only minutes to hit the missiles before they scatter their multiple warheads.

Some orbiting battle stations (6) fire intense laser beams of infrared (heat) radiation, focused by pivoting dish-shaped mirrors. Others fire beams of fast-moving electrically charged particles (7). Laser beams from ground stations (8) bounce off orbiting mirrors (9) that swivel to attack one missile after another. But the devices have to contend with attacks from enemy asats (anti-satellite satellites) (10).

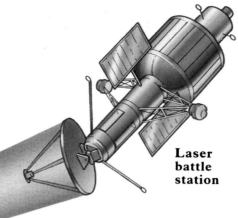

Laser battle station

Surface-launched missiles are the next line of defence. Submarines launch X-ray laser weapons (11), which convert the energy of small nuclear explosions into beams of X-rays that can destroy many missiles at once. Ground-launched anti-missile missiles attempt to destroy surviving warheads just before they explode.

A decision was made by the United States to develop this complex and costly system, in a programme called SDI (Strategic Defence Initiative). SDI has led to the successful Patriot anti-missile missile. It may be pursued further if relations between the superpowers worsen again, or if yet more countries acquire the ability to launch nuclear-tipped missiles.

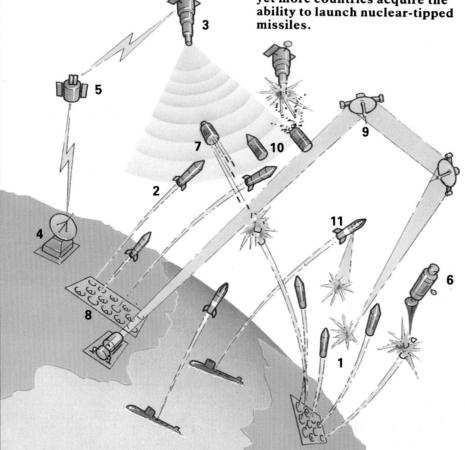

Space facts

One of the most amazing things about the coming of the Space Age was the speed with which it arrived. Only 27 years passed between the V-2's first flight and the landing of manned spacecraft on the Moon.

Man's knowledge of space has grown almost as fast. Here are some of the odder facts, events and theories to have come out of the years of discovery.

Because there is no wind or rain on the Moon to erase them, the footprints of the Apollo astronauts should, if left undisturbed, last for millions of years.

The most conspicuous features of the Earth as seen from space are its clouds. A visitor from space with eyesight similar to a man's would not see any sign of human life until he came within 250 km of the surface.

The first zero-gravity products were billions of tiny plastic beads made on a Space Shuttle. Because they were perfectly spherical, they were worth 2,000 times their weight in gold.

Intercontinental airliners of the future could switch from jet engines to rocket motors to go into space. They would land like normal planes.

Because the gravitational pull of the Moon is only one-sixth of that of Earth, athletes in a pressurized lunar stadium could (in theory) jump six times higher than they could on Earth. They might even be able to strap on wings and fly like birds!

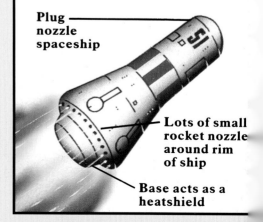

Plug nozzle spaceship

Lots of small rocket nozzle around rim of ship

Base acts as a heatshield

A new type of re-usable space rocket has been designed in America. Called the plug nozzle spaceship, it could take off and land vertically. This wingless single-stage rocket concept has a heatshield cooled by liquid hydrogen, surrounded by a ring of small rocket engines, which are used to drive it into orbit.

When it comes back to Earth, the heatshield protects it and the rockets fire backwards to brake it down gently to land.

The Pioneer 10 space probe was the first artificial object to leave the Solar System. Like its sister craft Pioneer 11, it carried a plaque bearing drawings of a man, a woman and the spacecraft to the same scale. There is also coded information about the Earth for the benefit of any alien beings who might discover the craft. Pioneer 10 should reach the neighbourhood of the giant star Aldebaran in the constellation of Taurus after 1,700,000 years.

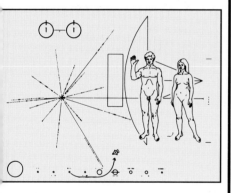

Message plaque carried aboard Pioneer 10

On July 20, 1969, Houston Mission Control put through the longest-distance telephone call in history. It connected Richard Nixon, then president of the United States, with the first men on the Moon. At the time, Neil Armstrong and Edwin Aldrin were setting up a base on the Sea of Tranquillity some 384,000 km from the Earth.

The Apollo spacecraft which carried astronauts to and from the Moon had nearly two million working parts. A large motor car has less than 3,000.

Space words

This glossary only includes words that are not fully explained anywhere else in the book.

You will find other rocket words explained on pages 4 and 5. Satellite terms are covered on pages 16 and 17, and Space Shuttle words on pages 18 to 21.

Centrifugal force
Outward force that arises when an object moves around another. When a satellite is in orbit, its outward, centrifugal force is exactly balanced by the inward pull of gravity.

Docking
Mechanical linking of two or more craft in space.

Elevons
Control surfaces on planes or spacecraft which can operate both as elevators (to make the craft climb or dive) or as ailerons (to make it bank left or right).

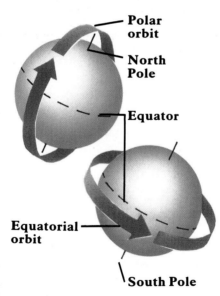

Polar orbit
North Pole
Equator
Equatorial orbit
South Pole

Equatorial orbit
Orbit around the equator. Polar orbit is an orbit which passes over the poles.

Fairing
Covering to protect inside parts of a rocket or satellite while it is passing through the atmosphere.

Heat insulating materials
In spaceflight terms, materials used to protect parts of spacecraft from extremes of heat and cold.

Hydroponics
Way of growing plants in water treated with nourishing chemicals instead of in soil.

Module
Section of a spacecraft.

Pallet
Platform for carrying research instruments.

Payload
The useful load launched by a rocket into space.

Permafrost
Permanently frozen subsoil in cold regions.

Propellant
The fuel and oxidizer of a rocket.

Re-entry
The return of a spacecraft into the Earth's atmosphere.

Retro rockets
Direction of flight

Retro rockets
Rockets which fire against the direction of flight to slow down a spacecraft.

Sensory ring
Base of a satellite or space probe used for mounting cameras and other sensors – information-gathering instruments.

Soft-landing
Slow-speed landing, after braking by parachute or retro rocket.

Synchronous orbit
Orbit 35,880 km high, in which satellites match the Earth's rotation, staying above a fixed point on its surface.

Thrust chamber
The combustion chamber of a rocket engine, in which fuel and oxidizer are burned.

Zero gravity
Condition of spaceflight in which astronauts and loose objects float weightlessly around.

Index

Books to read

Spaceships
by Gregory Vogt
Franklin Watts, 1990

Spacecraft Technology
John Mason
Wayland, 1989

Illustrated Dictionary
of Astronomy and Astronautics
Longman, 1987

The World of Space
by Cass R. Sandak
Franklin Watts, 1990

The Giant Book of Space
by Ian Ridpath
Hamlyn, 1989

Satellites and Space Stations
by M. Butterfield
Usborne, 1985

Space Shuttles: A New Era?
by Nigel Hawkes
Franklin Watts, 1989

THE USBORNE YOUNG SCIENTIST
JETS

SEPECAT Jaguar GR.1A 1972

Lockheed L-1011 TriStar

Birdproof windscreen

Weather radar

Flight deck

Forward entry door

Fuselage

Engine air intakes

Fin

Rudder

Starboard wing

Port wing

Nose undercarriage

Main undercarriage

Tailplane

Engine pod

Flaps

Elevator

Fairchild Republic A-10A Thunderbolt II

Credits

Written by
Mark Hewish
Revised text by
Christopher Cooper
Art and editorial direction
David Jefferis
Revised edition designed by
Paul Greenleaf
Text editor
Tony Allan
Educational adviser
Frank Blackwell
Revised by Alan Wright

Illustrators
Derek Bunce, Gordon Davies, Malcolm
English, Phil Green, Terry Hadler, John
Hutchinson and Michael Roffe
Copyright © 1991, 1982, 1976 Usborne
Publishing Ltd. Revised edition
published 1991

Acknowledgements
We wish to thank the following individuals and
organizations for their assistance and for
making available material in their collections.
Margaret Chester, Flight International,
Lufthansa Airlines; Neil Thomson, Rolls-
Royce Ltd, British Airways; L.F.E. Coombs,
McDonnell Douglas Corporation; Smiths
Industries; Airbus Industrie

First published in 1976. Revised and
updated 1982, 1991.
Usborne Publishing Ltd, Usborne House,
83-85 Saffron Hill, London EC1N 8RT,
England

The name Usborne and the device ⟨usborne⟩ are
Trade Marks of Usborne Publishing Ltd

Printed in Italy

On the cover: F16 'strike'
Falcon.
On this page: a flight of
Mirage F.1Cs

The experiments

Here is a checklist of the equipment you will need for the
experiments and things to do included in this book.

General equipment

Notebook and pencil
Ruler or tape-measure
Sticky tape★
Glue
Scissors
Watch (preferably with a second hand)
Rubber bands

For special experiments

Action and reaction (p.5): Balloon

Air compression (p.6): Plastic detergent bottle
Modelling clay

Glider (p.8): Drinking straw
Sheet of stiff paper at least 22.5 cm. long

Aerodynamic lift (p.9): Sheet of paper, roughly 15 x 20 cm.

Wing section (p.11): Three sheets of A4 paper (21 x 29.8 cm.)

Artificial horizon (p.13): Plastic pot (an empty cream carton is ideal)
Match with sharpened end

Sound power (p.19): Wide-necked glass bottle
Sheet of polythene
Sugar

★Cellophane tape

Weights and Measures

All the weights and measures used in this book are metric.
This list gives some equivalents in imperial measures.

mm. = millimetre
(1 inch = 25.4 mm.)

cm. = centimetre
(1 inch = 2.54 cm.)

m. = metre
(1 yard = 0.91 m.)

km. = kilometre
(1 mile = 1.6 km.)

k.p.h. = kilometres per hour
(1,000 m.p.h. = 1,609 k.p.h.)

sq. cm. = square centimetre
(1 square inch = 6.45 sq. cm.)

sq. m. = square metre
(1 square yard = 0.84 sq. m.)

A hectare is 10,000 sq. m.
(1 acre = 0.40 hectares)

kg. = kilogram
(1 stone = 6.35 kg.)

A tonne is 1,000 kg.
(1 ton = 1.02 tonnes)

1 litre is 1.76 pints

°C = degrees Centigrade
(Water freezes at 0°C and boils
at 100°C)

Contents

About this book

How do jet engines work? Why is there a bang when planes travel faster than sound? Why do jets leave vapour trails? Why do some planes have swing-wings?

Jets sets out to answer questions like these. It tells the story of the jet plane, from the beginnings in the 1930s to designs that are still on the drawing-board today. It explains the basic principles of jet flight. It describes what the most important instruments in an airliner cockpit are for, and how air traffic control works. It also covers such developments as supersonic airliners and vertical take-off, and the problems of noise pollution and jet-lag.

Jets also contains many safe and simple experiments that can be done at home with ordinary household equipment. They range from simple illustrations of scientific principles to projects like building a drinking-straw glider.

The first jets

It took a surprisingly long time for the jet engine to be invented, considering that the principle on which it works was known in ancient Greece. An inventor called Hero devised a sphere that was turned by escaping steam (see 1 below).

The idea of jet-propelled aircraft was first suggested in 1865, but the earliest planes to be built and flown were propellor-driven. Jet propulsion was not seriously considered again until 25 years after the Wright Brothers' first flight, when an English airman called Frank Whittle took up the idea.

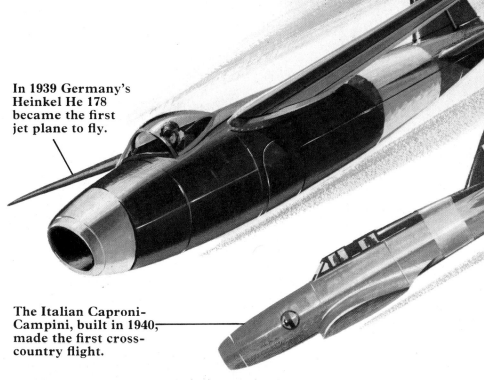

In 1939 Germany's Heinkel He 178 became the first jet plane to fly.

The Italian Caproni-Campini, built in 1940, made the first cross-country flight.

1. Hero's steam sphere

2. ▲ Pabst von Ohain, a German physicist, designed the engine for the world's first jet plane.

After taking a degree at Göttingen University in Germany, he began building working models of gas turbines. In 1936 he was employed by the aircraft manufacturer Ernst Heinkel.

A year later he successfully tested his first jet engine. An improved version of it was installed in the specially designed He 178 test plane in 1939.

3. ▲ Soon after dawn on August 27, 1939, Captain Erich Warsitz lifted the He 178 off the runway at the test base at Marienhe. He circled the airfield, then sideslipped in to land, completing the first jet flight ever.

6. ▲ On May 15, 1941, the E.28/39 took to the air for the first time, flown by Flt. Lt. P. E. G. Sayer. Whittle's engine gave the Squirt, on its first flight, a performance almost as fast as a Spitfire's, and it later reached 750 k.p.h.

7. ▲ The V-1 flying bomb was an offshoot of the development of the jet engine. It was powered by a pulse jet that allowed 'gulps' of air to pass into the combustion chamber, where they were mixed with petrol and ignited.

8. ▲ Heinkel's experience with the 178 led to the wood-framed He 162 Salamander jet fighter. It first flew in December 1944. Only 116 were built, though plans were made to build 4,000 a month. Few Salamanders flew in combat.

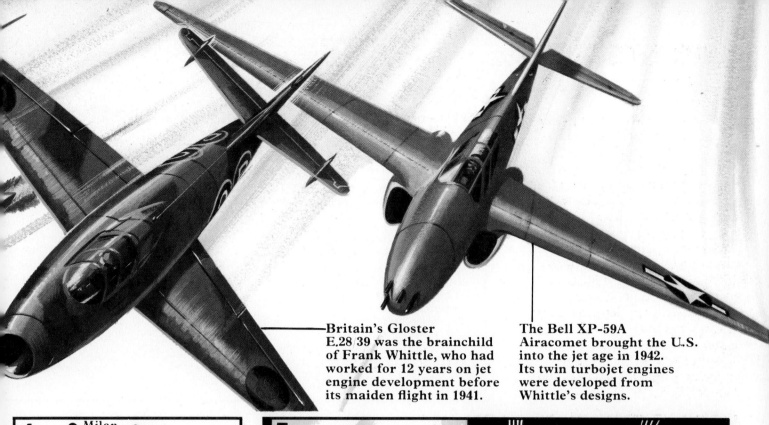

Britain's Gloster E.28/39 was the brainchild of Frank Whittle, who had worked for 12 years on jet engine development before its maiden flight in 1941.

The Bell XP-59A Airacomet brought the U.S. into the jet age in 1942. Its twin turbojet engines were developed from Whittle's designs.

4 Milan — Flight of the Caproni-Campini — ITALY — Rome

▲ The Caproni-Campini made its maiden flight exactly a year after the He 178. In 1941 it flew from Milan to Rome, a distance of 470 km. It was a slow flyer, though, with a top speed of only 375 k.p.h.

5

▲ Frank Whittle began thinking about jet propulsion in the late 1920s, when he was at the Royal Air Force College, Cranwell.

The Air Ministry rejected his designs, but in 1935 a friend raised the money to back his work, and Power Jets Ltd. was formed.

Their first working engine ran on April 12, 1937, and in July 1939 the company was awarded a contract to build an engine for the experimental Gloster E.28 39 – nicknamed the Squirt.

9 British Meteor
German Me 262

▲ The Me 262 and Meteor twin-engined warplanes both went into service in World War 2, but they never fought one another. The Me 262 had swept wings – a development pioneered by German aircraft designers.

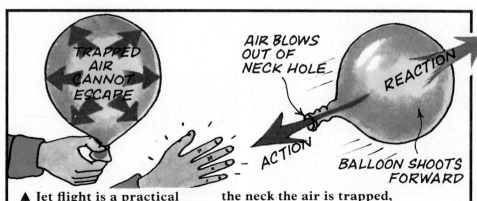

TRAPPED AIR CANNOT ESCAPE

AIR BLOWS OUT OF NECK HOLE

REACTION

ACTION

BALLOON SHOOTS FORWARD

▲ Jet flight is a practical application of the Third Law of Motion, which states that for every action there is an equal and opposite reaction. Try it for yourself by blowing up a balloon. While you hold the neck the air is trapped, but when you let go it rushes out. This action causes a reaction, so the balloon shoots forward in the opposite direction to the air. Jet planes speed along in a similar way.

Turbojet and turbofan

Early jet engines were pure turbojets. Air passing through them goes through four main stages. First it is sucked in through the intake. Then it is compressed. The compressed air is mixed with fuel and set alight. Finally the hot gases produced are forced back through the exhaust, driving the aircraft forward.

Some jets now use large fans to draw in more air. This kind of engine is called a turbofan.

Turbojet-powered Concorde

The turbojet shown opposite is the Rolls-Royce Olympus engine used in Concordes. Air entering the intake (1) passes through the compressor (2) – a series of vanes that pack it densely together. It is mixed with vaporized kerosene in the combustion chamber (3) and burned.

The hot gases this produces roar through the turbine (4), which spins round like windmill blades in wind, turning the vanes in the compressor as it goes. They then pass through a nozzle (5) into the afterburner (6), where more fuel is burned to provide extra thrust.

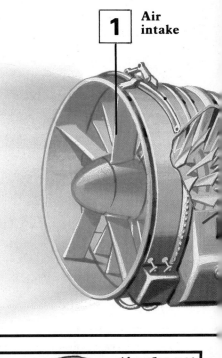

1 Air intake

1 Air compression

Jet engines have compressors to pack as much air as possible into the combustion chamber. The amount of thrust an engine gives increases as more fuel is used, and the fuel needs oxygen in the air to make it burn — so the thrust depends also on the amount of air that is sucked in.

Cold air is best, as it is denser than hot air. But air heats up as it is compressed. Try pumping up a bicycle tyre. You will soon find that compression and friction combined have warmed pump and tyre up.

2 PLASTIC BOTTLE
MODELLING CLAY
TAPE-MEASURE

▲ This is a neat and simple experiment which shows just how powerful a force compressed air can exert. All you need is an empty plastic detergent bottle, a piece of modelling clay, and a tape-measure.

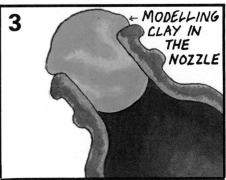

3 ← MODELLING CLAY IN THE NOZZLE

▲ Take the nozzle off the bottle, and ease a lump of modelling clay into the neck. Make sure the seal is airtight by squeezing the bottle gently and listening for air leaks. Take the bottle outside or into a large room.

4

▲ Lay the bottle on the ground, then jump on it! The pressure of compressed air will blow the modelling clay cork up to 20 m away. Mark the spot where it lands, then see which of your friends can make it go furthest.

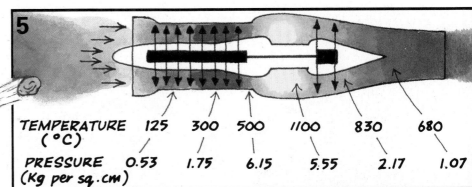

5

TEMPERATURE (°C)	125	300	500	1100	830	680
PRESSURE (Kg per sq. cm)	0.53	1.75	6.15	5.55	2.17	1.07

▲ This diagram shows what happens to the temperature and pressure of air as it passes through the Olympus turbojet of a Concorde flying at twice the speed of sound nearly 20,000 m up. The compressors increase the air pressure more than ten times, so that as much as possible is crammed into the combustion chamber. The air temperature, which has steadily increased in the compressor, is doubled when the fuel ignites, while the pressure starts to fall.

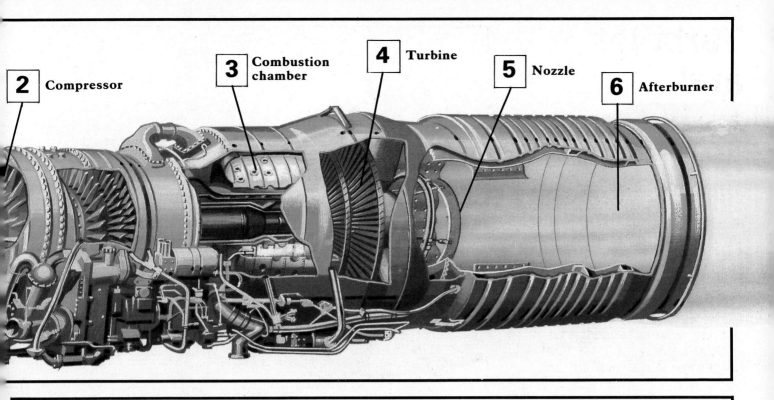

2 Compressor

3 Combustion chamber

4 Turbine

5 Nozzle

6 Afterburner

Turbofan-powered Lockheed TriStar

The Rolls-Royce RB 211 used in the TriStar is a turbofan engine. A turbofan is basically a turbojet with a big fan at the front or back. Most modern models use front fans. The fan (1) acts as a many-bladed propellor, drawing air into the compressor (2) just as a ventilator draws air into a room. The air then passes through the combustion chamber (3), the turbine (4) and the nozzle (5) as in a turbojet.

The 211 is a high-bypass-ratio engine, however. This means that a lot of the air (more than four-fifths of that entering the intake) is blown around the jet core. This air is not burned, but provides thrust as it blows back through the fan exhaust (6).

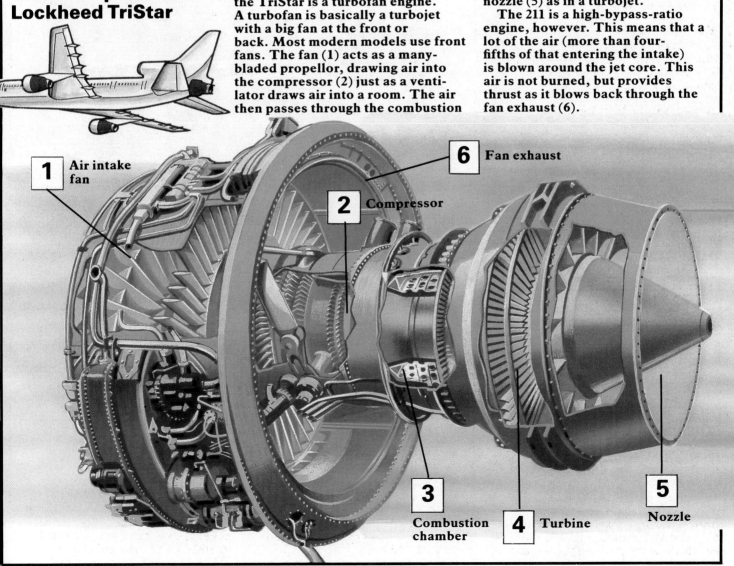

1 Air intake fan

6 Fan exhaust

2 Compressor

3 Combustion chamber

4 Turbine

5 Nozzle

How and why jets fly

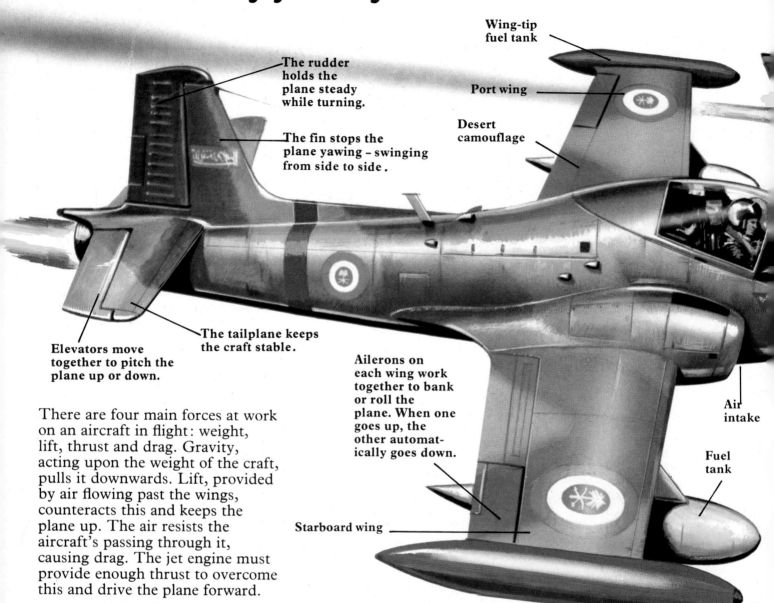

Wing-tip fuel tank

The rudder holds the plane steady while turning.

The fin stops the plane yawing – swinging from side to side.

Port wing

Desert camouflage

Air intake

Elevators move together to pitch the plane up or down.

The tailplane keeps the craft stable.

Ailerons on each wing work together to bank or roll the plane. When one goes up, the other automatically goes down.

Fuel tank

Starboard wing

There are four main forces at work on an aircraft in flight: weight, lift, thrust and drag. Gravity, acting upon the weight of the craft, pulls it downwards. Lift, provided by air flowing past the wings, counteracts this and keeps the plane up. The air resists the aircraft's passing through it, causing drag. The jet engine must provide enough thrust to overcome this and drive the plane forward.

How to make and flight-test your own aircraft

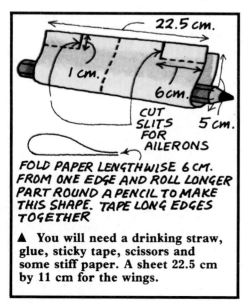

22.5 cm.

1 cm.

6 cm.

5 cm.

CUT SLITS FOR AILERONS

FOLD PAPER LENGTHWISE 6 CM. FROM ONE EDGE AND ROLL LONGER PART ROUND A PENCIL TO MAKE THIS SHAPE. TAPE LONG EDGES TOGETHER

▲ You will need a drinking straw, glue, sticky tape, scissors and some stiff paper. A sheet 22.5 cm by 11 cm for the wings.

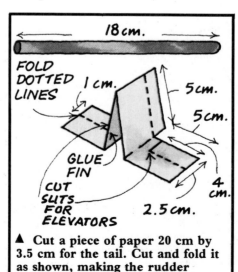

18 cm.

FOLD DOTTED LINES

1 cm.

5 cm.

5 cm.

GLUE FIN

CUT SLITS FOR ELEVATORS

2.5 cm.

4 cm.

▲ Cut a piece of paper 20 cm by 3.5 cm for the tail. Cut and fold it as shown, making the rudder extend 1 cm beyond the tailplanes.

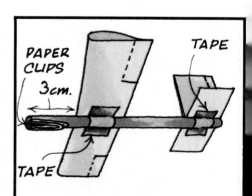

PAPER CLIPS

3 cm.

TAPE

TAPE

▲ Tape the wings and tail to the straw. Attach a paper-clip to the straw and test the glider. Go on attaching clips until the glider flies smoothly.

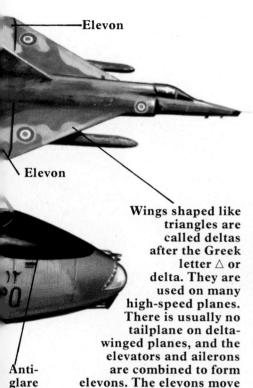

—Elevon

Elevon

Anti-glare panel painted in front of cockpit

Wings shaped like triangles are called deltas after the Greek letter △ or delta. They are used on many high-speed planes. There is usually no tailplane on delta-winged planes, and the elevators and ailerons are combined to form elevons. The elevons move together to pitch the plane up or down, and in opposite directions for banking and rolling.

The jet on the left is a British Aerospace (BAC) Strikemaster ground attack plane of the Saudi Arabian Air Force. The plane above is a Mirage fighter-bomber with French markings.

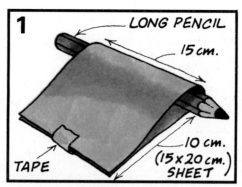

1 LONG PENCIL 15 cm. TAPE 10 cm. (15×20 cm. SHEET)

▲ To find out how lift works, take a thin sheet of paper, about 20 cm. by 15 cm., and fold it into a wing shape as shown. Tape the two loose edges together. Find a pencil more than 15 cm. long and slide it into the loop of paper.

2 BLOW HARD PAPER WING MOVES UPWARDS

▲ Hold the pencil so that the top edge of the 'wing' almost touches your lower lip. Now blow down over the outer surface. The wing will rise and remain level as long as you keep blowing. Your breath is acting like air over a plane wing.

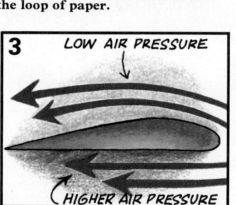

3 LOW AIR PRESSURE HIGHER AIR PRESSURE

▲ The upper surface of an aircraft wing is more curved than the lower surface, and air has to accelerate over the top to catch up with that flowing underneath. This 'stretches' the air on top, creating an area of low pressure that sucks the wing up.

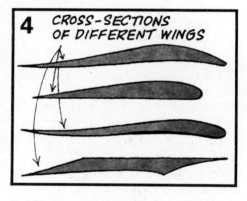

4 CROSS-SECTIONS OF DIFFERENT WINGS

▲ Wings, also known as aerofoils, have various shapes according to the sort of job they are designed for. They are usually thin on very fast planes, and may be flattened or wedge-shaped to increase lift under different conditions.

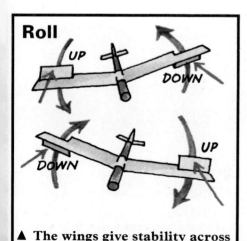

Roll UP DOWN DOWN UP

▲ The wings give stability across the plane. You can disturb the balance and make the plane roll by moving the ailerons as shown.

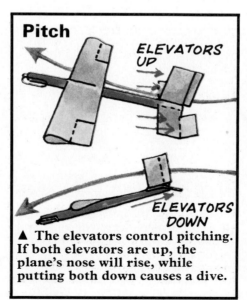

Pitch ELEVATORS UP ELEVATORS DOWN

▲ The elevators control pitching. If both elevators are up, the plane's nose will rise, while putting both down causes a dive.

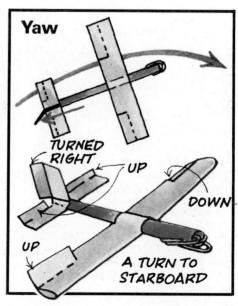

Yaw TURNED RIGHT UP UP DOWN A TURN TO STARBOARD

9

Jet-Age airliners

The age of the pure-jet airliner dawned on May 2, 1952, when a Comet 1 owned by the British Overseas Airways Corporation made its first scheduled flight, from London to Johannesburg. Jet services halved flying times on long-distance trips. In 1959 Pan American World Airways started round-the-world flights with Boeing 707s. Nowadays almost all airliners are jet-powered.

The Airbus series of jetliners began service in 1974. Parts for these aircraft are made in several European countries and assembled at Toulouse in France.

1 Fuel tanks, two to each wing. Fuel can also be stored in the wing centre section.

2 Ram-air turbine drops down from the starboard wing root in case of emergency. A small propellor on the front rotates in the airflow and generates electrical power.

3 Wide-body cabin can seat more than 300 passengers. It is 5.65 m. across.

4 Fuselage is made of aluminium alloy – as are the tail and wings.

5 Flight deck for pilot, co-pilot and flight engineer.

6 Radome protects radar equipment, which detects clouds and rain.

7 General Electric CF6 engine, one under each wing. The CF6 is a turbofan giving 23,133 kg. of thrust.

8 Underfloor freight holds can carry pallets, containers or loose cargo.

9 Main undercarriage has four wheels on each leg.

10 Auxiliary power unit in the tail is a miniature jet engine providing electrical power, and compressed air for starting the engines and for air-conditioning.

The Comet crashes

▲ The de Havilland Comet 1 was a great success when it went into service in 1952. It halved journey times, carrying 36 passengers in comfort at nearly 800 k.p.h. well above the worst weather. For two years things went well.

▲ In January 1954, disaster struck. A Comet crashed into the sea after taking off from Rome, and all 35 people on board were killed. Flights were suspended for a time. When they resumed, a second Comet went down in flames, killing 17 people.

▲ All Comets were grounded. Royal Navy salvage vessels were sent to the scene of the first crash – the second plane had gone down in very deep water – and with the help of divers they recovered nearly two-thirds of the sunken plane.

10

Make a wing section

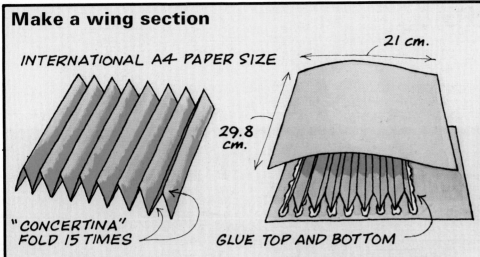

INTERNATIONAL A4 PAPER SIZE

"CONCERTINA" FOLD 15 TIMES

GLUE TOP AND BOTTOM — 21 cm. — 29.8 cm.

WEIGH EACH ITEM

▲ Aeroplane wings are not solid, but the honeycomb of metal struts that holds them together gives them great strength as well as low weight. You can make a surprisingly strong model wing simply by folding a sheet of paper.

▲ Do your best to make all the folds the same size, so that the load will be evenly distributed. Glue the folded sheet between two other sheets of the same size, placing it near one edge to give your wing the correct shape.

▲ Now test the wing to find out the weight that it can carry. You will find that it will take an unexpectedly heavy load without buckling. The model wing above could carry more than four-and-a-half kg.

The most complex wing ever?

The Airbus wing is designed to provide more lift over its rear section than normal wings, allowing a thicker but lighter wing to be used.

Flaps on the wing's trailing edge improve lift at low speeds, while there are twin ailerons for low- and high-speed flying. The spoilers, air-brakes and lift-dumpers can all be used to slow the plane down in flight and to allow low-speed approaches for landing.

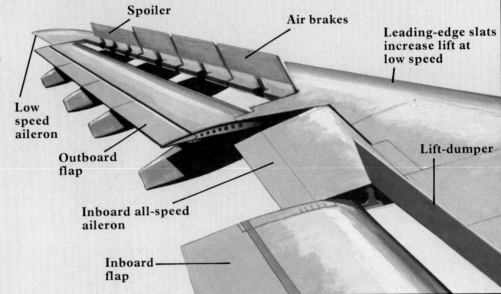

Spoiler

Air brakes

Leading-edge slats increase lift at low speed

Low speed aileron

Outboard flap

Inboard all-speed aileron

Inboard flap

Lift-dumper

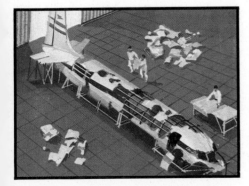

▲ The wreckage was sent back to Farnborough, England. It was reassembled on a frame the size and shape of a real Comet. Most of the fuselage, parts of the wings, and all four engines were found and wired into place.

▲ Another Comet was put in a tank, with its wings sticking out. Jacks bent the wings, while water was pumped into the fuselage to create strains equal to those of thousands of hours of flying. The fuselage eventually ripped apart.

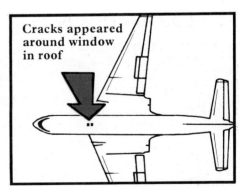

Cracks appeared around window in roof

▲ It was finally discovered that the crash had been caused by cracks spreading from a rivet hole, causing the pressurized cabin to explode. Jet design was altered as a result, and nowadays metal fatigue is kept under control.

Inside the cockpit

The A320 Airbus has an advanced computerized flight deck. There are two pilots, but no flight engineer is required to keep a watch on the aircraft's systems.

The controls

Flight controls. Side-stick controllers replace the traditional joysticks. Large pedals control the rudder, elevators, etc.

Flight instruments. Computer displays show course, speed, height, position of radio beacons, cloud and rain ahead, etc.

Aircraft systems displays. Fuel levels, flap positions, etc. are indicated — even if the cabin seat-belt signs are on.

Overhead panels. These carry controls and warning lights for the aircraft's fuel, electrical and hydraulic systems.

Engine controls. Throttles control the power of each engine separately. Other levers control flaps, slats and brakes.

Navigation display

In front of each pilot there is a display screen showing the aircraft's position, direction of flight, and route. The display is shown here in "compass rose" mode. Directions are shown as numbers that must be multiplied by 10 (21 means 210 degrees, etc.). The plane's autopilot is "locked on" to one ground radio beacon after another. These are called VORs (for VHF omni-directional range). Here there is a VOR at 144 degrees. The distance to a VOR is given by distance-measuring equipment (DME). Fixed points along the route are called waypoints.

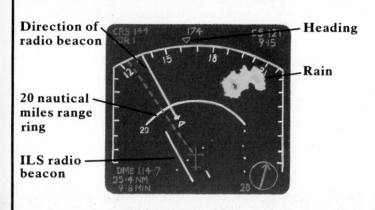

Radio beam

Ground speed

Distance to beacon

Time to reach beacon

Wind direction

Windspeed

Weather radar mode

The navigation display can be switched into weather radar mode. Information from the plane's forward-pointing radar is turned into a picture of the rain or snow ahead, with colours showing where it is heaviest. This can be switched off while the screen continues to show the plane's heading, speed and course. Circular arcs ahead of the plane symbol show distances — here, for example, there is one at 20 nautical miles (37 km). A planned route can be shown as a solid line from waypoint to waypoint. An alternative route can also be shown.

Direction of radio beacon

Heading

Rain

20 nautical miles range ring

ILS radio beacon

Primary flight display

Another screen mainly shows roll (the aircraft's tilt to left or right) and pitch (whether its nose is pointing up or down). The artificial horizon is controlled by a gyroscope which points in the same direction however much the plane rolls. To the pilot, sharing the motion of the plane, it looks as if the horizon line rolls while a bar representing the aircraft stays steady. Pointers moving along scales show height, airspeed, etc.

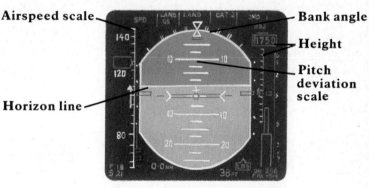

Airspeed scale

Horizon line

Bank angle

Height

Pitch deviation scale

Make a model artificial horizon

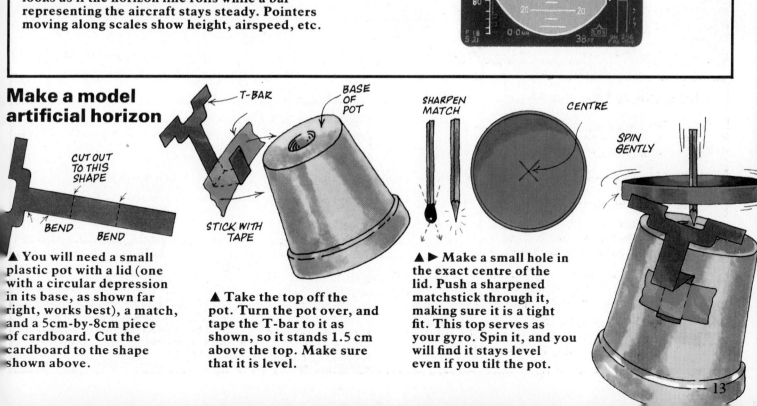

T-BAR

BASE OF POT

CUT OUT TO THIS SHAPE

BEND   BEND

STICK WITH TAPE

SHARPEN MATCH

CENTRE

SPIN GENTLY

▲ You will need a small plastic pot with a lid (one with a circular depression in its base, as shown far right, works best), a match, and a 5cm-by-8cm piece of cardboard. Cut the cardboard to the shape shown above.

▲ Take the top off the pot. Turn the pot over, and tape the T-bar to it as shown, so it stands 1.5 cm above the top. Make sure that it is level.

▲ ▶ Make a small hole in the exact centre of the lid. Push a sharpened matchstick through it, making sure it is a tight fit. This top serves as your gyro. Spin it, and you will find it stays level even if you tilt the pot.

13

Stand by for take-off

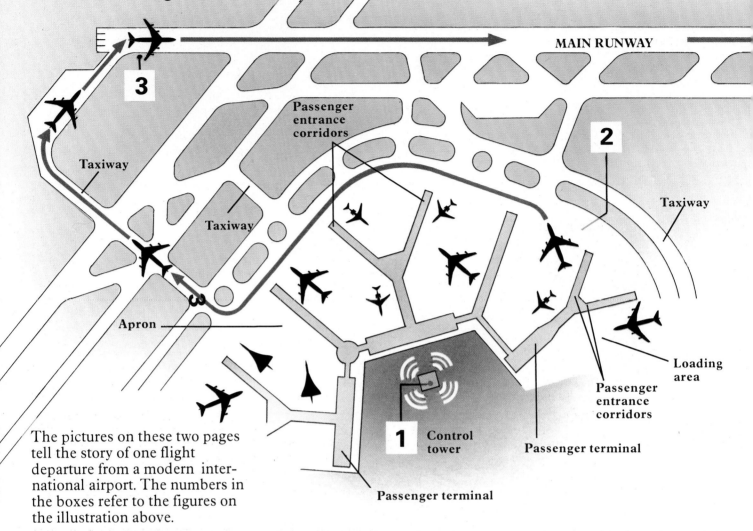

MAIN RUNWAY

3

Taxiway

Passenger entrance corridors

2

Taxiway

Taxiway

Loading area

Apron

Passenger entrance corridors

1 Control tower

Passenger terminal

Passenger terminal

The pictures on these two pages tell the story of one flight departure from a modern international airport. The numbers in the boxes refer to the figures on the illustration above.

1

▲ The most important building at any airport is the control tower. Behind windows with a clear view of all the runways, controllers pass instructions on taxiing and parking to pilots. Others control air traffic from radar screens.

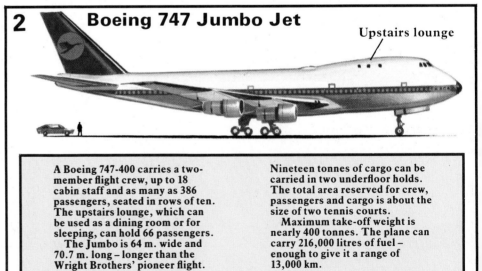

2 **Boeing 747 Jumbo Jet**

Upstairs lounge

A Boeing 747-400 carries a two-member flight crew, up to 18 cabin staff and as many as 386 passengers, seated in rows of ten. The upstairs lounge, which can be used as a dining room or for sleeping, can hold 66 passengers.
The Jumbo is 64 m. wide and 70.7 m. long – longer than the Wright Brothers' pioneer flight.

Nineteen tonnes of cargo can be carried in two underfloor holds. The total area reserved for crew, passengers and cargo is about the size of two tennis courts.
Maximum take-off weight is nearly 400 tonnes. The plane can carry 216,000 litres of fuel – enough to give it a range of 13,000 km.

▲ Before an aircraft can take off, the pilot has to file a flight plan and work out take-off speeds, which vary according to the plane's weight, weather conditions, runway length and the height of the airport above sea level. The plane

must be fuelled, food and drink put on board, and the cargo loaded
The passengers get on board afte clearing customs and passport control. Once they have fastened their seat-belts, the plane is ready to go.

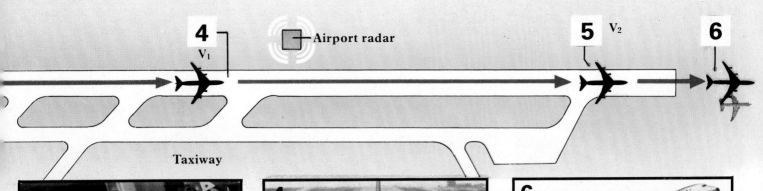

4 V₁

Airport radar

5 V₂

6

Taxiway

4

5

6

Levels out at 920 k.p.h. (Mach 0.84)

Speeds up to 600 k.p.h.

Climbs at 465 k.p.h.

10,000 m.
9,000
8,000
7,000
6,000
5,000
4,000
3,000
2,000
1,000
0

Lift-off – 293 k.p.h.

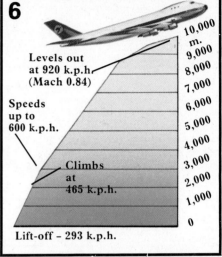

▲ The controllers give the pilot clearance to taxi to a holding point near the beginning of the runway. When checks have been completed, permission to take off is given. The aircraft taxis onto the runway and revs up its engines.

▲ The aircraft moves down the runway, gathering speed. Once V₁ is reached, the plane is going too fast to have room to stop. V₂ is safe flying speed. For a typical Jumbo take-off, these speeds are 265 and 293 k.p.h.

▲ As the plane climbs away from the runway it may have to throttle back to meet noise restrictions. Departure controllers guide the pilot onto the right course. On leaving the airport control area he set his course along an airway.

Keeping the engines supplied with fuel

A Jumbo Jet's four engines can gulp a total of more than 11,000 kg. of fuel every hour, but the plane is still one of the most economical forms of transport.

A separate tank is provided for each engine, but cross-feed valves allow all tanks to feed any engine.

No. 1 engine
No. 2 engine
No. 3 engine
No. 4 engine

Central fuel tank

Fuel-hungry jet liners

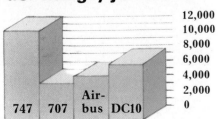

12,000
10,000
8,000
6,000
4,000
2,000
0

747   707   Air-bus   DC10

This chart shows how many kg. of fuel these aircraft use every hour of flight.

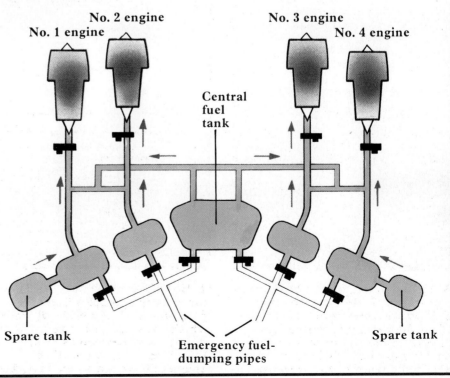

Spare tank

Emergency fuel-dumping pipes

Spare tank

Flight 593 to Perth

1 Local time 20.30 Body time 20.30

▲ Foxtrot Tango, a Boeing 747-400, takes off for Australia from Heathrow Airport. In each panel following, the clocks show local time (left) and "body time" (right) — the time in Britain, to which the passengers' bodies are still attuned.

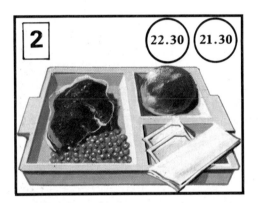

2 22.30 21.30

▲ Mealtime. The 18-strong cabin crew heat pre-packed frozen meals in fast-working microwave ovens in the Jumbo's 14 galley areas. After the meal, passengers can watch a film or listen to a choice of taped entertainment on headphones.

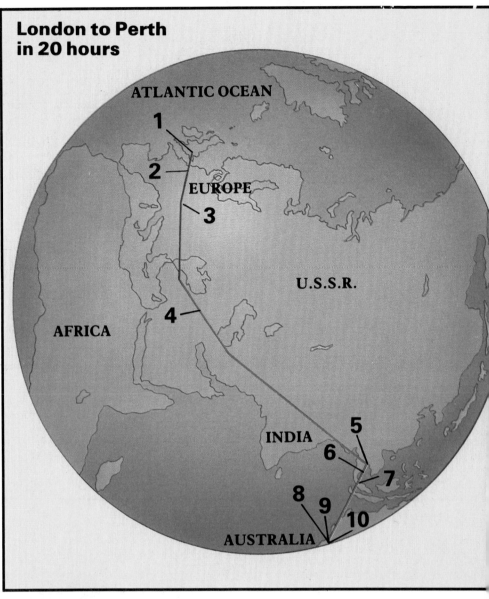

London to Perth in 20 hours

ATLANTIC OCEAN

1
2
EUROPE
3

U.S.S.R.

4

AFRICA

INDIA

5
6
7
8
9
10

AUSTRALIA

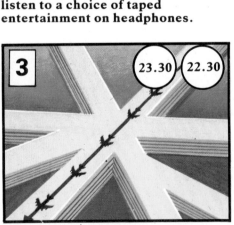

3 23.30 22.30

▲ The jet flies down an airway, a corridor in the sky marked out by radio signal beacons. Planes are separated by large distances horizontally and vertically. The jet is over Europe, where local time is one hour ahead of London time.

4 02.30 23.30

▲ The 747 flies 12 km high through the night. The air temperature outside is -57°C. Water vapour from the jet exhausts freezes into tiny ice particles, forming condensation trails. Body time now lags 3 hours behind local time.

5 14.25 07.25

▲ After nearly 11 hours' flying, Foxtrot Tango makes its first stopover, at Bangkok in Thailand. The aircraft is refuelled, and a new flight crew takes over. For safety reasons flight crews do not usually fly more than 11 hours at a time.

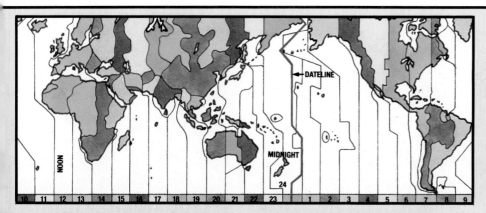

▲ As the chart shows, the hour of day at any one time differs around the world. One problem of long-distance jet flights is that they pass through several time zones too quickly for people to adapt.

Passengers like those on Flight 593, who land just past midnight feeling as though it were late afternoon are said to be suffering from jet-lag.

▼ Radar equipment is used throughout the flight to check on weather conditions ahead of the plane. It can warn the pilot of thunderstorms 200 km away, and can show him whether there is a cloud cover over the airport he is heading for.

The radar weather picture is displayed on a screen in the cockpit.

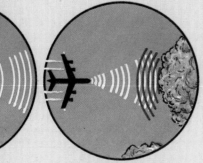

▲ Radar pulse is sent out from a dish in the plane's nose.

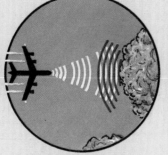

▲ Hitting a cloud, it bounces back towards the plane.

▲ Incoming pulses are transmitted from receiver to screen.

10 00.40 16.40

▲ A gentle touchdown, and Flight 593 is over. The passengers disembark after 20 hours with eight hours of jet lag. What seems to them to be afternoon is midnight in Perth. If they had flown the other way, the time difference would be reversed.

9 00.25 16.25

▲ The pilot's instruments use radio signals from ILS (instrument landing system) transmitters near the runway as the Jumbo comes down. Indicators show how far the plane is above or below, and left or right of, the correct approach path.

6 16.35 09.35

▲ After an hour the plane is on its way again. It is kept in straight and steady flight by the automatic pilot. The aircraft's position is constantly calculated by the onboard navigation system. The data is then fed to the autopilot.

7 18.35 10.35

▲ Foxtrot Tango lands for a second stopover, at Kuala Lumpur in Malaysia. Flight 593 has covered over 11,000 km, and there are over 4,000 km still to go. But they are now in their destination's time zone, so jet lag will not increase.

8 00.10 16.10

▲ Near the end of the flight's last leg, the 747 starts to descend while more than 100 km from its destination. Some aircraft are waiting to land at Perth, so the plane is 'stacked', circling a radio beacon while waiting for clearance to land.

17

The sound barrier

MiG-25 37 km. height record

30km.

25

SR-71 spy plane

Temperature constant at −56.3°C in the stratosphere

Mach 1 constant at 1,062.36 k.p.h. in stratosphere

STRATOSPHERE

20

Concorde

15

747

1,062

10

1,078

Mount Everest

1,094

1,109

DC-9

1,124

TROPOSPHERE

1,139

1,154

5

1,169

Mont Blanc

1,183

Speed of Mach 1 in k.p.h.

1,197

1,211

1

1,225

Sound travels at different speeds at different levels. At sea level its speed is about 1,225 k.p.h., but it slows down in the cold air higher up.

An Austrian scientist called Ernst Mach worked out a way of comparing speed through the air directly to the speed of sound which is called Mach 1 after him. Mach 2 is exactly twice the speed of sound, and so on.

Aircraft that travel faster than sound must pass through shock waves (see below) that slow them down. These waves are what is popularly known as the sound barrier.

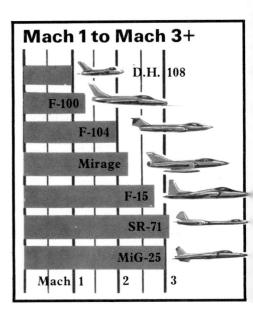

Mach 1 to Mach 3+

D.H. 108

F-100

F-104

Mirage

F-15

SR-71

MiG-25

Mach 1   2   3

Booming along on the shock cone

The illustration below shows three moments in the flight of a single jet, as it accelerates up to and beyond the speed of sound.

The nearly circular lines surrounding the aircraft (1) are the air disturbances its flight causes. They are known as pressure waves. As they move away from the plane they gradually get weaker, as

the ripples die away after a stone has been thrown into a pond. These pressure waves travel at exactly the speed of sound.

As the aircraft goes faster (2), it catches up on the pressure waves moving ahead of it. At Mach 1 it is travelling as fast as they are. It pushes all the air ripples that would previously have had

1

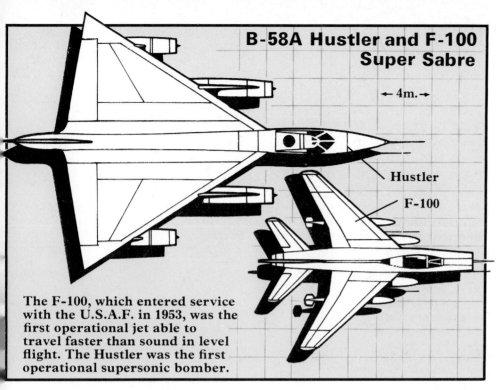

B-58A Hustler and F-100 Super Sabre

← 4m. →

Hustler

F-100

The F-100, which entered service with the U.S.A.F. in 1953, was the first operational jet able to travel faster than sound in level flight. The Hustler was the first operational supersonic bomber.

Sound power

The sonic boom is a spectacular example of sound power. Here is a small-scale sound experiment.

1 SUGAR
PIECE OF POLYTHENE
RUBBER BAND

▲ You will need a tin tray, an empty jar, some polythene and a little sugar. Put the polythene over the top of the jar, and fasten it with a rubber band. Smooth it down so that it is perfectly flat, and put a few grains of sugar on it.

ime to spread out ahead of it into ne vertical Mach wave (3).

When the plane is travelling aster than sound (4), it pushes he tip of the Mach wave with it, ending the wave into a cone shape. Where the lower edge of the cone eaches the ground, there is a udden increase in air pressure hat you can hear as a

double boom, or if the shock waves are very close together as one bang.

Supersonic planes trail the sonic boom in their wake over the entire region they pass over while travelling faster than sound. The area over which it can be heard is called the plane's 'carpet'. The carpet of Concorde, for example, is nearly 90 km. wide.

2

▲ Hold the tin tray about 10 cm. away from the jar, and hit it with something hard. The pressure wave that you hear as a bang will have the power to make the sugar jump. In the same way the sonic boom can damage windows and buildings.

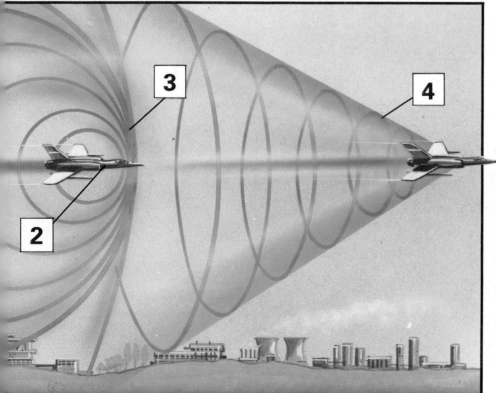

3

4

2

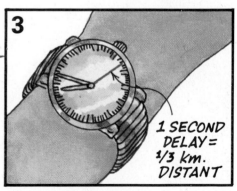

3

1 SECOND DELAY = 1/3 km. DISTANT

▲ Remembering the speed of sound can also be useful, for instance in a thunderstorm. To work out how many kilometres away it is, count the number of seconds between the lightning flash and the thunderclap and divide by 3.

Supersonic airliners

Supersonic military planes have been in service since 1953, but civilian supersonic transports (SSTs) took longer to develop.

The first SST to fly was the Russian Tupolev Tu-144, in 1968. The Anglo-French Concorde first flew two months later, and now regularly crosses the Atlantic. The Tupolev was soon withdrawn from passenger service.

The United States also laid plans for an SST in the 1960s. The project was eventually given up because of its cost, and as a result of public opposition based on fear of high noise levels and possible harm to the atmosphere.

Aircraft designers continue to work on a likely supersonic successor to Concorde. This design is for a 300-seat, trans-Pacific supersonic airliner which will travel at between two and two-and-a-half times the speed of sound. It should be in service by the beginning of the 21st century.

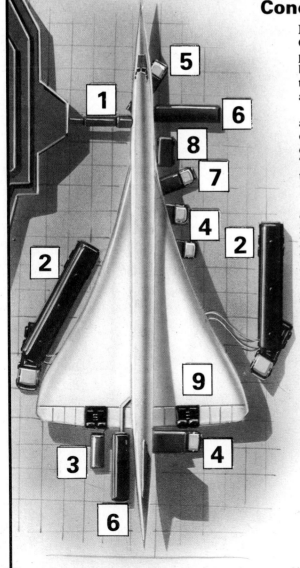

Concorde on the apron

It only takes 30 minutes for Concorde to unload its passengers and their baggage, to refuel, and to take on new provisions and a new load of passengers.

As soon as the jet stops, a jetway (1) noses up to the exit. All passengers disembark in five minutes. Two giant refuellers (2) take 18 minutes to pump in 120,000 litres of kerosene.

The air-conditioning cart (3) pumps fresh air into the passenger cabin. Baggage vehicles (4) unload the underfloor compartments at a rate of 135 kg a minute, and then put a new load aboard almost as fast.

The toilets are cleaned (5) and the drains checked. The plane's galleys are restocked with food, drinks and duty-free goods by special vehicles (6) which rise up to cabin level and 'plug in' to the doors. Drinking water is supplied by a bowser (7).

A ground power unit (8) supplies electricity while the jet's engines are shut off, and a similar truck restarts the engines (9).

By this time the new passengers are aboard with their baggage, and it's 'stand by for take off' again.

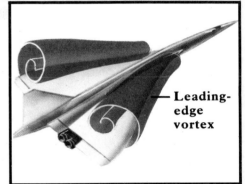

▲ The wings of the SSTs are ogival-shaped like a delta with the edges rounded off. A spiral current of air called the leading-edge vortex forms over them in flight. It stays there even at slow speeds, increasing lift.

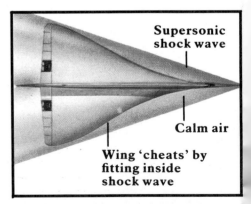

▲ As Concorde rushes through the air at Mach 2, a supersonic shock wave streams back from the nose. Its wings fit inside the cone of undisturbed air behind the shock wave, giving the plane and its passengers a smooth ride.

Aircraft and noise

All aircraft are noisy, and jets are noisier than most. Noise levels, particularly around airports, have mounted as more and bigger jets have come into service. Public criticism of jet noise has also grown, and designers now spend a lot of thought on finding ways of making jets quieter.

The roar of a jet engine is produced mainly by the violent mixing of its exhaust gases with the outside air. How loud it is depends on the speed at which the gases meet the air. It is greatest when the engines are run up to full power just before the plane takes off.

One way of reducing noise is to use turbofan engines in which much of the air taken in bypasses the combustion chamber, thus reducing the exhaust speeds. Turbofans are now used in most modern jet transports.

Inside the ear

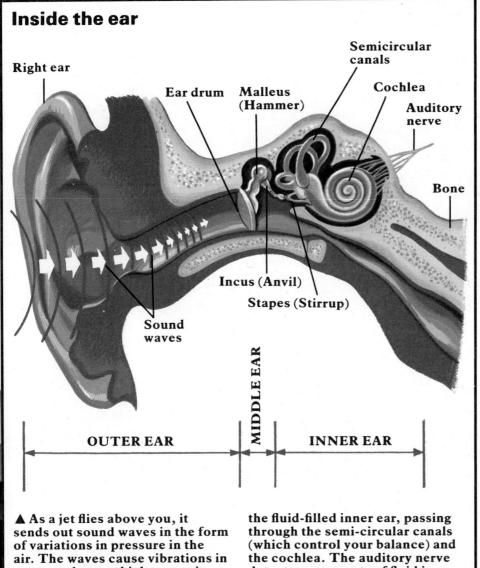

Right ear

Semicircular canals

Ear drum **Malleus (Hammer)** **Cochlea**

Auditory nerve

Bone

Incus (Anvil)

Stapes (Stirrup)

Sound waves

MIDDLE EAR

OUTER EAR | **INNER EAR**

▲ As a jet flies above you, it sends out sound waves in the form of variations in pressure in the air. The waves cause vibrations in your ear drum, which transmits them through three small bones — the hammer, anvil and stirrup — in the air-filled middle ear.

The vibrations next move into the fluid-filled inner ear, passing through the semi-circular canals (which control your balance) and the cochlea. The auditory nerve detects movements of fluid in the cochlea, and turns them into coded impulses. These pass to the brain, where the impulses are decoded and the sound is 'heard'.

Jet noise

Jet noise is usually measured in effective perceived noise decibels (EPNdB), which take into account the tone of a noise and how long it lasts as well as its loudness. The figures below are all given in EPNdB.

An increase of ten EPNdB means twice the amount of noise — so a sound that measures 60 EPNdB seems twice as noisy to the listener as one of 50 EPNdB, and so on.

The rustling of leaves in a gentle breeze.	**33**
Soft whispering between 1 and 2 m away.	**47**
Normal speech, or the noise in a busy shop.	**73**
The background hum in a crowded restaurant.	**78**
Loud music on a record-player in a large room.	**95**
The roar of city traffic. A diesel lorry 8 m away.	**105**
A Boeing 747 taking off overhead.	**107**
A motor-mower cutting a lawn, or an air compressor.	**112**
A Boeing 707 coming in to land at an airport.	**118**
Concorde taking off overhead.	**120**

Jet fighters

Jet fighters have come a long way since Me 262s and Meteors flew in World War 2. Subsonic Sabres and MiG-15s met in the first jet combats in 1950, during the Korean War, and now air forces throughout the world are equipped with advanced supersonic fighters

The aircraft shown here date from the Korean War to the present day. Other classic fighters include the Mirage F.1C (see p. 3) and the Tornado (see p.27). All but the Sabre and the MiG-15 use afterburning jet engines and carry target-detecting radar equipment.

The dates give the year of each plane's entry into service.

North American F-86 Sabre 1949

◄ The North American F-86 Sabre was the second American plane to break the sound barrier, and at one time held the world air speed record at 1,073 kph. It really made its mark in the Korean War, in which a total of 792 MiG-15s fell victim to its six 12.7 mm machine-guns and rockets.

◄ Russia's MiG-15, flown by Chinese pilots, was more than a match for early American jet fighters over Korea, being 100 kph faster than the U.S.A.F.'s F-80C Shooting Star and the U.S. Navy's F9F Panther. But it did not always win, and in its first week of use one was shot down to become the first victim of an all-jet combat.

Mikoyan MiG-15 1948

SEPECAT Jaguar GR.1A 1972

▲ This Anglo-French strike aircraft was first designed as a trainer and light attack aircraft. Its maximum speed is Mach 1.6, and it is very agile. It carries advanced electronics and can take off from rough airstrips with heavy weapons loads.

Lockheed F-104 Starfighter 1958

► The Starfighter has been nick-named 'the missile with a man in it' because of its slim, needle-nosed shape and small wings. The wings are so sharp that the leading edges have to be covered to protect ground workers from cutting themselves.

Saab JA-37 1978

▲ The Swedish Viggen (Thunderbolt) fighter was developed from the AJ-37 attack version. The JA-37 carries guns in a pack mounted under the plane's belly. Like the earlier versions it can operate from ordinary roads as well as airfields.

General Dynamics F-16 1979

▲ The U.S.A.F.'s air combat fighter, the Fighting Falcon, has also been selected by several European countries as a replacement for their Starfighters. It is one of the most manoeuvrable fighters ever built. There is a slightly lower-powered version which is known as the F16/79.

B.A.C. Lightning 1960

Detachable fuel tank

▲ The Lightning was the first supersonic plane to enter service with the R.A.F. It can accelerate from Mach 1 to Mach 2 in 3½ minutes.

The Lightning was outstanding as a high-level interceptor, being able to climb almost vertically, straight after take-off. At least one unsuspecting U-2 spy plane flying at 25,000 m has been pounced on by a Lightning.

McDonnell Douglas F-4 Phantom II 1960

▲ The Phantom is one of the world's most widely used advanced warplanes. It was developed because the U.S. Navy needed a twin-engined fighter to operate from aircraft carriers. Although no longer produced, well over 2,000 are still in service and are constantly updated.

The Phantom has a large radar for air combat and is armed with air-to-air missiles and a built-in six-barrelled cannon. It can also be used for ground attack with bombs, missiles and the cannon.

McDonnell Douglas F-18 Hornet 1982

► The Hornet is mainly flown from carriers by the U.S. Marine Corps, as either an interceptor or a ground attack aircraft. The plane can reach Mach 1.8 at high altitude.

Mikoyan MiG-23 1972

► Russia's swing-winged MiG-23 fighter-bomber flies from bases in Eastern Europe, and has also been supplied to Middle-East countries. The all-weather fighter version has a large nose to house radar equipment. There are also ground-attack and two-seat trainer versions.

Grumman F-14 Tomcat 1974

► The Tomcat is in service on the U.S. Navy's aircraft carriers. Its main purpose is fleet defence and tactical air support. An additional role is photographic reconnaissance. Its radar can detect targets 250 km away and can track up to 24 objects at the same time.

Bombers and strike aircraft

Until the 1960s bombers were designed to approach their targets at great height, making their final bombing runs in straight lines for the greatest accuracy. They were often unarmed, though the B-52 carried a tail gun. Then anti-aircraft defence relying on radar was improved. Now 'strike' aircraft are designed to fly low as well as fast to their targets, closely following ground contours, ducking under enemy radar, and taking advantage of radar-blocking obstacles such as hills. ECM (electronic counter-measures) equipment detects enemy radar and automatically sends back confusing signals of its own. The plane scatters radar-reflection foil ('chaff') and decoy flares that lure away incoming missiles. No human pilot could handle all this, so the aircraft is largely computer-controlled.

Body painted black reduce visibility

Engines buried in wings

'Beaver' tail

Sawtooth wing shape

British Aerospace Buccaneer S.2 1963

▲ When Britain abandoned its conventional aircraft carriers, this fast and powerful strike aircraft, originally intended for naval use, was assigned to the RAF It can carry four bombs in its weapons bay and four missiles under its wings. Because it is economical on fuel and can be refuelled in flight through the probe in front of the cockpit, it has a typical range of 3,700 km.

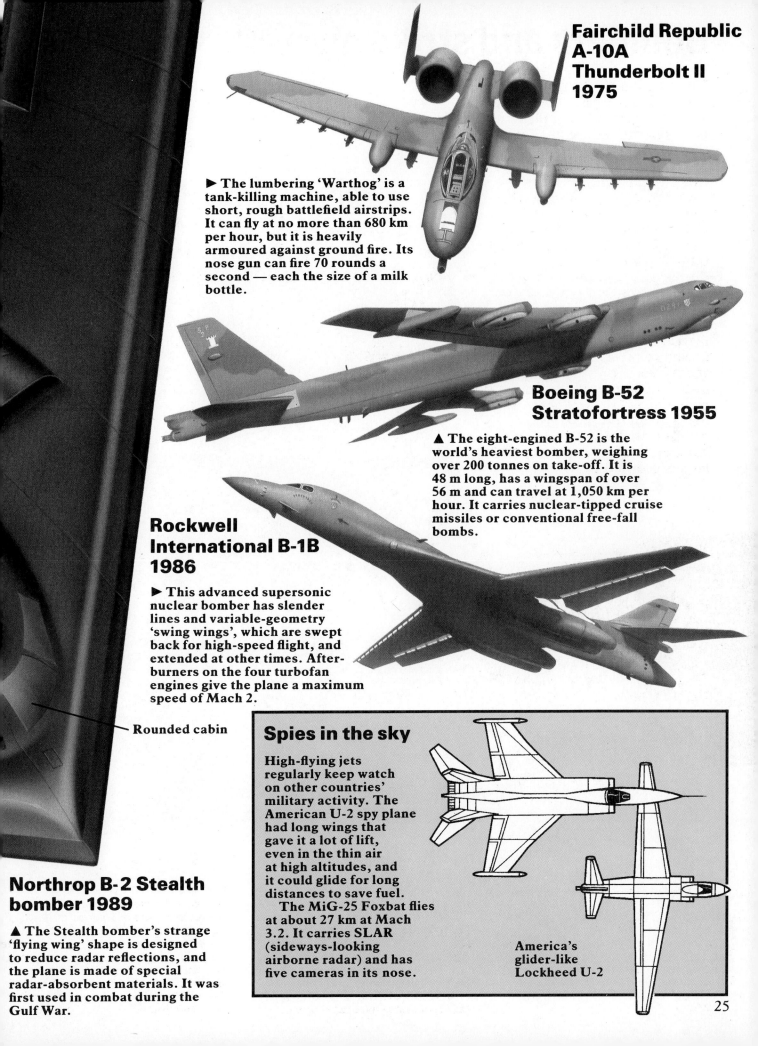

Fairchild Republic A-10A Thunderbolt II 1975

► The lumbering 'Warthog' is a tank-killing machine, able to use short, rough battlefield airstrips. It can fly at no more than 680 km per hour, but it is heavily armoured against ground fire. Its nose gun can fire 70 rounds a second — each the size of a milk bottle.

Boeing B-52 Stratofortress 1955

▲ The eight-engined B-52 is the world's heaviest bomber, weighing over 200 tonnes on take-off. It is 48 m long, has a wingspan of over 56 m and can travel at 1,050 km per hour. It carries nuclear-tipped cruise missiles or conventional free-fall bombs.

Rockwell International B-1B 1986

► This advanced supersonic nuclear bomber has slender lines and variable-geometry 'swing wings', which are swept back for high-speed flight, and extended at other times. After-burners on the four turbofan engines give the plane a maximum speed of Mach 2.

— Rounded cabin

Northrop B-2 Stealth bomber 1989

▲ The Stealth bomber's strange 'flying wing' shape is designed to reduce radar reflections, and the plane is made of special radar-absorbent materials. It was first used in combat during the Gulf War.

Spies in the sky

High-flying jets regularly keep watch on other countries' military activity. The American U-2 spy plane had long wings that gave it a lot of lift, even in the thin air at high altitudes, and it could glide for long distances to save fuel.

The MiG-25 Foxbat flies at about 27 km at Mach 3.2. It carries SLAR (sideways-looking airborne radar) and has five cameras in its nose.

America's glider-like Lockheed U-2

25

Jump-jets and swing-wings

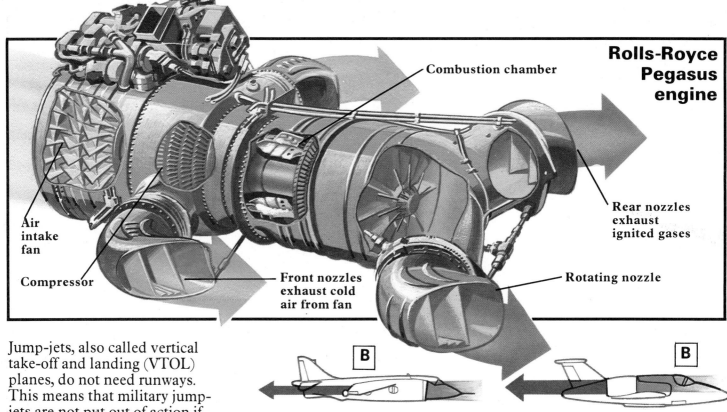

Rolls-Royce Pegasus engine

Combustion chamber

Rear nozzles exhaust ignited gases

Rotating nozzle

Front nozzles exhaust cold air from fan

Air intake fan

Compressor

Jump-jets, also called vertical take-off and landing (VTOL) planes, do not need runways. This means that military jump-jets are not put out of action if their airfield is bombed. They can also operate from decks of small ships without using catapults and arrester wires.

Early work on VTOL was done with the 'Flying Bedstead' (see page 30), and experimental VTOL craft have been built in America, Russia, France and Germany. The Hawker Siddeley Harrier, powered by the Pegasus engine shown above, was the first jump-jet to enter service, in 1969.

▲ The four exhaust nozzles of the Harrier's Pegasus engine point vertically down for take-off (A). They gradually swivel back until the plane is flying fast enough for its wings to keep it in the air (B). The process is reversed for landing.

▲ The projected McDonnell Douglas 260 had three fans, one in the nose and the other two above the wings. The company has since concentrated on an advanced version of the Harrier for the U.S. Marine Corps.

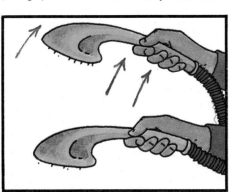

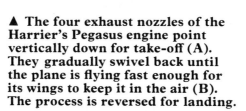

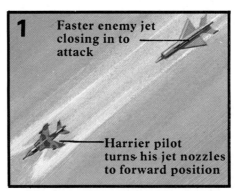

1 Faster enemy jet closing in to attack

Harrier pilot turns his jet nozzles to forward position

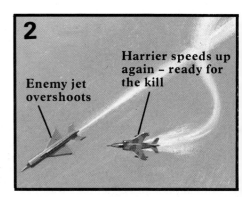

2 Harrier speeds up again – ready for the kill

Enemy jet overshoots

▲ VTO works just like normal jet flight, except that the jet is deflected downwards and so forces the aircraft up. Try holding a hand-shower over the bath, and turning it on fast. The force of the water gushing out will push your hand up.

▲ The jump-jet is at an advantage in air-to-air combat. If a Harrier is being chased by another fighter it can escape by a technique called V.I.F.F. (Vectoring In Forward Flight). The pilot swivels the nozzles from the fully back position

to as far forward as they will go. Its jets now slow the Harrier down much faster than air brakes can, so the pursuing fighter flies past. The Harrier pilot can then turn the nozzles back and get on the tail of the other plane.

Tri-national swing-wing – the Panavia Tornado

Germany
Italy
Great Britain

1
7
6
8
4
5
3
2
D-9591

The Panavia Tornado was the first European swing-wing to enter service. Training began in 1981 with aircraft equipping squadrons in 1982. The first swing-wing plane in military service was the General Dynamics F-111.

By using moving or 'variable geometry' wings, the Tornado combines the advantages of long straight wings for slow flying and landing with a fully swept layout for high-speed.

The part of the wing near the fuselage (1) is fixed, while the outer section (2) can swing backwards or forwards. The two RB 199 turbofan engines exhaust through thrust-reversing buckets (3) to shorten the landing run.

Weapons include two built-in 27 mm cannon (4), various air-to-surface missiles (5), and air-to-air missiles like the Sparrow (6). Fuel can be carried in tanks under the wings (7) as well as internally. There is also a probe (8) for in-flight fuelling.

▶The Tornado's pilot can vary the sweepback of his wings. Straight for take-off and landing, swept-back for high speed flight. The swing-wings are connected to a rigid box in the fuselage, and are moved by hydraulic jacks.

BELL X-5
U.S. AIR FORCE
01838

▲ The pioneer of swing-wing flight was the Bell X-5 research aircraft of 1951. It was based on Messerschmitt designs that came into American hands at the end of World War 2. Its success led, in 1953, to the development of the Grumman Jaguar, a carrier-borne fighter, but the project was abandoned after two prototypes had been completed.

Wing sweeps through this angle

Pilot to scale

Jets of the future

Tomorrow's jets will go faster and higher than today's, yet travel farther for each litre of fuel, and be quieter. They may one day be fuelled by liquid hydrogen, which would be non-polluting and plentiful, but would need to be refrigerated and would require huge fuel tanks.

A new generation of supersonic airliner, flying to Mach 3, may be built. Following these may come the spaceplane, propelled by a hybrid engine: it would be a fanjet, for take-off and low-altitude flight then a ramjet at altitude (see panel below), and finally a rocket, when at the fringe of space.

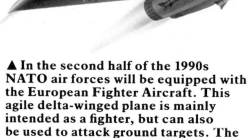

▲ In the second half of the 1990s NATO air forces will be equipped with the European Fighter Aircraft. This agile delta-winged plane is mainly intended as a fighter, but can also be used to attack ground targets. The nose winglets automatically correct the plane's flight as it is buffeted by turbulent air at high speed and low altitude. The EFA would instantly crash if it were not flown moment to moment by its computers. The pilot will control some functions by spoken commands.

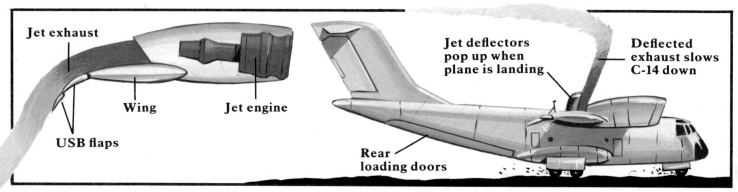

▲ A system called U.S.B. (upper surface blowing) makes planes capable of short take-offs and landings. The engines are mounted over the wings, as in the pioneering Boeing C-14.

U.S.B. works like this: Jet exhaust gases blow over the wing's upper surface. U.S.B. flaps curve down behind the wing's trailing edge, pointing towards the ground. The exhaust gases stick to the flaps and are deflected almost straight downwards, creating lift.

You can see what happens by holding the back of a spoon against the water from a tap. The gases stick to the flaps just as the water curves around the spoon. The effect is now put to work in some airliners — the Soviet An-72 and An-74, and the Japanese Asuka.

Hypersonic ramjets

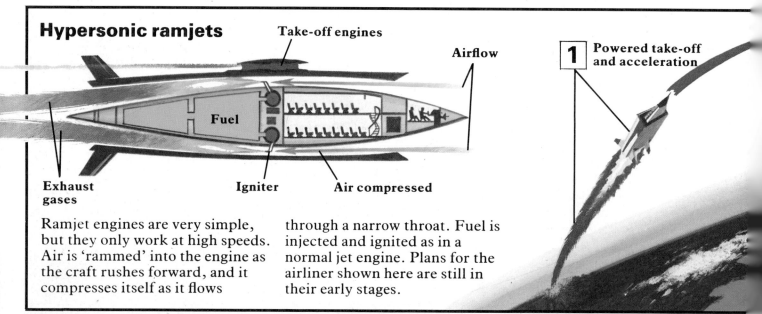

Ramjet engines are very simple, but they only work at high speeds. Air is 'rammed' into the engine as the craft rushes forward, and it compresses itself as it flows through a narrow throat. Fuel is injected and ignited as in a normal jet engine. Plans for the airliner shown here are still in their early stages.

Jet airliners may be growing propellers in the next few years. The unducted fan — also known as a propfan or ultra-high-bypass engine — is the latest development of the jet engine. Like a fanjet, (see page 7), it consists of a turbojet with a built-in fan, or propeller, either at the front or the back, which gives extra thrust. It differs from a fanjet in that a higher proportion of the intake air bypasses the turbojet core. The fan is mounted on the same axle as the turbine in the engine, which is rotated by the expansion of the hot exhaust gases.

A propfan engine is quiet and economical by comparison with a turbojet or fanjet of equivalent power. In fact the fuel costs over a 650-km journey of the McDonnell Douglas MD-80 testbed plane, shown here, could be half those of the company's comparable DC-9.

The blades of a propfan may be unducted — that is, exposed as here (right) — or ducted — placed inside a tube that gives greater protection from damage and also reduces the damage caused if a fan should break off.

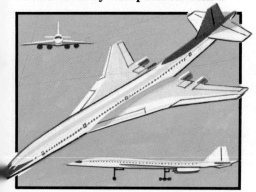

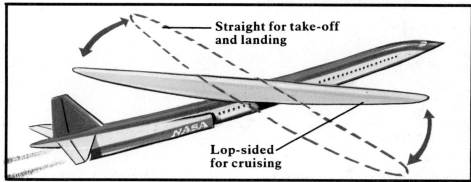

Straight for take-off and landing

Lop-sided for cruising

▲ This McDonnell Douglas design for a supersonic liner would carry 273 passengers at Mach 2.2. It has unusually shaped wings intended to cause less drag than ogival wings of the type used on Concorde.

▲ The weird, scissor-like swing-wing aircraft above is a design study by NASA. It would be an easy and lightweight way to give jet airliners swing-wings, because the design only calls for one swivel point — the heaviest part

of any swing-wing aircraft. The four turbofan engines are mounted in long ducts on the tail.

The idea is not new. German designers drew up similar plans in World War 2, for a fighter to be called the Blohm und Voss P 202.

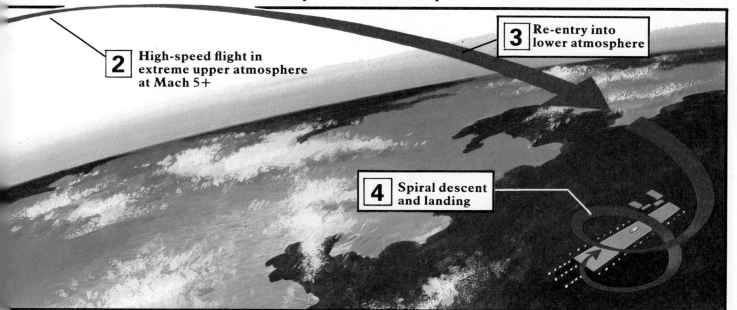

2 High-speed flight in extreme upper atmosphere at Mach 5+

3 Re-entry into lower atmosphere

4 Spiral descent and landing

Jet firsts

The first man to suggest jet air travel was the French balloonist Joseph Montgolfier. In 1783 he proposed (but did not succeed in) using the hot air that kept his balloons up to drive them forward. Here are some later pioneers from jet flight's short but crowded history.

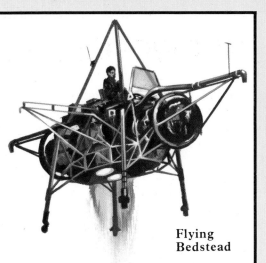

Flying Bedstead

1865
First real design for a jet-propelled plane drawn up by de Louvrié, a French engineer.

1865's jet

August 27, 1939
Capt. Erich Warsitz made the first jet flight, in a Heinkel He 178 test plane.

November 30, 1941
First cross-country jet flight, made in the Italian Caproni-Campini N-1 from Milan to Rome.

July 27, 1944
Gloster Meteors of the RAF made first jet combat flight, against V-1 flying bombs.

September 18, 1948
The Convair XF-92A research aircraft was the first delta-wing jet to fly.

July 27, 1949
The de Havilland Comet was the first pure-jet airliner to fly. It went into service in 1952.

November 8, 1950
First jet-vs.-jet air victory won by a Lockheed F-80 over a Chinese MiG-15 in Korean War.

August 3, 1954
First VTO jet flight, made by Rolls-Royce test pilot R.T. Shepherd in the 'Flying Bedstead'.

October 1959
First round-the-world jet passenger service started by Pan American, using Boeing 707s.

December 31, 1968
Russia's Tupolev Tu-144 made its maiden flight, becoming the first SST to fly.

April 1, 1969
Hawker Siddeley Harriers of the RAF became the first operational VTOL aircraft.

January 22, 1970
First Boeing 747 'Jumbo Jet' entered service on Pan Am's New York – London route.

January 21, 1976
Concorde made the first SST passenger flights. The Tu-144 had made mail flights earlier.

April, 1988
Airbus A320 enters service with the most advanced electronics of any airliner to date.

July 17, 1989
Northrop B-2 Stealth bomber, designed to be 'low observable' by radar, makes first flight.

Abbreviations

BAe	British Aerospace	**RAF**	(British) Royal Air Force
EPNdB	Effective Perceived Noise Decibels	**SLAR**	Sideways-Looking Airborne Radar
ECM	Electronic Countermeasures	**SST**	Supersonic Transport
Flt. Lt.	Flight Lieutenant	**STOL**	Short Take-Off and Landing
ILS	Instrument Landing System	**USAF**	United States Air Force
NASA	National Aeronautics and Space Administration	**VTOL**	Vertical Take-Off and Landing

Jet facts

Did you know that jet fighters can fly faster than the shells they fire, and that at least one jet has shot itself down? These are some other odd facts about jets and the men who fly them.

America's E-3A AWACS (Airborne Warning and Control System) is a flying command base, carrying 'look down' radar that can survey a battlefield from a safe distance. Each one costs $178 million, making it one of the world's most expensive planes.

The longest scheduled non-stop flight is from Brussels to Hawaii, a distance of 11,791 km., which takes 14 hours in a Boeing 747.

A modified MiG-25 Foxbat fighter has reached a height of 37.65 km., the world absolute altitude record. It can reach a height of 35 km. in 4 mins. 11.3 secs., at a climbing speed of 400 m. a second (well over Mach 1).

On December 20, 1968, United Air Lines carried 118,519 passengers in one day in its all-jet fleet of airliners.

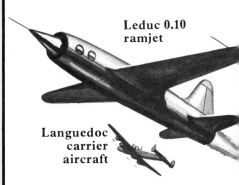

Leduc 0.10 ramjet

Languedoc carrier aircraft

Three prototype ramjets called Leduc 0.10s were built and successfully tested in France, making their first powered flight in 1949. They were air-launched from larger planes, and reached speeds of up to 800 k.p.h. on half-power. A later French research plane, the Nord Griffon, used a turbo-jet engine in the centre of a huge ramjet to provide power for take-off and climbing. The ramjet took over when the plane was flying high and fast.

Dornier Do31

One of the most interesting VTOL experimental aircraft was the Dornier Do31E military transport. It was powered by ten engines, with a Pegasus turbofan on each side of its fuselage and four lift-jets in removable pods on each wing-tip, and had a cruising speed of 650 k.p.h. The project was finally abandoned because of its cost and complexity.

The B-58 Hustler carried a giant-sized streamlined pod underneath its fuselage. This had two parts. The lower one was a fuel tank that could be dropped in flight once the fuel was used up. The upper part carried both fuel and a bomb or missile. This was dropped over the target zone, so that the Hustler could fly home faster and lighter.

The highest point from which airmen have made an emergency escape is 17,000 m. – nearly twice as high as Mt. Everest. On April 9, 1958, two crew members of an English Electric Canberra bomber that exploded at this height escaped unharmed. They fell 14,000 m. before their parachutes opened automatically.

The fastest jet flying-boat ever built was the Martin Seamaster, which could fly at nearly 1,000 k.p.h. Its four engines were mounted in pairs above the swept-back wings.

On December 29, 1974, a record 674 people were squeezed into a QANTAS airlines jumbo. They were being evacuated from disaster in Darwin, Australia after the town had been hit by a hurricane.

Jet words

The glossary only includes words that are not fully explained anywhere else in the book. You will find other engine words explained on pages 6 and 7, and flight words on pages 8 and 9.

Afterburning
A boosting system (also called reheat) in which fuel is injected and ignited in the jet exhaust to give extra thrust.

Dassault/Breguet Dornier Alpha-jet

Air brakes

Air brakes
Controls that increase drag, and so slow aircraft down.

Apron
Open space at an airport on which aircraft are parked for loading, refuelling etc.

Bowser
A tanker truck used for refuelling aircraft.

Console
An aircraft instrument panel.

Flight deck
An airliner's crew compartment.

Galley
Space for cooking food on board an airliner.

Glidepath
The path an aircraft follows as it comes in to land.

Interceptor
A fast, light warplane designed for cutting attacking aircraft or missiles off.

Jet core
The central part of the jet engine, made up of the compressor and fuel injection and ignition systems.

Leading edge
The front edge of the wing.

Operational
In service – the opposite of experimental.

Pallet
A platform for carrying cargo, with openings to fit the prongs of a fork-lift truck.

Prototype
The first model (or models) of a new make of aeroplane.

Radome
A protective covering for radar equipment.

Sensor
Any reconnaissance instrument that gathers information.

Skin temperature
The temperature on the outside of a plane.

Spoilers
Long metal plates that can be raised to disturb the airflow over wings, reducing lift.

Stacking
An air traffic control system by which aircraft approaching a busy airport are left circling a radio beacon at gradually descending levels until they are cleared to land.

Subsonic
Slower than Mach 1. Speeds between Mach 1 and Mach 5 are supersonic. Hypersonic means faster than Mach 5.

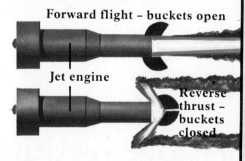

Forward flight – buckets open

Jet engine

Reverse thrust – buckets closed

Thrust-reversing buckets
Controls in the rear of a jet engine. They deflect the jet exhaust forwards, slowing the plane down.

Trailing edge
The rear edge of a wing.

Turbine
In jet engines, a wheel with curved blades that is turned by exhaust gases and itself turns the compressor.

Index

THE USBORNE YOUNG SCIENTIST
CARS

Contents

Credits

Written by Jonathan Rutland and Margaret Stephens
Art and editorial direction David Jefferis
Editorial revision Margaret Stephens
Text Editor Eliot Humberstone
Design Iain Ashman
Design revision Robert Walster
Technical consultant Roger Ames
Illustrators Malcolm English, Terry Hadler, John
Hutchinson, Frank Kennard, Jack Pelling, Michael
Roffe, Robert Walster, Sean Wilkinson, Hans Wiborg-
Jenssen, John Scorey and Chris Lyon.

Acknowledgements

We wish to thank the following individuals and
organizations for their assistance.

John Barker
Performance Car
Car Magazine
BMW (GB) Ltd
General Motors Ltd
Mercedes-Benz Ltd
Brands Hatch Racing Ltd
Citroën UK Ltd
Porsche Cars GB Ltd
Project Thrust

Usborne Publishing Ltd
Usborne House
83-85 Saffron Hill
London EC1N 8RT

Printed in Belgium

This edition published 1991
Based on the Young Engineers Book of Supercars,
published 1978.

The name Usborne and the device ♔ are trademarks
of Usborne Publishing Ltd.

Introduction

If you compare the sleek lines and speed of the latest Formula 1 racer with the clumsy design and spluttering performance of the first steam carriage, it is amazing that one grew out of the other. But that is exactly what happened.

From the first motorcars that crept along at a snail's pace puffing steam, to the development of the petrol engine and the latest top-speed dragster, the history of the car is fascinating and exciting.

In this book, you will find out about how a car works, learning to race, sportscars, the latest robot technology in car factories and what happens at the Formula 1 race track. You will also discover the world of dragsters and rally cars.

Everything is explained simply and there are experiments to show you the principles behind car engineering. You can even have a go at designing your own car.

This picture gives you a look at the parts which make up a modern rally car, the Lancia Integrale. Rally cars are always ordinary production cars, although with many changes and modifications.

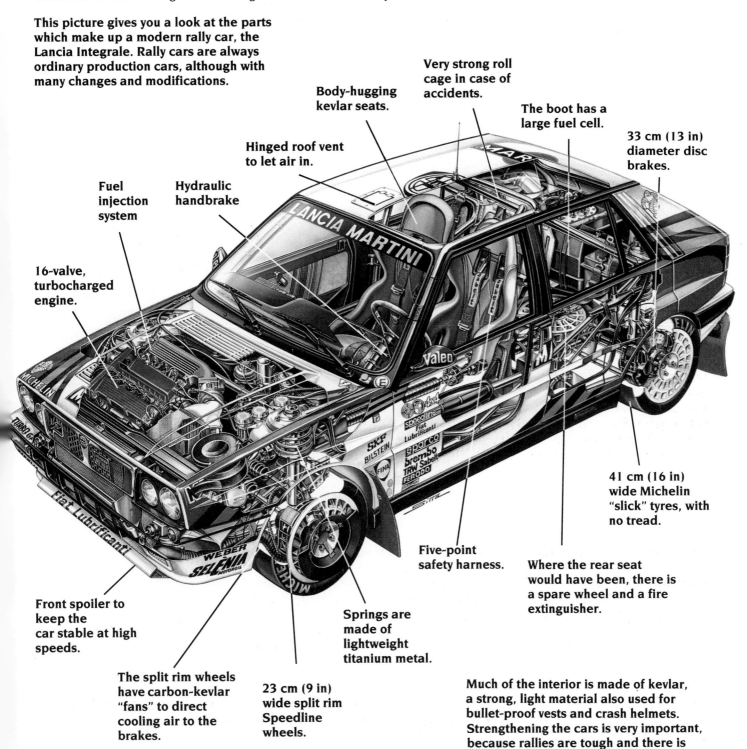

Very strong roll cage in case of accidents.

Body-hugging kevlar seats.

The boot has a large fuel cell.

33 cm (13 in) diameter disc brakes.

Hinged roof vent to let air in.

Fuel injection system

Hydraulic handbrake

16-valve, turbocharged engine.

Front spoiler to keep the car stable at high speeds.

The split rim wheels have carbon-kevlar "fans" to direct cooling air to the brakes.

23 cm (9 in) wide split rim Speedline wheels.

Springs are made of lightweight titanium metal.

Five-point safety harness.

41 cm (16 in) wide Michelin "slick" tyres, with no tread.

Where the rear seat would have been, there is a spare wheel and a fire extinguisher.

Much of the interior is made of kevlar, a strong, light material also used for bullet-proof vests and crash helmets. Strengthening the cars is very important, because rallies are tough and there is always the danger of an accident.

3

ly motorcars

t ancestor of the ... was built in the 18th century by a French engineer, Nicholas Cugnot. His first vehicle, shown on the right, was steam powered and not very successful.

In the 19th century, engineers tried to improve the design of these steam carriages, which were too slow and cumbersome to achieve widespread use. Then in 1885, there came a major breakthrough when Karl Benz, a German engineer, made the first vehicle powered by a petrol engine. This was the start of a revolution and soon petrol-powered vehicles were to replace horse-drawn vehicles and rule the road.

Cugnot's steam carriage of 1770 had a tank mounted at the front to boil water in. The steam power generated by the boiling water turned the vehicle's front wheel through a system of piston, cylinder, rods and cranks. It was designed to haul cannon for the French army, but proved of very little use. Top speed was 5 km/h (3 mph) and every 15 minutes it had to stop to build up steam again. The heavy tank made it hard to steer and Cugnot's first carriage crashed. He did make another, but by then the army had sensibly lost all interest.

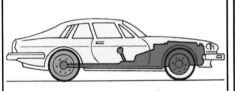

Front engine, rear wheel drive.

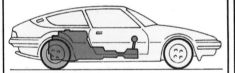

Mid engine, rear wheel drive.

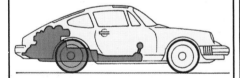

Rear engine, rear wheel drive.

Front engine, front wheel drive.

These diagrams show some of the different ways in which engines and driving wheels can be arranged. From top to bottom, the cars are: a Jaguar XJ-S, a Matra Bagheera, a Porsche 911 and an Alfa Romeo Alfasud. Front engine with front wheel drive is the most common design in modern cars.

This is a Renault leading the field in the first Grand Prix race, held in 1906 near Le Mans in France. The Renault completed the 1,238 km (769 mile) course at an average speed of 101 km/h (63 mph). Previous big events had been raced on public roads, but were banned as too dangerous. This was why closed circuit races like the Grands Prix were started.

4   In 1902, the French government tried to make motorists use alcohol fuel manufactured from potatoes.

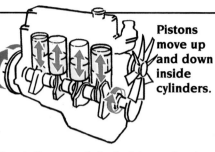

Pistons move up and down inside cylinders.

A rotating crankshaft drives wheels through a gearbox and driveshaft.

This picture shows the first car to run successfully with a petrol engine. It was built by Karl Benz in 1885. To the right is a diagram of a typical modern engine, based on the Benz principles. Petrol vapour is ignited at the top of each cylinder by an electric spark plug. The

explosions force down pistons which are inside the cylinders. The "up and down" movement of the pistons turns a rod and then a crankshaft, which provides turning power for the wheels. The pistons move one after the other in sequence to provide a smooth flow of turning power.

This 1891 Panhard Levassor had the layout used by many cars ever since. The engine was at the front under the bonnet. The car had a gearbox, foot-operated clutch, rear wheel drive and a radiator to cool the water. The basic principles have been the same for a hundred years.

The Ford Model T was the first car to be made on an assembly line. Before 1908, all cars had been hand made and were very expensive. Mass production techniques meant the time - and the cost - of car making could be drastically reduced.

As the car's popularity grew, so did the number of makes. Soon there were over 500 in the USA alone. The three badges shown above represent makes of cars that all became part of the American General Motors, now one of the world's biggest car makers.

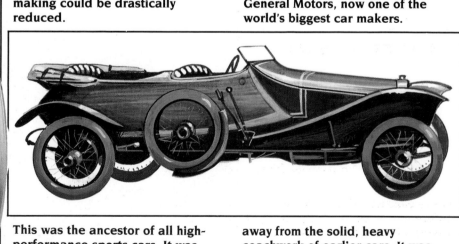

This was the ancestor of all high-performance sports cars. It was called the Skiff because of its boat-like appearance and was built in 1911 for the racing driver René de Knyff by Panhard Levassor. The Skiff's body was a revolutionary step

away from the solid, heavy coachwork of earlier cars. It was built to weigh as little as possible and had the lightweight construction of aeroplanes of that time. Spoked wheels were also used to reduce the weight of the car.

In 1896, Henry Ford's first car was the only car in Detroit. He had to chain it up when he left it unattended.

Understanding cars

The key to understanding how cars work is knowing that they are made up of seven systems. These are engine, transmission, body, steering, brakes, electrics and suspension - all shown on these pages.

The large picture is a skeleton view of a 1930 Bentley racing car. Compare this car with the modern cars pictured around it.

This is a side view of the 217 km/h (135 mph) Bentley.

Early cars had front wheels mounted on a single axle, linked to the chassis by springs.

Early cars had oil or gas lamps, which did not give out much light. Electric ones like this date from 1913 and are much more powerful.

The tyres are air-filled (pneumatic). The first cars had solid tyres. These gave a hard bouncy ride and poor grip, reducing cornering and braking power.

Engine

This is the power-house of the car. It is controlled by a floor-mounted accelerator pedal.

This handbrake, typical of the period, was mounted on the outside of the car. All cars now have handbrakes inside, usually between the front seats.

Transmission

Transmission links the engine to the driving wheels by clutch, gearbox, and differential.

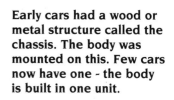

Propeller shaft

Early cars had a wood or metal structure called the chassis. The body was mounted on this. Few cars now have one - the body is built in one unit.

The capacity of the engine is measured in litres or cubic inches, depending on the country. The size refers to the total volume of all the cylinders.

Steering

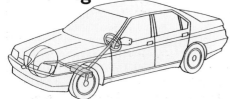

A rack and pinion steering system turns the wheels left or right. This is controlled by a steering wheel.

Brakes

Usually a floor-mounted pedal controls the brakes on all wheels. A hand brake is used for parking.

Electrics

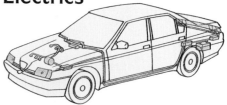

The alternator supplies all the electricity when the engine is running and charges the battery.

Body

In almost all modern cars, the body is made of welded pressed steel units.

The large fuel tank carries petrol, which is fed along pipes to the engine by an electric pump. For safety, modern tanks are placed in less exposed positions.

The differential unit is joined to the engine by a propeller shaft. The differential sends variable power to the two driving wheels. Most modern cars do not have a propeller shaft because they are front engine with front wheel drive.

Suspension

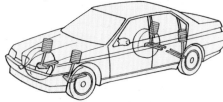

Springs and shock absorbers soak up road bumps, allowing a smooth comfortable ride.

Why a differential is necessary

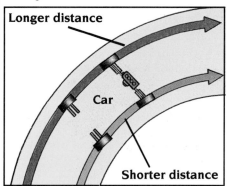

Longer distance

Car

Shorter distance

The differential is an essential component of a car. As a car travels around a bend, the inside wheels cover a shorter distance than the outside wheels. The differential adjusts the power to each driving wheel to cope with this situation.

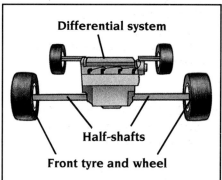

Differential system

Half-shafts

Front tyre and wheel

The driving wheels are attached to an axle split into two halves, called half-shafts. The differential, which is a gear system, lies in the middle. This allows the wheels to run at different speeds.

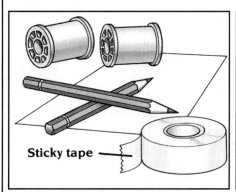

Sticky tape

You can see why a differential is necessary from this experiment. You need two pencils (or two ball point pens), a roll of clear sticky tape, two cotton reels and some paper. If you cannot get cotton reels, try plastic bottle tops.

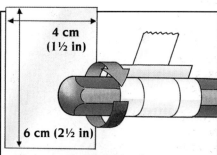

4 cm (1½ in)

6 cm (2½ in)

The pencil should be free to turn inside the sleeve.

Take a piece of paper and cut a shape 4 cm (1½ in) wide and 6 cm (2½ in) long. Wrap it round a pencil and fasten with tape. Make sure the tape does not touch the pencil. The pencil should be able to slide freely in its paper "sleeve".

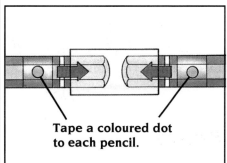

Tape a coloured dot to each pencil.

Cut two pieces of paper into a square, 1 cm (½ in) by 1 cm (½ in). Colour a dot on each and tape them to the pencils. Now jam the tips of both pencils firmly into the cotton reels, and slip the ends into the paper sleeve.

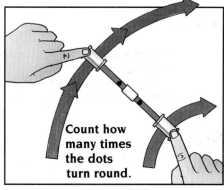

Count how many times the dots turn round.

Rotate your pencil and cotton reel assembly around a sharp bend. Count how many times the dot on the outer pencil turns. Count how many times the dot on the inner pencil turns. The outer dot should turn three times as much as the inner one.

In six years, an average car travels nearly 97,000 km (60, 276 miles). Each wheel will have turned 54 million times.

Classic cars

Motoring began as a noisy, uncomfortable and often messy adventure. But before long engineers began designing cars that gave a smoother ride and were more reliable.

In 1906, Rolls-Royce brought out the Silver Ghost which was the first of this new generation of cars. Other makers, like Mercedes-Benz and Jaguar, soon followed their example by producing cars with comfort, style, performance and reliability.

Many of these cars are now famous classics, and greatly sought after by collectors. Here we have chosen a selection of our own favourite classic cars.

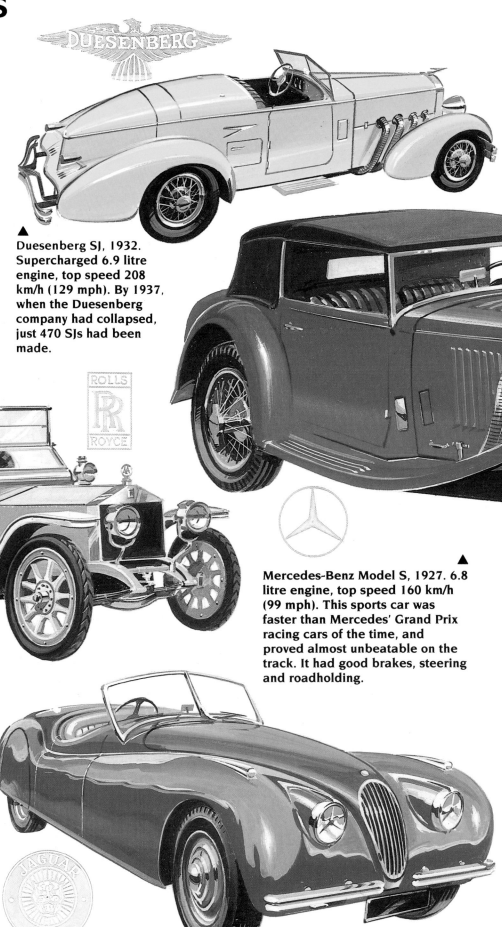

▲ Duesenberg SJ, 1932. Supercharged 6.9 litre engine, top speed 208 km/h (129 mph). By 1937, when the Duesenberg company had collapsed, just 470 SJs had been made.

▲ Rolls-Royce Silver Ghost, 1906. 7 litre engine, top speed about 125 km/h (78 mph). To show its superior quality, the first Silver Ghost was driven day and night for 24,120 km (14,988 miles). It had to make only one repair stop.

▲ Mercedes-Benz Model S, 1927. 6.8 litre engine, top speed 160 km/h (99 mph). This sports car was faster than Mercedes' Grand Prix racing cars of the time, and proved almost unbeatable on the track. It had good brakes, steering and roadholding.

Jaguar XK 120, 1948. 3.4 litre ▶ engine, top speed 212 km/h (132 mph). The first streamlined, high-performance sports car, it won race after race. It was also popular as a road car and fairly cheap to buy. Its engine design is still in use today.

To comply with different countries' various regulations, a Rolls-Royce has to pass more than 204 separate tests.

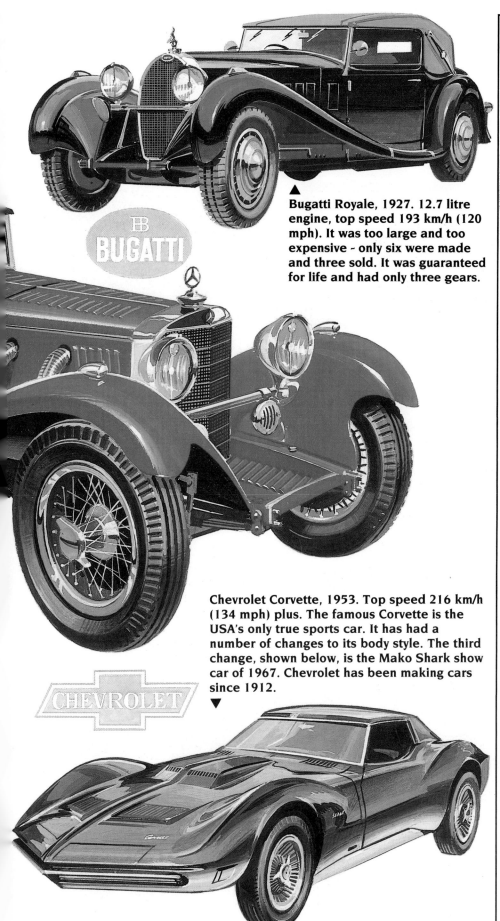

Bugatti Royale, 1927. 12.7 litre engine, top speed 193 km/h (120 mph). It was too large and too expensive - only six were made and three sold. It was guaranteed for life and had only three gears.

BUGATTI

CHEVROLET

Chevrolet Corvette, 1953. Top speed 216 km/h (134 mph) plus. The famous Corvette is the USA's only true sports car. It has had a number of changes to its body style. The third change, shown below, is the Mako Shark show car of 1967. Chevrolet has been making cars since 1912.

Classic cars revived

The Vicarage E-Type

Cars with the styling of famous classics from the past are a money-spinning part of the car-making business. This means that some classics you see on the road may be younger than they look. The Bugatti Royale, shown on the left, is a model that has been revived.

Vicarage Motorcars in the UK are specialists in creating almost brand new versions of classic Jaguars, including the Jaguar Mk ll and the most famous sports car of all time, the E-Type roadster.

The original E-Type was first produced in 1961, and designed by Malcolm Sayer, the engineer behind the Le Mans winning D-Type of the 1950s. Out of production now for many years, the E-Type has been revived by Vicarage with many new improvements. Girling brakes have been added and the steering and suspension have been improved. More supportive seats and a power hood are other modern additions. The car still has the famous E-Type body design, luxurious leather seats and a walnut dashboard.

How do Vicarage make a 30-year old car look brand new? First they take old Jaguar bodies and strip them to their bare metal. Then they shot-blast them for up to 48 hours to make sure the body is free of corrosion. Later, 17 to 24 coats of primer, undercoat, top coat and lacquer are applied to the bodywork. Then it takes two days to hand polish the painted body work. Every mechanical and electrical component is either made new or restored.

At Rolls-Royce a machine called IRMA "squirms" a million times to check that seats will not collapse.

Sports racers

Sports racers compete in the Sportscar World Championship. Famous car manufacturers, such as Jaguar, Porsche, Mercedes and Mazda, know that top performances in the these races will attract more customers to their ordinary production models. In the 1990 season, Japan showed 22 hours of sportscar racing on television. This was the year that the Sauber Mercedes Team won the World Championship. At the same time, the sales of Mercedes' passenger cars increased by 23%. Racing for such high stakes means competition is very fierce. The teams are always searching for new technology to give them the edge over their rivals.

In the Sportscar World Championship engines must have a maximum capacity of 3.5 litres. The races are 430 km (267 miles) in length, except for the 24-hour race at Le Mans.

This is the Sauber Mercedes. Versions of this car won the Sportscar World Championship in 1989 and 1990. It also won the famous French 24-hour Le Mans race in 1989.

Information about engine performance is transmitted during a race from the car to engineers in the pits.

The Sauber Mercedes was tested thoroughly in a wind tunnel, so all the sharp edges could be honed off the car to make it as streamlined as possible.

The body and the chassis of the car are made from carbon fibre reinforced plastic. This is extremely light and very rigid.

Different bonnets for different circuits

On racing circuits, airflow at speed can lift a car up and make it unstable. But car bodies are designed to give downthrust, so they stay firmly on the ground. Bonnet design is important. The successful Porsche 935 was designed with two different bonnets, one for slow track and one for fast track. This is because airflow acts differently at different speeds. On fast track, the 935 was given a lower more streamlined bonnet. The slow circuit bonnet provided downthrust at lower speeds than the fast circuit bonnet.

The Chaparall 2J sports racer of 1970 had a suction fan to "glue" it to the road around corners.

The ignition system and fuel injection are both electronic.

The roof of the car was tested with a weight of 8.5 tonnes (8.4 tons). There was only 2.6 mm (.1 in) movement. When the load was removed the roof returned to its original shape.

The car's design is very flat which gives it a low centre of gravity. The 12-cylinder engine is located as low as possible.

Porsche power

What is it like to sit behind the wheel of one of the world's most famous sportscars, the Porsche 911? First impressions are that the controls are all within easy reach. Starting is instant, the roar of the engine booming out of the back. Acceleration is fantastic and the car takes corners as if on rails. The suspension keeps the car flat on the ground and stable, but absorbs bumps well enough to give a firm, smooth ride. Top speed is 250 km/h (155 mph) and the faster it goes, the quieter it is. Truly this is a great sportscar!

In the World Championship, all sportscars that have raced 90% of the winner's distance are counted as finishers.

Grand Prix racing

Grand Prix racing cars are the kings of the track. Every year they compete for the Formula 1 World Championship and the cars have sleek streamlined bodies covered with bright advertising. Motor racing is an expensive business. Advertising sponsorship is vital to pay a racing team's huge expenses. If a team cannot afford the latest technology, then they will lose out to their rivals. Motor racing has three major categories. In the Formula 1, or Grand Prix, category cars have a maximum engine capacity of 3.5 litres. In Formula 3000 the maximum is 3 litres and in Formula 3 it is 2 litres.

In the cockpit, at the driver's fingertips, are an electronic turbo boost control switch, a multi-purpose visual display panel giving information about the state of the car's major components, a gear lever and rear light switch. GP drivers' racing suits are made out of a special fireproof material.

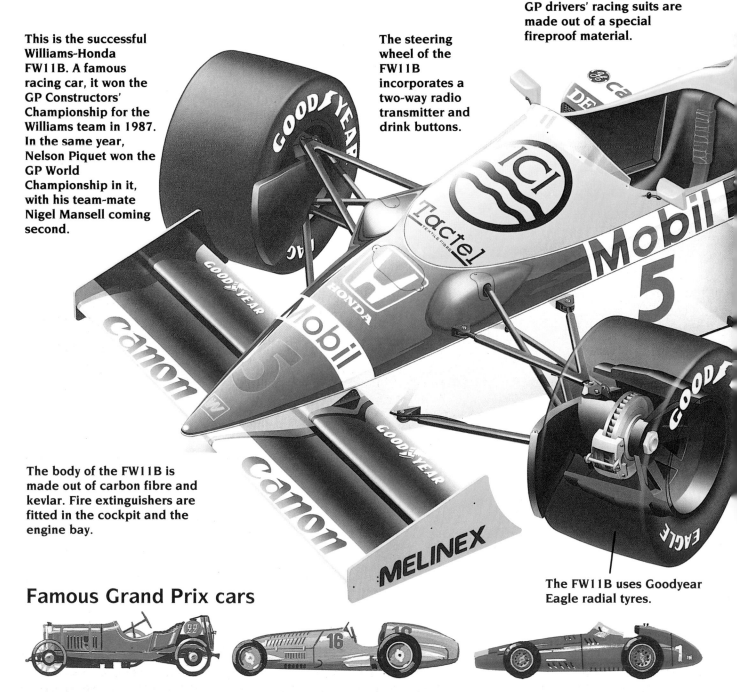

This is the successful Williams-Honda FW11B. A famous racing car, it won the GP Constructors' Championship for the Williams team in 1987. In the same year, Nelson Piquet won the GP World Championship in it, with his team-mate Nigel Mansell coming second.

The steering wheel of the FW11B incorporates a two-way radio transmitter and drink buttons.

The body of the FW11B is made out of carbon fibre and kevlar. Fire extinguishers are fitted in the cockpit and the engine bay.

The FW11B uses Goodyear Eagle radial tyres.

Famous Grand Prix cars

This handsome French Peugeot was one of the earliest racing cars, competing in 1912. Although its engine was very small, the car raced successfully against 14-litre Fiats.

The 1937 Mercedes-Benz W125, shown above, was the most powerful Grand Prix racer ever. Another successful car was the W196 which won 9 of the 12 GPs it entered.

This Maserati was an outstanding Grand Prix car of the 1950s. It was raced by two world famous drivers, the Briton Stirling Moss and the Argentinean Juan-Manuel Fangio.

12   The oldest driver to win a world championship race was Luigi Fagioli, who was 53. He was driving an Alfa Romeo.

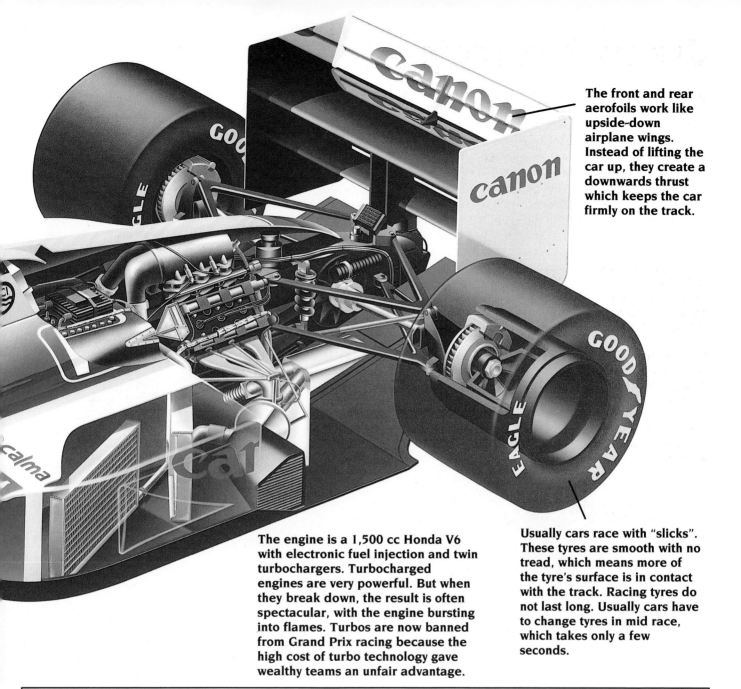

The front and rear aerofoils work like upside-down airplane wings. Instead of lifting the car up, they create a downwards thrust which keeps the car firmly on the track.

The engine is a 1,500 cc Honda V6 with electronic fuel injection and twin turbochargers. Turbocharged engines are very powerful. But when they break down, the result is often spectacular, with the engine bursting into flames. Turbos are now banned from Grand Prix racing because the high cost of turbo technology gave wealthy teams an unfair advantage.

Usually cars race with "slicks". These tyres are smooth with no tread, which means more of the tyre's surface is in contact with the track. Racing tyres do not last long. Usually cars have to change tyres in mid race, which takes only a few seconds.

Aerofoils

All Grand Prix cars are fitted with wings, called aerofoils to prevent them from lifting off the track at high speeds. Airflow around the aerofoils creates downthrust, pressing the car downwards. This experiment shows what happens to a car's roadholding when wings are added.

You will need a lump of plasticine or play dough and a model car, preferably made out of metal. Cut out a rectangular aerofoil 5 x 2.5 cm (2 x 1 in) from a piece of plastic, such as an empty detergent bottle.

You can use water to imitate the high-speed airflow on a race track. The principle is the same. Fill up a bath and send the model car whizzing down the sloping end. The car should slide along the bottom of the bath smoothly.

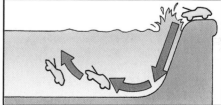

Dry the bonnet and fix the aerofoil on with the plasticine or play dough, angling it up as shown above. Watch how the aerofoil lifts the car up at the bottom of the bath. Now angle the aerofoil down and see how the car stays firmly on the bottom.

Learning to race

What is it like to drive round a Grand Prix racing circuit? To find out, we visited the Brands Hatch International Circuit, which runs a racing school.

Brands Hatch has several types of cars for would-be drivers. After training in a Ford Escort, we took to the circuit in a single-seater Formula First racing car (see the section below, Training to race). It was a real thrill to experience the twists and turns of the circuit, and the blue and white track markings became a blur as the racing car reached speeds of more than 161 km/h (100 mph). It was important to keep an eye on the red needle of the rev counter to make sure the engine was not over-revving. The car's tyres screamed as we rounded a bend and then accelerated out of it down the straight. If tyres get too hot under the strain of fast cornering, they lose their grip. An experienced driver eases off a little to allow them to cool down.

Motor racing is dangerous and the driving methods shown here are for a racing circuit only, not for public roads. Also, speed alone never wins a race. Skill, responsibility and safe driving are all required too. The diagram to the right shows the Brands Hatch circuit. The red line shows the fastest way to get round, and you can see the clipping points for each bend and the gears a driver will use.

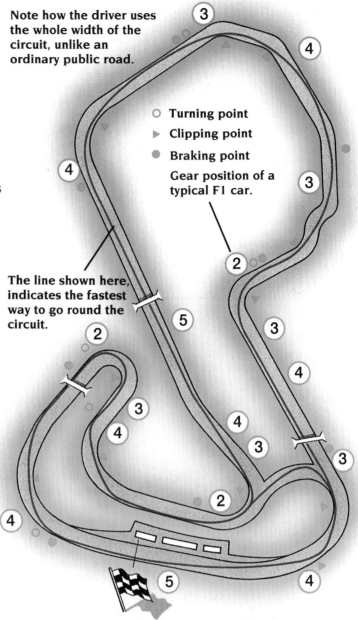

Note how the driver uses the whole width of the circuit, unlike an ordinary public road.

○ Turning point
▶ Clipping point
● Braking point
Gear position of a typical F1 car.

The line shown here, indicates the fastest way to go round the circuit.

Andy Rouse, British Touring Sportscar (Class A) Champion, driving his Ford Sierra RS 500 at Brands Hatch.

Training to race

Before their first outing on the Brands Hatch circuit, pupils receive instruction from professional racing drivers. Then they undergo training in Ford Escort saloons, learning the importance of braking in a straight line and clipping bends.

Next, pupils progress to a Formula First single-seater racing car, which is capable of more than 193 km/h (120 mph). It is vital to keep the car on the circuit under high cornering forces and to make sure the engine is not over-revved.

Safety is very important. Full-face crash helmets and full-harness seat belts are always worn. After much practice, pupils are set lap times to beat, so they become faster and faster until they are eventually ready for their first race.

Learning early

Road safety is vital. It is very important that young drivers are well-trained in controlling a car wisely and responsibly. Brands Hatch runs a scheme for pupils who are under the legal age limit to drive on public roads. In fact, there is no age limit at all for the scheme, you just have to be over 1.47 m (4 ft 10 in) - so you can see over the steering wheel and press the pedals at the same time! Pupils learn basic car control, how to cope with traffic lights and junctions, three point turns and hill starts. ▶

Points of a bend

To the right, you can see the three points that a driver must learn when taking bends on a racing circuit. To keep up the maximum safe speed, a good driver must know exactly when to brake, where to start turning and where to clip the bend. At the approach to the bend, the driver must brake when the car is still in a straight line. Then comes the turning point and after that he clips the bend. If he fails to clip the bend and goes wide, he may be overtaken on the inside by a car behind.

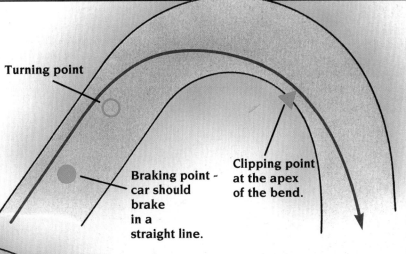

Turning point

Braking point - car should brake in a straight line.

Clipping point at the apex of the bend.

Sliding

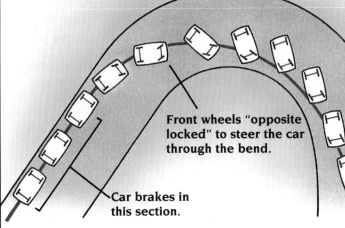

Front wheels "opposite locked" to steer the car through the bend.

Car brakes in this section.

As the car passes the turning point, the driver flicks the steering into the bend, pressing hard on the accelerator. This spins the back wheels, bringing the back of the car round. Then he turns the steering wheel the other way to keep the car on course. At top racing speeds, drivers can sometimes spin off the circuit when turning bends. There are many safety measures to prevent serious accidents, such as large bales of straw on either side of the circuit to absorb the impact of an out-of-control car.

Drifting

In a drift, all four wheels are sliding at an angle to the direction of travel. The front wheels are turned sharply into the bend. A well-controlled drift will result in the car passing the clipping point at the correct angle to accelerate down the next straight.

Study these three diagrams carefully, and the next time you watch racing on the television, see which drivers are the most skilled at turning bends. Notice how important bends are when a driver behind wants to overtake the car in front.

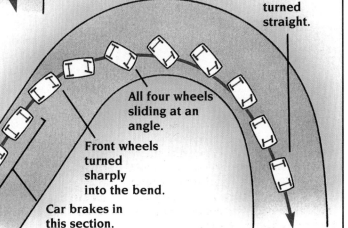

Front wheels turned straight.

All four wheels sliding at an angle.

Front wheels turned sharply into the bend.

Car brakes in this section.

The longest run was in 1935. Francois Leçot covered 400,000 km (248,560 miles) in daily runs of 19 hours.

At the race track

Grand Prix racing must be the noisiest sport in the world. The cars speed round the circuit with an ear-shattering scream. Apart from the noise, and of course the excitement of the race itself, the other remarkable thing about meetings nowadays is the super technology involved. Computers, electronics and even satellites all play an important part in a racing team's success.

Before the start, the cars will have raced against the clock. The car recording the fastest lap around the circuit is given "pole" position. That is, it will be in front of the others at the start.

This is just before the race starts. Race tactics will have been decided and the correct tyres chosen for the track and weather conditions. The driver is listening to last minute instructions from his support team.

During the race, a member of the support team will be in constant radio contact with the driver. The driver can communicate any problems and the team can advise him and let him know how the other competitors are doing.

Inside the team's control room, there is a massive computer. Important parts of the car, such as the fuel injection system or the brakes, transmit signals to a satellite. This satellite then relays information to the computer.

Cars make pit stops to refuel and have a tyre change only taking a few seconds. They also pull into the pits if they have mechanical trouble. The team will already know what the problem is from their computer.

Spectators at a race meeting often keep lap charts. These help you keep track of the drivers' positions. The drivers' names and numbers are entered on the left-hand side. After each lap, the car positions should be noted and recorded on the chart.

Nº	DRIVER	LAPS 1	2	3	
11	J. SMITH	6	6	6	6
20	N. HAUTA	20	20	20	10
10	J. SHUNT	11	11	10	20
28	E. FILLIE	10	10	28	28
6	M.				

Pit board

Although in radio contact with the driver, the team still hold up pit boards to show him his position.

Top row: he is lying seventh.

Middle row: 23 seconds ahead of the eighth man.

Bottom row: 9 seconds behind sixth man.

Control flags

At race meetings, another way of communicating with drivers is by waving different flags.

The flag of the country where the race is held ▶ starts off the race.

Held still, this flag means danger. Waved - more ◀ danger, prepare to stop.

Warns of a slippery surface. This is usually oil ▶ or petrol.

This flag is vital after an accident, as it tells drivers ◀ to stop instantly.

Indicates the danger that has occurred on the track ◀ is now clear.

Held still, car close behind. Waved, car closing ▶ fast or about to overtake.

This flag warns that ambulance or rescue ◀ vehicles are on the track.

A driver must stop at the pits when this flag is ▶ waved with his number.

 Waved for the winner. Held still to indicate race ◀ is now over.

Rally cars

Rally driving is a race against the clock and a test of endurance. Each car has a driver and a navigator. There is a set route which the teams have to follow and a number of check points along the way that they must call in at.

Competing in a world championship rally is not a simple task. Rally drivers have large back-up teams as there is much to do and organise. The team will have chase cars following the rally cars during a race, service vans and tyre vans. Often there will be a team aeroplane spotting problems that may lay ahead, such as traffic snarl-ups

The rally car on this page is the Citroën ZX that won the gruelling Paris-Dakar Rally in 1991.The Paris-Dakar Rally covers 8,047 km (5,000 miles), much of which is across broken track and sand dunes in the Sahara Desert.

The Citroën ZX carries a spare tyre for emergencies. It also has a rear spoiler to help keep the car stable at high speeds.

This is a 320 hp, 4-wheel drive, turbocharged car. The body is made out of kevlar and carbon fibre, light and strong to survive tough conditions.

Rally drivers need nerves of steel. During the Paris-Dakar Rally, the Citroën ZX survived a 15.2 m (50 ft) drop over a sand dune.

◄ Inside a rally car

Here we get a look inside the cockpit of a Lancia Integrale rally car. A display above the heater controls can show information, such as speed, oil pressure and oil and water temperature. A Halda rally computer is triggered by a foot switch to the right of the navigator's footrest. This calculates speed and times.

The Citroën ZX is also an ordinary production car. Travelling at speeds of 161 km/h (100 mph) in rough conditions, the rally version needed many modifications, such as improved suspension, special tyres and a roll cage to give extra protection in an accident.

The Lancia Delta S4 rally car was so powerful that ordinary drivers could not control it.

Dragsters

Dragsters are fast and furious. They compete against each other in drag races and are some of the most colourful and eccentric vehicles you will ever see. This is a typical mid-engined dragster. The machine is equipped with aerofoils front and back, and a strong metal frame.

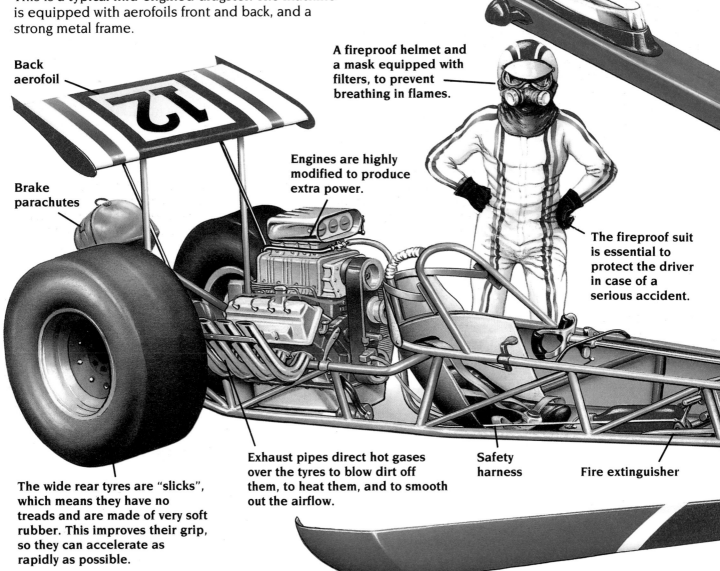

Back aerofoil

Brake parachutes

A fireproof helmet and a mask equipped with filters, to prevent breathing in flames.

Engines are highly modified to produce extra power.

The fireproof suit is essential to protect the driver in case of a serious accident.

The wide rear tyres are "slicks", which means they have no treads and are made of very soft rubber. This improves their grip, so they can accelerate as rapidly as possible.

Exhaust pipes direct hot gases over the tyres to blow dirt off them, to heat them, and to smooth out the airflow.

Safety harness

Fire extinguisher

The 5 second dash

Drag racing takes place all over the world. Dragsters race two at a time along a straight 400 m (¼ mile) drag strip. The kings of the strip, the AA fuel dragsters, look more like skeletons than cars. Any excess weight (panelling around the engine for example) is left off, and they burn a special fuel called nitro-methane to get maximum power from the engine. A fuel dragster's engine develops nearly twice the power of a "gasser", a gasolene (petrol) fueled car.

Cars smoke rubber as they start.

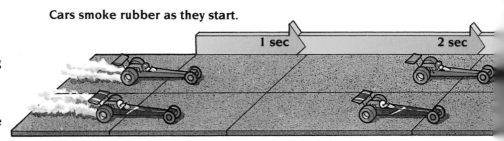

The "fire-up" road

This will give you an idea of what happens in a typical drag race.

The competing dragsters are push-started in the "fire-up" road. Then they make their burn-outs. For this,

the drivers lock the front wheels and spin the back ones. The heat and friction of the spinning back wheels warms the slicks and lays down twin strips of tacky rubber on the track.

Drag truck

This drag truck is festooned with aerofoils and covered with fancy paintwork. Very popular on the drag racing scene, these trucks are normally used for hauling heavy loads. This particular example is an American Kenworth, known as Super Boss. Production models of this truck are used for hauling heavy loads on the highways of the USA. It touched 232.9 km/h (144.7 mph) in its heyday and regularly performed at drag strips in the USA.

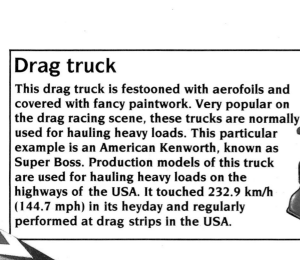

Body panels are necessary to protect the driver from the force of high-speed airflow when the dragster is going at top speed. They are detachable.

The front wheels have a metal insert to help the light beam timing equipment "see" the car and record its time. The latest dragsters have smaller wheels than shown here.

The driver sits in front of the engine, well clear of smoke and flame. In older designs, drivers sat right at the back behind the engine.

Tank carrying the super-powerful nitro-methane fuel.

The front aerofoil, like the back one, is important for the aerodynamics of the dragster.

Brake parachutes release to help slow cars down.

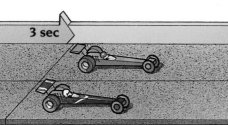

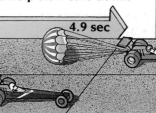

3 sec   4 sec   4.9 sec

This improves the slicks' grip, ready for take-off.

The dragsters now move to the start line. A series of lamps, called a Christmas tree, flash a countdown sequence. The last lamp to flash is green and this is the signal to start. If the cars get off to a good start, they will manage a time of about 4.9 seconds. Average speed will be about 290 km/h (180 mph). Electronic equipment records the time and speed. As the finish line is crossed, parachutes are released to slow the cars down.

The "Eurosting" dragster used nearly 23 litres (5 gallons) of fuel for its 400 m (¼ mile) run.

Weird wheels

The extraordinary creations on these two pages have one thing in common - they are all amazing!

Since the beginning of motorcar history, engineers have come up with odd ideas, like the motorized pram invented in 1922, with a platform at the back for a nursemaid to ride on. Or the 1941 Le Dauphin tandem which could use petrol, electricity or pedal power to turn the wheels.

The Vultee Aérocar of 1947 was a car and an aeroplane all rolled into one and even had a set of detachable wings.

◄ The French Leyat Aérocar was built in 1923. It had a wooden propeller which pulled the car along at speeds up to 160 km/h (99 mph). It had two brake pedals, one for each front wheel.

Rear wheel steering

Wooden propeller

Single rear wheel

Rear mounted engine

Passenger seating

▲ The vehicle above is the Dymaxion three-wheeler of 1933. It was designed by the famous American architect Buckminster Fuller. The overhanging section at the front made the car unstable, and the rear wheel steering made the car difficult to drive.

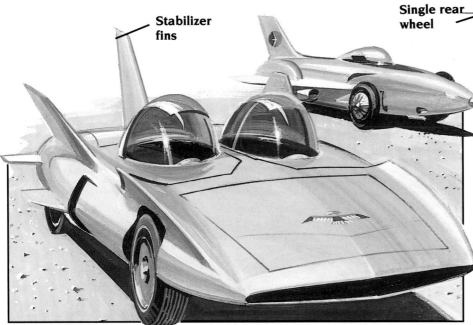

Stabilizer fins

◄ These experimental American cars were Firebirds, made by General Motors in the 1950s and 1960s. They were powered by gas turbine aircraft engines. One of these models had a single lever replacing the accelerator pedal, brake pedal and steering wheel.

Fuel for a world on the move

Nowadays some cars can run on electricity and solar power, but the most common motorcar fuel is still made from crude oil. Formed millions of years ago from the decayed remains of tiny plants and animals, the world's oil reserves lie deep under the ground or seabed. The sequence of pictures to the right shows the journey crude oil takes, from the moment it is brought to the earth's surface through to some of its end products, like jet fuel and bitumen. Each grade of oil has its own specialized uses.

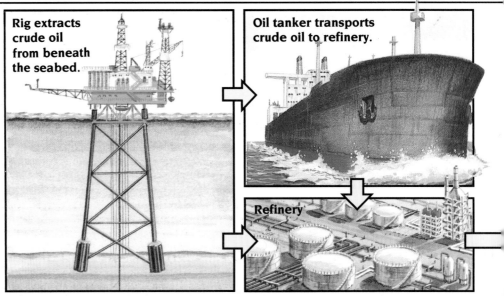

Rig extracts crude oil from beneath the seabed.

Oil tanker transports crude oil to refinery.

Refinery

A Lincoln Continental, built for the USA President, had more than 2 tonnes (2 tons) of armour plate.

The Panther-6 was designed as a unique and expensive car. The prototype shown here is a convertible two-seater. Production models had powered folding tops.

Aquaplaning and how to avoid it

At low speed on a wet road, a tyre's tread channels water out of the way, keeping it in contact with the road. At high speed, so much water can build up that not all of it is channelled away. The tyre then loses its grip and rides up on a film of water. This is called aquaplaning and can mean a total loss of control.

The Panther-6 had a six-wheel layout. The car's first set of front wheels swept the water to one side, so the second set could get a good grip.

This picture shows how the Panther's unique wheel layout allows safer driving in wet weather.

First set of front wheels aquaplaning, but still channelling water aside.

Second set of front wheels stay in road contact.

▲ This "orange" bubble car was built as a publicity stunt to advertise a firm importing oranges. The shell was made of glass fibre, built up on the chassis of a British Leyland Mini. Several "oranges" were made and were fully roadworthy.

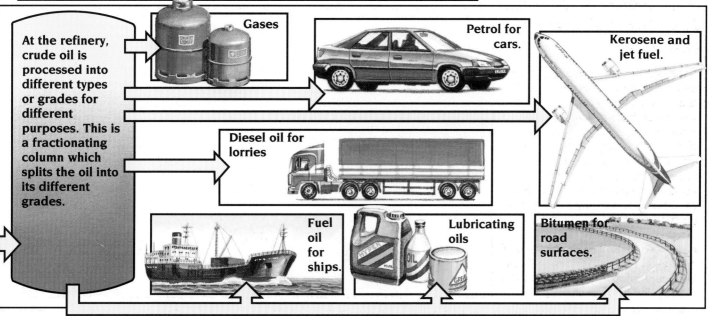

At the refinery, crude oil is processed into different types or grades for different purposes. This is a fractionating column which splits the oil into its different grades.

Gases

Petrol for cars.

Kerosene and jet fuel.

Diesel oil for lorries

Fuel oil for ships.

Lubricating oils

Bitumen for road surfaces.

A tyre rolling on a wet road at 80 km/h (50 mph) has to channel away over 5 litres (1.1 gallons) of water a second.

Car design

At international car shows, companies display their latest models together with special vehicles, called concept cars or prototypes. These cars are usually "one-off" experiments, testing different design and engineering ideas. Sometimes they go on to become production cars that are sold to the general public.

The Ghia Saguaro, shown on the right, was a concept car that appeared on the Ford stand at the Geneva International Motor Show. It was an experiment in designing a futuristic car for everyday use. It did not become a production car, but some of the ideas would have been included in other Ford models.

Big tyres, 531 mm (24¾ in) in diameter, for off-road as well as on-road driving.

The Ghia Saguaro

This concept car was developed in Ford's design studio at Turin in Italy. Here you can see the designers' pictures of their idea for the finished car. It had seating that could take from two to seven people and a large area at the back, like an estate car, when the back three seats were folded down. The back tailgate extended deep into the roof, to load very large objects.

Be your own car designer

The first rule when designing a car is to make sure that there is room inside for people. This means your first step must be to assemble the mannikin, shown on the right. Trace the body parts and transfer your tracings to a piece of cardboard. Cut out the shapes and assemble the mannikin as shown in the blue box. Now create cardboard car components in the same way and you will be ready to design your car. On the opposite page is a small sports car we designed.

How to assemble your mannikin

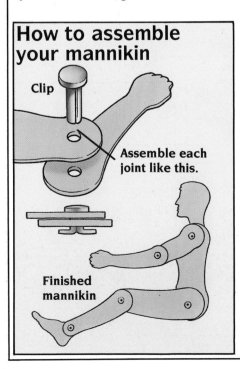

Clip

Assemble each joint like this.

Finished mannikin

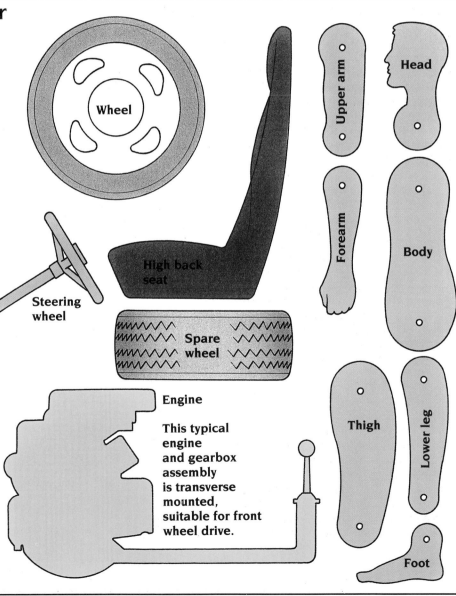

Wheel

Steering wheel

High back seat

Spare wheel

Engine

This typical engine and gearbox assembly is transverse mounted, suitable for front wheel drive.

Upper arm

Head

Forearm

Body

Thigh

Lower leg

Foot

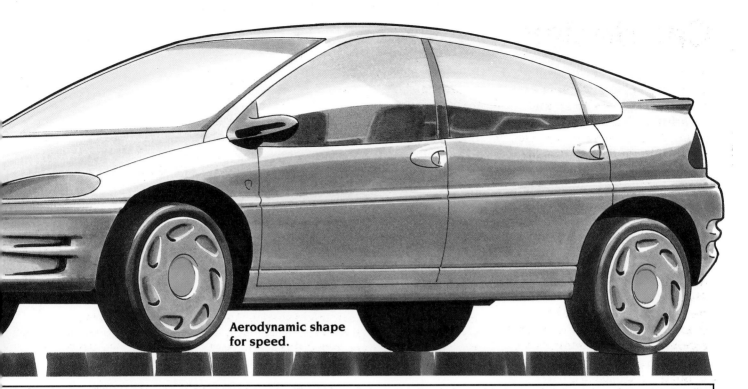

Aerodynamic shape for speed.

Three steps to a sports design

First of all, decide what type of car you want to design. For our sports car, we decided on a front-wheel drive, front engine and four seats. The spare wheel was stowed at the front. Good streamlining was essential, to improve the car's top speed and fuel economy. The basic components were put in position together with the driver mannikin.

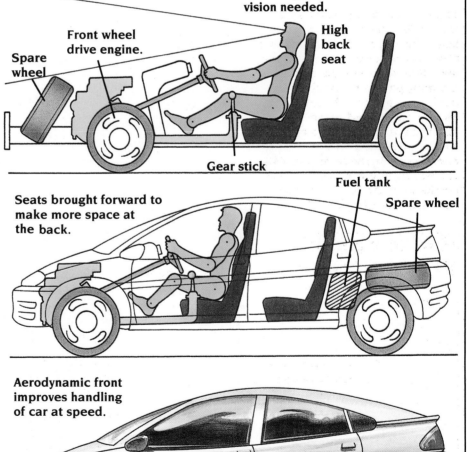

Good angle of driver's vision needed.

Front wheel drive engine.

High back seat

Spare wheel

Gear stick

Here the design has progressed a little, with the car body shape sketched in. We brought the seats forward to create a larger load space at the back. Then we moved the spare wheel to the back, so the nose could be lower and sleeker. The fuel tank was also placed at the back, in a lower position and protected by the crash bulkhead.

Fuel tank

Spare wheel

Seats brought forward to make more space at the back.

The final design has tinted windows and large front and back lights. The bumper strip all round gives good bodywork protection. The back door frame hides a tough roll-over cage to protect the driver and passengers in a crash. The tyres have a reflective coating, so the car is clearly seen from the side at night.

Aerodynamic front improves handling of car at speed.

The largest engine ever built for a road racing car was a 26.4 litre four-cylinder Dufaux of 1905.

Car production

A motorcar is made up of at least 15,000 different parts. To make these complicated machines quickly and efficiently, today's car factories are as modern and automated as possible. Usually cars are put together step-by-step on an assembly line. A conveyer belt moves lines of cars down the assembly line, so each worker or robot can add their part to each vehicle. Producing cars very quickly like this is called mass production. BMW in Germany use many robots for jobs that workers once did, like welding, drilling and painting. On these pages you can see car production in BMW factories.

1

More than 6,000 scientists and engineers work at the BMW Munich Research and Development Centre. This is where cars are designed and tested. Computers here are connected to computers in the factories.

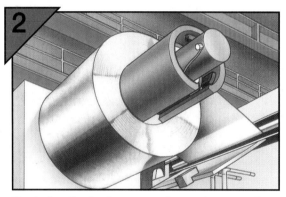

2

Parts for the body are made on the press lines. At the start of a press line is a roll of sheet metal. A section, called a "crude sheet" is cut from the roll. This then travels down a conveyer belt to be pressed into shape.

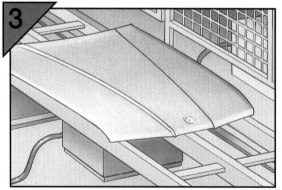

3

The pressed sheet, like a bonnet or hood, eventually moves on to the body production line. This is where different parts of the body are put together. There are 288 robots at the BMW Dingolfing factory doing this job.

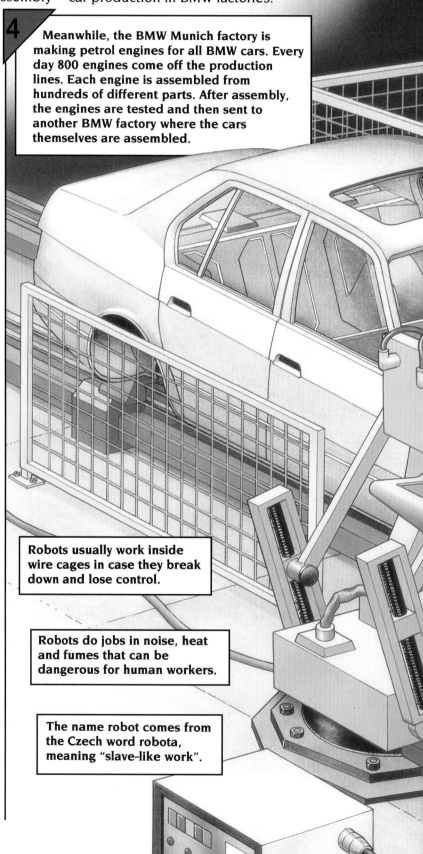

4

Meanwhile, the BMW Munich factory is making petrol engines for all BMW cars. Every day 800 engines come off the production lines. Each engine is assembled from hundreds of different parts. After assembly, the engines are tested and then sent to another BMW factory where the cars themselves are assembled.

Robots usually work inside wire cages in case they break down and lose control.

Robots do jobs in noise, heat and fumes that can be dangerous for human workers.

The name robot comes from the Czech word robota, meaning "slave-like work".

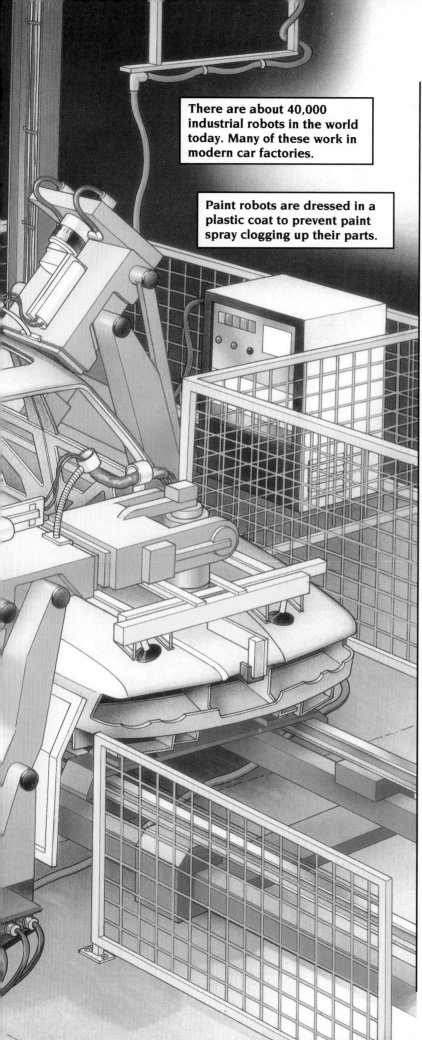

There are about 40,000 industrial robots in the world today. Many of these work in modern car factories.

Paint robots are dressed in a plastic coat to prevent paint spray clogging up their parts.

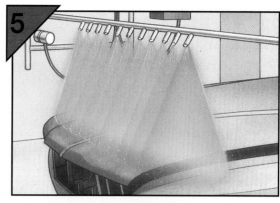

The body joins the paintwork line. Here it is cleaned before the primer is applied. Next it moves into the drying tunnel, where the primer is burnt on. Automatic spray guns and robots paint it and the last step is a drying oven.

All the different parts of the car, such as engine, seats, windows and headlights, are added to the body on the assembly line. All these pieces are fed onto the assembly line by electric suspension tracks and hoists.

The entire production process from the pressing lines to a brand new vehicle is complete. Now the cars must be inspected. The electrical system is checked from top to bottom. The brakes and axles are thoroughly tested. The fuel and engine oil are added and waste gases coming from the exhaust are measured. Finally, the blue and white BMW logo is fixed to the hood and a layer of protective wax is added to the body.

Green cars

Petrol engines emit waste gases which can be very damaging to the environment, such as nitrogen oxide. This gas mixes with moisture in the air to become an acid. Clouds absorb the acid and when it rains, this acid rain kills trees and poisons rivers.

Exhaust car gases are not the only problem. Car production uses much energy and many raw materials. Recycling would protect the earth's resources. On these pages you will see how new technology is giving us a greener motorcar.

The Impact

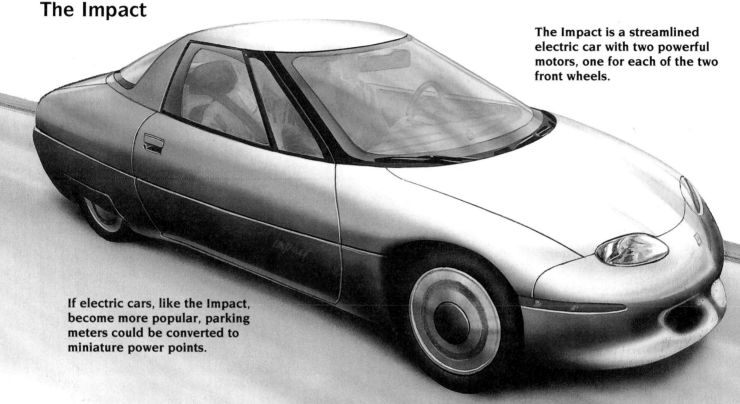

The Impact is a streamlined electric car with two powerful motors, one for each of the two front wheels.

If electric cars, like the Impact, become more popular, parking meters could be converted to miniature power points.

Electric cars are one way of avoiding the harmful gases given out by petrol-engined cars. Up until recently most electric cars were very slow and could only travel short distances before running out of energy.

General Motors have now produced a test car called the Impact. This electric car can accelerate like a sportscar from 0-100 km/h (0-62 mph) in eight seconds, and it has a top speed of 161 km/h (100 mph).

Electricity to recharge its batteries comes from a power station that may be burning fuel and creating pollution. This means that although the car itself is not producing harmful gases, the power station is. But electric cars can be recharged overnight, using only surplus energy. If most of the cars in New York were electric and the batteries were recharged overnight, the power stations would not have to burn more fuel.

Recycling

As raw materials, like wood, rubber and metals, get scarcer, recycling is vital. By the year 2000 about 2.8 million cars will have been scrapped in Germany alone. This is a terrible waste of raw materials. Car manufacturers are now doing their best to preserve resources and avoid the waste. BMW has a factory to break up old cars. The BMW 3 Series car, shown here, has many plastic components that can be broken down and made into parts for new cars.

This is a BMW Series 3 car, partly made of recyclable plastic.

Blue: made of recycled materials.

Green: made with the best recyclable plastic.

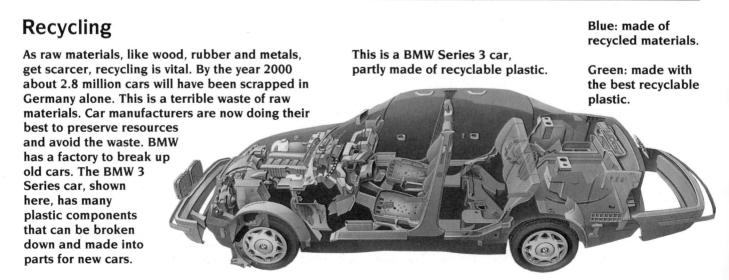

Cars emit carbon dioxide. Too much of this in the atmosphere traps heat making the earth too warm.

Catalytic converters

When scientists discovered that cars were causing a lot of dangerous pollution, they began to try and find a way of reducing the poisonous gases coming from car exhausts. Eventually they devised a simple piece of equipment fitted to the exhaust called a catalytic converter, which can get rid of most of the poisonous gases. This means that a car's pollution can be reduced by as much as 90%. In the USA, all new cars must have a catalytic converter.

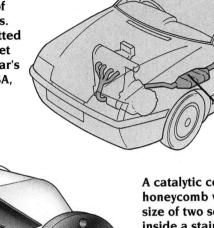

Position of catalytic converter.

Poisonous gases from the exhaust are changed by chemicals in the catalytic converter to become less harmful.

There are no moving parts in the catalytic converter and it needs no servicing.

A catalytic converter is like a honeycomb with a surface area the size of two soccer pitches. All this is inside a stainless steel box about 30 cm (1 ft) long and 23 cm (9 in) wide. Waste gases from the exhaust pass through the honeycomb structure, which causes chemical reactions that change most of the poisonous gases and make them harmless. The chemicals in catalytic converters are destroyed by lead, so all cars with this equipment must run on unleaded petrol.

Sunraycer

Cars in the future may use energy from the sun and not emit poisonous exhaust gases. The General Motors Sunraycer entered a race in Australia for cars powered by this solar energy. It ran by converting the sun's energy into electricity, with the help of a special magnet in the motor. Solar panels at the top of the car trapped the sun's energy. The car was a very odd shape. This was to make it as aerodynamic as possible. The race was run over 3,138 km (1,950 miles) from Darwin to Adelaide. First past the post was the Sunraycer.

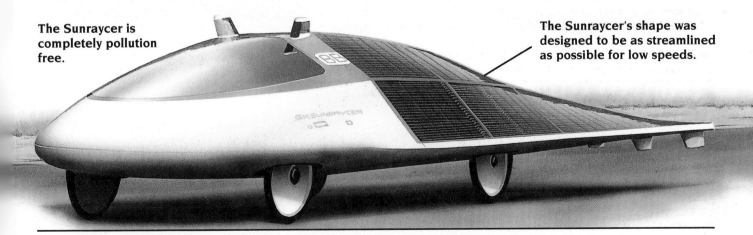

The Sunraycer is completely pollution free.

The Sunraycer's shape was designed to be as streamlined as possible for low speeds.

Unleaded petrol

Lead is added to petrol because it helps engines run more smoothly. But it passes through the engine and out through the exhaust into the air that we breathe. Lead is a poison that can cause brain damage, so it is a dangerous pollutant. People living in cities are the most seriously affected, especially children. Nowadays governments all over the world are encouraging motorists to use unleaded petrol, that is petrol without the extra lead in it. Eventually all petrol should be unleaded. This will cut most of the lead pollution.

Every car produces nearly four times its own weight of the greenhouse gas, carbon dioxide, every year.

The world land speed record

In 1983, Richard Noble from Britain broke the world land speed record. This was the first time it had been broken for 13 years. His car, Thrust 2, travelled at an average speed of 1,019.63 km/h (633.60 mph). Richard beat the previous record set by the American Gary Gabelich in Blue Flame by just 18.01 km/h (11.19 mph). This new land speed record came after nine years of planning and hard work.

When competing for the world record, a car must make two runs over the same measured 1.6 km (1 mile). Both passes must be made within a period of 60 minutes. Speed is calculated from an average of the two runs. Cars gather speed before the starting post. This is called a flying start. The top speed Thrust 2 achieved was 1,047.46 km/h (650.89 mph).

Thrust 2 was a one-off vehicle built just to break the record. A Rolls-Royce Avon 302 engine was used from a Lightning fighter aircraft.

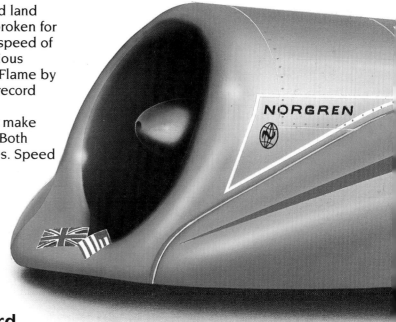

La Jamais Contente

In 1899, the bullet-shaped electric-powered La Jamais Contente (French for "The Never Satisfied") became the first car to travel over 100 km/h (62 mph). It must have been a very bumpy ride with those big wheels.
▼

Bluebird

Donald Campbell broke the world land speed record in 1964. He reached a speed of 645 km/h (401 mph) in his car Bluebird on the dry bed of Lake Eyre, in Australia. The car's power came from a gas turbine engine. Donald Campbell's father Malcolm also held the world land speed record and won the title many times during the 1920s and 1930s.
▼

Thrust 2 won the record on the mud flats of Black Rock Desert in Nevada, western USA.

Streamlining for speed

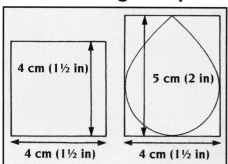

4 cm (1½ in)

4 cm (1½ in)

5 cm (2 in)

4 cm (1½ in)

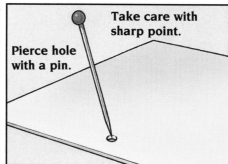

Take care with sharp point.

Pierce hole with a pin.

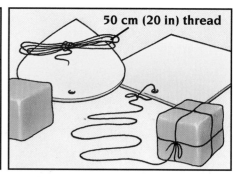

50 cm (20 in) thread

Streamlining is the science of creating smooth, sleek shapes that pass through water or air with the least drag or resistance. The less drag cars and boats have, the faster they go. This experiment shows how streamlining works.

Cut a piece of cardboard 4 x 4 cm (1½ x 1½ in). Cut another piece 4 cm x 5 cm (1½ x 2 in) and then cut it again to the shape shown in the first picture. Using a pin, pierce a hole in the centre of each shape, 1 cm (½ in) from what will be the front.

Cut two small cubes of plasticine about 1 cm (½ in) square to act as weights. They should both be exactly the same size to weigh the same. As shown above, tie the weights to the cardboard shapes with pieces of thread about 50 cm (20 in) long.

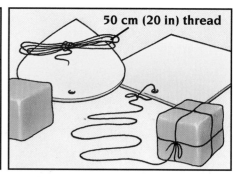

28   In 1966, Art Arfons crashed his car, Green Monster, at 967 km/h (601 mph). He survived.

Thrust 2

To reduce drag, the engine and all the other parts were wrapped up in a smooth aluminium skin. This streamlined body was important to give as little air resistance as possible.

Richard Noble sat in a safety cage to the right of the engine. Steel firewalls separated him from the engine and fuel tanks. The seat was made especially to fit him.

Rubber tyres can disintegrate at very high speeds. So solid aluminium wheels were used instead.

A right-hand foot pedal operated the accelerator, the HP cock (admitting fuel to the engine) and after-burner. The left-hand foot pedal operated the wheel brakes. The steering wheel had thumb buttons which released the drag parachutes. These helped the car slow down.

Blue Flame

◄ Gary Gabelich's Blue Flame, which won the world land speed record in 1970, was powered by a rocket motor like many other record holders. This meant power was not sent to the wheels, the car being propelled by the backward thrust of the rocket motor. This was mounted in the tail section and burned a mixture of hydrogen peroxide and liquid natural gas.

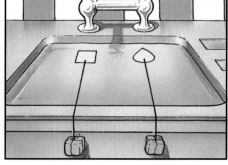

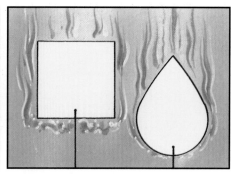

Fill up the kitchen sink with water, as high as it will go without overflowing. If you want to see the ripples your two cardboard shapes make, sprinkle tea leaves - or a fine powder, such as talcum, that floats - evenly on the surface of the water.

Carefully place the square shape and the streamlined tear-drop shape at the far end of the sink. The plasticine weights should dangle over the edge of the sink. It may help if a friend holds the weights while you position the shapes.

Now let go. Did your streamlined shape whizz past the square one? Its smooth lines give much less resistance to the water. Compare the turbulent ripples made by the square shape with the smoother ripples of the streamlined shape.

The White-Triplex record breaker of 1928 had three airplane engines, one in the front, two at the back.

Record breakers

Although the fastest car in the world now travels at 1,019 km/h (633 mph), it is by no means the fastest vehicle. Nowadays planes and rockets claim that record. Yet curiously enough, in 1906, for one year only, the fastest vehicle of all was a car. Called the Stanley Wogglebug, this steam-powered car set the record at 196 km/h (122 mph). It once reached 241 km/h (150 mph) before crashing on a beach. Speed records and championship races are big business now. The humble Wogglebug cost much less than the millions Ferrari or McLaren-Honda spend on their top-class Grand Prix racers.

The Grand Prix champions

Grand Prix racing has changed a great deal since Giuseppe Farina won the first GP World Championship in 1950. Crash helmets were not compulsory and protective clothing was unheard of. Later, names like Juan-Manuel Fangio, Jack Brabham, Niki Lauda and Ayrton Senna would claim their place in racing history by winning the Grand Prix crown. The cars they drove were to become more and more complex and safety as much as speed became a big consideration. Drivers wear flame-resistant suits and full-face crash helmets. Cars must be designed to resist the impact of a crash, and aerofoils are compulsory to keep cars firmly on the track at high speeds.

Year	Driver	Car
1950	Giuseppe Farina (Italy)	Alfa Romeo
1951	Juan-Manuel Fangio (Argentina)	Alfa Romeo
1952	Alberto Ascari (Italy)	Ferrari
1953	Alberto Ascari (Italy)	Ferrari
1954	Juan-Manuel Fangio (Argentina)	Maserati & Mercedes-Benz
1955	Juan-Manuel Fangio (Argentina)	Mercedes-Benz
1956	Juan-Manuel Fangio (Argentina)	Lancia-Ferrari
1957	Juan-Manuel Fangio (Argentina)	Maserati
1958	Mike Hawthorn (England)	Ferrari
1959	Jack Brabham (Australia)	Cooper-Climax
1960	Jack Brabham (Australia)	Cooper-Climax
1961	Phil Hill (USA)	Ferrari
1962	Graham Hill (England)	BRM
1963	Jim Clark (Scotland)	Lotus-Climax
1964	John Surtees (England)	Ferrari
1965	Jim Clark (Scotland)	Lotus-Climax
1966	Jack Brabham (Australia)	Brabham Repco
1967	Denny Hulme (New Zealand)	Brabham Repco
1968	Graham Hill (England)	Lotus-Ford
1969	Jackie Stewart (Scotland)	Matra-Ford
1970	Jochen Rindt (Austria)	Lotus-Ford
1971	Jackie Stewart (Scotland)	Tyrell-Ford
1972	Emerson Fittipaldi (Brazil)	Lotus-Ford
1973	Jackie Stewart (Scotland)	Tyrell-Ford
1974	Emerson Fittipaldi (Brazil)	McLaren-Ford
1975	Niki Lauda (Austria)	Ferrari
1976	James Hunt (England)	McLaren-Ford
1977	Niki Lauda (Austria)	Ferrari
1978	Mario Andretti (USA)	Lotus-Ford
1979	Jodi Scheckter (South Africa)	Ferrari
1980	Alan Jones (Australia)	Williams-Ford
1981	Nelson Piquet (Brazil)	Brabham-Ford
1982	Keke Rosburg (Finland)	Williams-Ford
1983	Nelson Piquet (Brazil)	Brabham-BMW
1984	Niki Lauda (Austria)	McLaren-Tag
1985	Alain Prost (France)	McLaren-Tag
1986	Alain Prost (France)	McLaren-Tag
1987	Nelson Piquet (Brazil)	Williams-Honda
1988	Ayrton Senna (Brazil)	McLaren-Honda
1989	Alain Prost (France)	McLaren-Honda
1990	Ayrton Senna (Brazil)	McLaren-Honda
1991	Ayrton Senna (Brazil)	McLaren-Honda

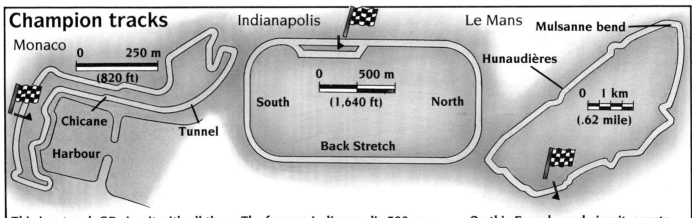

Champion tracks

Monaco
0   250 m
(820 ft)
Chicane
Tunnel
Harbour

Indianapolis
0   500 m
(1,640 ft)
South   North
Back Stretch

Le Mans
Mulsanne bend
Hunaudières
0   1 km
(.62 mile)

This is a tough GP circuit with all the twists and turns in what are Monaco's public roads. Passing is difficult so the driver who starts at the head of the race has the best chance of winning.

The famous Indianapolis 500 race, over a distance of 805 km (500 miles) takes place on this American circuit. Unlike GP circuits, there are only four corners and two huge straight stretches.

On this French road circuit, sports cars, such as Mercedes-Benz and Porsche, compete in the famous 24-hour endurance race. The car which covers the greatest distance in the 24 hours wins the race.

Champion speeds

The world land speed record always attracts a lot of interest. In some years, several people tried to break the record, but only a few succeeded. The chart here lists the fastest record-holders and their speeds, at the end of each year in which the record was broken.

Sir Malcolm Campbell was a Briton who became famous for breaking the world land speed record and the world water speed record many times. His son Donald (see page 28) also raced cars and boats, aiming to be the fastest in the world.

All Malcolm Campbell's racing machines, for land and water, were given the name Bluebird after the play of the same name by Maurice Maeterlinck

Year	Driver	Car / Speed
1898	G. de Chasseloup-Laubat	Jeantaud 63.15 km/h (39.24 mph)
1899	C. Jenatzy	Jenatzy 105.88 km/h (65.79 mph)
1902	M. Augières	Mors 122.00 km/h (75.81 mph)
1903	A. Duray	Gobron-Brillié 136.36 km/h (84.73 mph)
1904	P. Baras	Darracq 168.20 (104.52 mph)
1905	V. Hémery	Darracq 176.46 km/h (109.65 mph)
1906	F. Marriott	Stanley 195.64 km/h (121.57 mph)
1909	V. Hémery	Benz 202.69 km/h (125.95 mph)
1910	B. Oldfield	Benz 211.98 km/h (131.72 mph)
1922	K. Lee Guiness	Sunbeam 215.25 km/h (133.76 mph)
1924	M. Campbell	Sunbeam 235.22 km/h (146.17 mph)
1925	M. Campbell	Sunbeam 242.80 km/h (150.88 mph)
1926	J. Thomas	Thomas Special 275.23 km/h (171.03 mph)
1927	H. Segrave	Sunbeam 327.96 km/h (203.79 mph)
1928	R. Keech	White-Triplex 334.02 km/h (207.56 mph)
1929	H. Segrave	Irving-Napier 372.46 km/h (231.45 mph)
1931	M. Campbell	Napier-Campbell 396.04 km/h (246.10 mph)
1932	M. Campbell	Napier-Campbell 408.72 km/h (253.98 mph)
1933	M. Campbell	Campbell Special 438.48 km/h (272.47 mph)
1935	M. Campbell	Campbell Special 484.62 km/h (301.14 mph)
1937	G. Eyston	Thunderbolt 502.11 km/h (312.01 mph)
1938	G. Eyston	Thunderbolt 575.34 km/h (357.52 mph)
1939	J. Cobb	Railton 594.97 km/h (369.72 mph)
1947	J. Cobb	Railton 594.97 km/h (369.71 mph)
1964	A. Arfons	Green Monster 863.75 km/h (536.73 mph)
1965	C. Breedlove	Spirit of America Sonic 1 966.57 km/h (600.63 mph)
1970	G. Gabelich	Blue Flame 1,001.62 km/h (622.41 mph)
1983	R. Noble	Thrust 2 1,019.63 km/h (633.60 mph)

The youngest drivers to start in a GP were Pedro Rodriguez (1961) and Chris Amon (1963). They were both 19.

Index

Going further

There are many books and magazines about all aspects of cars and motoring. Some cover the history of motoring, others deal with Grand Prix racing, sportscars or classic cars. A few of the most useful are listed here.

Books

The Eyewitness Guide to Cars (Dorling Kindersley)
Car Talk Nigel Fryatt (Simon & Schuster Young Books)
The World's Fastest Cars Alex Gabbard & Graham Robson (Haynes)

Sporting Supercars Walton & Cadell (McDonald Illustrated)
The World's Fastest Cars Giles Chapman & John McGovern (Apple Press)
The Observer's Book of Cars (Penguin)

Magazines

Car
Performance Car
Grand Prix
Motor Sport
Autocar

THE USBORNE YOUNG SCIENTIST
MOTORBIKES

Contents

Credits

Written by Philip Chapman and Margaret Stephens
Art and editorial direction David Jefferis
Editorial revision Margaret Stephens
Text editor Eliot Humberstone
Design Iain Ashman
Design revision Robert Walster
Technical consultant Bob Currie
Illustrators Terry Hadler, Christine Howes, John
Hutchinson, Frank Kennard, Michael Roffe, Robert
Walster, John Scorey, Stephen Gardener, Chris Lyon
and John Barker.

This edition published 1991.
Based on The Young Engineers Book of Superbikes,
published 1978

Acknowledgements

We wish to thank the following individuals and
organizations for their assistance.

Special thanks go to Tony Greener of Positive
 Images.
Matt Oxley
Auto-Cycle Union
Robert Cross
Dunlop Ltd
Griffin Helmets Ltd
Richard Powell
Glenn Wilson
Gerard Brown
Christopher Pick

Usborne Publishing Ltd
Usborne House
83-85 Saffron Hill
London EC1 8RT

Printed in Belgium

The name Usborne and the device ♟ are trademarks
of Usborne Publishing Ltd.

Introduction

Motorbikes have been a favourite form of transport for over 100 years. Many famous historical figures rode motorbikes. Lawrence of Arabia, for instance, had a Brough Superior and the first man to cross the Atlantic Ocean by plane, Charles Lindbergh, rode a Harley-Davidson. Today, motorbike riding is just as popular, but the variety of bikes you can buy has increased enormously.

In this book you will find a whole range of different motorbikes, from a stunning high-powered 900 cc sports roadster to a nippy little 125 cc trail bike. Tyres, brakes, engines - they are all explained clearly, together with tips on choosing your first bike. There is even a section that starts you off on the road to becoming a safe and competent rider.

This picture gives you a first look at the parts which make up a modern motorbike. The bike is a 1,000 cc BMW K1, with the fairing cut away to reveal the engine.

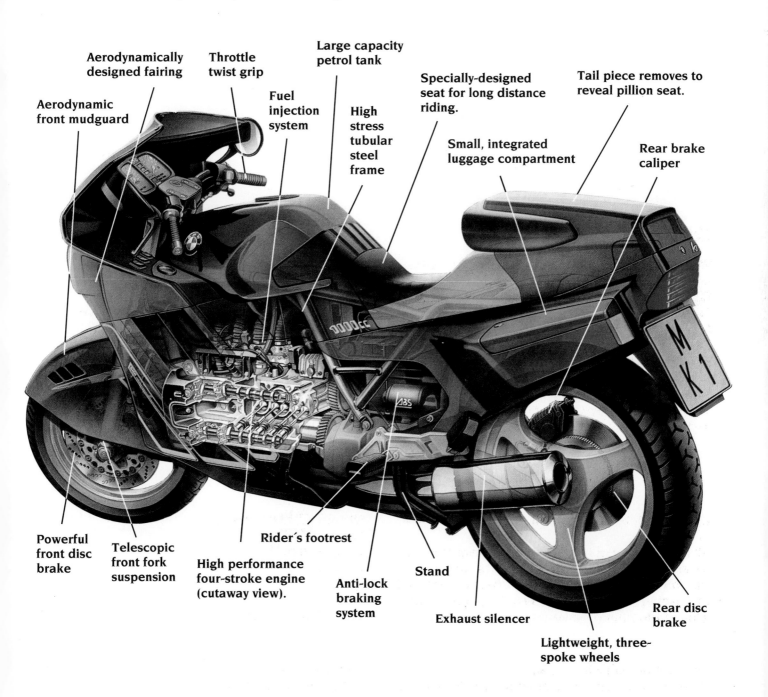

Aerodynamically designed fairing

Throttle twist grip

Large capacity petrol tank

Aerodynamic front mudguard

Fuel injection system

High stress tubular steel frame

Specially-designed seat for long distance riding.

Tail piece removes to reveal pillion seat.

Small, integrated luggage compartment

Rear brake caliper

Powerful front disc brake

Telescopic front fork suspension

High performance four-stroke engine (cutaway view).

Rider's footrest

Anti-lock braking system

Stand

Exhaust silencer

Lightweight, three-spoke wheels

Rear disc brake

Motorbike testing

Motorbikes start life as experimental prototypes which are ridden mercilessly over special test tracks. They are also tested on long distance runs in all types of weather and traffic conditions. The aim is to discover any weak points and correct a bike's design accordingly. Next the assembly lines for mass production are prepared. The first bikes off the assembly line are called pre-production models and these too are thoroughly tested. When the manufacturers are finally satisfied with the design, actual production begins. Motorbike magazines publish road test reports on new bikes to help prospective customers. This test, on a fast roadster, was written specially for this book.

Kawasaki GPZ900R road test

The Kawasaki GPZ900R is a fast bike - and looks it. The full fairing was designed in a wind tunnel and gives the bike its sleek lines. Many of the bike's features have originated from the Kawasaki Grand Prix racing bikes.

Sitting in the saddle, you can immediately appreciate how compact the bike is, especially the incredibly narrow engine. Four-cylinder, in-line engines are usually quite bulky, but by using liquid cooling and repositioning the generator, overall width has been trimmed considerably. This means the engine can be mounted low in the frame, without reducing cornering clearance.

Starting and stopping

A touch of the starter button and the engine springs into life. Vibration is virtually non-existent, but choke is needed for about 1.6 km (1 mile) as the engine warms up to operating temperature, which is regulated by the radiator.

The front wheel with a radius of 43 cm (17 in) means that steering is light, even in heavy traffic, and gives excellent straight line stability.

Road-holding and braking are superb thanks to the grippy wide section tyres, the dual 300 mm (12 in) semi-floating discs and the anti-dive, air-assisted front fork which stops the front end dipping suddenly under fierce braking.

The Kawasaki GPZ900R sports bike built for high speeds.

The GPZ900R's diamond frame

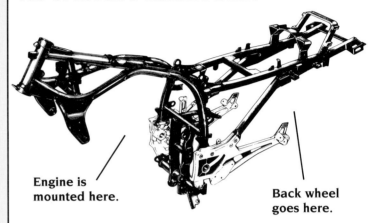

Engine is mounted here.

Back wheel goes here.

The lightweight diamond frame is massively strong and acts as an excellent "backbone" for the bike. An alloy subframe is bolted on to it at the rear. The engine is mounted low down on the frame, giving a low centre of gravity, which means the bike is better balanced and road handling improves. It is possible to mount the engine so low due to the lack of down tubes, and tubes below the crankcase. This has allowed the exhaust pipes to be tucked in, giving room for the engine closer to the ground.

Good handling at speed

The GPZ900R is a sports bike built for high speeds. In 1984, its first year of production, it set new performance standards and finished 1, 2 and 3 in the Isle of Man TT Production Race.

It is on winding, traffic-free roads that the bike really excels. The low-set handlebars provide a comfortable crouched riding position. This is important at high speeds because the more a rider can tuck in behind the fairing, the less he interferes with the fairing's specially-designed aerodynamic shape. Another important reason for such a position is that the fairing can protect a rider in bad weather conditions.

Rear suspension is Kawasaki's championship-winning Uni-Trak system. This employs a single shock absorber with progressive action. Hitting a pothole at high speed will not cause the suspension to bottom out and throw the bike off course. Small irregularities in the road are easily absorbed to give the rider a smooth, comfortable journey.

With all these features and its lightweight chassis, the GPZ900R is a machine that handles exceptionally well. Straight-line stability is perfect, and the light, quick steering means that a series of bends can be taken safely at high speed.

Power

Maximum power on the first production bikes was a massive 110 hp. Kawasaki no longer state power outputs for their bikes, but we do know that today the GPZ900R's output is less, because of restrictions on noise and exhaust emissions. More important than power output is the spread of power available, which is excellent in this bike due to the use of four valves with each cylinder.

Naturally, big horsepower and top performance like this must be paid for and you cannot expect the fuel consumption of a moped. About 14 km per litre (39 mpg) is average, and gentler use of the throttle will give a maximum of about 19 km per litre (54 mpg).

The engine

This was the first Kawasaki engine to use four valves with each cylinder. Note the camchain is mounted outside the cylinder block. This means it is more accessible for service and cuts the engine width to 451 mm (18 in). Another feature helping to reduce the width of the engine is the position of the bores. The liquid cooling has allowed them to be placed close together. The balance shaft is mounted below the crankshaft.

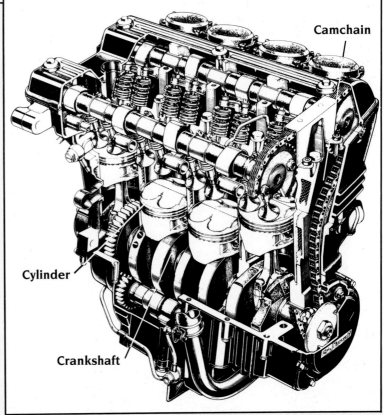

Camchain

Cylinder

Crankshaft

Ten international motorbike magazines voted the GPZ900R "Superbike of the Year" in 1984.

5

The first motorbikes

The first motorbikes ever invented were powered by steam and had three wheels. Then in 1869, Ernest Michaux from France developed a two-wheeled version, but it still had a steam engine. Michaux's motorbike was not a success. The engine was slow to start and not very powerful. The solid tyres made journeys very bumpy and worst of all, the engine's red hot boiler was far too close to the rider. Steam must have been a problem too, so the motorbike gave a very hot, sticky ride.

A far more practical model was developed in 1877 by the German engineer Nicolaus Otto. This motorbike had a petrol-driven internal combustion engine.

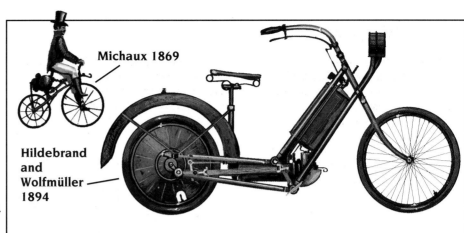

Michaux 1869

Hildebrand and Wolfmüller 1894

To the left is Michaux's steam motorbike. On the right is the world's first commercially made motorbike, the Hildebrand and Wolfmüller. This had a huge twin cylinder engine of 1,488 cc, which still holds the record for the largest engine on a production bike. The rear mudguard held water to cool the engine. There was a single brake, but the rider also used his foot to operate a steel lever which scraped against the ground. Top speed was 45 km/h (28 mph).

The first motorbike designers experimented with many different positions for the engine. The two designs here show the engine in rather bizarre positions. The most commonplace was above the wheels.

This is a 1901 Werner 262 cc. It was the first production bike with an engine placed between the wheels. Other manufacturers were quick to copy this design and modern bikes still have the same basic layout.

In 1901, this bike was built by George Hendee in the USA and called an Indian. Hendee only built three in 1901, but in the next two years produced a total of 568. The Indian was a classic American bike.

By 1907, motorbike speeds had passed the 200 km/h (124 mph) mark. Glenn Curtiss, an American who owned an airplane company, rode this machine on a beach in Florida, USA, at nearly 220 km/h (137 mph). Many people refused to believe that the bike was capable of such a speed, so the "record" was never made official. Curtiss had designed the engine for one of his airplanes, and fixed it to a motorbike frame to test it. The bike was never intended as a road-going machine.

Riding on air

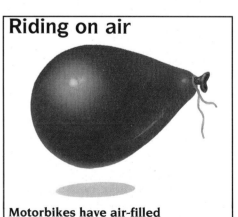

Motorbikes have air-filled pneumatic tyres which absorb bumps to give the rider a smooth ride. Blow up a balloon, fasten it securely and then gently sit on it. The cushion effect works in the same way as a tyre.

Since the early days of motorcycling more than 2,000 different makes of bike have been produced.

Motorbikes at war

Motorbikes have been useful during wars. In World War I, dispatch riders carried messages into battle zones where radio and telephone communications were few or non-existent.

Motorbikes even went into battle themselves, with machine guns mounted on sidecars. The picture below shows a BMW R75, first built in 1940. Over 16,500 R75s were used during World War II, and spearheaded blitzkrieg ("lightning war") attacks. They had a top speed of 95 km/h (59 mph). The Russian Army still uses a similar design today, called the K-M72. The diagrams below show the back, side and front view of the R75.

Classic bikes

From the early days of motorbikes until modern times, there have been some special machines that became famous for smooth performance, speed or other unique design features. These bikes are called "classics".

None of the bikes shown here is in production any more, but they will always be remembered as classic bikes of their time.

Choosing a selection of famous bikes is difficult as everyone has their own favourites. Make your own list and see how far you agree with the ones here.

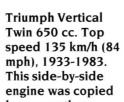

Harley-Davidson WLA 45, 738 cc, V-twin. Top speed 120 km/h (74.6 mph), 1937-1952. This powerful and reliable bike became well-known in World War II when 90,000 were issued to US and British troops.

Triumph Vertical Twin 650 cc. Top speed 135 km/h (84 mph), 1933-1983. This side-by-side engine was copied by many other manufacturers. One famous copy, the Triumph Bonneville had a top speed of 192 km/h (119 mph).

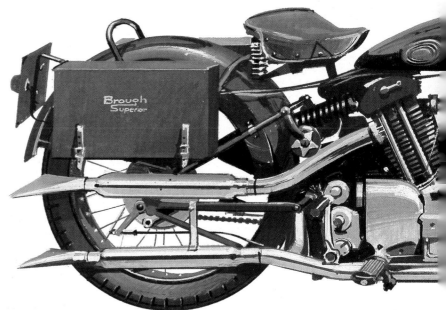

Ariel Square Four 500, 600, 1,000 cc models. Top speed 161 km/h (100 mph), 1929-1958. The "Squariel" engine was basically two parallel twins with their crankshafts geared together. This design gave excellent balance.

Vincent Black Shadow 998 cc V-twin. Top speed 197 km/h (122 mph), 1948-1955. This was the fastest production bike of the 1950s. It was famous for the superb quality of its craftsmanship and smooth performance.

Motorbikes have been made all over the world since the 1890s. But in the 1990s, Japan dominates the market.

Brough Superior

Brough Superior SS 100, 980 cc V-twin. Top speed 161 km/h (100 mph), 1924-1939. This was a luxury bike built mostly by hand and renowned for its smooth performance and craftsmanship.

Norton

Manx Norton 490 and 348 cc single cylinder. Top speed 195 km/h (121 mph), 1932-1962. The frame was known as a "featherbed" because it allowed great comfort at high speeds. A rigid steering head meant it handled well on corners.

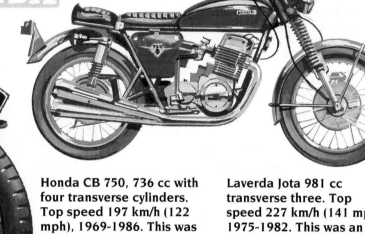

Honda CB 750, 736 cc with four transverse cylinders. Top speed 197 km/h (122 mph), 1969-1986. This was the first of the modern Japanese motorbikes, it had an electric starter, a high cruising speed and excellent acceleration of 0-100 km/h (0-62 mph) in under 6 seconds.

Laverda Jota 981 cc transverse three. Top speed 227 km/h (141 mph), 1975-1982. This was an extremely fast road bike, well-known for its excellent handling at high speeds. It was originally developed by Laverda's British importers and was hand-built in Italy.

BMW R69S, 594 cc horizontally opposed twin engine. Top speed 161 km/h (100 mph), 1960-1969. This was a classic touring bike because it gave a fast comfortable ride with its rubber mounted engine, a vibration damper on the crankshaft and great suspension.

The first chromium plated metal parts of a motorbike appeared on a Rudge speedway machine in 1929.

Piston power

There are two sorts of motorbike engine - two-stroke and four-stroke. Both types are explained on this page. Engines have one or more pistons, which move up and down inside the cylinder. They are powered by a gassy mixture of petrol and air. In a four-stroke engine, this mixture enters the top of the cylinder and there it is exploded by a spark from the spark plug.

The explosion forces the piston down, and this action then pushes down a connecting rod which turns the crank. A crankshaft runs through the centre of the crank and this turns too. The crankshaft transmits its circular motion to the back wheel by a chain or driveshaft.

Four-stroke engine

The cam and valve system opens and shuts the ports in the correct sequence.

A mixture of petrol and air enters the cylinder through this inlet port.

Piston rings make the piston a gas-tight fit in the cylinder. Oil is used as lubricating fluid.

Most modern bikes have four-stroke engines which are more robust and emit less pollution than two-strokes.

The crank rotates moved by the connecting rod. The crank's rotating speed is measured in rpm - revolutions per minute.

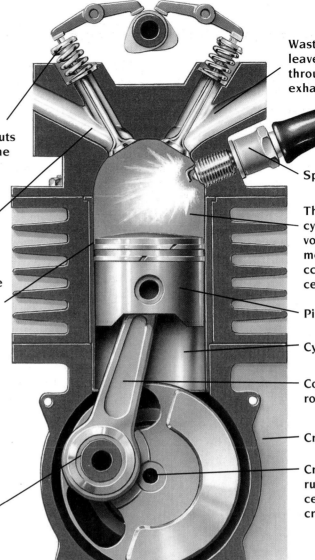

Waste gas leaves cylinder through this exhaust port.

Spark plug

The cylinder's volume is measured in cc - cubic centimetres.

Piston

Cylinder

Connecting rod

Crankcase

Crankshaft runs through centre of crank.

The two-stroke engine

In a two-stroke engine the piston moves up and down twice between each spark. The petrol-air gas enters the crankcase below the piston. The piston moves down and pushes the gas up through an opening to the top of the cylinder. When the piston rises again it compresses the gas and a spark creates an explosion which pushes the piston back down, rotating the crank.

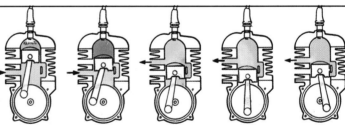

1 POWER - spark plug ignites gas mixture. Fresh gas in, waste gas out.

2 COMPRESSION - gas by the piston.

The four-stroke engine

The four-stroke engine moves up and down four times between each spark.
1. "Induction" stroke: gas is drawn through the inlet port into the top of the cylinder.
2. "Compression" stroke: the piston rises squashing the petrol-air gas. 3. "Power" stroke: a spark explodes the gas, pushing the piston down. 4. "Exhaust" stroke: waste gas is pushed out of the exhaust port.

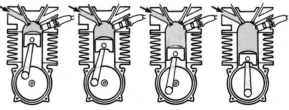

1 INDUCTION - gas mixture is drawn into the cylinder.

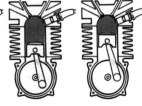

2 COMPRESSION - gas piston.

Arranging the cylinders

Motorbike engines vary in the number of cylinders. Generally, the more cylinders they have, the smaller the engine vibration and the smoother the ride. Shown below are many different designs.

Flat twin BMW R100S ▶

◀ Parallel twin
Triumph Bonneville

Transverse triple
Suzuki GT 750 ▶

◀ V-twin Moto Guzzi 850

Flat-four
Honda Gold Wing ▶

◀ Transverse four
Kawasaki 650

Transverse six
Benelli Sei ▶

◀ Square four
Suzuki RG 500

Keeping parts apart

The magnified view on the right shows where the sides of the piston and cylinder come together. It is absolutely vital that they never actually touch each other. If this happened, the friction created would quickly destroy their surfaces.

Keeping them apart is oil, which acts as a lubricant. This experiment shows how a lubricant can reduce friction.

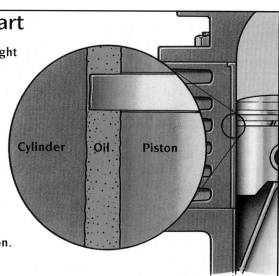

Cylinder Oil Piston

Experiment

You need a small plastic cup and a tray. These will represent the cylinder and piston surfaces.

Try skating the cup across the dry tray surface. Now place two large spoonfuls of water on the tray.

Skate the cup across the puddle. You will see that it goes much further and much faster than before because the water has acted as a lubricant and reduced friction between the surfaces.

Small plastic cup

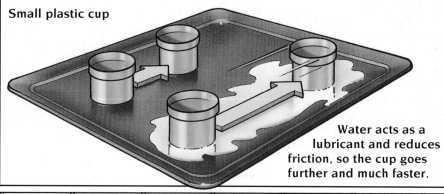

Water acts as a lubricant and reduces friction, so the cup goes further and much faster.

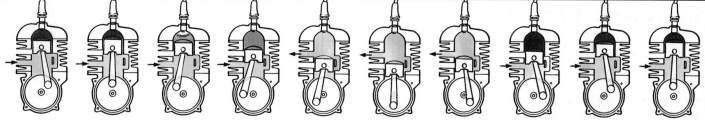

mixture is squashed Fresh gas in.

1 POWER - spark plug ignites gas mixture. Fresh gas in, waste gas out.

2 COMPRESSION - gas mixture is squashed by piston. Fresh gas in.

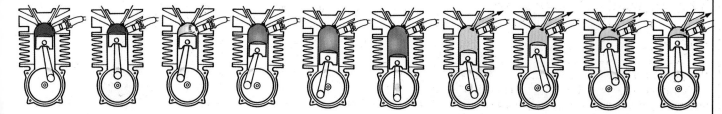

is squashed by the

3 POWER - spark plug ignites gas mixture. Explosion forces piston down.

4 EXHAUST - piston moves up pushing waste gas out.

In 1856 Moto Guzzi made a racing engine with 8 cylinders - the most ever.

Tyres and brakes

Tyres and brakes are the two most important pieces of equipment on a motorbike. If either become faulty then the life of a motorcyclist can be seriously endangered.

The front and rear tyres on a bike are of a different size and tread pattern as they have different jobs to do. The smaller front tyre is designed to resist slipping sideways on corners. It is also designed to pump water away from the rear tyre's path on a wet road. The bigger rear tyre is harder wearing and transmits the power of the engine onto the road. Most modern bikes have hydraulically operated disc brakes on both wheels.

The rear brake is operated by a pedal under the rider's right foot. On a good road surface 70% braking pressure should be applied to the front brake and 30% pressure to the rear brake.

A tyre's "rubber" part is often a mixture of natural rubber and butyl plastic. The tread is mostly butyl, but the side walls have up to 60% natural rubber.

Under-inflated tyres overheat at high speeds which shortens their life. Over-inflated tyres have a smaller area in contact with the road, causing instability.

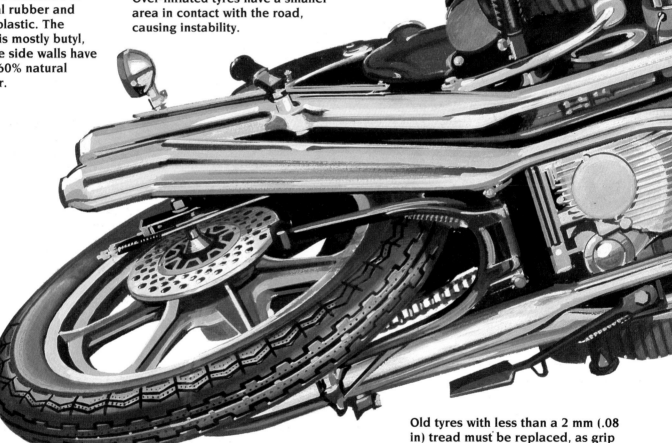

Old tyres with less than a 2 mm (.08 in) tread must be replaced, as grip will be seriously impaired.

Disc brake stopping power

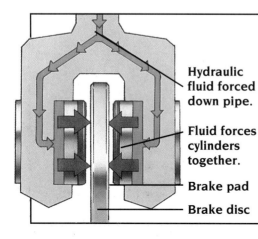

Hydraulic fluid forced down pipe.

Fluid forces cylinders together.

Brake pad

Brake disc

Hydraulic discs are fitted to motorbike wheels. When a rider operates the brake lever and brake pedal, the brake fluid is put under increased pressure. This fluid then presses on the brake pistons, forcing them along cylinders. The pistons are backed with brake pads. These push against the disc, creating friction and slowing the wheel down. With hydraulic brakes, it is important to keep the brake fluid topped up. Watch out for leaks and check regularly for wear and tear, replacing all worn parts.

Take a large coin and roll it on a smooth surface. Catch it between your finger and thumb. This is how two brake pads stop a moving wheel.

Rear tyres on racing bikes get very hot - up to 125°C when accelerating around banked bends.

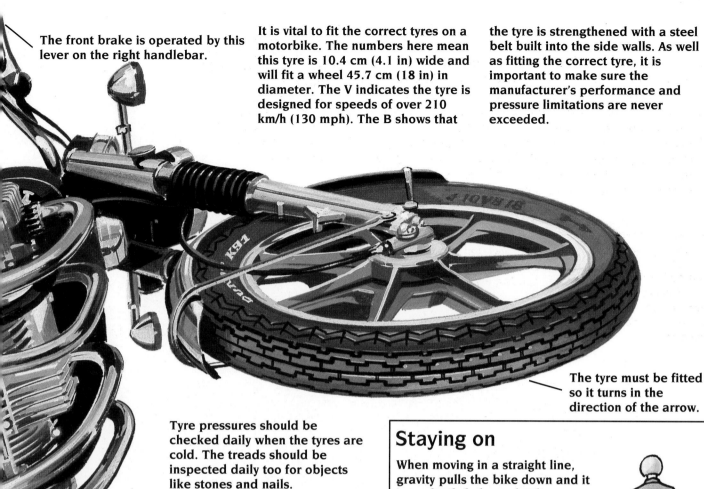

The front brake is operated by this lever on the right handlebar.

It is vital to fit the correct tyres on a motorbike. The numbers here mean this tyre is 10.4 cm (4.1 in) wide and will fit a wheel 45.7 cm (18 in) in diameter. The V indicates the tyre is designed for speeds of over 210 km/h (130 mph). The B shows that the tyre is strengthened with a steel belt built into the side walls. As well as fitting the correct tyre, it is important to make sure the manufacturer's performance and pressure limitations are never exceeded.

The tyre must be fitted so it turns in the direction of the arrow.

Tyre pressures should be checked daily when the tyres are cold. The treads should be inspected daily too for objects like stones and nails.

In 1888, John Dunlop invented the first inflatable tyre when he joined a length of hosepipe and fixed it around the wooden rim of a bicycle.

Staying on

When moving in a straight line, gravity pulls the bike down and it is perfectly balanced. When turning into a bend, an outward force pulls at the bike and rider. It is important the rider leans the bike into the bend and aligns

his centre of gravity with the bike's. The weight of the bike and rider will then counteract the outward force.

The tyres slip if the bike leans too much.

The bike and rider will tip over when the rider does not lean enough.

Types of tyre

To the right is the profile of a standard tyre. The tread pattern is designed to drain water away and grip the road. The tread goes up around the sides so the tyre can still grip when leaning into corners.

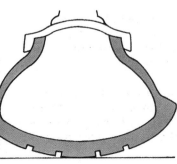

To the left is a "racing slick" which has a smooth surface. It is also "low profile", having a reduced depth compared to ordinary tyres. Both features mean more tyre comes into contact with the track giving big, powerful racing bikes extra stability.

Giacamo Agostini holds the record for Grand Prix world titles, winning 15 between 1966 and 1975.

Protecting the head

In a motorbike accident, the head is the most vulnerable part of the rider's body. A human head weighs about 4.5 kg (10 lb). But if it hits something at 48 km/h (30 mph), the impact weight becomes 136 kg (300 lb) - rather like being hit with a massive hammer. It is vital that motorbike riders and passengers wear helmets.

Nowadays there are two types of crash helmet. The open-face helmet, like the 1950s design below, is less claustrophobic and usually cheaper. However, the full-face helmet, like the picture to the right, gives greater all-round protection.

Evolution of the crash helmet

Since motorbikes were first invented, the design of crash helmets has changed enormously. The pictures below show three of the major designs in motorbike history.

The pudding basin was made originally from leather. This design was first used in the 1900s.

This jet style open-face helmet was first used in the 1950s and is still worn today.

This is a modern full-face BMW System helmet which complies with the world's toughest safety standards.

Anatomy of a full-face helmet

This picture gives you an idea of the careful design that goes into the making of a modern full-face crash helmet. Safety standards for new designs are very tough, and all helmets undergo rigorous tests before they can be sold to the public.

A piece of grit hitting your eye at 40 km/h (25 mph) could blind you. This is why visors are essential. Scratches can give a distorted, dazzling effect at night. So all visors should have an anti-scratch coating. A few drops of washing-up liquid rubbed gently onto the inner surface will help prevent misting.

Never buy a second-hand helmet. Always spend as much as you can on a modern design. Fit is very important. Choose a helmet and then try it on before buying. Does it fit comfortably? When securely fastened does it move much, either backwards and forwards or side to side? If the answer is yes, then it is too big.

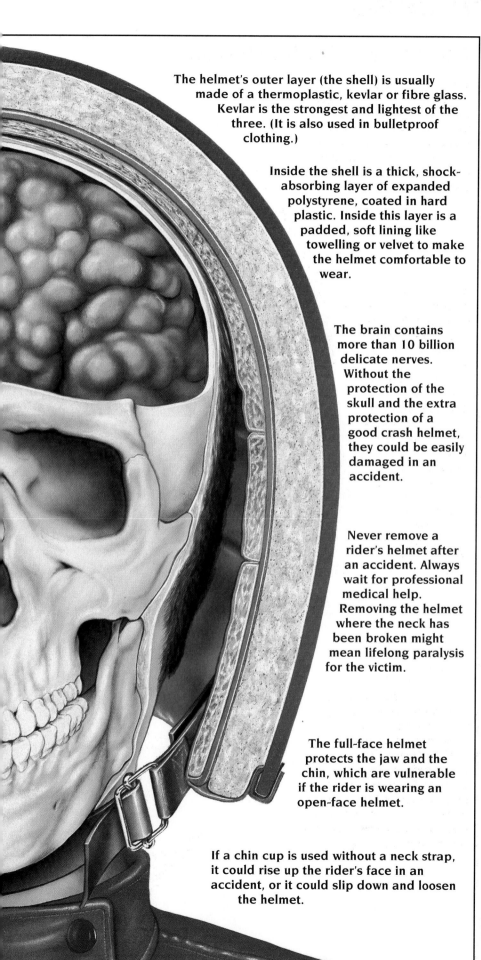

The helmet's outer layer (the shell) is usually made of a thermoplastic, kevlar or fibre glass. Kevlar is the strongest and lightest of the three. (It is also used in bulletproof clothing.)

Inside the shell is a thick, shock-absorbing layer of expanded polystyrene, coated in hard plastic. Inside this layer is a padded, soft lining like towelling or velvet to make the helmet comfortable to wear.

The brain contains more than 10 billion delicate nerves. Without the protection of the skull and the extra protection of a good crash helmet, they could be easily damaged in an accident.

Never remove a rider's helmet after an accident. Always wait for professional medical help. Removing the helmet where the neck has been broken might mean lifelong paralysis for the victim.

The full-face helmet protects the jaw and the chin, which are vulnerable if the rider is wearing an open-face helmet.

If a chin cup is used without a neck strap, it could rise up the rider's face in an accident, or it could slip down and loosen the helmet.

Easy riding

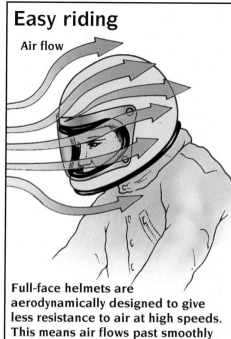

Air flow

Full-face helmets are aerodynamically designed to give less resistance to air at high speeds. This means air flows past smoothly at high speeds, which reduces noise and buffeting.

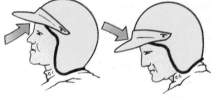

With an open-face helmet, air-flow at high speeds can catch under the peak (left), jerking up the helmet and head, which can be dangerous. If the driver has his head down, air can press down on the peak, straining the forehead and neck muscles (right).

A vision problem

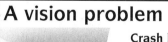

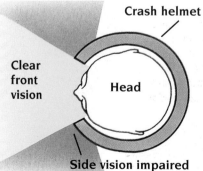

Crash helmet

Clear front vision

Head

Side vision impaired

The first full-face helmets only had small eye slits which impaired side vision. Later designs developed wider openings, but side vision is still not as good as with open-face helmets.

Motocross and trail bikes

These bikes are designed for rough conditions and must have excellent suspension and powerful engines to cope with the lumps and bumps of cross-country riding. Motocross bikes are special off-road racers ridden in club competitions. Motocross is an exciting sport with ditches that riders jump, steep downhill turns and usually a water splash at the bottom of a gully that turns into thick mud. Similar to motocross bikes, trials bikes are raced in cross-country trials events. But riders are timed instead of racing against each other as in motocross. Enduros are similar to trials but run over hundreds and sometimes thousands of kilometres or miles of country tracks and public roads. Trail bikes are modelled on motocross bikes but can be used on or off the road. These machines can perform as well over rough land as in busy city streets.

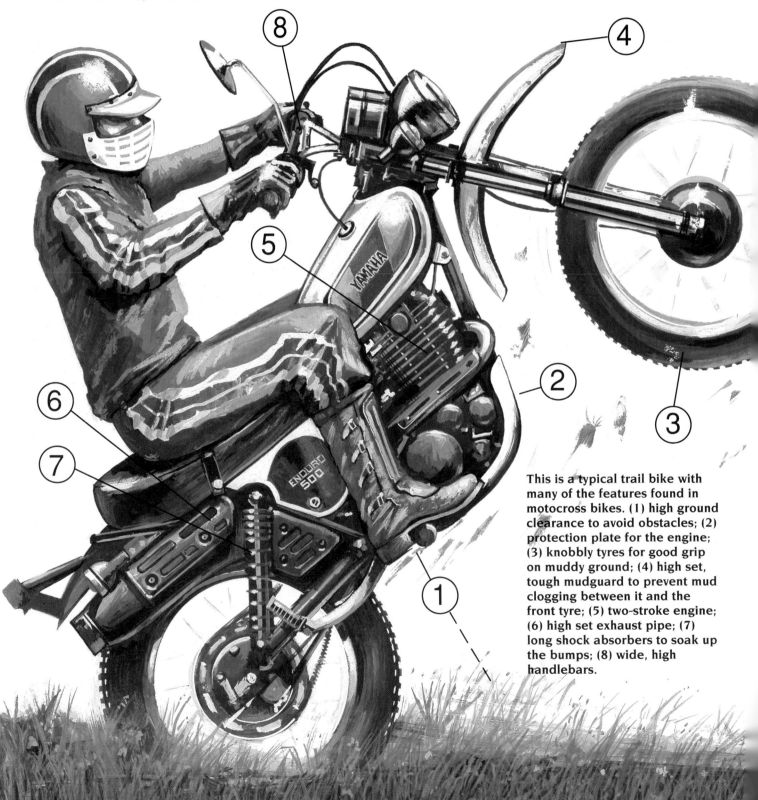

This is a typical trail bike with many of the features found in motocross bikes. (1) high ground clearance to avoid obstacles; (2) protection plate for the engine; (3) knobbly tyres for good grip on muddy ground; (4) high set, tough mudguard to prevent mud clogging between it and the front tyre; (5) two-stroke engine; (6) high set exhaust pipe; (7) long shock absorbers to soak up the bumps; (8) wide, high handlebars.

Absorbing the bumps

Shock absorbers have two main parts - a steel spring to absorb bumps and a piston connected to it. The piston slides up and down in an oil-filled cylinder. Its job is to slow down the bouncy movements of the spring. The diagram below shows an inside view of a rear shock absorber.

Oil or gas in cylinder.

Piston moves up and down with spring. Oil in the cylinder slows it down. This in turn damps the bounciness of the spring.

Spring compresses to absorb the shock of hitting a bump in the ground.

A modern trail bike

Suzuki DR 800

The Suzuki DR 800, otherwise known as Dr Big, has the world's biggest and most powerful single cylinder, four valve engine. With an engine capacity of 779 cc, the thumping power unit gives excellent turning power (torque) and top speed. Dr Big, like all trail bikes, is an off and on the road machine.

With dual spark plugs and an electronic self-starting system, the engine springs to life with first time reliability.

The superb suspension, the low centre of gravity, extra-slim frame and light weight make the bike easy to handle and very nimble over rough countryside. The centre of gravity is kept low by the position of the 29 litre (6.4 gallon) fuel tank.

One of the problems with trail bikes is the noisy engine, but Dr Big has an exhaust system which is fitted with twin mufflers to reduce noise levels.

The bike is designed in a snazzy colour scheme, and the comfortable seat is built for a passenger and rider, and specially designed for long rides. The seat has a luggage carrier and a grab rail for the passenger.

Other points of interest are hand protectors on the handlebars, a sump guard to protect the engine and gearbox from loose stones and a powerful halogen headlight.

Home-made shock absorber

Paper clip

Wind paper clip round pencil

A shock absorber spring is one long piece of steel wound up to form a coil. The longer the coil, the more it can compress when the wheel hits a bump. The amount a coil can compress is called "travel".

Make your own mini shock absorber by straightening out an ordinary paper clip. Then wind it around a pencil, like in the picture above. When you take it off, you should have a small, springy coil.

Drag bikes

Drag bikes are the ultimate in racing machines. They are fast and furious, often with more than one engine, and race down a track that is only 402 m (¼ mile) long.

Riders compete against the clock in solo races, or against each other in pairs. Drag racing started in Britain during the 1920s, but it is now popular the world over, especially in the USA.

As the rider here revs up his machine at the start, fuel has been poured onto the track and set on fire to soften the tyres. This will improve their grip.

This bike is the "Atcheson Topeka and Santa Fe", ridden by Russ Collins. Russ held the 402 m (¼ mile) record in the 1970s with a time of 7.86 seconds.

This machine had no less than three engines. The 12 cylinders and 3,000 cc of power accelerated the bike to nearly 300 km/h (186 mph) in about 8 seconds. Competition solo drag bikes use fuels like methanol and nitro-methanol.

Drag racer controls are similar to an ordinary bike. But to cope with the enormous power, a heavy-duty clutch is fitted.

Countdown to a quick getaway

The riders are revving up and watching the "Christmas tree". This is a series of lights, one for each rider, which counts them down to the start signal. Light 1: approach the start. Light 2: bikes almost at the line. Light 3: bikes ready to race. Light 4: false start. Lights 5, 6, 7: ready, steady, go! Light 8: false start. As the bikes blast off they cross a light beam (A) starting an electronic clock. 402 m (¼ mile) later they cross the finish light beam (B). The clock then records the time. Light beam (C) is 1 m (3 ft 3 in) after the finishing line. The clock records the bikes from B to C to calculate their speed.

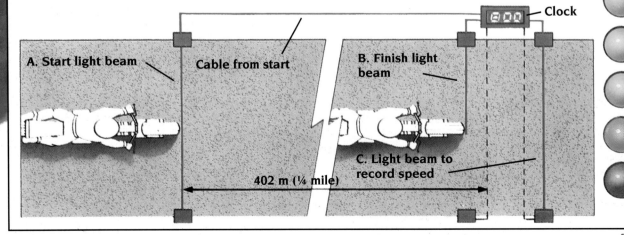

A. Start light beam

Cable from start

B. Finish light beam

Clock

C. Light beam to record speed

402 m (¼ mile)

1
2
3
4
5
6
7
8

The "Timetraveller" drag bike went from a standing start to 97 km/h (60 mph) in two seconds.

Speedway

Speedway is an exciting and popular sport staged in special stadiums all over Europe, Australia and the USA. Riders usually compete in teams and leagues rather like soccer. Races are run in quick succession, about one every five minutes, anti-clockwise around four laps of the track. The winning team is the one scoring most points.

The best riders in a team are called "heat leaders". The next best are "second strings" and the remainder are called "reserves". The fuel is pure methanol.

A speedway rider balances his bike by applying great power to the back wheel and opposite lock to the front wheel.

Most speedway bikes are single cylinder, four-strokes with a clutch and twist-grip throttle. If race leaders braked quickly, nasty pile-ups could result. So the bikes have no brakes.

The speedway rider

Riders rev up their engines behind a starting tape which only lifts when the referee judges everyone to be ready. Riders always hug the track's inside line and ride at a furious rate, sliding through corners with their front wheels turned sideways.

Speedway bikes have no gears.

Front suspension is minimal compared to other bikes .

Speedway racing is exhilarating and very dangerous. Riders must have excellent balance to judge bends accurately. Like many other sportsmen, they need to be good tacticians too, reading the race correctly and predicting what other competitors might do. Speedway is tough physically, and good all-round physical fitness, perfect eyesight and perfect hearing are musts.

Most important of all though is lengthy experience on a speedway bike. The bikes are so unlike other machines, as they are light but very powerful, and no rider can get used to controlling a bike without brakes in a short space of time.

Speedway riders must have all-in-one leather riding suits, strong crash helmets and special boots. The left boot has a steel sole for sliding through corners. Another expensive necessity, apart from the bike itself, is a vehicle to transport the bike to races.

During the time it takes you to read this sentence a drag bike can accelerate from 0-300 km/h (186 mph)

Grand Prix

Grand Prix road racing takes place all over the world. There are four different classes depending on the engine capacity of the bike - 80 cc, 125 cc, 250 cc and 500 cc. A fifth class is for 500 cc bikes with a sidecar.

The winner of each race is awarded 20 points; second place earns 17 points and then a sliding scale of points - 15, 13, 11, 10, 9, 8, 7, 6, 5, 4, 3, 2 and 1 - is awarded down to 15th place. Each year, every class has a world champion. This is the rider who scores most points, although only the points from his seven best races throughout the year count towards the championship.

This is the Honda NSR500, a 500 cc world championship winning bike. It has been developed over eight years. One of the newest features of the motorbike is an on-board computer which controls engine timing and the exhaust valve.

The NSR500 weighs less than 120 kg (265 lb). Ground clearance is 105 mm (4 in) and overall width is 600 mm (2 ft). Fuel tank capacity is 30 litres (6.6 gallons).

The Honda factory in Japan is always improving the aerodynamics of the NSR500. The bike's air resistance (the drag factor) has been greatly reduced over the eight years of its development. This has been achieved by streamlining the bike's overall shape.

The youngest world champion ever is Johnny Cecotto. He won the 1975 350 cc title when only 19.

To take part in Grand Prix racing, a rider must have an international racing licence. Licences are only given to those scoring a certain number of points in national races.

The fairing, seat, rear brake disc and exhaust silencers are all made from lightweight carbon fibre. The lighter the bike, the faster it can go.

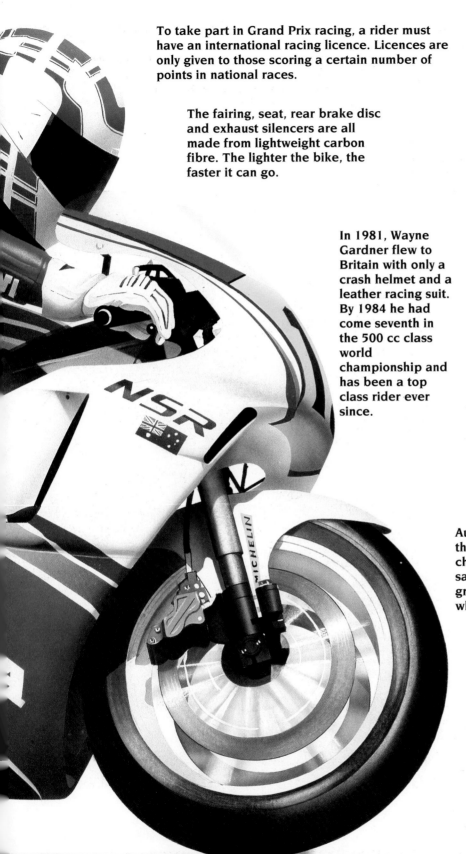

In 1981, Wayne Gardner flew to Britain with only a crash helmet and a leather racing suit. By 1984 he had come seventh in the 500 cc class world championship and has been a top class rider ever since.

Wayne Rainey ▲

Wayne Rainey from the USA won his first 500 cc world championship in 1990. Riding a Yamaha YZR500, he led the series from the first round and won seven Grands Prix in all. Out of the 44 Grands Prix he has raced so far, he has only failed to finish on three occasions which is a fantastic record for consistency.

Australian Wayne Gardner is shown racing the NSR500 here. Wayne won the 500 cc championship in 1987 on a version of the same bike and came second in 1988 to his great rival, the American Eddie Lawson, who was riding for Yamaha that year.

Grand Prix road racing is an expensive business. In 1984, when Honda were testing Wayne Gardner on the 500 cc Grand Prix circuit, he had to pay his own way. After coming seventh in the world championship that year, Honda gave him full financial backing. Most riders join a team like Honda, Yamaha Kawasaki or Suzuki.

Victory in the popular 500 cc class gives motorbike manufacturers valuable publicity for the bikes that they sell to the public. Companies like Shell or Michelin also get publicity by sponsoring the Grand Prix teams. In exchange for this advertising, the sponsors either pay or donate their product to the teams free of charge.

In 1989, Eddie Lawson joined Honda and began to ride the NSR500 with great success, winning the world title for the second year running.

Wheel sizes, front and rear, are 432 mm (17 in). Wheels are fitted with Michelin tyres.

The oldest world champion ever is Hermann-Peter Müller. He won the 250 cc title in 1955 at the age of 46.

Highway patrol

A modern city police force would be lost without a fleet of motorbikes. Weaving in and out of heavy traffic, motorbikes can speed medical assistance to road accidents and pursue escaping criminals down back roads or motorways. They also provide an escort service, like guarding cars carrying VIPs. Traffic control is another important duty and they deal with traffic jams and small traffic offences.

American Harley-Davidson - Electra Glide

Harley-Davidsons are said to be the best bikes in the world for police work. They can keep up with most vehicles on the road and have a lot of sophisticated law enforcement equipment. The latest Electra Glide has a four stroke, air cooled, 1,340 cc V-twin engine. The seat is a "solo saddle" with air suspension for comfortable riding during long shifts.

At the rear, the Electra Glide can be fitted with a strobe light and an electronic 100 watt siren system. Officers communicate with their base by radio - a microphone is at the front of the bike.

The heaviest production bike in the world, without accessories it weighs 323 kg (712 lb). If it falls over, getting it upright again is a two man job.

The fuel tank has a capacity of 22.73 litres (5 gallons). In the city, the bike runs at 13.6 km per litre (38 mpg).

Strobe light

Radio equipment

A day in the life of a police motorcyclist

A typical duty for motorbike policemen is dealing with minor traffic offences. Here a motorbike rider has been stopped for going through a red light. The officer can act swiftly in heavy traffic.

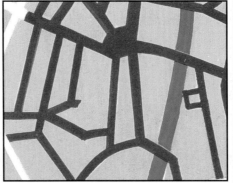

Officers on bikes do not simply cruise about looking for trouble. They are assigned a "beat" and patrol a fairly small area. This one covers a major traffic junction and the approach roads leading to it.

A bank robbery has been committed and the criminals are about to flee the scene of the crime in a getaway car. Motorbikes will form a vital part of the police team in pursuing and stopping the runaways.

In May 1976, in Sydney, Australia, 14 policemen and 3 police women all rode on one bike - a 750 cc Honda.

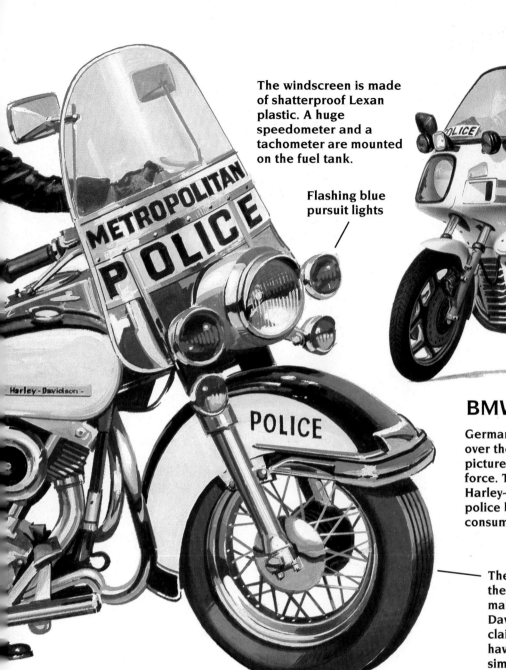

The windscreen is made of shatterproof Lexan plastic. A huge speedometer and a tachometer are mounted on the fuel tank.

Flashing blue pursuit lights

BMW police bikes ▲

German BMW police bikes are popular all over the world. The BMW R80 RT in the picture above is used by the British police force. This bike is less powerful than the Harley-Davidson, but is still ideal as a police bike, with easy handling, low fuel consumption and a comfortable ride.

The tyres are tubeless which means they are stronger and need less maintenance. Although Harley-Davidsons are expensive, they claim to consume less fuel and have lower maintenance costs than similar bikes.

The bank staff contact the police, giving details of the car. This information is radioed to all units near the bank, including officers on foot patrol, police cars and bikes, and sometimes even helicopters.

A patrolman hears the details on his VHF radio. He spots the car and calls HQ. His job is to trail the car and keep HQ informed. He will not intercept it as his bike could be damaged by the getaway car.

Guided by the patrolman, police cars move in and intercept the getaway car. In a dangerous situation like this, police cars are much better suited to stop and capture escaping criminals like these.

In the USA, one patrol cut its response time from 45 minutes in a squad car to 5 minutes on a Harley-Davidson.

Your first bike

When choosing your first bike decide how much you can afford and what you really want to use the bike for. Then pick a style that suits you best.

Remember, bikes with a small engine capacity cost less and have smaller running and maintenance costs. If you go for a sports roadster or trail bike, their good looks will cost more.

Always test the machine of your choice. Can you physically handle the bike? Can you walk it round in a circle with ease? Do you feel comfortable on it?

Suzuki AE50 Style. Two-stroke 49 cc engine. No gears. Seat height 610 mm (2 ft). Fuel tank capacity 4 litres (.9 gallon). This scooter is ideal for commuting around town, with no gear changes to worry about. Scooters like this are cheap to buy and run.
▼

Suzuki GP100. Two-stroke 98 cc engine. Five-speed gear box. Seat height 750 mm (2 ft 6 in). Fuel tank capacity 14 litres (3.1 gallons). An advantage with this bike is its large seat. A passenger can ride behind once you have passed your test.

◄ **Kawasaki KDX 125SR.** Two-stroke 124 cc engine. Six-speed gear box. Seat height 860 mm (2 ft 10 in). Fuel tank capacity 9 litres (2 gallons). This trail bike has the high, wide handlebars of a motocross machine.

Yamaha TZR125. Two-stroke 124 cc ► engine. Six-speed gear box. Seat height 765 mm (2 ft 6 in). Fuel tank capacity 12 litres (2.6 gallons). The frame is designed to give maximum strength with minimum weight, and was first used on Grand Prix racing bikes.

◀ Honda NSR125. Two-stroke 124 cc engine. Six-speed gear box. Seat height 780 mm (2 ft 7 in). Fuel tank capacity 12 litres (2.6 gallons). Honda say that the bike's technology was developed on the Grand Prix racing circuit. The fairing makes it look very similar to a racing bike.

Kawasaki AR50. Two-stroke 49 cc engine. Five-speed gear box. Seat height 785 mm (2 ft 7 in). Fuel tank capacity 9.6 litres (2.1 gallons). This sportster has low handlebars for comfortable sports riding, good suspension for rough roads and lightweight cast alloy wheels. ▼

Remember!

Every country has different rules governing the type of bikes that young people can ride and how old they must be before being allowed on the road. It is essential that you check these details before buying your first bike.

There are other important details to sort out too. You will need a licence for yourself and tax and insurance for the bike. Remember, the bigger the engine capacity, the bigger your insurance costs.

Another important decision is how to pay for the bike. Cash is the best way, but if you need to borrow money then a bank loan or hire purchase may be necessary.

Learning to ride a motorbike

The most important lesson when learning to ride a motorbike is "safety first". This means wearing the correct clothing - a helmet, boots, eye protection, gloves and a tough weatherproof riding suit are essential.

Safe riding also means you must learn and obey all the rules of the road and take lessons from professional instructors. Frequent checks on engine oil, brakes, tyre pressures and back lights are also important.

Here are some of the things you must learn before riding on public roads. The bike in these photographs is a Suzuki TS 125R.

The first thing to learn is the layout of the controls. Motorbikes now have standard positions for the clutch, throttle, gear lever, front and rear brakes. Positions of minor controls like horn and light switches vary from maker to maker.

Most bikes have an electric starter, but you should learn how to kick start the engine into life, in case your starter motor fails or you have a flat battery. You can kick start either standing at the side of the bike, or astride it as shown here.

On a dry road apply 70% braking pressure to the front brake (above) and 30% to the rear brake. Never grab at the front brake lever. Use both brakes at once, but apply the front brake a fraction of a second before the rear brake.

It is easier to control a motorbike when going fast. On an instruction course you will be taught good bike control by riding slowly in a circle made from traffic cones. The clutch should be fully open and speed adjusted with the rear brake.

A slalom course develops your bike control skills even more. You will weave in and out of the cones as slowly as you can. Moving the cones even closer together tests how expert you are. You will need all these skills for slow road traffic.

Remember, as well as using your flashing indicator lights, you must still make hand signals when about to turn a corner. Always look behind before making a hand signal. Otherwise you might get your arm taken off by a car.

This is an emergency stop. The front suspension is compressed and the rear suspension is fully out. When making an emergency stop it is important to avoid applying the rear brake too fiercely as it may lock and then the tyre will skid.

! Do's and don'ts

● Wear a retro-reflective fluorescent overjacket if you can. This shines in the light of headlamps at night and glows brightly during the day.
● Buy the best helmet you can.
● Check that the bike is in neutral before starting the engine.
● Take extra care if the road is wet or the light is poor.
● Never overtake or change direction without checking the traffic behind.
● Never overtake on a bend or near the brow of a hill.

With the engine now running, move off by pulling in the clutch lever (picture 3) and pressing down the gear lever (picture 4) into first gear with your left foot. Then transfer this foot to the ground and bring up the right foot to cover the rear brake.

Open the throttle (picture 5) a little, gently releasing the clutch at the same time. As you start moving off, slow down the rate at which you are releasing the clutch and open up the throttle more. When you have pulled away you can release the clutch

completely. Co-ordinating the clutch and throttle can be difficult for beginners, so you will need to practise this. Before moving off always look behind and signal your intention to move out.

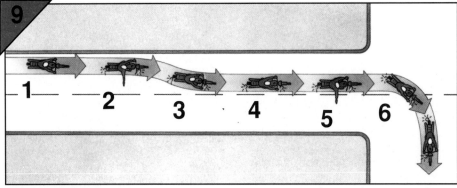

To turn a corner across oncoming traffic, first check the traffic behind (1) and signal that you want to cross to the centre of the road with your rear indicator (keep this on until you have turned the corner) and a hand signal (2). When it is safe, move to

the centre of the road (3). Now slow down using the brakes and change gear as you approach the corner (4). Check behind you that it is still safe and give another hand signal (5). Turn the corner with both hands on the handlebars (6).

Almost all bikes have flashing indicator lights at the rear which signal which way you intend to go. Also at the rear are a brake warning light and a rear lamp for night-time riding. All lights, both rear and front, must be checked regularly.

The Suzuki TS 125R

This trail bike is light in weight and ideal for the learner rider. The 124 cc, water-cooled, two-stroke engine gives increased turning force (torque), and the front fork suspension is designed for bumpy off-road riding and the odd hole in the road. The chassis has good rear suspension.

The expansion chamber, fuel tank and radiator are positioned low down - all these features give the bike a low centre of gravity which is important for stability and handling.

The large, wedge-shaped knuckle guards help protect the rider's hands and a rear side grip is for pillion passengers to hold on to.

The world speed record

The world motorbike speed record is held by Californian Don Vesco. On 28 August 1978, Don and his bike Lightning Bolt managed a record of 512.7 km/h (318.6 mph).

Don Vesco has actually been the title holder since 1975 when he set a record of 487.5 km/h (302.9 mph) with the same bike, then called Silver Bird. Lightning Bolt was 6.32 m (20 ft 8 in) long and powered by two turbocharged Kawasaki Z1000 engines.

High-speed runs need a long track with a perfectly level surface. This was created for Lightning Bolt on the Bonneville Salt Flats in the USA, and stretched for 17 km (10.6 miles).

The 1975 version of this record-breaking bike, Silver Bird, had two Yamaha TZ750 two-stroke engines. Don Vesco tuned these engines to produce more power than their original capacity, and they ran on a mixture of petrol and oil.

To maintain good aerodynamic design, the exhaust pipe exited through a recessed hole at the top of the body.

A tail fin helped to keep the bike in a straight line and prevented instability during the high-speed runs.

The body was crafted from 1.5 mm (.06 in) thick aluminium. Lynn Yakel, the designer, later worked on Challenger, the US Space Shuttle.

The bike had two brake parachutes tucked into its rear end. These were essential after a high-speed run. One opened out to 3.7 m (12 ft) wide and ran out on an 11 m (36 ft) line. A larger 5.5m (18 ft) parachute was also carried.

The aluminium wheels were specially made for the bike and fitted with tubeless Goodyear tyres. The tyre on the rear driving wheel wore out after only two runs at top speed.

The body was mounted on a strong chrome-alloy frame.

Six steps in a motorbike speed record

Don Vesco eased his way into the cockpit for the 1978 world speed record attempt, while his crew made final adjustments. The two "skids" either side of the bike prevented it from toppling over at this stage.

A truck towed the bike along the track until it had gained enough speed to stay upright. At 80 km/h (50 mph) the tow cable was cast off and the truck then swiftly pulled clear of the track.

As the bike accelerated down the track, the "skids" retracted into the body. Don Vesco's right foot worked the throttle, while his left foot operated the clutch and his left hand changed gear.

Don Vesco lay in the bike. The distance between his body and the ground at the nose end was a mere 38 mm (1½ in).

The Flats are 1,310 m (4,298 ft) above sea level. So, engines were adjusted for low air pressure.

The best time to make a record-breaking attempt on the Flats is always in autumn after they have dried out over the summer.

A "skid" on each side kept the bike upright when at a standstill and at low speeds. The valve for the air pressure retraction system was in the left of the cockpit.

Safety at speed

This is the Kawasaki powered Lightning Bolt. Safety was a vital feature of the project and Don Vesco wore gloves, boots, a crash helmet and a fireproof suit. He was also strapped in with a five point seat belt and shoulder harness. The cockpit was lined with a 13 mm (½ in) thick shock absorbing material and there were two strong, anti-crush roll bars around the cockpit area. A freon-gas fire extinguisher was fitted with two outlets in the engine compartment and one in the cockpit. Electrical system isolating switches and fuel shut-off switches were installed to help avoid fire or an explosion in case of an accident.

The bike had to maintain its speed over a 1.6 km (1 mile) section in the middle of the track for the record to become official. Two runs were completed in each direction and the average became the world record.

At the end of the measured section the bike was slowed down by a high-speed parachute. If this parachute failed then an emergency chute was in reserve. The bike also had a single disc brake on the rear wheel.

After shattering the world record, the bike slowed down and the "skids" were lowered. Instruments on the bike showed approximate speed, but the electronic timing device on the track gave the official time.

Record Breakers

Between 1909 and 1978, the world motorbike speed record was broken 44 times. It was pushed up from 123 km/h (76.4 mph) to almost 513 km/h (319 mph).

Since then the world record holder Don Vesco has managed to achieve faster times, but never in both directions of the track, which is the rule for a world speed record.

The superior performance of engines and gear boxes and improved design giving better streamlining have made modern bikes much faster and safer. Many of these developments have come from lessons learned in racing and record breaking.

On these two pages you can read about some of the records, races and people who have earned their place in motorbike history.

Speed records

Early motorbike speed record attempts were made on race tracks and public roads.

As machines got faster, riders needed longer and straighter tracks. Greater length was needed because modern bikes take more time to develop maximum speed and it is only at maximum speed that a rider wants to cross the starting line of the timed section. Another reason for increasing the length of track was to give the fast bikes more slowing down distance.

Straight track is important, as going around bends slows bikes down and is highly dangerous at modern world-record breaking speeds. Most speed attempts are now run on the long, straight stretch of the Bonneville Salt Flats in Utah, USA.

In the chart on the right are some of the world speed records.

Year		
1909		W. E. Cook GB NLG
1914		S. George
1920		E. Walke
1924		H. Le Vack
1930		
1935		
1937		
1951		
1955		
1962		
1970		
1975		
1978		
?		

The first track

Brooklands race track, situated near London, was the first racing circuit specially built for cars and motorbikes in the world. Brooklands opened in 1909 and was the centre of car and motorbike racing in England up until 1939, when the site was taken over for airplane production during World War 11. By 1939, the average lap record stood at 200 km/h (124.3 mph).

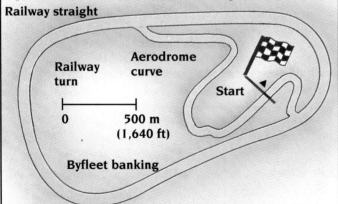

Railway straight
Railway turn
Aerodrome curve
Start
0   500 m (1,640 ft)
Byfleet banking

The longest circuit

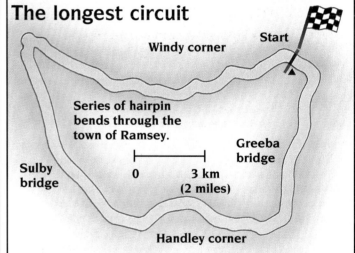

Start
Windy corner
Series of hairpin bends through the town of Ramsey.
Greeba bridge
Sulby bridge
0   3 km (2 miles)
Handley corner

One of the most famous events in the racing calendar takes place in the Isle of Man, UK. Starting in 1907, the TT (Tourist Trophy) races were originally for ordinary bikes straight from the factory. The mountainous circuit of about 61 km (38 miles) covers twisting, hilly roads.

The fastest circuit

The Salzburgring in Austria is known as the fastest circuit in the world. It also has the reputation of being one of the most dangerous. Set in the mountains it is designed with many fast sweeping corners and has staged many exciting Grands Prix. Kevin Schwantz from the USA holds the record for the fastest lap. In 1990, he raced round the 4.24 km (2.63 mile) circuit at 195 km/h (121.2 mph), riding a Suzuki.

The fastest man for 14 years

Tailfin

Air inlet

Ernest Henne's 1937 world speed record of 281.35 km/h (174.83 mph) was set at Darmstadt in Germany on one of the first fully streamlined motorbikes. It is shown on the left. This was the last of the seven world records that Henne set in the 1920s and 30s. It lasted for 14 years.

.99 km/h (76.43 mph)

151.43 km/h (94.10 mph)

ndian 167.76 km/h (104.25 mph)

gh Superior JAP 192.86 km/h (119.84 mph)

ght GB OEC-Temple JAP 244.20 km/h (151.75 mph)

E. Henne Germany BMW 257.74 km/h (160.16 mph)

E. Henne Germany BMW 281.35 km/h (174.83 mph)

W. Herz Germany NSU 291.76 km/h (181.30 mph)

R. Wright New Zealand Vincent HRD 299.70 km/h (186.23 mph)

W. Johnson USA Triumph 363.69 km/h (225.00 mph)

C. Rayborn USA Harley-Davidson 430.09 km/h (267.26 mph)

D. Vesco USA Yamaha 487.52 km/h (302.94 mph)

D. Vesco USA Kawasaki 512.73 km/h (318.61 mph)

?

The standing km

Don Vesco's world speed record is timed over a "flying" km (.6 mile), a measured section of track that the rider approaches very fast after a long run-up. A "standing" km (.6 mile) has no run-up and the rider is timed from the moment his bike starts to move, although he is allowed to rev up his engine. Drag bikes are used for this record.

Date	Rider	Machine	Speed
1967	Alf Hargon	JAP 1,149 cc	188.14 km/h (116.9 mph)
1972	Dave Lecoq	Volkswagon Dragwaye 1,286 cc	191.48 km/h (118.99 mph)
1975	Henk Vink	Kawasaki 1,081 cc	195.39 km/h (121.42 mph)
1977	Henk Vink	Kawasaki 984 cc	215.83 km/h (134.12 mph)
1986	Christian Le Liard	Honda Elf 1,000 cc	181.32 km/h* (112.67 mph)

* This is according to the new 1978 method of speed calculation.

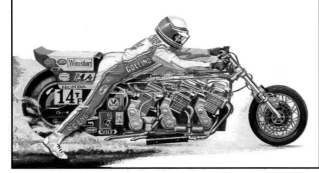

500 cc world champions

Since 1949, motorbike Grands Prix have been organized by the FIM (Fédération Internationale Motorcycliste). There are different classes based on engine capacity and the fastest and most exciting class is 500 cc.
I = Italy; GB = Great Britain; R = Rhodesia; USA = United States; Aus = Australia.

1953 G. Duke	Gilera GB	1972 G. Agostini	MV	I
1954 G. Duke	Gilera GB	1973 P. Read	MV	GB
1955 G. Duke	Gilera GB	1974 P. Read	MV	GB
1956 J. Surtees	MV GB	1975 G. Agostini	MV	I
1957 L. Liberati	MV I	1976 B. Sheene	Suzuki	GB
1958 J. Surtees	MV GB	1977 B. Sheene	Suzuki	GB
1959 J. Surtees	MV GB	1978 K. Roberts	Yamaha	USA
1960 J. Surtees	MV GB	1979 K. Roberts	Yamaha	USA
1961 G. Hocking	MV R	1980 K. Roberts	Yamaha	USA
1962 M. Hailwood	MV GB	1981 M. Lucchinelli	Suzuki	I
1963 M. Hailwood	MV GB	1982 F. Uncini	Suzuki	I
1964 M. Hailwood	MV GB	1983 F. Spencer	Honda	USA
1965 M. Hailwood	MV GB	1984 E. Lawson	Yamaha	USA
1966 G. Agostini	MV I	1985 F. Spencer	Honda	USA
1967 G. Agostini	MV I	1986 E. Lawson	Yamaha	USA
1968 G. Agostini	MV I	1987 W. Gardner	Honda	Aus
1969 G. Agostini	MV I	1988 E. Lawson	Yamaha	USA
1970 G. Agostini	MV I	1989 E. Lawson	Honda	USA
1971 G. Agostini	MV I	1990 W. Rainey	Yamaha	USA

Index

Going further

Bookshops and libraries are full of books about motorbikes and there are many magazines on the subject too. Here is a small selection of the publications available:

Books

Observers' Book of Motorcycles, Penguin
Custom Motorcycles, Andrew Morland, Osprey Publishing Ltd
First Bike, Kris Perkins, Osprey Publishing Ltd
Motorcycle Parade, Bob Holliday, David & Charles

Harley-Davidson - a celebration of the dream machine, Graham Scott, Hamlyn

Magazines

Classic Bike
Classic Motorcycle
What Bike
Motorcycle News
Classic Racer
Bike

THE USBORNE YOUNG SCIENTIST
TRAINS

Contents

Credits

Written by Jonathan Rutland and Margaret Stephens
Art and editorial direction David Jefferis
Editorial revision Margaret Stephens
Text editor Eliot Humberstone
Design Iain Ashman and John Jamieson
Design revision Robert Walster
Illustrators Malcolm English, John Hutchinson, Frank
Kennard, Michael Roffe, Robert Walster, Sean
Wilkinson, John Barker, Hans Wiborg-Jenssen, Abdul
Aziz Khan, Keith Talbot

Acknowledgements

National Railway Museum in York
Rail Magazine
SNCF
British Rail
German Railways
Japan Rail
Canadian National Railways
Airfix Products Ltd
Beatties of London Ltd
Dowty Hydraulic Units Ltd
Energy Equipment Co. Ltd
Airfix Products Ltd

Usborne Publishing Ltd
Usborne House
83-85 Saffron Hill
London EC1N 8RT

Printed in Belgium

This edition published 1991
Based on The Young Engineers Book of Supertrains,
published 1978.

Introduction

This book is full of amazing trains. As you turn the pages you will find fast trains, powerful trains, slow trains and astonishing trains. You will also discover that each train has a personality all of its own, whether this means it flies above the track without touching the rails, or has long legs which go under water.

There are tunnels, bridges, tracks and freight yards to read about too. Where is the longest tunnel in the world? Which bridge has the longest steel arch span? How do freight containers load onto rail wagons?

All the facts are explained very simply and there are experiments to help you really understand how things work. There is even a step-by-step guide to how a steam locomotive works, and a cutaway picture of the latest high-speed, magnetic levitation train.

This book will really show you how exciting and intriguing the world of trains can be.

Introducing the steam locomotive

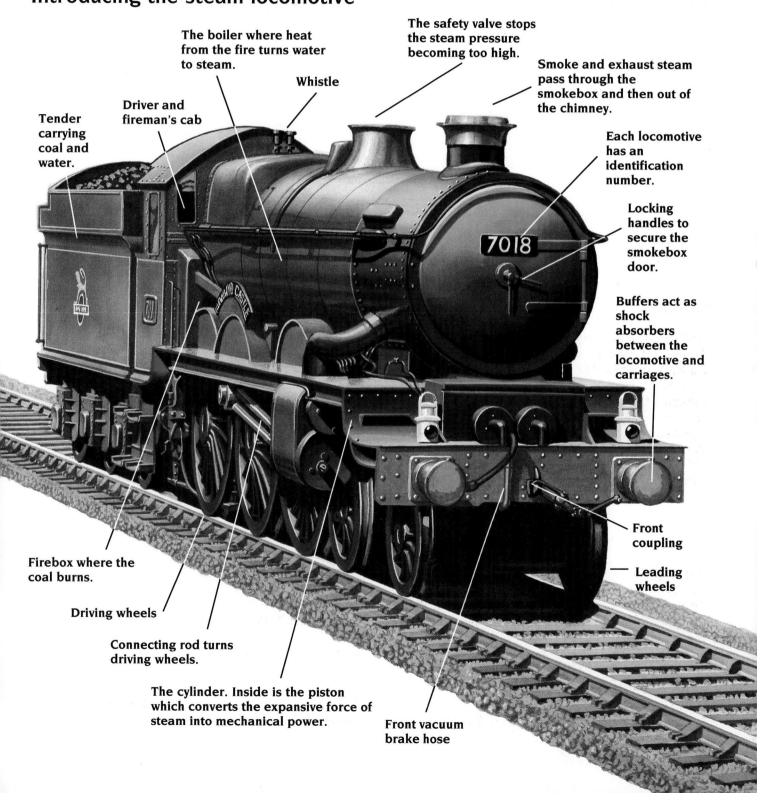

The boiler where heat from the fire turns water to steam.

The safety valve stops the steam pressure becoming too high.

Whistle

Smoke and exhaust steam pass through the smokebox and then out of the chimney.

Driver and fireman's cab

Tender carrying coal and water.

Each locomotive has an identification number.

Locking handles to secure the smokebox door.

7018

Buffers act as shock absorbers between the locomotive and carriages.

Firebox where the coal burns.

Front coupling

Driving wheels

Leading wheels

Connecting rod turns driving wheels.

The cylinder. Inside is the piston which converts the expansive force of steam into mechanical power.

Front vacuum brake hose

The magic of trains

The four famous trains shown here come from Great Britain, France and the USA. Great Britain and the USA were the first to develop modern railways. But nowadays France is one of the leading countries in railway technology and while other countries are running down their railways and closing routes, France is laying new track and building the fastest trains in the world.

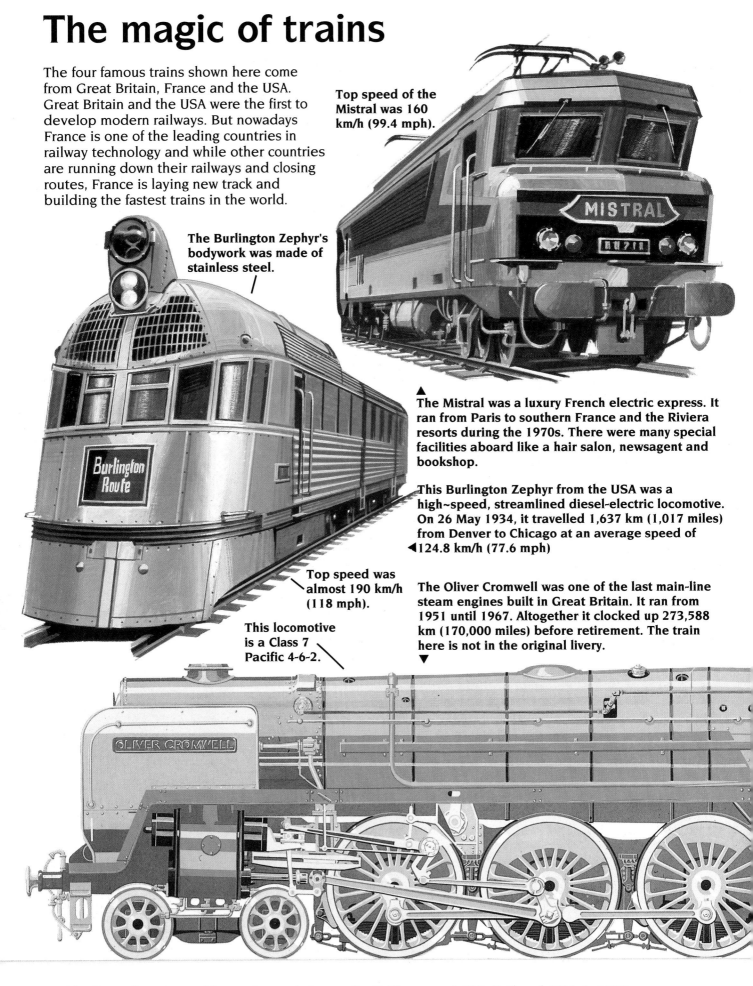

Top speed of the Mistral was 160 km/h (99.4 mph).

The Burlington Zephyr's bodywork was made of stainless steel.

The Mistral was a luxury French electric express. It ran from Paris to southern France and the Riviera resorts during the 1970s. There were many special facilities aboard like a hair salon, newsagent and bookshop.

This Burlington Zephyr from the USA was a high~speed, streamlined diesel-electric locomotive. On 26 May 1934, it travelled 1,637 km (1,017 miles) from Denver to Chicago at an average speed of ◀124.8 km/h (77.6 mph)

Top speed was almost 190 km/h (118 mph).

This locomotive is a Class 7 Pacific 4-6-2.

The Oliver Cromwell was one of the last main-line steam engines built in Great Britain. It ran from 1951 until 1967. Altogether it clocked up 273,588 km (170,000 miles) before retirement. The train here is not in the original livery. ▼

The first railway to provide meals on a train was the Baltimore and Ohio Railroad, USA, in 1853.

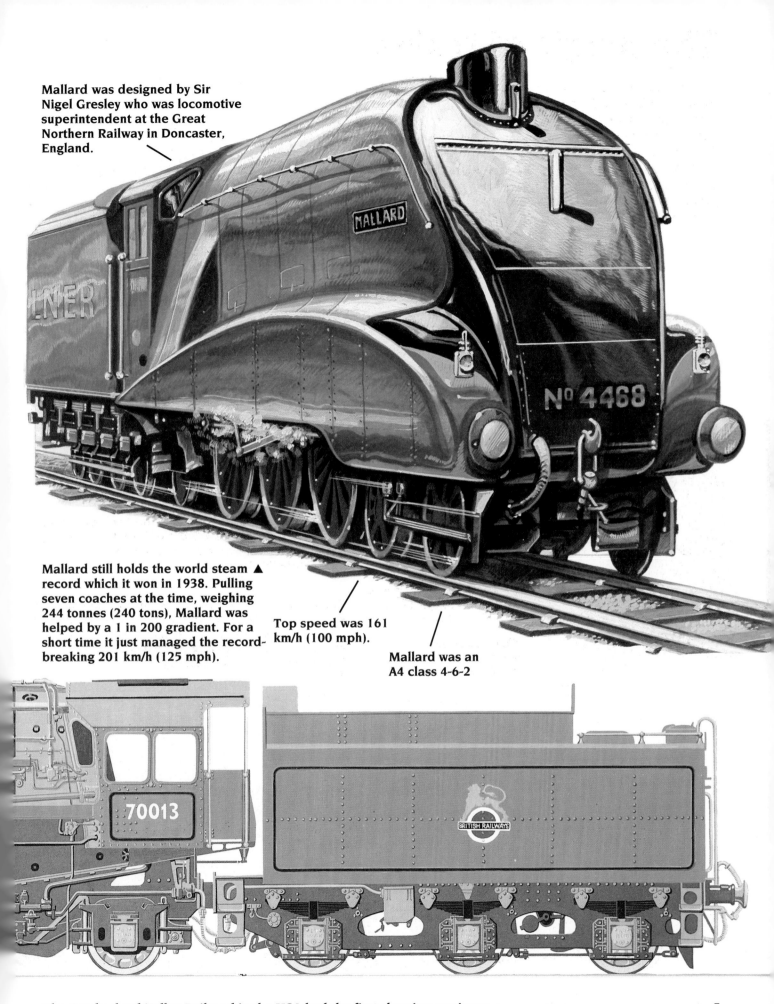

Mallard was designed by Sir Nigel Gresley who was locomotive superintendent at the Great Northern Railway in Doncaster, England.

MALLARD

Nº 4468

LNER

Mallard still holds the world steam ▲ record which it won in 1938. Pulling seven coaches at the time, weighing 244 tonnes (240 tons), Mallard was helped by a 1 in 200 gradient. For a short time it just managed the record-breaking 201 km/h (125 mph).

Top speed was 161 km/h (100 mph).

Mallard was an A4 class 4-6-2

70013

BRITISH RAILWAYS

The Cumberland Valley Railroad in the USA had the first sleeping carriages.

The first trains

About 3,000 years ago, the Ancient Greeks made grooves in stone paths to guide wagon wheels. These wagonways were the simple forerunners of the track you now find in modern railways. Nearly 2,500 years later, wooden rails were being used for mine railways. Coal wagons had wooden wheels, with flanges (rims to keep them on the rails). Horses walked between the rails pulling the wagons along the track. Later some metal rails were flanged too, in an "L" shape.

Much later, metal was laid over the wooden rails to save them from wear and tear. Then by 1800, metal rails were invented. Today's rails are made of steel.

The power of steam has been known for more than 2,000 years, but the first steam engine was only invented in 1712. It pumped water out of flooded mines. In 1804, Richard Trevithick of Cornwall in England built a steam locomotive that pulled passengers and freight at 8 km/h (5 mph). Many engineers all over the world then began to design their own steam locomotives. One of the most famous of these early railway engineers was Robert Stephenson, who designed and built many trains and railway bridges.

The Best Friend of Charleston, 1830 ▶

This locomotive ran on the first regular train service in the USA. Once its boiler exploded when the fireman tied down the steam valve because the noise of escaping steam was annoying him.

This oddity, a sailing rail car, ran on America's Baltimore and Ohio Railroad in 1830. It was a success only when the wind blew the right way. One day the sailing master forgot to brake at the end of the line, and crashed into a bank.

▲ The Rocket, 1829

In 1829 a competition was held to find the most reliable locomotive for the new Liverpool to Manchester Railway. There was a £500 prize. George Stephenson and his son Robert, who was 26 years old, entered Rocket. Robert had in fact done most of the design work on Rocket. Their locomotive won easily. It made 20 trips of 2.8 km (1.7 miles) each, at an average speed of 20 km/h (12.4 mph), pulling wagons weighing 13.2 tonnes (13 tons).

Der Adler, 1835 ▶

This locomotive was used on the first German railway, from Nuremberg to Fürth. Der Adler was built by Robert Stephenson's company, at Newcastle-Upon-Tyne

One of Rocket's rivals in the 1829 competition was powered by two horses turning a treadmill.

Rolling on rails

A loaded wagon rolling along level track at 100 km/h (62 mph) can freewheel for at least 8 km (5 miles) before stopping. On a road, a lorry of the same weight stops after only 1.5 km (nearly one mile). Smooth metal wheels roll much more easily on smooth metal rails than rubber tyres do on roads. This is why locomotives can haul such enormous loads. The first wheels and rails were wood, but modern metal wheels and rails mean trains can go faster and the track is more hard wearing.

You can see the difference a smooth surface makes with this experiment. Collect together a model train wagon, some track, plasticine, cotton thread and a towel.

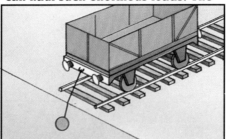

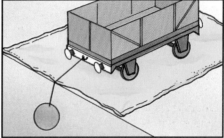

Put the model wagon on some track at the edge of a table. Tie the wagon's coupling to 40 cm (16 in) of cotton thread. Fix a ball of plasticine to the other end of the thread. Hang the plasticine ball over the table and adjust the weight so it just starts the wagon rolling.

Now place the towel on the table and smooth it down flat. Take the wagon off the rails and put it on the towel. Try again to find the weight of plasticine that starts the wagon rolling. You will discover that it does not move unless you use a much bigger piece of plasticine.

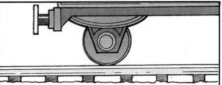

This is a metal wheel on a metal rail. As the wheel turns it meets little resistance, as both the rail and wheel are smooth. This means it needs less weight to pull it along.

When a wheel meets the towel's rough surface, resistance is much greater, so the wagon needs a heavier weight to pull it. This resistance is called friction.

The first steam locomotive on the Baltimore and Ohio Railroad in the USA was a strange looking contraption called Tom Thumb. It was built in 1829 but first ran in 1930. The boiler was vertical and the locomotive had one cylinder.

Some inventors came up with the idea of steam road carriages that ran without rails. This one was built in 1832. It needed someone hanging on the back to feed the fire with coal. The design was very similar to the horse-pulled coaches of those times.

in England. It had three pairs of wheels, one more than Rocket, which meant it could carry a large boiler.

The first passenger railway in the world started in Wales in 1807. Horses pulled the wagons.

Steam power

From Rocket to the present day, the basic design of steam engines has remained the same. The remarkably simple principles of steam power can be seen in this cutaway picture of a classic American locomotive.

About 20,000 of these locos were built between 1840 and 1890, and the 4-4-0 wheel code is known as an American. The engines usually burned wood because only a few coal mines were operating at the time. Just 4% of the fire's heat was used to pull the wheels. Most of the heat went up the chimney, which was designed to catch sparks from the burning wood. The large oil lamp on the front of the locomotive helped the driver to see animals on the track at night.

Another hazard at night was the danger of ambush, and the light's strong beam was essential to spot criminals waiting by the track. As cows could derail a train, the wide cowcatcher on the front was designed to sweep away animals straying onto the track.

Pulling a 150 tonne (147.6 ton) train at 65 km/h (40.4 mph), the firebox used 45 kg of wood per 1 km (163 lbs per mile).

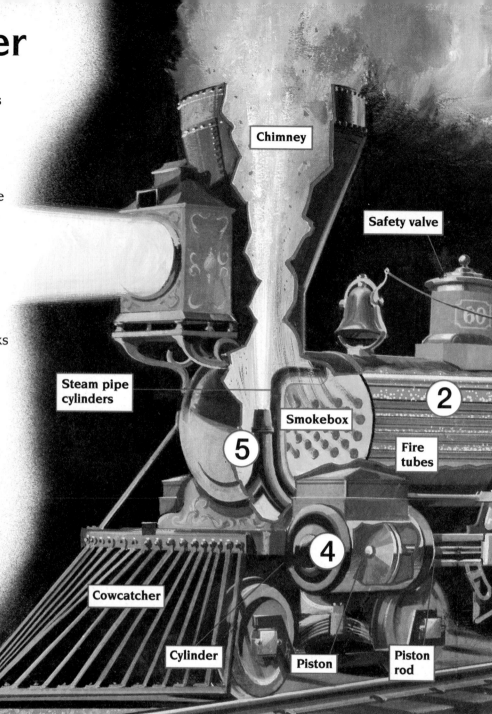

Chimney

Safety valve

Steam pipe cylinders

Smokebox

2

Fire tubes

5

4

Cowcatcher

Cylinder

Piston

Piston rod

Wheel codes

A steam locomotive's wheel code shows how many wheels it has and what job they do. The first figure in the code gives the number of leading wheels, the second the driving wheels, and the third the trailing wheels.

This system is known as the Whyte notation because it was invented by railroad official Frederick Whyte in the USA, in 1900.

2-6-0
Mogul

2-6-2
Prairie

2-6-4
Adriatic

2-8-0
Consolidation

2-8-2
Mikado

2-10-0
Decapod

2-10-2
Santa Fé

4-4-2
Atlantic

4-6-2
Pacific

4-6-4
Hudson

4-8-2
Mountain

4-8-4
Northern

1 The firebox
The firebox contains the engine's coal or wood fire. The heat from the firebox is used to boil water in the boiler, which creates steam.

2 The boiler
The boiler is really a large metal barrel of water. Inside are lots of hollow fire tubes heated by hot air coming from the firebox. As the water in the boiler come in contact with the tubes it begins to boil. Steam is generated by the boiling water and collects in the dome.

3 The dome
As steam collects in the dome, pressure begins to build up. When the pressure is high enough, the driver opens the regulator valve by working a regulator handle in his cab. Steam then passes through the steam pipes and rushes into the cylinders. These are mounted on each side of the locomotive over the bogie with the leading wheels.

Tender

Connecting rod

Crank

4 The cylinder

Slide valve

Piston

Steam inlet

Steam outlet

Inside each cylinder is a piston. Steam (orange) is fed into the cylinder first on one side of the piston and then on the other, controlled by the slide valve. In this way the piston is pushed backwards and forwards. This action, linked through a connecting rod and crank, turns the driving wheels. At the end of each piston stroke, exhausted steam escapes through the blastpipe and out of the chimney. Each puff of a steam train is made by a rush of steam up the blastpipe.

5 The blastpipe

Piston

Blastpipe

When exhaust steam from the cylinder is forced up the blastpipe, this draws hot air from the firebox along the fire tubes which heat up the water. At the same time, a draught is created in the firebox, which makes the fire burn well.

In Tasmania, Australia, in 1836 people paid a shilling to ride in trucks pushed by convicts.

Modern locomotives

Passenger carriages

Diesel engine

Fuel tank

Modern trains rarely use steam to power their engines. Diesel and electricity have taken over as the two main sources of energy. Steam trains look splendid, but their engines are very wasteful. Only about 9% of the fire's energy is used to drive the wheels. Steam trains are very dirty and emit a lot of atmospheric pollution too.

Diesel and electric power are much more efficient. Overall, electric locomotives are more costly to run than diesel ones, because the installation of trackside equipment is high. So electric locos are only profitable on routes with lots of passengers.

Diesel power

This is British Rail's High Speed Train (HST). Top speed in service is 201 km/h (125 mph). The locomotives at either end of the train are diesel-electrics. This means that the power actually turning the wheels is electricity.

The engine burns diesel, which is pumped up from tanks beneath the locomotive. The power from the burning diesel then turns a generator which produces electricity. This electricity is passed to the traction motors which turn the driving wheels.

One of the problems with fast trains is braking within a safe distance. HSTs have disc brakes on all carriage and locomotive wheels.

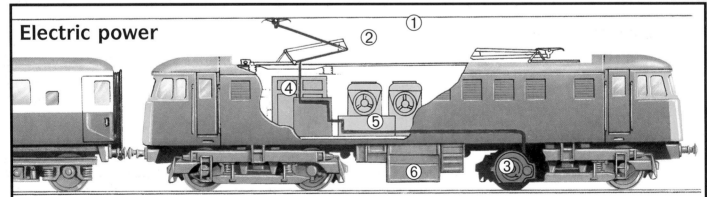

Electric power

This British Rail locomotive, Class 85, runs on electricity. The power supply comes from overhead wires (1) and is fed into the engine by pantographs (2) which stretch up from the locomotive's roof. The pantographs press firmly against the wires, and can be lowered when necessary. A very high, mains current voltage is transmitted through the pantographs. As low voltage motors (3) are easier and cheaper to run than high voltage ones, the current is changed to low voltage by transformers (4) and a rectifier (5). Class 85s have batteries (6) which power the control circuits and lighting. The locomotive's roof panels are removable to allow the installation and taking out of equipment.

The first public electric railway ran near Berlin, Germany, in 1881. It carried 26 passengers on each journey.

Exhaust vents

Aerodynamic shape reduces air resistance at high speeds.

Diesel-electric locomotive

Driver's cab

Electric traction motors

Driving wheels

Gas-turbine power

The first locomotive with a gas-turbine engine was built in 1941 for the Swiss Federal Railways. Since then a few have run in North America and Europe. Gas-turbines have never been as popular as electric and diesel locomotives. The engine of this Canadian National gas-turbine loco works like a jet-propellor aeroplane. Air is sucked in through the air intakes (1). Then it is compressed and mixed with vaporized kerosene. This produces hot gases which turn the blades of a turbine (2). The rotary action of the turbine is transmitted to the main gear box (3) by way of reduction gears. These are needed because the turbine rotates at a very high speed. A driveshaft (4) then takes the power to the wheels.

Between 1940 and 1967, the proportion of diesel pulled trains in the USA rose from under 1% to 99%.

Light rail transit - monorails

Light rail transit systems carry large numbers of passengers on short journeys, in the quickest possible time. They are electrically operated and usually found in cities where they help ease congestion on busy roads. Modern automatic systems can carry 50,000 passengers an hour. Trams, tubes and monorails are all examples of light rail transit. Monorails can look ugly built over city streets, and they make a lot of noise, but they are cheap to build. The train either runs on top of the rail, or it hangs from beneath. The first passenger monorail was built in 1876.

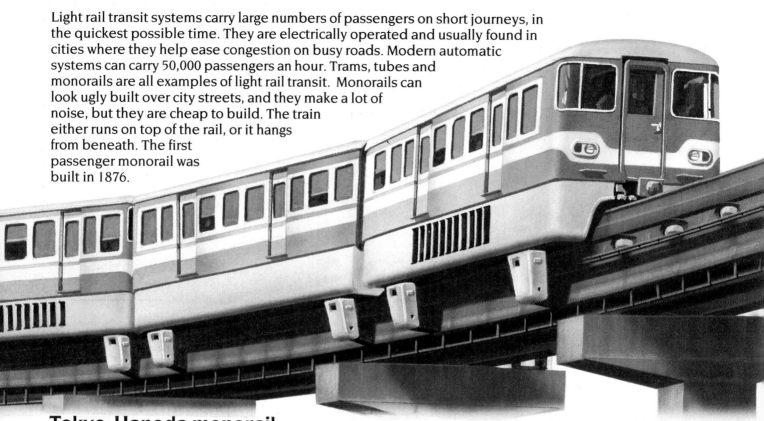

Tokyo-Haneda monorail

The Tokyo-Haneda monorail runs 13.1 km (8.1 miles) between Tokyo and the Haneda international airport, in 15 minutes. The train straddles a concrete beam. This method is known as the Hitachi-Alweg system. The track stands on concrete pylons which elevate it above the countryside. The train has two running wheels which propel it along the track. There are guide and stabilizing wheels too, that grip the side of the track, to keep the train balanced and secure.

Wuppertal Schwebebahn

The Wuppertal Schwebebahn is a suspended, cranked-arm type monorail. Most of the track runs over the Wupper River in Germany. From 1901 to 1960 it carried 1,000 million passengers. This monorail has a system where sections of movable track switch position, so trains can turn for the return journey.

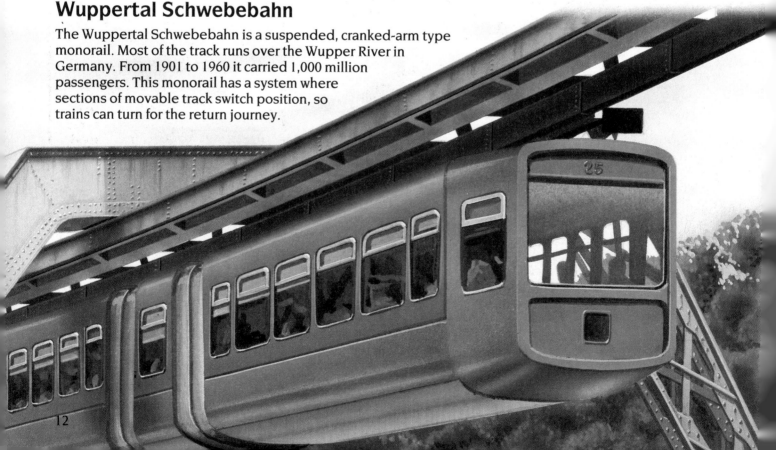

Light rail transit - trams and tubes

Underground railways, or tubes, are the most common type of light rail transit. Many cities throughout the world have a tube. In Paris it is called the metro and in New York, the subway. Trams have carriages that look more like buses than trains, and they run on rails which can be laid on roads, or have their own special track.

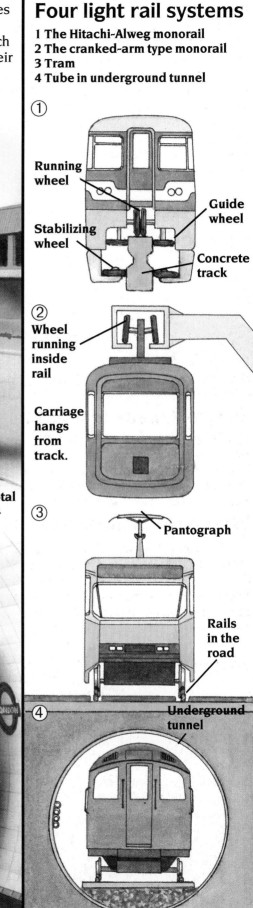

Four light rail systems

1 The Hitachi-Alweg monorail
2 The cranked-arm type monorail
3 Tram
4 Tube in underground tunnel

① Running wheel
Guide wheel
Stabilizing wheel
Concrete track

② Wheel running inside rail
Carriage hangs from track.

③ Pantograph
Rails in the road

④ Underground tunnel

Melbourne tram

▲ The tram above runs in the city of Melbourne in Australia, which has the largest system in the southern hemisphere. The city has converted under-used railways to tramways.

The London Underground below carries 815 million passengers a year. All the routes put together total 408 km (253.5 miles). 167 km (104 miles) of this is below ground. ▼

London underground train

City 57
72
2001

MORDEN
053

Ups and downs

Railway engineers are faced with many problems when they lay track. Locomotives run best on level straight track. So how do they build track across a river or steep ravine? How can they avoid hills? How can they avoid bends, which slow a train down?

Sometimes track can be laid over a different route to avoid the problem. If this is impossible viaducts or bridges are built to carry trains over valleys and rivers, and cuttings are made in hills to straighten out bends. Tunnels are built too, through hills and under rivers.

Other ways of overcoming the problems of steep gradients are to increase the grip of wheels by fitting gears, dropping sand on rails, or using a rack and pinion system. Zig-zag track reduces the gradient in steep mountainous areas, but increases the travelling distance and running costs as trains travel backwards and forwards up the zig-zags. Tunnels that loop, climbing gently through mountains, can solve these problems, but are costly to build.

To the right is a section of the Landwasser Viaduct in Switzerland. It is part of the Rhaetian Railway and has six masonry arches. The track is 65 m (213 ft) above ground.

The Channel Tunnel

When the Channel Tunnel opens between France and England in 1993, it will be the second longest tunnel in the world at 49.4 km (30.7 miles). (For the longest see page 31.) The tunnel will also be about 100 m (328 ft) below sea level.

There will be two rail tunnels at 7.6 m (24 ft 11 in) in diameter, and one service tunnel at 4.8 m (15 ft 10 in) in diameter. Three types of train will run through it, a tunnel shuttle, a high-speed passenger train and a freight train.

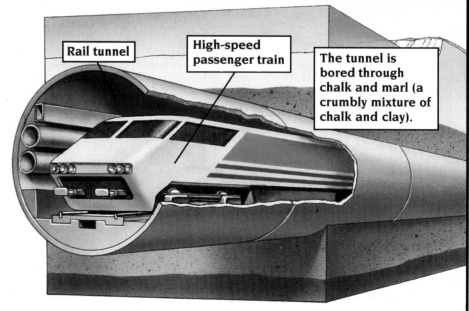

Rail tunnel

High-speed passenger train

The tunnel is bored through chalk and marl (a crumbly mixture of chalk and clay).

Sydney Harbour Bridge

Steel arch span

North shore

South shore

Sydney Harbour is very deep.

Tower supporting bridge.

Sydney Harbour Bridge in Australia stretches 1,149 m (3,770 ft) from the north to the south shore. It is a vital rail and road link between the two, with an eight-lane road, two rail tracks and a footpath. The famous steel arch span is the longest in the world at 503 m (1,650 ft). There were engineering problems of deep harbour water and the absence of any natural supports, like an island. Two massive towers, faced with granite, were built on both shores to support the bridge.

Getting it straight

A train uses lots of energy to build up speed. Once it has done so, little power is needed to keep it rolling on a straight and level track. Climbing gradients uses up much more power, and wheels slip easily on smooth metal. Laying track around hills is costly because it takes longer and uses up more materials. Track can be laid as straight and level as possible by cuttings, bridges, viaducts and tunnels.

Viaduct

Cutting

Bridge

Tunnel

Hillclimbers

The Pilatus line in Switzerland is the world's steepest railway. To stop wheels slipping it has a rack and pinion drive. Toothed wheels (the pinions) turn in a toothed rail (the rack) to pull the train uphill.

Another way to stop wheels slipping on hills is by using gears. These help the engine turn the wheels more slowly. This increases their grip. The geared locomotive here hauled timber in America.

Many steam locomotives had a device for pouring sand on the rails in front of the driving wheels to improve grip. The Indian train here carried men on the front to sprinkle sand on the rails.

The Chengtu-Kunming railway in China holds the world record for the greatest number and length of tunnels.

Rails and tracks

Baseplate

Fishplate joins rails together.

Wood or concrete sleepers

Spike - can be one of several designs

Steel T-rail

The sleepers are laid on ballast which is usually made of broken stone like granite.

Rails are vital to guide trains along a route. Concrete, steel or wood sleepers rest on stony ballast.

T-shaped steel rails are laid on the sleepers. Most rails are continuously welded, but fishplates sometimes still join different sections. In hot lands, continuously welded rail is stretched before laying, so it does not buckle by expanding in high temperatures.

The distance between rails is a gauge. A standard gauge of 1.435 m (4 ft 8½ in) is the most common worldwide. George Stephenson developed this gauge, basing it on the track mostly used for horse-pulled coal wagons.

Multi-gauge track

Some countries have several different gauges. This means loads have to be transferred from one train to another where gauges change. The diagram below shows the multi-gauge track of South Australia which handles three different sized trains, each using separate pairs of rails.

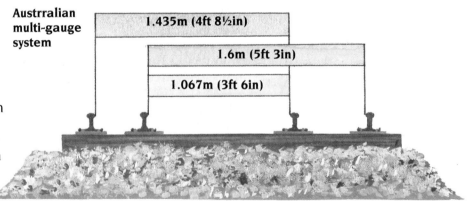

Austrralian multi-gauge system

1.435m (4ft 8½in)

1.6m (5ft 3in)

1.067m (3ft 6in)

Locomotive weight distribution

High-speed locomotives depend on their design and the quality of track for safety. As locomotives take sharp bends, they tend to be thrown outwards, which can be very dangerous. To counteract this, most of their weight is distributed low down near the base of the engine, because the higher their weight, the more chance there is of them tipping over.

A good way of testing this is to run a model train too fast. The experiment here shows the effect of different weight distribution.

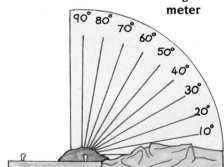

Angle meter

First make this meter to show the angle at which the train overbalances. Use stiff cardboard and draw angles from 0 to 90 like in the picture above. Prop up the meter with plasticine.

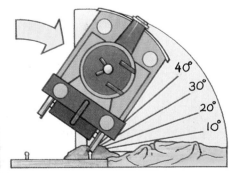

Use a model train, or a block of wood, and gradually tip it. When it starts to overbalance, note the angle on the meter. If you use a model train have a piece of soft cloth under it in case it falls.

Different trains for different gauges

Hiawatha Express

North Star

Romney, Hythe and Dymchurch locomotive

60°
50°
40°
30°
20°
10°

Now wedge a piece of plasticine on top of the train. Start tipping it again and you will notice that it overbalances more quickly at a smaller angle. A higher distribution of weight has made it less stable.

The British steam locomotive to the left above was the Great Western Railway's North Star. From 1838 to 1892 it ran on the widest gauge in railway history - 2.134 m (7 ft).

To the right of this train is the tiny locomotive that runs on the Romney, Hythe and Dymchurch Railway in England. This train runs on a gauge of 3.81 cm (1 ft 3 in).

The railway holds the rail speed record for a narrow gauge. A locomotive with 14 coaches ran without stopping for 43.2 km (26.8 mph) with a time of 73 mins 22 secs, and at an average speed of 35.4 km/h (22 mph), in 1982.

The huge locomotive above and below is an Atlantic with a 4-4-2 wheelcode. Atlantics were built in the USA between 1935 and 1937. This oil-fired loco ran on standard gauge and pulled the Hiawatha Express at a speed of 161 km/h (100 mph). Top speeds reached were up to 193 km/h (120 mph). Only four of these streamlined locomotives were ever built.

On standard gauge track in Britain, each kilometre of track weighs 111 tonnes (each mile weighs 151 tons).

Technology takes over

Railways need the latest computer and engineering technology so that trains can compete with other modern transport like planes and cars. New inventions can make railways faster and also make them more convenient and comfortable.

Some trains now have computers instead of drivers. The Docklands Light Railway in London, shown on the right, has driverless trains. A computer on board knows exactly where to coast, accelerate and brake between stations.

If there are problems, an operator in the control centre can take over by transmitting messages to the train.

By operating a push button in the Docklands Light Railway control room, a supervisor can stop a train instantly in an emergency.

BART

BART stands for the Bay Area Rapid Transit system, which operates in San Francisco and Oakland on the west coast of the USA. The line runs above, on, and under the ground as it threads its way through towns and suburbs. The BART carriages are made of lightweight aluminium alloy. Using advanced computer technology, everything is completely automated. Passengers put their money into automatic fare collection gates and enter the train through doors operated by computers.

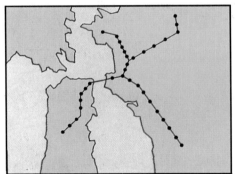

This map shows the 120 km (74.6 mile) long BART system. Part of it travels under the waters of San Francisco Bay. The 5.8 km (3.6 mile) underwater tunnel is made of pre-cast concrete sections.

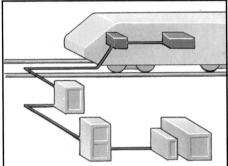

A computer in the cotrol centre sends messages to a transmitter. The transmitter then passes these messages down wires on the track. A train's electronic sensors picks up the messages and feeds

them into its control box. A driver still sits in the cockpit, but the control box changes speeds and stops and starts the train. If anything goes wrong the driver or the controller can take over.

CATE

If you want to know which train to catch, then ring CATE (Computer Assisted Timetable Enquiries). All you do is phone and tell the computer operator where you want to go from, your destination, and the date and approximate time of your journey. Two seconds later the computer will have worked out the times and the best way to go. CATE will also tell you if your train has any food on board or a phone, and of course how much your ticket costs. These complex systems can operate on huge rail networks with thousands of stations, routes and trains.

From: Poole
To: Gloucester
Departing after 17.35 on WEDNESDAY 7th October 1992 in a maximum of three changes.

POOLE	DEP 19.46
BASINGSTOKE	ARR 21.21
	DEP 21.25
READING	ARR 21.50
	DEP 22.35
SWINDON	ARR 23.07
	DEP 23.12
GLOUCESTER	ARR 00.01

British Rail - scientific research

British Rail has a special scientific research centre that invents and tests the latest railway technology. Seven hundred scientists and engineers work on projects there. One project is an electronic signalling system linking train drivers to control centres which supervise train traffic. Paved concrete track without sleepers and ballast is another invention. They can match paints by computer too (like the picture here), and have invented a special chemical formula to stop bridges corroding.

Canadian ATCS

Canadian National Railways have a way of guiding and controlling freight trains, called ATCS (Advanced Train Control Systems). At Jasper Station in Alberta, a train carrying 92 grain wagons begins a journey. As it gathers speed, underneath the train electronic sensors start scanning the track. They are looking for a transponder. When the sensors pass over a transponder, the transponder feeds a message through the sensor to the train's computer. This message is then transmitted by the train's aerial to a computer control centre. In this way the control centre always knows exactly where all their trains are and the speed at which they are travelling.

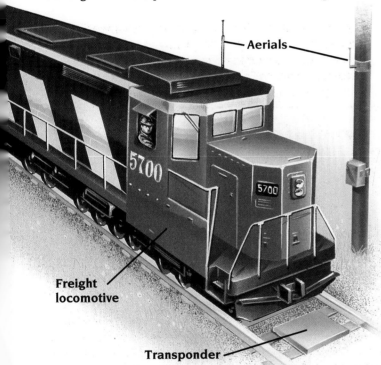

Aerials

Freight locomotive

Transponder

Computerized control

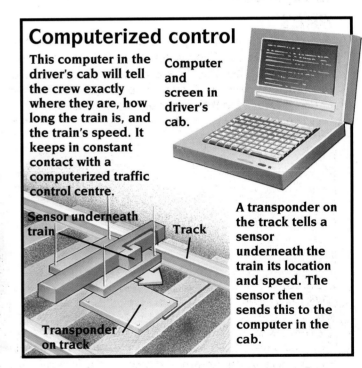

This computer in the driver's cab will tell the crew exactly where they are, how long the train is, and the train's speed. It keeps in constant contact with a computerized traffic control centre.

Computer and screen in driver's cab.

Sensor underneath train

Track

Transponder on track

A transponder on the track tells a sensor underneath the train its location and speed. The sensor then sends this to the computer in the cab.

TGV wind tunnel

This is a computer model of the French TGV in a wind tunnel. Wind tunnels test the flow of air around trains. Air can behave rather like water. An oar with the blade turned sideways is easy to pull through water. It is much harder when the wide flat part of the blade is pulled through water, as this creates more resistance. Resistance happens when trains travel through air too, and slows them down. It is important that fast trains are as aerodynamic as possible by being long and slender, like the TGV.

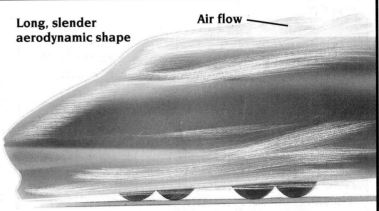

Long, slender aerodynamic shape

Air flow

If the crew of an ATCS train forget to brake in time, the computer in the cab will apply the brakes for them.

Maglev trains

Maglevs are trains of the future that will give passengers a smooth, silent ride. They operate on the principle of magnetic levitation, which means the trains are suspended above the track. As they never come in contact with the track there is less friction so they can go faster, and there is much less wear and tear which saves money on maintenance. Two types of maglev have been developed. The Japanese Linear Express operates in a guideway by magnetic repulsion and attraction, and the German Transrapid and the Birmingham maglev operate suspended over a track by attraction. The Birmingham maglev is in service now and the Japanese maglev starts in the year 2000.

Japanese Linear Express

Side magnet

The Japanese Linear Express

The Japanese Linear Express will probably be the fastest train in the world when it finally comes into service. Japan Rail promise that it will run at an average speed of 500 km/h (311 mph), with a top speed of almost 600 km/h (373 mph). One problem is the effect of the strong magnets, which can cause sickness among passengers.

Magnetic power

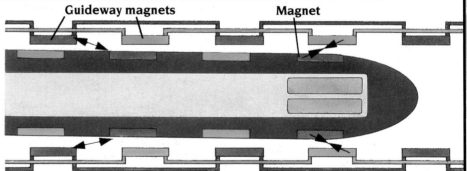

Magnet **Magnet**

Magnets

Levetation coil

Guideway magnets   **Magnet**

The Linear Express runs in a guideway. As it gathers speed, magnets in its underside create an electrical current in coils in the guideway floor. These then become magnetic too and repel the train's

magnets, lifting it off the track by 10 cm (4 in), at 100 km/h (62 mph).

The train moves by magnets in the sides of the guideway and train. These have alternating north and south poles, controlled by computer.

The attraction and repulsion forces created propel the train. Repulsion forces act from the back and attraction forces act from the front, to push the train forward through the guideway.

The German Transrapid has a solid track mounted on pillars which elevates the train across the countryside.

Birmingham maglev

The British Birmingham maglev travels at about 53 km/h (34 mph), from the city's airport to its railway station. The track is T-shaped and the bottom of the train slots into the top flat bit of the "T". The part of the train beneath the track is attracted upwards by magnets on the underside of the track. This attraction pushes up the main body of the train above the track for a friction free ride. The German Transrapid also works on this principle, but is much faster.

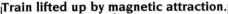
Train lifted up by magnetic attraction.
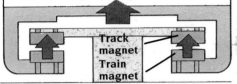
Track magnet
Train magnet

Aerodynamics

The Linear Express is aerodynamically designed to make it as streamlined as possible. It is a long pencil-shaped train with a pointed oval nose, built to achieve the highest speeds.

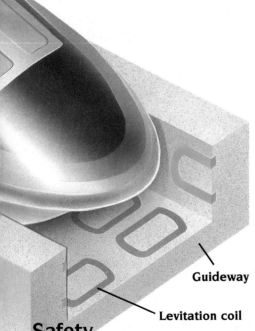

Guideway

Levitation coil

Safety

The attraction and repulsion forces of the side magnets also keep the Linear Express running safely in the centre of the guideway. If a train moves to one side, repulsion and attraction forces act to move the train back to the centre. This principle works even better at high speeds.

Maglev experiment

This simple experiment will show you how magnetic repulsion forces lift the Japanese Linear Express from the floor of its guideway.
   Collect together two horseshoe magnets, two pieces of stiff cardboard and some strong glue.

The ends of each magnet are either a north or south pole. If two identical poles come together they repel. Two different poles will attract. Glue the ends of each magnet firmly to the centre of each piece of cardboard.

Pick up each piece of cardboard by its magnet. Slide one cardboard over the other. What happens when the magnets meet in the middle? Do they repel or attract? Try it again, but switch one piece of cardboard round. When the same poles meet the two pieces will repel each other and push apart. This is what happens when the maglev lifts up from the floor of its guideway.

Cardboard   Magnet

Glue

When north and south poles meet the pieces of cardboard will attract each other.

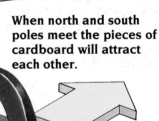

When the same poles meet the pieces of cardboard will repel each other.

The Birmingham maglev holds 34 people standing and six sitting. Its track measures 623 m (1,709 ft).

Freight handling

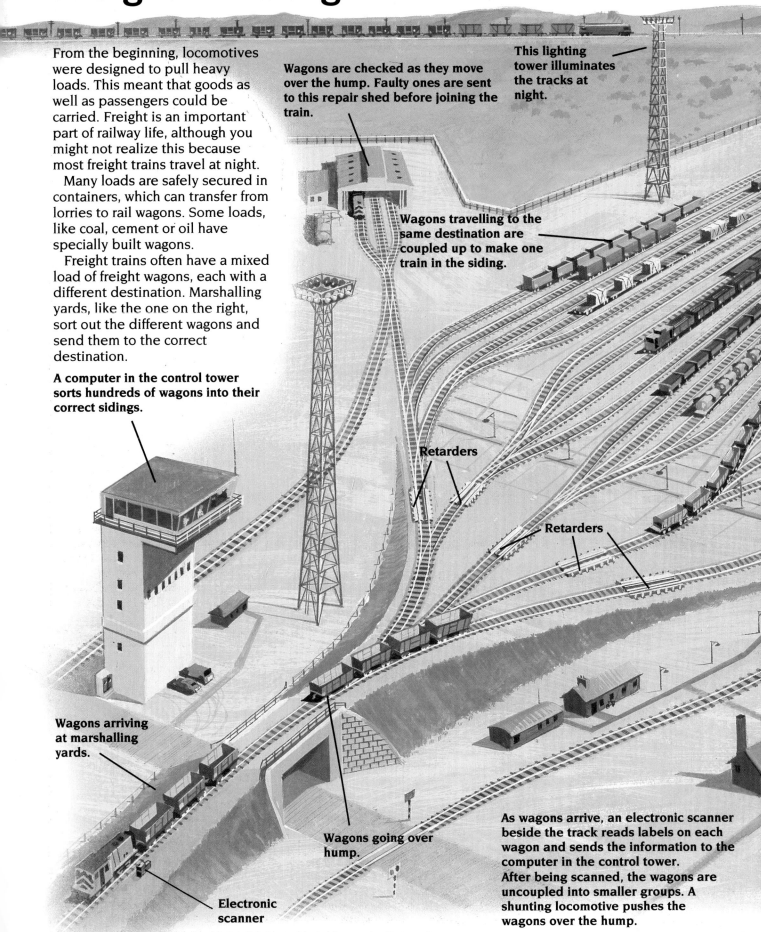

From the beginning, locomotives were designed to pull heavy loads. This meant that goods as well as passengers could be carried. Freight is an important part of railway life, although you might not realize this because most freight trains travel at night.

Many loads are safely secured in containers, which can transfer from lorries to rail wagons. Some loads, like coal, cement or oil have specially built wagons.

Freight trains often have a mixed load of freight wagons, each with a different destination. Marshalling yards, like the one on the right, sort out the different wagons and send them to the correct destination.

A computer in the control tower sorts hundreds of wagons into their correct sidings.

Wagons are checked as they move over the hump. Faulty ones are sent to this repair shed before joining the train.

This lighting tower illuminates the tracks at night.

Wagons travelling to the same destination are coupled up to make one train in the siding.

Retarders

Retarders

Wagons arriving at marshalling yards.

Wagons going over hump.

Electronic scanner

As wagons arrive, an electronic scanner beside the track reads labels on each wagon and sends the information to the computer in the control tower. After being scanned, the wagons are uncoupled into smaller groups. A shunting locomotive pushes the wagons over the hump.

Freight carrying containers were first used as early as 1849 on the Camden and Amboy Railroad, USA.

A train leaves to join the main line.

As wagons roll downhill from the hump, the computer in the control tower operates points and retarders (see below) to send the wagons in the correct direction. This means each wagon rolls gently into the correct siding.

Transporting goods in containers

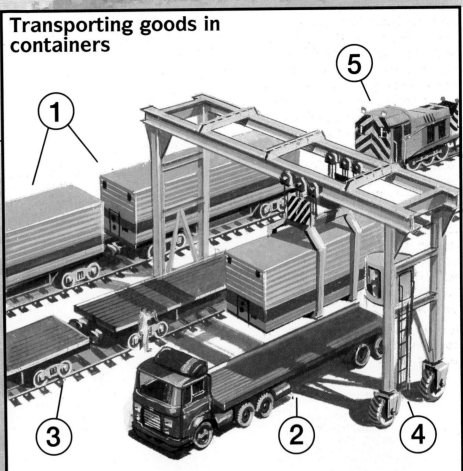

Containers 1 are like giant packing cases. Each container is a standard size that fits onto container lorries 2, rail wagons 3, and into the grabs of container cranes 4. Packed containers are sent by road to a road-rail container terminal. There they are transferred to a rail wagon by the crane. A shunting locomotive 5 then takes the wagon off to join a container train. Containers arriving at docks after a sea journey are loaded straight onto wagons.

Slowing down wagons

Retarders go down and then up as wheels roll over them. If the wagon is travelling too fast, a piston inside the retarder stops it being pressed down so quickly. As the retarder resists the wheels, it slows the wagon down.

A French kangaroo

Lorry with container load.

Wheeled container rolls down into pouch.

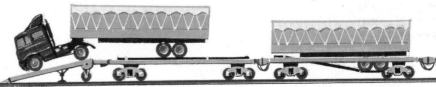

This picture shows a French container system. French railways have a lower loading gauge than other railways. This means the distance from the wagon floor to the ground is smaller, so containers can be loaded onto the wagons by a lorry. Each wagon has a kangaroo-style pouch. As you can see in the picture, the container's wheels drop neatly into the pouch, which hangs underneath the wagon. The bottom of the container then rests firmly on the wagon floor.

A hydrocracker reactor of 558 tonnes (549.2 tons) holds the record for the heaviest freight ever carried on rails.

Giants on rails

The largest and heaviest steam engines were the 4-8-8-4 Big Boys, built for the Union Pacific Railroad from 1941 to 1944 in the USA.

The Big Boys were articulated, with a front set of wheels that swivelled when going around bends. A huge Russian locomotive, with an unarticulated rigid frame, was so restricted around bends, it had to be taken out of service.

To get round sharp bends, Big Boys had a leading set of eight driving wheels pivoted under the boiler, and a four-wheel swivelling bogie at the front.

Giant truck chains

Big Boys hauled long loads over the 1 in 67 gradient found in parts of the Wasatch Mountains in the USA. The train here has 70 trucks.

Garratts, like the Australian one shown below, were also giant articulated locomotives. They had one boiler in the middle, with sets of driving wheels at each end. The biggest Garratt ever was built in England in 1932 for the USSR railways. It was 5.2 m (17 ft) high.

Big Boys were 3.4 m (11 ft) wide and 4.9 m (16 ft) high. They were 39.9 m (131 ft) long, and with their tenders (not shown here) they weighed 508 tonnes (500 tons).

The rear set of eight driving wheels was fixed to the frame. Steam for the pistons and cylinders of all the driving wheels came from one gigantic boiler.

The firebox grate had an area of almost 14 square metres (151 sq ft). It could burn 22 tonnes (21.7 tons) of coal an hour. Mechanical stokers had to be used.

Mechanical stokers are usually Archimedes' screws - spiral screws of metal inside a hollow tube. As the screw turns, coal is drawn up around the thread.

Heavyweight trains on lightweight tracks

Giant locomotives like the Big Boys were so heavy there was a danger of the track collapsing. Engineers increased the length of these locomotives to spread their load and so reduce strain on the track.

The experiment here will show you the effect of spreading load on track. You will need a piece of paper (about 290 x 210 mm or 11 x 8 in in size), four drinking straws, scissors, glue, stiff cardboard, and a pile of books.

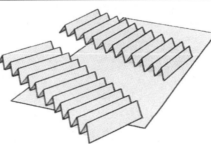

Fold the piece of paper into a zig-zag concertina. 15-20 folds will do. Try and get the folds as even as possible. Close the concertina up tightly and cut in half, to make two concertinas. These will be the track base that supports the rails.

Glue the straws lengthways on the concertinas, as shown above. These will be the rails and it is important that they each have the same gauge. About 5 cm (2 in) apart is the best gauge. Put the track to one side and leave to dry.

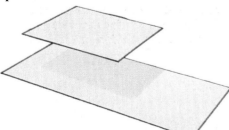

Cut two rectangles of cardboard to represent a long and short load. One must be 9 cm (3½ in) long and 6 cm (2½ in) wide. The second must be 18 cm (7 in) long and 9 cm (3½ in) wide and will represent the long wheelbase of the Big Boy engine.

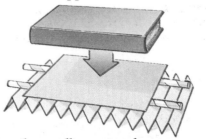

Lay the smaller rectangle across one set of concertina track. Gently start loading books onto it until the track collapses. In our tests the track collapsed under a weight of 1.9 kg (4 lbs 3 oz). Check and record your own "collapse weight".

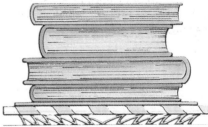

Now do the same with the second set of track and the longer rectangle. It should take the "collapse weight" of the smaller rectangle easily. Add more books until this track also collapses. Our "Big Boy" prototype collapsed at 4 kg (8 lb 13 oz).

The longest ever train pulled 500 wagons of coal in the USA. It was about 6.5 km (4 miles) long.

Strange trains

Railway engineers have come up with some amazing ideas. But their strange inventions were not always successful, and sometimes more of a fantastic experiment than a useful, working locomotive.

To make trains faster and to lay track more cheaply, these are the main problems facing engineers, who often found some weird solutions.

Some of the inventions create problems themselves, like the double-funnel train which needed mobile steps to help passengers across the track. Others flopped badly when unforeseen problems arose, like the British Advanced Passenger Train (APT). It took corners at top speed by tilting. This worked well, except that passengers always felt sick.

The underwater railway

Nicknamed Daddy Longlegs, this electric train, with 7 m (23 ft) high legs, ran on a 4.4 km (2.7 mile) track at Brighton Beach. Storms damaged the rails so it closed after five years.

The giant-wheeled train ▲

This Crampton-type Norris engine ran in the USA during the 1850s. Pistons turn big wheels as quickly as small ones, but one turn of a big wheel drives a train further than one turn of a small wheel. This is how large driving wheels achieved high speeds. Top speed was 110 km/h (68.4 mph).

The camelback train ▲

Camelbacks earned their name from the position of the driver's cab which lay over the top of the boiler. The fireman stood on a platform at the back. The firebox was wide with a large grate to burn slack coal. This 1854 camelback ran for almost 50 years on America's Baltimore and Ohio Railroad. It had six driving wheels and a four-wheel swivelling bogie.

The largest railway waiting rooms in the world are at Beijing in China.

The vacuum-tube train

The vacuum-tube train ran in south-west England in the 1840s. It did not have locomotives hauling the carriages. Instead it was powered by a series of pumps, which sucked air out of a vacuum tube that lay between the rails. Air pressure behind the piston pushed it into the vacuum. The train was attached to the piston and drawn with it along the rails. But rats ate the leather flaps which sealed the tube. This meant air leaked, the vacuum was lost and the train ground to a halt.

Driver

Vacuum tube

Piston

The propeller-driven ▲ train

The Kruckenburg (above) was a German single-car train which broke the world record in 1931 when it maintained a speed of 230 km/h (142.9 mph) for a distance of 10 km (6.2 miles). Its propeller was powered by a Maybach diesel engine used in Zeppelin airships. The train was built as an experiment to test stability and streamlining at high speeds.

The double-funnel ▶ train

This locomotive (right) was invented by Charles Lartigue, a Frenchman, and ran on the Listowel and Ballybunion Railway in Ireland, from 1888 to 1924. It had twin boilers and ran on top of an A-shaped track that could be laid cheaply and quickly.

There were supports either side of the track to stop it tipping over and loads had to be balanced.

In London in 1891, the Great Eastern Railway assembled a locomotive in a record time of 9 hours, 57 minutes.

Superspeed trains

Modern high-speed trains are some of the most exciting in the world today. France, Germany, Britain and Japan are all developing new technology to make their railways faster and more competitive. Modern motorways and jetplanes mean that passengers can travel quickly and comfortably to their destination. So, to compete successfully the latest long-distance trains must have high speeds and provide a relaxing and comfortable journey. The importance of speed was understood from the time of Rockèt, which won the world record at 46.8 km/h (29.1 mph) in 1829. But 161 years later, in 1990 the French TGV raced down its specially built track in a test run, achieving a record-shattering speed of 515.3 km/h (320.2 mph). The Japanese Maglev Linear Express may reach 600 km/h (373 mph) by the beginning of the 21st century - Thirteen times faster than the Rocket.

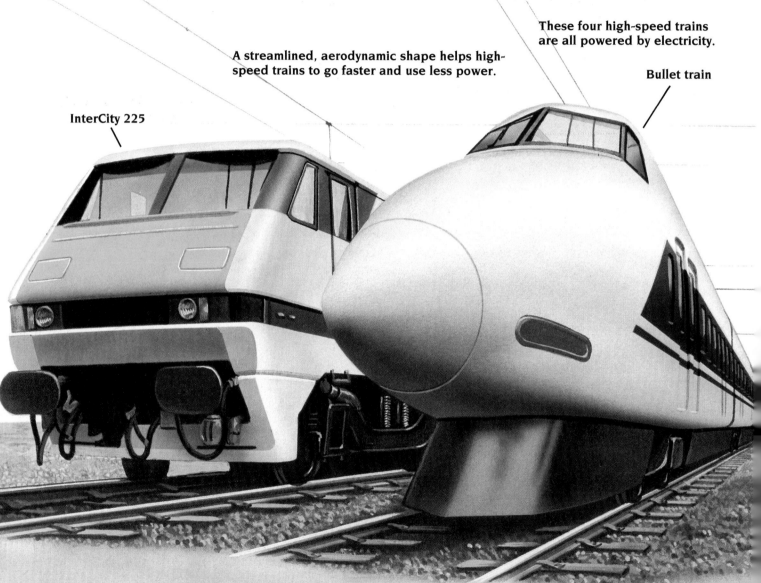

These four high-speed trains are all powered by electricity.

Bullet train

A streamlined, aerodynamic shape helps high-speed trains to go faster and use less power.

InterCity 225

InterCity 225 (Britain)

The InterCity 225 has Britain's most powerful ever locomotive, a Class 91 electric designed to run at a maximum speed of 225 km/h (139.8 mph). The Class 91 is at one end of the train and a Driving Van Trailer (DVT) at the other end. When the DVT is leading, the driver controls the Class 91 from the DVT. New technology means the driver can select a speed and the Class 91 will accelerate to it under computer control, saving energy and giving a smoother ride.

Bullet train (Japan)

The famous electric Bullet train is a gleaming, stream-lined train that travels at top speeds of 220 km/h (136.7 mph). A speed of 319 km/h (198.2mph) has been recorded on test track. The train runs on the Shinkansen line from Tokyo to many other Japanese cities and carries thousands of passengers each day. The record for passengers carried on one day was 807,875 in 1975, and over 300 million people were carried in the ten years from 1980 to 1990.

The world speed record for diesel traction was set in 1987 when a British prototype reached 283.4 km/h (176 mph).

TGV (France)

The French TGV (Train à Grande Vitesse, which means "high-speed train") is the world speed record holder at 515.3 km/h (320.2 mph), and has an average speed of about 300 km/h (186.4 mph). A streamlined, electric train, the TGV has a network of routes covering much of France. It even reaches into Switzerland. At low speeds the TGV travels on normal railway lines, but at high speeds switches to specially designed and built track. The trains have a locomotive at either end, and power is transmitted to the engine by pantographs picking up electric current from overhead wires. Computers play a large part in the running of the train. High-power brakes work with a computer controlled anti-lock system for each axle, and the driver has a computer screen in his cab to warn him of technical problems. He is also linked by radio with the signalling and control post in Paris, which controls all TGV traffic.

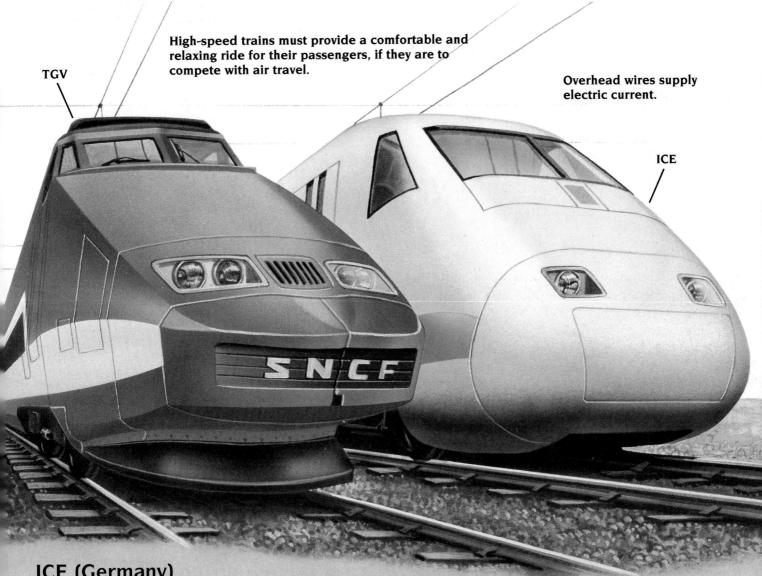

High-speed trains must provide a comfortable and relaxing ride for their passengers, if they are to compete with air travel.

TGV

Overhead wires supply electric current.

ICE

ICE (Germany)

The new German ICE (InterCity Express) has already been tested at more than 400 km/h (248.6 mph), and when it goes into service in 1992 will run at up to 250 km/h (155.3 mph). There are two locomotives at either end of the train, and pantographs send electric current to the engine. Like all high-speed trains it has good aerodynamics with a sleek, streamlined shape. With fast journeys and a high level of comfort, it is expected that the ICE will steal passengers from airlines flying between German cities. There are many luxuries on board like phones and lounges, and attached to each seat is a system which provides travel information and entertainment. From 1993 ICE carriages will be designed for use in France and other parts of Europe. This means that passengers will be able to travel in one high-speed train across many different countries.

In France in 1971, L'Aérotrain, reached a speed of 427 km/h (265 mph)

Rail records

From 1829 to 1990 the world railway speed record rose from 46.8 km/h to 515.3 km/h (29.1 mph to 320.2 mph). Speed is practical as well as exciting. Every extra 2 km/h (1.2 miles) in speed can bring a 1% increase in passengers.

High-speed rail travel is very safe compared with roads. On the New South Wales railway system in Australia, from 1963 to 1977, there were no deaths at all, while road deaths were in the thousands.

The world slow-speed rail record must be held by a train from Texas. In mid journey, the track was washed away, stranding the train. Seven years later new track was built and the train finally reached its destination.

Speed records

Name	Type	Speed
Rocket, England, 1829	Steam	
Great Britain, England, 1848	Steam	
999, USA, 1893	Steam	
Siemens & Halske, Germany, 1903	Electric	
Borsig, 05.001, Germany, 1935	Steam	
CC 7107, France, 1955	Electric	
ICE, Germany, 1988	Electric	
TGV, France, 1990	Electric	

0   50   100

The fastest thing on rails

In 1959 this rocket-powered sled zoomed along the Supersonic Naval Ordnance Research Track (SNORT) in New Mexico, USA. It reached an amazing 4,972 km/h (3,090 mph) during high speed tests. Instead of rolling on wheels, like normal locomotives, it slid along on metal shoes. The shoes fitted snugly into slots on the rails to keep it on the track. The nose-section was taken from a B58 Hustler aircraft.

Most luxurious train

In 1883 a train steamed away from Paris bound for distant Romania. It had two luxurious sleeping cars, a dining car and a smoking lounge. When it reached its destination King Charles of Romania entertained the passengers. This was the first journey of the Orient Express.

Today the train is as luxurious as ever, running between London and Venice with stops in Paris, Zurich, Innsbruck and Salzburg. There are 11 sleeping cars and three restaurant cars. Passengers can even listen to live music in the piano bar.

Each cabin has hot water, a bed, special soap and writing paper.

The longest railway in the world

The Trans-Siberian Railway was completed in 1916 and stretches 9,297 km (5,777 miles) from Moscow to Vladivostok. The entire journey takes seven days and two hours.

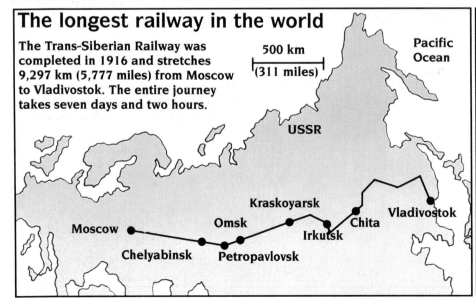

500 km
(311 miles)

Pacific Ocean

USSR

Kraskoyarsk
Omsk
Irkutsk
Chita
Vladivostok
Moscow
Chelyabinsk
Petropavlovsk

The longest straight

AUSTRALIA
Brisbane
Nullarbor Plain
Adelaide
Perth
Melbourne
Sydney

The Trans-Australian Railway includes the longest section of straight track in the world. This 478 km (297 miles) of standard gauge straight track crosses part of the treeless Nullarbor Plain.

The longest railway bridge in the world is the Huey P. Long in New Orleans, USA. It stretches 7,082 m (23,235 ft).